THREE
LIGHT-YEARS

THREE
LIGHT-YEARS

ANDREA
CANOBBIO

Translated from the Italian by
Anne Milano Appel

FARRAR, STRAUS AND GIROUX | NEW YORK

Farrar, Straus and Giroux
18 West 18th Street, New York 10011

Printed in the United States of America
Originally published in 2013 by Giangiacomo Feltrinelli Editore,
Italy, as *Tre Anni Luce*
English translation published in the United States by Farrar, Straus and Giroux
First American edition, 2014

Library of Congress Cataloging-in-Publication Data
Canobbio, Andrea, 1962–
    [Tre anni luce. English]
    Three light-years : a novel / Andrea Canobbio ; Translated from the
Italian by Anne Milano Appel.
        pages   cm
    Originally published in 2013 by Giangiacomo Feltrinelli Editore, Italy,
as Tre Anni Luce.
    ISBN 978-0-374-27890-8 (hardback) — ISBN 978-0-374-71010-1 (ebook)
    I. Appel, Anne Milano, translator.   II. Title.

PQ4863.A545 T7413 2014
853'.914–dc23
                                                                    2013039909

Designed by Abby Kagan

www.fsgbooks.com
www.twitter.com/fsgbooks • www.facebook.com/fsgbooks

10   9   8   7   6   5   4   3   2   1

TO
Pier Vittorio Tondelli
AND
Daniele Del Giudice

I know, however, of a young chronophobiac who experienced something like panic when looking for the first time at home-made movies that had been taken a few weeks before his birth.

—VLADIMIR NABOKOV,
Speak, Memory: An Autobiography Revisited

CONTENTS

PART I

(2002)

A DECLINE IN THE BIRTHRATE

Memory is an empty room. Gone are the bookshelves littered with journals, gone are the chairs and table, the paintings, the calendar, and the computer screen filled with words. My father is gone, too, effaced by thousands of identical moments, deleted by the same repetitive gestures day after day, as he sat there tapping the keys.

That's how he would have remained, an empty man in an empty room, like a cipher, for who knows how long, if Cecilia hadn't appeared and asked for his help. It was six o'clock on an evening in late March. The pediatricians' lounge became a stage on which a young woman in a white coat hurried in, alarmed, complaining about not being able to find anyone. Her eight-year-old son had been admitted to the ward a few days earlier and she was looking for a doctor, or at least someone dressed as a doctor, who could persuade him to eat. My father noticed the name of another hospital sewn on the woman's coat, noticed her red, chapped hands, her unmanicured nails, and the absence of rings. He observed her hands in detail, to the point where he could recall them years later, because he could not look at her face: already in those first moments her eyes disturbed him.

Had the woman stolen the coat or was she wearing it because of some bizarre trend even though she wasn't a doctor? No, she was describing the situation in very precise terms; she spoke like a physician. The child was undergoing parenteral nutrition; electrolyte balance and renal function were returning. But he had to start eating on his own. He had taken a dislike to the head nurse, and perhaps a man could persuade him: the attending physician the day before had managed to. The boy was fed up with having women around him—his mother, his grandmother, his sister. All he wanted was to be left in peace. Like everybody else, my father thought—the ones who are always hungry, and the ones who are never hungry. All they ask is to be left in peace.

He told Cecilia he'd help her and followed her into the first room on the ward. Not that he had any high hope of success: it wasn't his specialty, he wasn't a pediatrician, and he didn't know how to deal with children. He was sure that a nurse would soon come along to relieve him.

The boy was sitting on the middle bed with his back to the door, his legs dangling. He was wearing a blue hooded sweatshirt over his pajamas and had an open book in his lap, while his meal, semolina porridge and applesauce, had been left on the cart apparently untouched. The full plates told the story: the nurse must have ordered him to eat in the usual commanding tone that so impressed parents, but had no effect at all on children. Not wanting the scene to repeat itself, and not wanting her child to be forced, Cecilia had panicked.

My father paused in the doorway, motioned for her to stay outside, then went in with a distracted air, absently examining the charts at the foot of the beds. A sullen-looking little boy occupied the bed near the door, and a child with a mop of red hair had the one next to the window. A woman, presumably a mother, was sitting in the far corner, knitting. There were still women who knitted, then; you saw them in waiting rooms, in the wards, mysterious and comforting like childhood scars you rediscover on your skin from time to time.

Cecilia's son was watching the red-haired boy maneuver two dinosaurs on the bed in a noisy, never-ending battle. He looked a lot like his mother; his face was hardly sunken, he didn't seem emaciated. On the bedside table, next to a bottle of mineral water and a glass, four toy cars rested on a sheet of graph paper on which the diagram of an angled parking lot had been drawn with great precision. My father thought the child must love things that were done just so, that he must love any form of order.

The book in the boy's lap was called *Supercars*. My father asked to see it. As he leafed through it, his eye fell on an old Aston Martin. "The car James Bond drove," he said contentedly. He told a story about a miniature model that they'd brought him from London when he was little, from which the passenger could be ejected by pushing a lever. Meanwhile, he sat down on the bed next to the child. He picked up the spoon and began to stir the steaming porridge, stirring and talking, stirring and talking. This went on for a while, my father describing the gadgetry found in James Bond's Aston Martin, the bulletproof rear shield, the smoke screen, the machine guns, the tire slashers projecting from the wheel hubs, and the boy listening in silence, not missing a word.

Finally my father said he had to go. Maybe he'd come back tomorrow to tell him about 007's skirmishes with SPECTRE.

"What's SPECTRE?" the boy asked.

"Very bad people."

"Crooks?"

"Thieves and killers, but James Bond always beats them."

"Why is it called SPECTRE?"

"To scare people."

Behind them, the sullen little boy offered another explanation: "Because they're invisible." As if it were something obvious and well known.

My father viewed the scene from above, like the eye of a hidden camera hanging from the ceiling. The room captured by the eye's slow whirl, people and things suspended in space but all of them drawn down to the bottom, where Cecilia's son had declared cold war on his supper.

My father turned to the other bed. He asked the red-haired boy the names of his two dinosaurs, but the child didn't know or was too shy to answer. The sullen little boy, more interested in being a know-it-all than pouting, spoke up again: they were a *Tyrannosaurus rex* and a *Diplodocus*. His mother, over in the corner, smiled without looking up from her knitting needles.

He'd better go; what did he think he'd accomplish by staying. He started toward the door. To gain a bit of time he asked the sulky boy what music he had downloaded on his iPod. He stuck the earbuds in and began listening to a band called Punkreas at a deafening volume. Cecilia's son had begun to eat. He didn't see it with a hidden camera, didn't perceive it through a sixth sense, and didn't hear the sound of the spoon clinking on the plate. He saw him reflected in the empty IV bag still hanging on its stand, between the two beds.

He followed the meal, bit by bit, so focused on the small convex image that he managed to tolerate the music's impact on his eardrums with surprising ease. At the end he removed the earbuds and told the boy that Punkreas was interesting. "Don't keep the volume too high, though," he added, perhaps only to make himself credible and reassume the mantle of a boring adult.

He turned and retrieved the cart without looking directly at the child, resisting the temptation to say "that's a good boy." When he went out pushing the trophy of empty plates, he found Cecilia beside the door, leaning against the wall. She stared at him with a faint smile and shining eyes. She didn't say a word, just held an open hand out in front of her as if to stop him from speaking, as if to keep him at a distance.

My father walked to the kitchen with the cart, and when he

got back to the hallway Cecilia had already gone inside to the child. The corridor and the ward were sucked into oblivion, devoured by time; rejected, my father went out through the glass door, unable to create any more memories here and resigned to never seeing her again.

I think back to that chance meeting, the origin of it all, and its fortuitousness. It never ceases to amaze me. What is my father doing in Pediatrics? He's an internist, but his best friend works in Pediatrics and they have a computer—an old machine, easy to use, regardless of, or maybe thanks to, its grimy plastic and scratched screen—on which he is correcting some proposed new guidelines.

My father often spends time in the department. It's no accident that Cecilia finds him there. It's no accident, nor is it fate, there's no such thing as fate, you shouldn't believe in destiny, in the existence of a soul mate, in eternal love, or in eternity either. Not because of metaphysical conviction, but out of simple reserve.

Anyway, nothing has happened in his life for ten years, and if something has happened he doesn't remember it. No rite of initiation, no epiphany led him to that evening. But when Cecilia enters and sees him and asks him for help, a story begins and becomes part of memory. The pale wooden table with the blue Formica top, the yellow credenza from the fifties that somehow ended up in that corner of the hospital, the aluminum chairs and glass-doored cabinets filled with samples of expired medicines, the calendar from the missionary group with a bunch of African children on a green tractor, the naïf paintings with huge red and yellow peppers, the metal carts littered with folders to be filed away—everything suddenly reappears because Cecilia is a spotlight projected on the dark scene, Cecilia is the sun that illuminates the heavenly bodies, Cecilia creates the things around her, gives them substance and color, and she creates my father as well, my father, too, shines with her light.

The astronomical hyperbole is dedicated to him, though he wouldn't have approved of it, because he never let himself get carried away, almost never; even if he could have read the future and known how that woman would change his life, he would never have compared her to a star. You are a distant flame that shines in the night, you are pure spring water, you are the heart that beats inside things . . . after all, why *not*? Because the images are banal? Or because no image can ever be a substitute for reality? Or because real women are infinitely more precious and desirable than ideal women?

Maybe because there's only one thing worse than a lack of moderation and that's its verbal expression. So never utter excessive words, never ask excessive questions (Does eternity exist? Does happiness exist?). Never reveal yourself.

But the next day he went back to visit the child and began chatting with him. The boy's name was Mattia. He had a large notebook on his knees and he was sketching a parking lot on graph paper. He had drawn an elongated shape with a meandering outline and he was trying to fit as many parking spaces in it as possible: rectangles or parallelograms depending on whether they were straight or angled, whether they were for cars or special spots for motorcycles and bicycles. My father asked him why he liked parking lots so much. Did he have a lot of toy cars to park?

"No, I want to be a designer," he said. He showed him other pages with irregular shapes and parking spaces inside them. My father immediately noticed that all the shapes were similar; they could be different attempts to reproduce a real place from memory. Beside each sketch Mattia had noted the number of spaces he had managed to fit in. Every now and then he also drew cars inside the grid, but in profile.

And which plan did he like best? Mattia showed him one. It looked like the outline of a goose, or a round mirror with a handle.

"What is this? Is it a place you know?"

"It's the park near our house."

"Why do you want to turn it into a parking lot?"

"For when I get big."

"But then there will be other children who will want to go and play there."

Mattia said no, there wouldn't be any more children, his sister had told him so.

"Not even one?"

Mattia shook his head: "It's because of something called *birthrate*, I think, but it's not really a disease."

My father ran a hand through his hair and murmured: "The declining birthrate, of course, there won't be any more children . . . I've heard about it, too." He'd heard about it and he thought about it continually, as if he were the person primarily responsible for the drop in the number of births. If he were to have a son at that moment, he would be fifty-six years old when the boy entered high school, sixty when he came of age, sixty-five when he got his college degree (unless he specialized in medicine or didn't finish on time). In fact he might never see him graduate. Certainly he would never see him marry, and he would never know his grandchildren. Because his son would have inherited a certain difficulty when it came to procreating.

He was afraid it was too late.

The child's presence gave my father one more reason to visit the ward. At least once a day he'd go and exchange a word or two with him. In school they had given him *Pinocchio* to read, one of the few books that my father remembered almost scene by scene. Here's an idea that had always struck him: planting coins to make money grow. But that was something the Cat and the Fox made up, Mattia objected; money didn't really grow on trees! Of course . . . still, it would have been wonderful. And waking up one morning with donkey ears? They laughed. They tried to feel if their ears were hairy. They really were! And the bogus funeral with the four coffin-bearing black Rabbits, what a sad sight; and the girl with the azure hair who appears at the window, she was so mysterious . . . Why did she say she was dead?

"I was always struck by it," my father said, not noticing how much the boy was struck by that expression.

"Were you *struck* when he goes to the Field of Wonders?" Mattia asked.

"Yes, it always struck me."

"And did the donkey's ears *strike* you?"

"Oh yes, very much, they always scared me a little."

"But *what* was it that *struck* you the most?"

Each time he would have to recall a new episode of the book that had truly struck him. Until the day came when my father, running out of things to say and not stopping to think, mentioned the pear skins and cores that Pinocchio ate out of desperate hunger. "That really struck me," he said, and the moment he said it he was mortified. Mattia looked at him, rapt, motionless; my father could already imagine the boy's outraged mother barging into the room to confront him, to throw him out. Why talk about a stubborn, bratty puppet? As if the child didn't already feel guilty enough. But by then he couldn't stop and he went on to explain all the extraordinary nutrients found in the skin and seeds of a pear; he described the strange things that are never eaten even though they're good for you: skins, rinds, seeds, stems, flowers . . . Mattia nodded and for the first time said: "Yes, that really *struck* me, too," and my father, unable to contain himself, hugged him. The other children in the room were watching them, but Mattia didn't seem embarrassed.

"I really like canned pears," he said. "I like the delicious syrup that's left at the bottom of the can. Pears or peaches, I ate them with my grandfather. Mama says the fresh ones are better."

"Your mother is right," my father confirmed.

He managed to see Cecilia again. At first it never seemed like the right time to strike up a conversation. She would be talking with the pediatricians or sitting on the bed, playing with her son, and my father didn't have the nerve to approach her. Attributing his own difficulties to others was an old habit: maybe in his heart he knew the truth, but he preferred to think that Cecilia was embarrassed for not having even thanked him.

Bumping into her one evening, he was disturbed by the attraction he felt. Staring at the freckle-dusted triangle of skin revealed by her neckline, he realized he wanted to touch her, right then and there, in the middle of the hall. But the specter of improperly putting his hands on a near stranger made him slip away without raising his eyes (studying the floor, the way he always did). After hugging the son, imagine embarrassing himself by hugging the mother, too.

After a couple of weeks they ran into each other at a café. My father was eating a plate of boiled vegetables, sitting at a table behind a column, the place where he had lunch every day, where he could keep an eye on the entrance without being seen. She appeared all of a sudden, nearly falling over him, as if she thought the chair would be empty, and burst out laughing. Later she would confess to him that she, too, always sat at out-of-the-way tables, she, too, preferred to be out of sight, but that day my father thought she was laughing at him: she was a young woman making fun of an antisocial, somewhat awkward man hiding behind a column. A young woman, beautiful and bursting with vitality. Surprised by seeing her suddenly materialize before him, surprised to see her laugh for the first time, not out of nervousness or to be polite but heartily and impulsively, my father was finally obliged—was finally permitted—to look at her. Obliged and permitted, he did not lower his eyes for a full two minutes. When he was able to face the world and look it in the eyes, for a moment it was like a miracle: his gaze saw through people and things, and the part of him that was hardest to bear was released, and he felt lighter.

Cecilia Re is thirty-four years old and the first thing you notice about her is the wavy brown hair that she keeps short, trying to restrain it in a stunted ponytail at the nape of her neck, until after a while the wisps come loose—first the strands over her eyes, then those twined behind her ears. Her eyes are light brown and big and almost always alarmed or darkened by a frown, so that when she relaxes and lets herself go she seems to light up with joy. With certain expressions her face seems childlike: beneath the adult woman you can still see the little girl she once was. As a child she wanted to become a champion swimmer, she spent hours in the pool (hence the habit of wearing her hair short), but she left that behind fifteen years ago.

She apologized, laughing, saying that he'd startled her, she hadn't expected that . . . What, what hadn't she expected? As if my father weren't the most predictable man in the world. Was that what she meant, she hadn't expected that he would surprise her?

She hadn't expected the table to be occupied. Her purse had slipped off her shoulder; she had a roasted-pepper-and-anchovy sandwich in one hand and a glass of orangeade in the other. She set the glass down on the table and adjusted the bag on her shoulder. The smile, the laugh, were disappearing—how to make them linger? How to trigger them again? My father found the right moment to get a word in between the choppy phrases and invited her to sit down.

They started out talking about the boy, who was better and getting stronger. Cecilia was happy because that morning she'd caught him eating cookies on the sly. He'd made a small slit in the package so you couldn't tell it had been opened. He was a clever child. My father said it was nice to see her smile. "Yes," she said, "I think things will only get better now. And I never thanked you for that evening, you were really good with—" Her voice died in her throat.

To change the subject, my father confessed that at first he thought she worked at another hospital, then he discovered that she had recently started working in the ER. Cecilia told him that she didn't have a spare coat and occasionally used her old ones. My father knew one of the chief surgeons in the hospital where she'd done her residency; he'd been his professor twenty years earlier. They smiled, imitating some of the man's pompous expressions; he was the first extra to appear in the film of their conversations, the first excuse to talk and be together and joke.

They discussed various places to eat during the lunch break, which was not a real break for her, because she had six-hour shifts and usually ate around two. With surprising presence of mind, my father pretended that this was his routine as well, and in a way it was true because he kept to it unfailingly for the next two years. They remarked on the outrageous parking situation around the hospital, went over the most convenient transportation options for getting to work, and described the neighborhoods where they lived.

Cecilia lived behind a large church dedicated to Our Lady, built in the late nineteenth century as an absurd replica of a famous monument of ancient Rome. The windows of her house overlooked the circular piazza in whose center the monstrosity rose. You get used to anything.

"You get used to anything, it's true," my father agreed.

And before he realized what he was doing, he found himself telling her, with a naturalness that was unthinkable for him, about the bizarre living situation he'd been in for the past ten years. My father was not yet my father; he was a divorced man with no children (a man who thought of himself as a man with no children, destined to remain so, to end his life without children, secretly anguished by this seemingly inevitable fate, even though he didn't believe in fate). He lived on the fifth floor of a building that housed his elderly mother, who lived on the second floor, and his ex-wife, Giulia, who lived on the third floor with her new husband and six-year-old son. Giulia loved her mother-in-law as a daughter would, perhaps even more so, and when she separated from my father after just three years, amicably, with no regrets, in perfect friendship, she had rented an apartment in the same building. She'd gone on living there with her new husband as well. Thanks to a short-circuiting of imaginary family relationships, Giulia's son called my father "uncle" and called *my* grandmother Marta, "nonna." (I did not yet exist to challenge and reclaim that title.)

My father couldn't complain about the situation. He'd lived in that building for forty years, as a child, a young bachelor, a husband, and a divorcé; it was his home. *It's your choice, you have to decide whether to keep it all together or divide things up, money, ID card, driver's license, credit card, ATM card, you can carry a wallet, a planner, a briefcase and spread out the risk, keeping it all together is riskier, if you lose your wallet you lose everything, but it's an apparent risk, because you actually pay more attention and focus your attention and vigilance on one single object.* But over time he'd begun to feel uncomfortable there among them, as if he were the real intruder. "It's become difficult to have a private life," he said, smiling, even as he realized, in telling the story to a practical stranger, that there was nothing very funny about it.

Cecilia listened to him, serious and attentive. Her eyes were her secret weapon; with those eyes she could conquer anyone willing to let himself be conquered. Eyes that waited, watchful and concerned, never evasive, following you to a diagnosis. They went back to talking about her, about the neighborhood where she lived, along the river, which, the church notwithstanding, was a lovely area. Perhaps my father expected Cecilia to immediately tell him all about her life as he just had. But time was up and she said she had to go, she was already late. My father's eyes, orphaned by

Cecilia's as she turned away, followed her to the doorway of the café, then slid over the empty orangeade glass, the half-eaten plate of boiled vegetables; he stared at the abandoned chair in front of him. He hadn't felt so alone in a long time.

Beguiled, *struck*, captivated not only by the mother, but also by the child. Each captivating in different ways and for different though related reasons; clearly related, even to someone as dense in the area of family relations as he. Not that he had never heard of eating disorders in children, but he hadn't seen a specific case. He wasn't even sure it was an unusual case. And why should he have known more about it? He dealt almost exclusively with old people. Antonio, his pediatrician friend, would have been able to cite similar cases, but the topic had never come up. Antonio had two sons who ate like pigs, Omasum and Abomasum he called them. "You're costing me a fortune!" he said to them, pleased and proud. Pride in a child who eats eagerly. As if the child were endorsing his parents. My father knew nothing about that. He didn't even remember what it had been like to eat when he was eight years old. He remembered his mother's words, though: "to enjoy a healthy appetite."

He had a memory, incorrectly set in adolescence: his mother, Marta, distracted by something, worried or depressed for some reason, had stopped cooking, had stopped doing the grocery shopping. Incorrectly assigned to the period following his father's death in order to explain the behavior, and because something like that had happened after his father's death as well. He remembered a time of grim hunger, or thought he remembered it. He'd buy himself huge slices of pizza from the bakery before going home from school and eat them sitting on a bench with a classmate. But it hadn't lasted, and perhaps it wasn't a period of time but an episode or two, transformed by resentment into a recurring incident. He was familiar with those memories and continually tried to put them into perspective because they seemed improbable. What could his mother have done to him that was so terrible?

He thought about the child. Viberti was more and more drawn to foods that were white and bland. Ricotta, boiled fish, vegetable broths. He wanted to know what it was the child saw on his plate. He sat at the kitchen table with a packet of prosciutto in front of him and tried to imagine disgust or indifference. He rolled the ham into small cylinders and ate three or four slices plain, without bread. Or he cooked himself the kind of tasteless dishes the child must have had to eat in his first few days at the hospital; semolina porridge, thin soup with stelline pasta, applesauce. Circling around in the bowl, the spoon sketched a tangle of lines in the porridge which disappeared immediately and sank into the depths like a probe. It was possible to make the same whorl, but with more distinct lines, appear by dipping a piece of bread in a pool of olive oil, at the center of a blue plate.

He was tempted to buy the child a present, and one day he went into a toy store near his apartment. The toy shops from his child-hood no longer existed; this one was a kind of warehouse where the merchandise was displayed like in a supermarket—long shelves and long aisles, a place where someone like my father was bound to be bewildered, worried as he was that someone might spot him. He had no children; he had no grandchildren; he was an impos-tor. After wandering around for twenty minutes he gave in and asked a salesclerk if they had any toy garages. The clerk led him to a garage that my father examined in detail for half an hour, reading all the labels on the box, then bought out of desperation. He knew that wasn't the garage he was looking for, the garage he had been given when he was eight years old: that one was much more carefully made and more detailed, much more realistic. As soon as he got home he realized that the "3+" on the box meant that the model was suitable for children over three, and therefore probably meant for children no older than four or five. The rounded shapes and strictly primary colors should have made him suspect as much. Now the fact that it was intended for children much younger than Mattia seemed so crystal clear and glaringly obvious to him that he wondered how he could have made such a mistake. An elderly person like his mother could have bought that garage. He never considered taking it back and exchanging it. He tossed the box in a corner and tried to forget it existed.

They fell into the habit of eating together three or four times a week. At first, being unable or unwilling to ask about the specific times of her shifts, my father would arrive at the café around a quarter to two. If Cecilia was working the afternoon shift, she would already be there munching a sandwich; if she was coming off the morning shift, she would arrive half an hour later. They never stayed more than twenty minutes, sitting at the table behind the column. Regularity was important, eating at regular hours, even just a bite, but unhurriedly, chatting about relaxing topics. Maybe Cecilia simply had to get used to wanting a connection again, friendship or something more, accepting it a little more each day, just as her son was getting used to eating again. And my father's situation, though his divorce went back more than ten years, wasn't all that different.

Incredible that the woman came back day after day to the same café knowing that he, too, would be there. He'd heard from Antonio that Cecilia was separated or practically divorced, or maybe actually divorced. The news hadn't surprised him, in fact he'd mumbled, "Yes, I know," all the while aware that he hadn't known it at all, no one could have told him. He reflected on the lie for an entire evening, and the next day, when he saw Cecilia again, he wondered what could have heightened his scant intuitive capacities. He wasn't good at reading people, particularly their feelings; he specifically couldn't tell if they were married or engaged or committed in some way. Maybe intuition had nothing to do with it, maybe it was only wishful thinking. She simply had to be free. She *was* free. Actually, now that he knew for sure, he didn't feel any better. Now came the difficult part, his homeopathic plan to make her fall in love with him.

And he liked her more and more. He liked it when she tucked a strand of hair behind her ear, how it revealed that small, perfect pink conch. He liked it when they were eating and she touched her lips with two fingers, searching for a nonexistent crumb or indicating that she couldn't speak at that moment, her mouth was full. He liked the way her eyes widened an instant before she laughed. She had a mole in the hollow at the base of her neck. She had a very lovely neck. She had a green spot in the iris of her right eye (did she know?).

They talked a lot about work. My father complained about having to spend a lot of his time chasing after his patients' children, who were always and forever trying to put off the day of their elderly parent's discharge. Daughters who hadn't slept for weeks because their nonagenarian mothers cried out for help all night had them hospitalized for dubious bronchial asthmas and then claimed they couldn't take them back home and couldn't afford caregivers to look after them (sisters or brothers refused to contribute to the cost of assistance because the sibling in question lived in the parent's house without paying rent). The greater the number of children and grandchildren, the greater the likelihood that no one wanted to take care of the elderly family member. At the other extreme, an unmarried son, an only child, living with his parent was dependable—until he became a threat: this was around the time my father had been accused of negligence by a seventy-two-year-old man following the death of his ninety-seven-year-old mother. *Dear Doctor,* the son had written in very large letters that slanted precariously forward, as though the words were about to drop off the right edge of the paper at any moment, *you killed my mother. I will never forget the grief you caused me. When I admitted my mother to the hospital I placed her in your hands and you did not take care of her. My mother entered the hospital to die and for this I will never forgive you.* And on and on for four pages. His six hours a week in the endocrinology outpatient clinic were an oasis of peace.

Cecilia described the strangest, most convoluted cases, both dramatic and comical; in the ER, anything could happen. There was a lot of boredom, a lot of drug addicts and drunks; but also, on the one hand, the inexhaustible list of howlers and absurdities made up by patients and their families, and on the other, the act of challenging death, that, too, never ending. My father asked questions; he liked to hear her laugh and talk, not just because of the passion apparent in her stories, but because they showed her competence. Each time, he was amazed by the accuracy of her diagnoses, and by how sound and sensible her treatments were. He thought that sooner or later, at least once in a lifetime, a doctor like him (diligent, caring, mediocre) was bound to meet a true natural talent. There was no envy, it was pure admiration. Maybe he was deluding himself about his role in Cecilia's bravura, deluding himself about being the first to discover it. The only resource he could claim, experience, could be measured by age; it was less mysterious than talent, but more bitter, because to a great extent you earned it by making mistakes.

One day Cecilia arrived at the café and said she wasn't hungry; she needed to talk and felt like walking, did my father want to keep her company? They went out and he asked her what had happened, because it was clear that something had happened, something had upset her. Cecilia said she had just *laid out* a patient. "I laid him out" meant "he died in my hands," a common expression among doctors, though a bit brutal, and one which perhaps implied an admission of guilt, even if no one was to blame. Coming from someone else, my father wouldn't have thought anything of it, but "I laid him out" sounded strange and moving coming from her. Not that he didn't lay out patients, frequently, constantly, one after another: it seemed to be his specialty.

A suspected recidivous ulcer had arrived in the emergency room. But the patient had intense chest pain, was pale and sweaty, and had a reading of 180 in one arm and 80 in the other. So Cecilia had sent him to have a CT scan, because she was thinking about the aorta. The man, a very tall, thin, elderly fellow with a bewildered look, was left lying on the stretcher until they came to take him. They had exchanged a few words. He was in pain and he was thirsty. "I'm dying of thirst" he kept saying. He remembered a fountain where he used to go to get water as a child, in the countryside, and he remembered the water was so cold that when he filled the bottle the glass fogged up. Ten minutes later they called her from Radiology: he had died while they were scanning him. "But I just sent him to you," she told the radiologist. She didn't think he would go so fast.

She was afraid she'd never forget that image, his final memory, the bottle fogged up by the icy water. My father listened in silence. He was ashamed of having once told her that he couldn't stand his patients' relatives, that until people got sick they didn't learn anything from life. He'd said his department was full of unstable or inattentive relatives who expected the doctors to work miracles or perform some kind of undetectable euthanasia before the holidays. He told her that the living didn't want to see dead bodies anymore, that rather than cure people, hospitals served to cover up death. He was ashamed of having told her that the old people in his care were treated like broken appliances. He was ashamed to have spoken only about the most grotesque side of his work, as if the rest didn't exist. He'd left out all that was noble, left out himself as a doctor; by leaving himself out of the picture, except as a victim of the relatives' stupidity, he'd meant to leave out illness and death. Was this, too, something he'd done out of reserve? He sensed that with her he would learn to be less reserved.

One evening in early May my father came out of the locker room on the ground floor. In the corridor he passed an elderly woman, out of breath, barefoot, carrying her shoes, one shoe in each hand. Two nurses had stopped to look at her, but her eyes were focused straight ahead and she wasn't paying attention to what was going on around her. The large windows that overlooked the inner court-yard were open; it had just stopped raining and the air was awash with that hospital smell, usually imperceptible, now intensified by the dampness: a mixture of disinfectant, scented ammonia, and kitchen odors. In the courtyard was a parking area scattered with saplings with reddish leaves, the cars parked regularly between the tree trunks as if this, instead of white lines, were the natural system of marking the spaces, as if this had been planned from the beginning.

It looked like one of Mattia's sketches, but blurry, badly drawn. And in the drawing, vibrant and unexpected, was Cecilia. Stand-ing beside a Scénic, rummaging in her bag for the key. How had she managed to get in? To park inside? A privilege granted only to a few and never to the younger doctors—the woman definitely had hidden resources. To get a better look at her, to see what she was up to, my father had to lean over and peer through the new foliage of a tree. He didn't want to expose himself too much because he'd noticed some people who'd stopped to talk on the other side of the courtyard. He didn't want them to see him spying on a colleague, but he couldn't tear himself away from the win-dow. The people in the distance were mere shadows at the edge of his field of vision, but cautiousness and fear made them loom larger. Cecilia meanwhile activated the remote door opener, but the smart key fell to the ground, landing in a puddle. Leaning over even farther, my father saw that the cause of Cecilia's difficulty was the couple of packages she was juggling in addition to her handbag. To free herself from the packages she set them on the roof of the car, then picked up the key and dried it off with a tissue. At that point, as if inspired by a spirit and will of its own, the key dropped a second time, into the same puddle.

She didn't pick it up right away. She leaned against the Scénic and stared at it. And my father stared at her staring at the key. The ground floor was about five feet above the level of the courtyard, and from where he stood he could see her quite well. He tried to read the expression on her face. He couldn't make it out. There was a trace of sadness in her eyes, but also something that simply didn't make sense: tenderness, affection. Toward the key that had fallen? Toward herself? She didn't seem like the type of person to feel sorry for herself, nor someone who would take an incident like that as a sign of bad luck. He would have liked to see a face like that every morning when he opened his eyes (my father thought for the first time). No, that wasn't right. Not a face *like* that—*that* face. Sudden, overwhelming desire: he wanted to leap down from the windowsill—swoop down like an angel in an ex-voto—and wheel around her, glide down to grasp her and snatch her away, save her from an impending danger. What had come over him? Were a pair of tender, somewhat mournful eyes all it took for him to start having visions? Of all the faces in his life, why *that one*? As if the others had paled and dulled. Why such joy, such hope? It made no sense, any more than feeling sorry for an object made of plastic and metal that keeps falling.

Across the courtyard, meanwhile, the small group of people had gone their separate ways, and a man and child had emerged from the glass door of the building opposite. They walked slowly, approaching the parking lot. My father was afraid they might see him if they looked up, but he couldn't make himself budge. Cecilia's eyes, staring down at the key, were now desperate. It was strange that someone so competent and self-confident would get so disheartened over something so trivial. He thought of calling to her—to say hello, to shake her out of her reverie, to prevent strangers from catching her in that moment of despair. He, too, felt paralyzed by the fallen key. When he was a boy, soon after his father's death or shortly before, coming out of his room in his pajamas one Sunday morning, he found himself in the doorway of the kitchen. His mother, sitting at the table with a cup of coffee in front of her, hadn't heard him approach. She was staring blankly, her right hand gripping her left wrist. And he didn't know whether to leave or stay, whether to go in and pretend he hadn't noticed or hug her, comfort her, if she needed to be comforted. What had he decided to do, in the end? Impossible to remember. But he remembered the floor being cold underneath his bare feet.

As they came closer, the boy holding hands with the adult looked more and more like Mattia. He must have recently been discharged. He hadn't had time to say goodbye and already he missed him. They walked firmly toward the Scénic, and my father desperately tried to identify the man leading the child as a pediatrician, but with every step that became more and more unlikely. He was tall and rather good-looking despite an angular face and a big nose.

How does the face of a teenager turn into the face of a man? It doesn't. Time was, people became adults, and you could tell. Now we're born with more or less adult faces and we keep them our whole lives, because life isn't as draining as it used to be. So you had aging children, like Cecilia, graying young men, like my father, and mature adults, who at forty reached the age suited to their features.

How could he have been so naïve. As if a person suddenly disappeared just like that from someone's life. He didn't disappear. As if inertia didn't govern everyone's relationships. It did.

In the space of a few seconds, Cecilia looked up, saw her son and husband (or ex-husband), picked up the key, and opened the car door. She greeted them, kissing her son on the head and the man on the mouth, grabbing the back of his neck and pulling him to her, laughing. The sadness of a moment ago seemed to have left no trace. The man walked to the other side of the car and opened the passenger door so the child could climb in. Last of all, Cecilia retrieved the packages from the roof of the car. They got in, closed the doors, and the Scénic pulled out.

My father stayed there awhile looking out at the deserted courtyard, undecided whether to focus his acute, intense jealousy on the child or on the mother. He'd always thought he was incapable of reading people and he was right. But it was more than that. It was as if everything around him lacked a dash of imagination.

So then: at the beginning, an empty room like a stage; in the middle of it, a man hidden behind a column, observing the world; finally, a window. The idea is more or less the same. Sitting in the audience, he watched. Hidden, looking out, he watched.

Looking out at the world was my father's preference. His name was Claudio Viberti, but everyone in the hospital just called him Viberti, and over the years he, too, came to think of himself by that name, as if it were his first name.

Writing is what the son prefers, the son who in those days didn't exist and so had no name yet. No one can keep me from it, there is no present that is of greater interest to me than that distant past that I did not experience, about which I know almost nothing, and which I continue to imagine, fabricating other people's memories.

PART II

(2003)

ABANDON ME ON THE ICE PACK

For some months Marta had been experiencing memory problems. She would repeat the same question or the same story three or four times in a row, she forgot where she'd put her keys or glasses just moments before, and now she had started leaving pots and pans to scorch on the stove. Giulia had noticed it and, worried, had pointed it out to Viberti, who acted as if he weren't aware of it. But pretending is a subtle art that requires a lot of practice, guile, and nerves of steel, and Viberti wasn't up to it. Giulia made him confess that, yes, he had noticed his mother's memory lapses and had ignored the facts, deciding that there was nothing that could be done. Always the wrong tack to take. So Marta was taken to a geriatrician, and the tests ruled out Alzheimer's but not senile dementia. In a woman of eighty-two the course of the illness was unpredictable; she might not recognize anyone in three or four years' time or she could die at the age of a hundred with the same minor issues.

A year after having met Cecilia in Pediatrics, Viberti, returning home one evening in May, stopped by to see Marta, as he often did, though never frequently enough to allay the feeling that he was neglecting his elderly mother, who lived just three floors below him. It sometimes seemed to him that his ex-wife had set-tled in a nearby apartment with the goal of fueling that guilt (guilt was the alimony Viberti paid to Giulia). Marta's kitchen was plas-tered with notes written by Giulia or by Angélica, the Peruvian woman who looked after her. *Prosciutto and stracchino cheese in the refrigerator; Heat for 4 minutes on High; This envelope contains six (6) Ibuprofen tablets, given to Marta today, April 23, by Giulia, which must last until Sunday evening (April 27?)*, the last parentheses added in Marta's rounded, ornate handwriting. The table was littered with old photographs on the backs of which Marta had been adding cap-tions for months now. *In the chalet at Montenegro Bagni, Marta is holding her "dear" puppy Haile, it was a "fashionable" name because Italy had just "conquered" Abyssinia.* Or: *Excursion to San Colombano. Pietro displays a "trophy" of porcini mushrooms.* On virtually every photo there was at least one word in quotation marks. Giulia claimed that the proliferation of quotes was due to a specific neuro-logical problem: Marta no longer remembered whether certain ex-pressions could be used in certain contexts, everything seemed out of place and uncertain to her; better to distance herself from them.

Viberti's visits might last a few minutes or more than an hour. That evening they'd started talking about Stefano Mercuri, an old family friend, a doctor, who had been like an adoptive father and spiritual guide to Viberti. Mercuri had long since retired and lived on the Riviera di Levante, where Viberti visited him from time to time. Marta listened absently to the latest news of their friend, then changed the subject and started retelling a story by Chekhov or Maupassant or Tarchetti, which she called "scandalous." The name of the protagonist (who may have been Russian, French, or Italian) was Cecilia, and the chance appearance of that name on his mother's lips seriously upset Viberti, though the story left him somewhat indifferent (some kind of incest)—especially since his mother's narration was even less consistent than usual.

———

After a restless night he awoke with the conviction that he could no longer put it off; he had to speak to Cecilia or stop seeing her. He was forty-three years old. At forty-three, one could have a child of fifteen or twenty, at fifty, one could become a grandfather, at seventy-five, a great-grandfather. His father and mother had married late; he was the son of elderly parents and now he, too, was getting on in years; he'd lost some time but his time wasn't up, it was at a standstill, dormant, adrift, stagnant and swampy.

He began the day with the sole intention of finding ten free minutes to go down to the ER as soon as possible to find her. He never did that—usually they would agree to meet from one day to the next or they'd send each other messages, but the previous afternoon, saying goodbye, Cecilia had mentioned she wasn't sure she'd be able to eat with him the next day. He scrambled to put off his outpatient visits, raced down the stairs, dashed into the ER, and looked into the ward where Cecilia was on call. She barely raised her eyes from the desk and told him she'd be busy at lunch.

Viberti left the ER without knowing where he was going or why. The thought that he couldn't stand this torment much longer crossed his mind, and he was immediately surprised. It was the first time in his life that he'd described an attraction or feeling with the word "torment," the first time he'd doubted his ability to carry on. He'd always believed he was capable of enduring the most painful trials, certainly more painful than an infatuation or falling in love. Should he call it that? He wasn't sure. But precisely because he was a loner, as his mother had described him the night before, precisely because he was acquainted with and dwelled in solitude, he didn't need anyone, he'd never needed anyone, he was self-sufficient and then some. In any case, and this he was sure of: it was important to never feel sorry for yourself, ever.

He kept walking briskly as if he were trying to run from the prospect of making a fool of himself, but in fact after two right turns he found himself returning to the ER via Radiology. That department must have been built or renovated in the fifties: the wooden moldings, baseboards, windows, and doors were pale, with shiny blue Formica panels, and the contrast between the two materials dated the work. For some reason that type of workmanship had become a mark of modernity and for a period of several years had been used extensively in schools and hospitals, only to later be replaced by metal and plastic. The work might have been done by the hospital's on-site carpentry shop, which had existed until the early seventies, when Viberti, on a school trip to the hospital, had visited the workshop with his class to see how the lathe and milling machine worked. He had a clear recollection of the strong, pungent smell of the wood, the unbreathable air, the two carpenters who had been transplanted up north from Tuscany, craftsmen who in their spare time built inlaid furniture and bric-a-brac but who out of necessity had taken more practical jobs. When a classmate asked if they also made wooden legs for amputees there were several stifled laughs, and he, already quite shaken by their visit to the operating rooms, had fainted. When he came to, he found himself lying on the ground, his feet elevated on a low stool and his head resting on a soft bed of sawdust and wood chips. He'd never passed out like that again. And that might have been during the period when Marta was trying to starve him to death.

Seeing that he'd come back after just a few minutes, the nurse at the reception desk looked at him with surprise. Cecilia was showing a medical student how an EKG in the cardiology textbook looked like the one they had just performed on a patient. Her tone was playful. Trust me, she said, things are often simpler than they look. The student walked away, somewhat troubled and still skeptical, and Cecilia looked at Viberti, smiled at him, and said: "Sometimes they don't believe us." Viberti slid the book left open on the desk over to him, turned to the blank flyleaf, and in the space hidden beneath the jacket flap wrote: *I need to talk to you. Let's eat together.* Then he shoved the book back to Cecilia.

She didn't understand at first that it was a message, that she

THREE LIGHT-YEARS | 31

should read it, and when she read it she seemed uncertain and vaguely embarrassed. "What's wrong?" she whispered, as if someone were spying on them, though the nurse nearby didn't seem very interested in their business.

He hadn't expected Cecilia to have any doubt about the nature of their talk—his blush, his uneasiness, his look gave him away. An overture like that, for him, was virtually the height of intimacy. He felt exposed, and though the clues were obvious, she was far from the answer and getting colder.

"Nothing," Viberti stammered, "there's no hurry . . ."

Cecilia looked at him, confused. She told him she had agreed to eat with two colleagues. "See you tomorrow, okay?"

He went to eat alone behind the usual column and brooded over the situation, hardly raising his eyes from his plate of boiled vegetables, analyzing and retracing each and every moment of the scene in the ER. What had he been thinking? Why that particular day, why not a month ago, or a year ago, or six months after he'd met her? For a year he'd acted as if nothing had happened, and then suddenly he'd realized that the woman had become irreplaceable.

He'd spent the long weekend of April 25, Liberation Day, with three friends and their families. Had it been the children who'd made him feel his failure more intensely?

Had it been the story by Chekhov or Maupassant or Tarchetti that pushed him over the edge? Or Marta's condition, or the fear of growing old alone . . . ? But if any of these were the case he would have been better off enrolling in a tango class or taking Spanish lessons, or bridge, or he could have taken a trip, a singles cruise. If he wanted to find a mate, anything would have been better. And besides, she might not even be his type (especially since Viberti had never really understood what the expression meant).

"She's not your type," Antonio Lorenzi, his pediatrician friend, had remarked a few months earlier, "why are you attracted to her?"

Viberti mumbled that he didn't know. As if a person always knew why he did things.

"Yes, but there must be something about her that appeals to you."

"At first I didn't like her much," he lied. "She's one of those doctors who call you from the ER asking for a bed and won't leave you alone until you give it to them. But then we became friends and I started to want to see her."

"Do you talk about work?"

"That, too. She's very good."

"Good as a doctor?"

Viberti nodded.

"And what do you want from her, do you want to talk about medicine with her? You talked about medicine with Giulia, too."

"I like her because there's something about her that isn't quite right . . . She dresses funny, her T-shirts are always tight and her pants baggy . . ."

"They all dress like that."

"Yes, but she'll put on a perfect white blouse, and then she'll wear a shapeless sweater, full of holes, over it."

Antonio burst out laughing and Viberti told him to go to hell.

They were a group of friends, old schoolmates, most married with children, Antonio separated with children, Viberti divorced with no children—though according to the others, Viberti's divorce was an annulment in disguise, it didn't count as a divorce and it didn't count as a marriage. It hadn't been like Antonio's blood-sweat-and-tears separation, it hadn't been a marriage with passion, bickering, long faces, joy, satisfaction, and frustration like the marriages of the other three. Every so often they played tennis together, and in the teasing that took place week after week, on the courts or in the locker room, in the endlessly repeated gibes and wisecracks that only they understood and were allowed to toss at one another, in the oral repertoire of their friendship, Viberti's soubriquet was "Claudio, who didn't consummate."

Unconsciously, not ever having spoken to one another about it, let alone to him, the group preferred that he remain a bachelor. He was their mascot. When he went on vacation with them it was only for brief periods of time—any longer and it didn't work. Whether or not their children came along, it didn't work, they all knew it. His friends' idea of his private life was nebulous. Yes, he'd had a couple of affairs after the divorce; one woman refused to sleep at his house because she said there was a "ghost" there. But they didn't know much more.

Since his own divorce, Antonio took it for granted that he and Viberti would be a steady couple. Every Tuesday or Wednesday evening that winter, Antonio invited Viberti over to watch the game. Wednesday, Antonio had his two sons. The house was a mess; a housekeeper came three mornings a week—to "ward off the threat of disease"—but Antonio refused to run the dishwasher and washing machine, or do any cooking or cleaning. Every now and then it was Viberti who summarily tidied up the kitchen, during a break in the game. Maybe when he talked about Cecilia, Antonio was simply worried that his friend might remarry. Maybe he was jealous.

When he said, "Besides, not everyone thinks Cecilia is so great," it occurred to Viberti that he might be jealous.

"Who thinks she isn't?"

"Her colleagues say that—"

"Who?"

"They say she's overly meticulous, sometimes she argues with the nurses."

"I don't believe it."

"She's obsessed with rules."

"But that's good."

"And she gets angry because some of the other doctors' handwriting is illegible."

They both laughed. "She gets angry because doctors have bad handwriting?"

"Apparently."

"Well, that makes her even more likable," Viberti said.

Antonio looked at him, smiling. "We're getting old."

"I don't feel old."

"This is your first senile infatuation."

"I'm forty, leave me alone."

"Forty-three. Don't get upset. I have some good news for you."

"What?"

"She's separated from her husband again, this time for good, they say."

It was the end of February; he'd known her for almost a year.

This time he didn't pretend he already knew it—he hadn't known and he was too stunned to lie. He didn't recall having noticed anything different in Cecilia's behavior recently. She didn't seem more worried or more relieved than usual. He was annoyed that he didn't know, disappointed to find out from Antonio, but then again, why on earth would Cecilia have told him?

The next day, when he meets her at their café, at their table, he's concocted a perfect substitute speech: plausible, urgent, and innocuous. "I have to have my mother looked at, I don't quite trust the geriatrician I made her visit, do you know anyone else?" But seeing her there in front of him, reading anxiety and discomfort in her eyes rather than expectation and curiosity, he realizes that the woman is worried because she knows exactly why he's asked to meet her. She's also had time to analyze and brood after the scene in the ER, and ruling out the less likely hypotheses, has arrived at the truth. It makes no sense to back off now, he doesn't want to look like a coward; better to appear ridiculous. Better to make her uncomfortable than be vilified. He looks at her hair, her mouth; then he lowers his eyes. Today Cecilia is wearing a purple T-shirt with a pair of blue linen trousers, and the edge of the shirt's neckline is a little ripped.

He says, almost in one breath: "I don't know how I could have let things get this far, it doesn't make sense, and it's my fault. I thought about the fact that we've been seeing each other for a year and I felt so anxious. I should have told you sooner, or decided not to eat with you anymore. I don't know, is it normal for us to have lunch together every day?"

Cecilia shakes her head: "I don't know what you're talking about."

Viberti sighs, starts over again: "I don't know how it happened, but I think one of the main reasons is the respect that I have for you as a doctor. I know you don't feel the same attraction, I would have noticed, but in the last few months you've become a kind of torture, so I thought that if I told you maybe I'd be able to stand it, I don't know, maybe it's a stupid idea, I'd like to get over it." He immediately regrets using the word "torture," but he didn't prepare the little speech he's giving now. "Well, torture is an exaggeration, sorry, I meant fixation, obsession, in a positive sense . . ." He's complicating his life, making things worse. He takes a sip of water.

He can't help glancing at her, if only briefly. Cecilia's lips are parted, her chin is quivering a little, she's wide-eyed. Viberti looks away, to the half-empty room of the café. He's not sure he saw her right, maybe she doesn't have that look of absolute astonishment. He glances at her again. She does.

He lied when he said he knew she didn't feel the same attraction—he doesn't know that and indeed continues to hope that the opposite is true. "Look, I didn't mean to make you so uncomfortable, please don't think I want to saddle you with any kind of responsibility. Put it this way: you're both the illness and the doctor, tell me there's no hope, it's better you tell me right away."

Cecilia doesn't smile and Viberti thinks they'll never leave that café. It's a very hot day, not a breath of air, a false spring that's already summer, and a sense of anticipation has hung over things since early afternoon; nothing will ever be resolved with all that light.

"Please, don't make that face," he smiles. "You make me feel like I'm crazy."

"No, I don't think you're crazy," she says at last. "It's just that . . ." She breaks off, opens her hands in a gesture of helplessness.

"You don't know what to say to me, I expected it, you're like me, if I were in your situation I would be afraid of hurting someone and making him suffer, too, but I, well . . . it's what I'm asking you, it's better to hear it directly from you."

Cecilia shakes her head. "It's my fault. I should have told you more about what was going on with me. I've been through some tough months, that much you know. I separated from my husband, I think this time for good. And it was very painful. Now I'm completely drained. Even if there were attraction, I wouldn't have the strength to act on it."

"But there isn't."

"Well, I never thought about it . . . I guess I knew you liked me, but these lunches were too important for me, and I didn't want to give them up."

Important, why? No one has ever insisted on eating with him, not even his mother.

"I'm very confused right now, but you're right, I don't want to lead you on . . . I really never thought of you . . . that way . . . in those terms . . . But I think about you a lot."

"Of course, I realized that . . . I wasn't hoping."

And the fact that he wasn't hoping seems to make Cecilia feel much better and that at least is something Viberti actually does realize. He suddenly feels empty; he has nothing more to say and would like to get up and leave.

They're silent for a time that, to both, seems to stretch on and on.

"I disappointed you."

"No, you didn't disappoint me. I'm disappointed, but it's not your fault."

"You won't talk to me anymore."

"I'll talk to you."

"Will we still be friends?"

"Of course, what do you think?"

"You're a special person."

She's recovered, her eyes are shining, her cheeks have their color back.

"You're very important to me, you know?"

"Don't feel like you have to say these things."

"No, I'm serious. You're an important friend . . ."

Viberti shakes his head, but Cecilia is undeterred and continues her speech. It seems more and more like a eulogy.

". . . you have no idea how many times a day I feel like I want to talk to you, want to tell you about something; I never talked so much with anyone in my life."

The pain he didn't experience when she said no, he's experiencing now. He has to stop her before she adds something else, something irrevocable, as if "friend" weren't enough.

"I'm not sure I like these compliments, you're saying I'm a good listener, a kind of confessor . . ."

"That's not all I meant, and you know it."

"Okay, I exaggerated."

"I meant you're one of the few human beings I've met in this hospital."

Viberti finally relaxes. Yes, he likes that. *The real challenge for a physician is to continue treating patients as human beings year after year and not just as cases because, you see, after a while it's natural for everyone to say things like "tonight a bad case of pneumonia came in" or "the angina in bed 5" or "number 20 is a refractory decompensation," they're formulas of self-defense to depersonalize the illness, but one must defend oneself from this self-defense.* He likes being a human being.

"The others belong to a different species. They're seals and walruses. Hens, barnyard chickens."

Viberti smiles. "I sometimes feel like a dog."

"Why?"

"Eager to obey, too faithful, in need of a master."

"Every now and then it's okay. Every now and then it's all right to be an animal, but not all the time."

"You're a cat."

"God, no. One of those obnoxious ones? Then we can't get along."

Now they're bantering, complicit; he can't let it die. "I'll never forget your expression."

"When?"

"Before. Your expression when you didn't know what I was talking about, and then when you realized."

"What was my expression like?"

"Your mouth was open."

"Impossible, I never have my mouth open."

"I swear, you were wide-eyed and gaping."

"Come on!"

"You weren't expecting it."

"No, I wasn't expecting it."

"Not from such an important *friend*."

"Actually, I was wrong. You're the only one. I have no other friends. Really." She pauses. "But no, I wasn't expecting it. When did you decide to tell me?"

"I didn't decide. Yesterday morning I thought, now I'll tell her that I have to talk to her. And I told you."

"You wrote it to me."

"I wrote it to you."

"Why?"

"I hadn't yet made up my mind whether to really tell you everything."

"But why did you write it?"

He shakes his head. "I don't know."

"And what were you thinking of telling me?"

"Instead of what I told you? I thought maybe I'd tell you something else. Something about my mother, maybe."

"When did you decide to tell me the truth?"

"When you came in and sat down. I thought it was silly for things to keep going like this."

"How long has this been going on?"

"From the beginning. More or less. Ever since I met you. But I didn't know it. Then I had to admit it."

"Had to?"

"I would rather have kept telling myself that I admired you."

She smiles. "You admire me?"

"As a doctor."

"How do you know what kind of doctor I am?"

"I know."

"But it wasn't admiration."

"Not just admiration."

"But do you admire me or not?"

"Very much."

"So then it's been going on for about a year now."

"For a year."

"And all of a sudden you decide to tell me."

"I don't know why. Last night my mother told me a crazy story. My mother is eighty-two. She probably has the beginnings of senile dementia."

"What are her symptoms?"

"She doesn't remember what she just said. She leaves stuff on the stove."

"I'm sorry."

"It's hard to worry about her. Because she's actually in very good health. Then, too, dementia is difficult to diagnose. She took the Mini mental test and scored twenty-nine out of thirty. She came out boasting, saying that even her university professors, the bastards, always gave her twenty-nine. The progression is so slow you tend to think it's inevitable."

"Isn't it?"

"It is, but maybe we shouldn't admit it."

"And the crazy story?"

"The crazy story was by some writer or other, it was the first time she'd mentioned it to me, who knows, it may be that she actually read it, she was a big reader, although I got the impression that she was confusing it, mixing up two different stories. But the funny thing is that the main character's name was Cecilia."

"Did you talk to her about me?"

He smiles. "I don't talk about women with my mother."

When they get up to leave it's as though they'd met to celebrate a birthday; they're sorry that the party is over, but all in all everyone's in a good mood. Viberti pays for the two mineral waters and puts the receipt in his wallet along with the extra passport photo from when he renewed his ID card. He says goodbye to Cecilia with a handshake, smiling. The passersby seem to be smiling also, as do the faces on the billboards, and the grilles of the cars.

I bet at home, cooking himself some pasta *al ragù*, he's whistling. I bet he's not depressed, he's not disappointed, and he's not embarrassed about having been rejected. I have no way of knowing that, I don't know anything, but I'd swear that, for him, having declared his love was actually cause for euphoria; as though everything else, like experiencing it and hoping it might be returned, would follow as a result. Not least because deep down, very deep down, in the unexplored depths of his consciousness, he doesn't for a minute believe that he's been rejected. (Sixteen years later he would use the same blend of self-deception and premonition with me when, at the height of my adolescent rebellion, I told him I didn't want to see him again. He went away whistling after grumbling that I couldn't be serious, that I'd have second thoughts and that he'd always be ready to welcome me back.)

Between an ordinary May 8 and an equally ordinary June 3 they continued meeting at the café at lunchtime. Viberti pretended that the confession had cured him of a foolish infatuation, Cecilia seemed satisfied that he had been cured. But it didn't add up. If they weren't uncomfortable, why was it necessary to act like they weren't? On some days appearing nonchalant became a contest.

They talked about the past year as if it were in the distant past, its memory confused, an Arcadia in which they had been young and innocent. Cecilia confessed that Viberti, with his boiled vegetables, shamed her, made her feel guilty, since she, on the other hand, liked rather peculiar sandwiches, peppers and anchovies, curried chicken, smoked salmon. Once, thinking he wouldn't be there, she'd been caught with gorgonzola and walnut. Viberti confessed the system he had engineered to increase the probability of finding her at the café, always arriving at a quarter to two. He confessed that before he met her he went to eat at twelve thirty, one at the latest. By noon he was usually terribly hungry; he would chew on a piece of gauze to get over it.

They didn't mention his declaration again, but it was as if his declaration enabled them to speak about new, more intimate things. Cecilia apparently felt freer to talk about what she really cared about—her children. Viberti spoke of his mother's illness, voicing a sadness that previously he hadn't wanted to admit he felt.

Meeting elsewhere was out of the question. During those weeks he tried inviting Cecilia to dinner, to the movies, but she told him she couldn't: "Maybe in five or six years," she explained. She smiled but she wasn't joking. All of her time was devoted to her children, and when she spoke of them, when she talked about being locked up in the house with them, she seemed to be describing the valiant resistance of a city under siege or the life of a small community quarantined by the plague.

She said she had a strained but civil relationship with her husband, she said there were no scenes in front of the children when he came to take them for the weekend; it didn't feel like an exchange of prisoners, no, everything was restrained and disciplined, just as the separation had been restrained and disciplined, after the initial phase. The pain shoved to the back of the closet like an unsightly dress. She said, at first, they went to the park along the river to argue. Viberti pictured them walking, free to raise their voices, hurling insults at each other, as he imagined couples did when they separated, quarreling violently. He imagined them far away from the children's microscopic surveillance, like secret agents forced to be wary of confined spaces.

"After the initial phase" and "at first" meant that the separation had gone through different stages and only the first had been confrontational and violent. Viberti was too struck and confused by these confidences to wonder if they made sense. There seemed to be no motivating trigger that had prompted them, no betrayal or growing irritation, and Cecilia, on that subject, was silent. But what did he know about real separations, his hadn't had a motivating trigger either, he hadn't consummated, he hadn't sullied himself with wrongs and recriminations, insults and accusations, words to regret and be ashamed of. He felt ashamed, every now and then, though he didn't tell anyone: he didn't remember why he had married Giulia, he didn't remember why they'd split up.

The motivating trigger was missing from Cecilia's account, and Viberti had no desire to probe. All that mattered was that they had separated for good. He often lingered over another notion: replacing the husband, in the wife's bed and in the children's hearts; becoming a father to them. On the whole, though, since he'd never met the little girl, his fantasies revolved around Mattia. He imagined reading him books in the evening. On Sunday they would go to the stadium and he would explain the plays to him. They would bring a big notebook and sketch the actions and movements of the players on the field. Then he would feel dejected. He knew nothing about those children. He knew nothing about children, period.

It was difficult to picture the children, plus every time Cecilia described them she revised her description, upsetting the tentative image newly formed in Viberti's head; she seemed to do it on purpose to derail him. The children had suffered a great deal on account of the separation and they reacted in different ways. The children had different temperaments and each had reacted in his own way, in the only way two children could react, by trying to forget. The children would never forget, it was impossible. The children had acted too much like adults, they had shown a maturity that their parents didn't possess. The children had acted like children, they had denied and repressed so as not to suffer too much. The little girl had taken on the duty of raising her mother's morale, the boy had become serious and conscientious, "the man of the house." The girl was irresistibly appealing, but after wearing you out with her fussing she left you with only one wish: to strangle her. The girl was petulant and self-centered, she never stopped talking, but in the evening, at dinner, after listening to her for half an hour, pretending to be amused, a surge of tenderness would wring your heart. On the one hand the boy, silent, with no appetite, dignified and never capricious, on the other the sister, who tried so hard to submerge everything in a sea of words. On the one hand the obstinacy of the little ingrate who fought back using hunger as a weapon, on the other the mercilessness of the other little ingrate who wouldn't forgive the mother for having made the father run off.

"Michela thinks it's your fault?" Viberti asked.

"They both think it's the fault of whoever stayed with them, the one who went away was thrown out, he's the victim,"

but then,

"They think it's their fault, they think they did something wrong,"

but then,

"She takes her anger out on her brother, but that's not the biggest issue, I think,"

but then,

"They think he wants to start a new family and have other

children; sooner or later they'll ask me how they should act toward those new siblings,"

but then,

"They don't think anything."

Viberti asked (trying not to sound concerned),

"Does Michela mistreat her brother?"

"No, she's gentle and protective, they play together, they get along very well, only sometimes she lets off steam and starts shouting, and won't let him go into her room anymore,"

but then,

"She has a strange way of excluding him, even when she's not angry with him, every now and then she won't talk to him and I can hear him asking her the same question ten times,"

but then,

"She helps him do his homework, puts away his toys when she sees him lying on the bed reading, she's actually very caring— she acts a bit like a mother but she won't let me cuddle with him, she pesters me until I make him get off my lap,"

but then,

"I don't think she's forgiven me for bringing him into the world!"

Viberti asked (wondering if he was overstepping his bounds),

"How can they think that your husband wants to start a new family? Who could have told them that?"

"No one told them, it's not true, I think it's the last thing he wants,"

but then,

"No one suggested it to them, the fear of having to share him with other children is so strong they just think that, that's all,"

but then,

"Their grandparents, his parents, may have told them that nonsense and then forgotten it a moment later,"

but then,

"If you think about it, though, that's not the strangest thing, the strangest thing is that they're not worried that I might want to start a new family, they take it for granted that I'll always be with them, alone, don't you see?"

"And is that true?" He blushes.

"It is, it is." She stares into his eyes. "They think that because I let them know it, without having to tell them, for fear of losing them I made them understand."

One day, during those weeks, and for the first time since he'd met her, Viberti reconstructed the chronology of Cecilia's life, going back in time: she must have qualified at thirty, had Mattia when she was twenty-six, graduated at twenty-four, had Michela at twenty-three, married at twenty-two. Married at twenty-two. It seemed incredible to him, and even more incredible was the fact that he hadn't thought about it before. He asked her to confirm his calculations, and she did, and started laughing. "You look shocked, what's wrong?" Yes, he said, he was rather shocked. Where had she found the energy to do all those things at once? Cecilia smiled again, and didn't answer.

To tell her about Marta, Viberti began with the nightly homecoming scene. For twenty years, ever since he'd moved to another apartment in the building where he was born and grew up, he'd dropped by his mother's almost every night, at least to say hello, often remaining in the doorway, just to find out if everything was okay, to let her know that everything was okay. Even after his marriage he hadn't changed that routine; in fact, Giulia often stayed to chat with Marta, and seemed happy in the company of the older woman, who encouraged her, advised her without pressuring her, was a friend to her. When their marriage ended, for Marta almost nothing changed; she received visits from both of them, brought them together by inviting them both to dinner at least once a week.

Years passed and Viberti still went home every night faced with the same dilemma: whether to stop by and see his mother or for once pretend he hadn't thought of it. If he was very hungry and couldn't wait to make himself something to eat, he'd hop into the elevator and press the button for the fifth floor, but then he would stop in front of his door and jingle the keys in his hand, making up his mind whether to go in or not. Especially in spring, when the afternoons seemed to go on forever, the light at seven o'clock took on a mellow, tender tone that wore him down, enveloped him, left him helpless.

All he had to do was drop by and say hello, a matter of minutes, but that was exactly what stopped him, the ease with which he could go down three flights of stairs, ring the bell, exchange a few words. Something held him back, a vague desire that surfaced through his resignation, and he didn't want to give in. Yes, he'd go into the apartment and cook himself the steak he'd bought, put the frozen potatoes in the oven, open a new jar of mustard, uncork a bottle of wine, because the evening meal was the only real meal of the day, at lunchtime he never ate more than a salad or a plate of boiled vegetables. *Remember that digestion begins at the time the meal is consumed, never eat too fast, there is no hunger or emergency or work or play that can justify devouring a cup of yogurt in ten seconds, theoretically a mouthful should be chewed at least fifty times, but forty may be enough.* Reluctantly, he put the keys back in his pocket and went down to the second floor.

Gathering his forces to ring the bell, he stood in front of his old door, his first door, the door par excellence, the mother of all doors. And magically, without his ringing the bell, the door opened and his mother appeared in the flesh, mainly bones, with a small watering can in her hand.

"Claudio."

"Ciao, Mama."

Then mother and son turned their gazes to the plants that adorned the light-filled hallway and together they saw the flowerpot saucers overflowing with water, the soil moist, drenched. Marta made an annoyed gesture with her free hand: "Giulia must have watered them," she said. Viberti nodded.

They stayed in the doorway, and he began apologizing for not having come by to see her, even though they had actually seen each other two nights before. She said nothing, prudently, because by continuing the conversation she might be forced to try to remember when she'd last seen her son.

"You haven't come to eat, have you?" she asked in alarm.

"No, Mama, thank you, I have everything ready at home. I just wanted to say hello."

"Everything all right at work? Are the glands se-cre-ting? Dear God, what a difficult word."

"They're secreting, all right!" Viberti replied, smiling.

If they went into the house, by then he'd be sitting at the kitchen table while she went out on the balcony to get rid of the watering can. Though she didn't cook anymore since Giulia had forbidden her to use the stove, the kitchen continued to be her command center.

"Can I offer you anything?" she asked when she returned.

"No, thank you," Viberti replied.

"Have you heard from Giulia?"

"No, not since dinner Sunday evening."

"Did you eat at their place Sunday night?"

She'd been there, too, but Viberti never pointed out her mistakes; he thought it wouldn't do any good, would only humiliate her. Giulia, on the other hand, thought that continually correcting her would serve to stimulate her memory. Giulia was a gastroenterologist, Viberti an internist and endocrinologist, but since he dealt almost exclusively with old people he felt he was more qualified to speak about geriatrics.

Hanging in the kitchen (on the refrigerator, usually, with the same colored magnets that held up Giulia's notes) were recent photos of the two children that Angélica, the caregiver, had left in

Peru, and Viberti made some pleasant comment about how nicely they were growing up. For Marta, those were "grandchildren," too.

Often Viberti would update her on Stefano Mercuri's latest. Marta wondered if the weather was nice on the coast, and Viberti always answered yes, though he never discussed the weather with his old friend. The conversations between them no longer followed the same patterns they had in the past: Viberti would talk solely about politics and medicine, Mercuri would describe the satisfaction he got from tending his vegetable garden.

"Can I offer you anything?"

A pigeon landed on the balcony railing, swiveled his head around his purple-and-emerald neck as though performing a relaxation exercise, and stared goggle-eyed at Viberti.

"No, thank you."

"Pigeons are one of the world's great mysteries," Marta said, shaking her head. She gestured to shoo him away and the movement of her hand was so frail that she seemed to want to detain him, invite him into the house with them.

If Viberti mentioned an old acquaintance he'd accidentally run into at the hospital, Marta would speak up immediately. "I remember him perfectly," she would gush with a triumphant smile, and begin telling her son everything the familiar memory had passed on about the man. It was a simple enough trick—all you had to do was steer her toward the most distant memories, because terra firma lay in the past, whereas the present meant stormy waters where nothing remained afloat for long.

That's why Giulia was wrong; it was pointless to torment Marta by making her feel at fault, it wasn't true that all conversation had become impossible, it was just a matter of finding a safe topic to explore.

"Can I offer you anything?"

The formula itself was strange, even more than its repetition. Never would his mother, in full possession of her faculties, have used the word "offer" with her son, so formal, so distant, as though the metamorphosis of the lexicon were an early sign of a more general metamorphosis by which all things, plants, animals, and human beings, would one day become new and unfamiliar, an entire planet of aliens, virgin territory to be classified, identified, treated with aloof politeness.

"A glass of water, thanks," Viberti said.

"You didn't come to eat, did you?"

"No, thank you, Mama, everything's ready at home." He drank a sip of water. "In fact, I'm going now."

Marta went out onto the balcony and came back in with the watering can in her hand.

"I'll come with you, that way I can water the plants on the landing."

"All right," Viberti said.

Going out ahead of her, he commented that the flowerpots seemed wet already, maybe Giulia had seen to it. Marta nodded, disappointed. She went back inside and closed the door, forgetting to say goodbye to him.

His mother's world. Not yet an alien planet, actually, not yet a virgin land of new and unfamiliar objects. For now, familiar, battered objects that suddenly appeared where they shouldn't be. The pots on the stove, for example, charred turnips and carrots, dried-up soup, evaporated water, red-hot metal. Who'd turned on those burners? She had, but in a parallel universe, which she'd left without retaining any memory of it. Standing outside the door, Viberti tried to imagine his mother's mind, to envision the effect of those sudden apparitions. Of those sudden disappearances. Impossible to remember where she'd placed her glasses just a few moments ago. Impossible to find the money she'd hidden away in a safe spot. It was a world of objects with a life of their own. The life that little by little was slipping away from her.

Viberti went up the stairs, stopping at each landing to glance out the windows. In the courtyard the light had taken on the shade of spent embers. He looked at his watch; some evenings barely ten minutes would have passed since he'd gone down.

When I try to put myself in his shoes, that's how I imagine him: standing between one floor and another, in a no-man's-land, as if, having left his mother's house, he doesn't yet have the right to enter adult life. And I want to say to him, come on, hurry up, because I'm there waiting for you in that adult life, you have to turn your attention to me, don't put it off. But he doesn't move. Staring at his watch, he studies the hand's blithe sweep between seven and nine, stubbornly, firmly indifferent to his mother's fate, and to his.

Cecilia had a vital gift: her attentive gaze. Viberti's stories really seemed to interest her. One day, he even managed to speak to her about his father. He didn't remember ever having spoken to anyone about his father's death.

Cecilia had walked into a café where he was having a cup of coffee. Not the usual café, and Viberti had immediately thought that she was looking for him, that she wanted to talk to him. But no, she had nothing in particular to say.

He asked her, "Did you follow me?"

"You betrayed our café."

"If I know you're not there, I can't bring myself to go in anymore."

Cecilia smiled. "I didn't follow you. I saw you from a distance and you looked sad."

"I'm not sad."

Did she feel guilty for making him miserable, was she troubled by not having noticed anything for a year? He didn't want her pity. Maybe he should tell her, "Don't feel guilty."

But she changed the subject: "Sometimes I wonder why I studied medicine, why I chose this profession. Do you ever feel like that?"

"Always. Not every single day, but often."

"Was it because of your father?"

"Because of my father?"

"You told me he died when you were little."

"Not really little, I was fourteen . . . Why would you think I did it for him? He didn't think very highly of doctors."

"You told me he died of a malignant lymphogranuloma."

"I don't remember telling you that."

"A few months ago, remember that man . . ."

"Sure, now I remember. But my father died in '75."

He began to feel a strange crawling sensation in the pit of his stomach.

"We talked about it because you told me that back then they were incurable, for the most part. Today they would have saved him."

"I think so. But what does it have to do with my decision to study medicine?"

"To save him, to be able to save him in the future." She broke off, gesturing as she tried to explain. "I mean, to save him in your mind."

"Oh. Well, could be."

The thing that surprised him—he realized later, on his way home—was that the woman had thought of him. That she had reflected on the matter for days, trying to find an explanation for him, to come up with a story that *explained* him.

Every so often he imagined his father dying in his parents' old bedroom. The precise moment. Since that time he'd had occasion to witness the deaths of numerous patients. "Death rattle," an appalling term, a frantic tumble down the final slope, "you've taken a turn for the worse." He hadn't been present when his father drew his last breath, because during the long months of the illness he'd been gone a lot, encouraged by his mother to stay away, to take his mind off things. Marta wanted the boy to remember his father healthy, but there wasn't much to remember.

As if reading his mind, Cecilia asked, "Was it a long illness?"

"Yes, quite a few months, but I don't remember it clearly, I must have repressed it." He paused. "No, I don't think I became a doctor because of that. I wanted to follow in someone else's footsteps, a friend of my father's I'm very close to."

Cecilia had never met Stefano Mercuri, but she'd heard about him at the hospital, and had read some of his articles.

"And you, why did you become a doctor?"

"I don't know. I really don't know. When I was younger I wanted to swim."

"Oh, yes, you told me."

She stared at his coffee cup resting on the counter the way she'd stared at the Scénic's fallen keys on the ground a year ago.

Viberti touched her shoulder lightly. "Thank you for following me to talk to me. I'm happy when you talk to me."

Cecilia smiled. "I didn't follow you."

On the morning of Monday, June 3, Viberti wakes up drenched in the relentless light of day and feels an intense desire for fog. Still, he knows that even if it were November he'd have no hope of being satisfied, since these days the fog isn't what it used to be. The climate has changed, the pollution level has changed, the city has changed. When he was a boy, on his way to school at eight in the morning, he would sometimes be afraid of getting lost. He couldn't see a thing ten steps in front of him. Figures would emerge suddenly, as if out of the blue, hazy and featureless and chilled. He'd never again encounter such dismal figures, irritated and fearful, and not only because of the fog. Actually, fog and fear weren't necessarily related in this memory, which was a reassuring, or maybe just nostalgic one; in the fog you could hide, pretend not to see anything and turn the corner. When he got home, Mercuri, the Communist, would often be there. You could discuss things with Mercuri and try to understand what was happening, partly because, unlike other adults, he had no ready-made answers he passed off as "experience," and his misgivings made things easier to grasp. Reflecting on Mercuri's misgivings and what politics were like in the seventies and on politics in general, he gets up and, standing in front of the mirror, remembers that he has to go to a critical union meeting that day: the hospital administrator is out of control, somebody has to stop him.

In the late afternoon he settles into the pediatricians' lounge to fill out a self-evaluation form. The sun cuts diagonally across the long blue table and Viberti sits in the most shaded corner, away from the whitish glare. He spent the weekend at Mercuri's and fell asleep on the beach, getting a sunburn. For three days he thought of nothing but Cecilia; the visit to his old friend made him feel his solitude more painfully (perhaps because Mercuri was alone all his life and has now solved the problem by marrying his housekeeper). He'd like to confess his tenacious obsession to the older man, or better yet he'd like to have him meet Cecilia, introduce her to him and receive his blessing. He'd like to hear him say: "She seems like an excellent doctor." Why is it so important to him that Cecilia be an excellent doctor?

Today he saw her again at lunch and it calmed him. They joked about his sunburn. Seeing her every day is absurd and comforting. The self-evaluation poses a difficulty. There's a question, the last one, which last year he wasn't able to answer: *How do you rate the overall level of your performance?* It's a bit like when you go to the United States and they make you fill out that green card where you have to declare that you are not a terrorist, a murderer, or a thief. The year before, Antonio and Giulia had suggested he write: *Fair, but I can always improve.* They were joking, but he took them seriously and responded in just those words. Then he regretted it, because the personnel office probably thought he was being sarcastic. So today he goes straight to the final question and without thinking twice writes *Fair*, the answer he'll continue to give in the years to come, until the last self-evaluation before his retirement.

He turns the pages and starts the questionnaire from the beginning. The door opens and Cecilia comes in. The doctors' lounge, as it did a year ago, now becomes the scene of future memories, at least as long as the minds in question are able to retain and recall them.

Cecilia isn't wearing her doctor's coat. Time shifts gear, all the moments spent with this woman race by too swiftly, she is too quick to appear and disappear.

"I thought you'd left."

"I'd forgotten a TB case report."

"And you came back specially?"

Cecilia goes over to the window. Outside, the wide tree-lined boulevard is teeming with rush-hour traffic, and beyond it lies the river with two solitary rowers paddling, and beyond the river the green woods of a hill that rises steeply, houses set among the trees.

"Is something wrong?"

Cecilia shrugs. Something's wrong, but what? She turns, looks into his eyes, goes over to him, maybe it was him she was looking for, maybe she wants to talk to him.

She sits down beside him. The collar of her blouse is a little crooked, Viberti would like to straighten it but he restrains himself.

"The sunburn looks worse, you should put some lotion on it."

"Yes, I can feel myself burning."

Cecilia lifts her arm, straightens the collar of his white coat. What a coincidence! He's about to tell her, "Your collar is a little crooked too, let me fix it for you," but she doesn't lower her arm. She slides her fingers to the lapel, just above the pocket. She seems to want to take one of his pens or maybe the stethoscope that Viberti still has around his neck. It's unclear whether that arm is a bridge about to unite them or the measure of a distance keeping them apart.

Then Cecilia leans forward, pulls him to her, and kisses him on the mouth. Viberti is too stunned to part his lips; Cecilia breaks off, but doesn't move away.

They remain close, their breaths mingling, hardly any space between their faces. Five seconds and Viberti recovers. He grabs Cecilia by the back of her neck and sticks his tongue in her mouth with a groan of relief, because this is the time and place to fulfill a desire that has traveled far, was presumed lost and mourned for dead. He kisses her with an impetus that would amaze or disconcert or amuse or excite those who know him, a determination to stay in that hot, moist mouth, to make it his permanent residence, because he has to punish her for making him wait so long, because he's afraid she might change her mind, because he likes it and knows that no matter how long it lasts it will never be enough.

They break off suddenly, both looking toward the door. But the sound was only in their heads. There's no one there.

"Let's get out of here," Viberti says.

Cecilia nods, looking at him as if she wants to kill him. This woman is scared, this woman scares him, this woman isn't scared of anything.

He gathers his papers, gets up, and remembers that he's supposed to go to the union meeting with Antonio. He takes out his cell phone, calls him: "I screwed up, sorry, I'll see you tomorrow." Antonio sighs: "I can't make it either," but he hadn't thought of telling him. Maybe he wouldn't have let him know either, if it weren't *this* that was keeping him from going, but in any case he doesn't have time to think about it now.

They leave the doctors' lounge. Two nurses down the hall greet them with a nod and they respond by raising the same arm, as coordinated as a pair of synchronized swimmers.

"I screwed up?" Cecilia whispers, smiling, as Viberti takes off his white coat in the locker room. Right, he actually said "I screwed up." What was he thinking? Why not "I have an appointment" or "I don't feel well, I'm going home"? If he really wanted to make an excuse. But why does he need to make excuses?

He kisses her again, pushing her against the metal lockers. He wants her to feel how turned on he is, but her backpack is between them. Viberti thinks her mouth is exactly the right size, that their mouths were made to fit together. She pushes him away. "Let's go."

They leave the hospital. They walk quickly; they're fleeing, or chasing something, they're late, they have to make up for lost time. They look around. They don't run into any of their colleagues, but if they had they wouldn't have noticed.

"My car," he says. He points to the other side of the boulevard like a military commander; neither of them smiles at the gesture.

On the opposite sidewalk they pass by their café. "I need something to drink," Cecilia says.

"Yes, but not here."

They get into Viberti's Passat, stop after a couple of blocks, check out a café from the outside, it seems too dismal, they look for another one, they find one. Viberti double-parks alongside some green garbage bins, gets out and goes around the car, and only when he's already on the sidewalk does he realize that Cecilia hasn't gotten out, she's jammed in, she can't get the door open even though she's slamming it rather persistently against a Dumpster. He gets back in the car, shifts into reverse, makes sure the door is clear so Cecilia can get out, then moves forward again, gets out, and locks the car. During all these maneuvers neither of them comments or jokes or smiles even for a second; they're serious and focused as if they were about to rob the café instead of getting something to drink.

This time they don't drink mineral water. Cecilia orders a Campari and, although he doesn't particularly like the taste of Campari, Viberti has one, too. They're sitting at a table in the back of the room, facing the wall. Viberti, leaning forward, strokes the inside of Cecilia's thigh as she spreads her legs and slides toward him on the chair, looking at him languidly, her eyelids half-lowered and her lips parted. She is the picture of a woman who wants to fuck, Viberti thinks, he must have seen it in some film, then immediately corrects himself: no, not a picture, it's she herself, she's the woman who wants to fuck, in the flesh, and it's him she wants to fuck. Can it be? It seems so, but it's still strange. They stammer words of little importance and almost no meaning: "How did it dawn on you," "I don't know what's the matter with me," "All of a sudden like that."

They drink the Campari quickly—as soon as they set their glasses down on the table they pick them back up to take another sip, they toss them down in five minutes. Their thoughts are very confused, not so much about what they want but about how to get it. They get back in the car. They come out on one of the streets bordering the hospital, they end up in a traffic circle, they make two complete turns around it, with no comment, not a smile, not even when the tires screech during too sharp a turn. *Like with all spare parts, it's not worth trying too hard to save money on tires, better to replace them at regular intervals, every year and a half, every two, every three years, depending on how much you use the car; there's nothing worse than having to change a tire yourself, and it's impossible to know when they're worn through, you can't trust the tire guys, obviously, just decide for yourself how long they'll last and then don't worry about it.* Viberti then turns onto a bridge, crosses the river, and drives into a wooded area surrounding a school. Antonio lives not too far away, the neighborhood is familiar to him, and around the corner Viberti knows a dead-end street lined with plane trees, fairly quiet and secluded, where they can talk. Where they can calmly decide where to go to do what they want to do. They should go farther away from the hospital to make sure no one sees them, but what the hell, Viberti thinks, if she's not worried about it why should he be worried? Besides, they're only stopping to talk, that is, essentially to decide what to do and where to go, that is, Viberti is essentially going to try to persuade Cecilia to go straight to his house to have sex, even though getting into his building without running the risk of being seen by Giulia will be a whole other story, but they'll face one problem at a time. But as soon as the Passat is safely parked on the dead-end street, deserted at that hour as it always is, as soon as the engine is turned off, the windows lowered to let in the cool air of late afternoon, as soon as they find themselves close and alone, seemingly alone, safe from prying eyes and unwelcome encounters, Cecilia and Viberti don't start talking.

Without a word they cling to each other and kiss each other and suck each other's lips and bite and touch, pressing and rubbing, they undo buttons and loosen belts and slip their hands under shirts and into jeans. Viberti grabs a breast and squeezes the erect nipple between his thumb and forefinger, Cecilia pulls out his dick and whips her hand up and down, scratching his stomach with her nails, Viberti (in thirty seconds, leaning out of the driver's seat with a contortion that he'll look back on for months with pride and disbelief) manages to lower her jeans and panties to mid-thigh and dives in to kiss and lick the triangle of brown fluff that looks like a stylized drawing of a cunt between closed legs, the drawing of a horny teenager, but this isn't a drawing, down here there's a real cunt, can it be? Yes, it seems it can, and although Viberti has seen a cunt or two in his life, it's as if he were about to see one for the first time. It's like the mythical first time he never had because he preferred to erase the real, disappointing first time from memory, if only the damn panties would come down lower so she could open her legs, if only the legs would open and let him see and kiss and lick what he wants to see and kiss and lick, if only she would slide down on the seat and raise her legs on the dashboard, if only they were in a bed instead of in a car, but suddenly Cecilia pushes him off and screams loudly, loudly enough to be heard at the hospital emergency room: "Stop!"

Viberti raises his head and she hugs him, hiding her face against him and resting her cheek on the patch of chest exposed by his unbuttoned shirt; she's breathing heavily. They're both breathing heavily now that they've stopped, and Viberti, rather alarmed, rather worried, is trying to figure out what could be the matter. "Sorry," he says finally, "I'm sorry, I didn't mean to." But he really did mean to, and she really meant to also, so why is she shaking her head, she's shaking her brown hair against him and holding him even tighter, so what's the problem?

"There's someone back there."

Viberti turns his eyes to the rearview mirror and sees a man with a dog ten yards from the Passat, in silhouette, the unmistakable image of a dog walker with an animal that can't make up its mind to do its business. He's not a Peeping Tom; on the contrary, he's turned his back because he must have seen that there was someone in the car. Viberti could wait, but the man seems vaguely familiar to him. Who does he know who owns a dog? If it were winter, it would already be dark at that hour. There's too much light.

He starts the car and leaves by driving onto the wide sidewalk between the trees and the houses so that the dog walker, across the street, won't be able to see their faces even if he wants to. Meanwhile, Cecilia has straightened her clothes again, she's pulled up her jeans and is buttoning her blouse, concealing the superb splendor she'd shown. "Don't worry," Viberti says, "he didn't see us."

"Did you recognize him?"

"No, why? Who was he?"

"I don't know, I didn't see him."

"It was nobody."

"Somebody from the hospital."

"Is it so bad if they see us? Let's go to my house, we'll feel safer."

"And maybe we'll run into your ex on the stairs . . ."

"She has office hours until eight."

Cecilia shakes her head. "No, I have to go now, it's late."

"Please."

She squeezes his arm, and smiles. "I want to, too, but I can't. We'll talk about it with cooler heads tomorrow."

Viberti isn't sure that a cool head will encourage the realization of his desires, but he nods: "All right."

He takes her to where she left her car, and despite the fact that they are nearly across from the hospital and she's evidently afraid of being seen, Cecilia gives him a long, passionate kiss, or at least that's how it seems to Viberti. Otherwise maybe, when he watches her get out and head toward the Scénic, he wouldn't think: That woman is mine, that woman is mine, that's my woman.

Viberti was right, a cool head never encourages the realization of certain desires, because the next day Cecilia came to the café all worked up, explaining that she hadn't slept a wink all night, but that she'd come to an important decision.

"You don't look tired, or maybe insomnia makes you even more desirable," he said. The words were so unlike him that the panic he was feeling was even more evident. It wasn't the assumed self-assurance of an actor, it was like flailing your arms as you fall through space, a useless conditioned reflex.

Cecilia had thought and thought about what had happened, tossing and turning in bed, and had decided that it was all wrong. It was wrong because she couldn't afford to, she was no longer mistress of her life, plus she wasn't being honest with him, he was an important friend, but he would never be anything more. "I was an idiot, no, more precisely I was a shit, people shouldn't act like that, I don't know what came over me, or maybe I do know—anyway, I'm terribly sorry, now you'll hate me, and you're right, you're absolutely right, you *should* hate me." A speech delivered unhurriedly, calmly, almost in a subdued undertone.

Viberti was stunned, he hadn't seen it coming, it struck him head-on. Not that he felt he had found the woman of his life (or at least the second part of his life), not that he imagined being able to actually marry her, but he certainly hadn't thought it would end so quickly, before it even began. And it certainly seemed like it was really over, the tone and composure used to announce dire decisions proved it.

"Last night I was upset, I felt like I was someone else, I didn't know why I'd done it, and why I then suddenly wanted to take it all back, not just for me, not for what it meant for me, but because I realized what I'd done to you. I'll never forgive myself."

Speaking softly, Viberti said there was no need for forgiveness, there was nothing to forgive, and he certainly wasn't capable of hating her, but he didn't understand and maybe he shouldn't even try to, they would talk about it later (with cool heads? How cool-headed did they need to be?). He told her it was best to let a few days go by, so that both of them would be thinking more clearly.

"All right, but I'm already thinking clearly, that's what I want you to understand. I'm quite clear about the situation. I did some-thing foolish and you shouldn't expect it to happen again; please, tell me you won't expect anything from me anymore, because it won't happen, and it would be worse if you kept . . ."

Interrupting her, Viberti stood and said he had to go back to the hospital, and although he was beginning to get irritated he managed to take her hand and tell her almost affectionately that he didn't expect anything, he was a big boy, inured to this kind of thing, and he didn't expect anything from anyone.

"But don't desert me now," she said.

"What do you mean? It seems to me it's the other way around."

"No, no, don't desert me, you don't know how important you are to me, don't desert me, let's keep seeing each other, keep being friends."

"All right."

"No, don't say 'all right' like that. Promise me."

"I promise."

"We'll see each other at lunch tomorrow?"

"Tomorrow."

He left her in front of the café rummaging through her back-pack, looking for the car key. He took off nearly at a run; he didn't believe in a fit of madness, he didn't believe it had been a slip. He'd like to force her to take another look at herself: not just the kisses and embraces and caresses, not just what she had done or would have been ready to do, but *how* she had done it. A long close-up of her face from the moment they'd shared their first kiss until they'd parted: passion and abandon weren't a lapse, they weren't a mistake, they weren't foolishness. He wanted to force her to open her eyes. Her real face was *that* face, not the wooden mask she'd just shown him.

But he, at least, had to remain calm, not sedated as Cecilia seemed to be, calm and responsible; he had to think and decide for two, since she was wholly incapable of seeing clearly and knew so little about herself. He had to remain calm, but he was so worked up that without realizing it he passed right by someone who'd stopped to say hello.

"Claudio."

Viberti was finally wrenched from his trance; turning, he saw Antonio. He immediately noticed his mischievous expression.

"Hey, I saw you acting like a dirty old goat."

Viberti smiled blankly.

"I have a dog! A present for the boys, I don't know what I'm going to do with it . . . You want it?"

"A dog? You don't have a dog."

"I was out walking the dog and I saw you wrapped around her like a python, I recognized your car. Unless you lent it to someone."

"When?"

"Yesterday afternoon. It's a Dalmatian. He seems really dumb. Come on, don't pretend you don't know what I'm talking about, I can tell from your eyes that it was you."

"Did you see me?"

"Well, I couldn't very well go and put my face up against the window, I'm not a Peeping Tom. Besides, the dog couldn't make up his mind to take a crap. But tell me, is she who I think she is?"

He didn't seem at all jealous, actually. He had already replaced him with the dog and was using those animalistic expressions: acting like a dirty old goat; wrapped around her like a python.

"And you leave him in the house?"

"On the balcony, the house isn't set up, it's already a pigsty. I'm on my way to walk him now, gotta run." He smiled at him again, but this time it wasn't a mocking smile. It was an affectionate look. "You'll tell me about it later," he said, knowing full well that Viberti would never tell him anything. Viberti watched him walk away, thinking he couldn't stand the idea that he'd been discovered, though he didn't know why.

He would've liked to *talk politics*, at least occasionally, find someone to argue with, the way you look for someone to play tennis with, because playing in front of a wall is no fun. But arguing with Antonio, the only likely candidate, was impossible. Antonio was quick to lose his patience. No matter where you started from, he always ended up at the same old place: the idea that they were trying to turn hospitals into corporations, that no one could stop them and that everything else was just talk. Viberti then assumed his hangdog expression and mumbled that, even so, it was important to discuss things, and it was important to try to change things. Antonio would calm down, maybe worried that he'd offended his friend, or maybe he regretted what he had said, and would assure him that the hospital administrator wouldn't have an easy time of it.

Years ago, when he really felt like talking politics, Viberti would take off for the coast, in search of Mercuri. He'd gone to see him the previous Saturday and they'd dined by themselves beneath a grapevine-covered pergola, watching the sea tossed by the vestiges of the previous few days' mistral. Mercuri's wife had prepared *trofie* pasta with pesto and batter-fried zucchini blossoms. Was it an accident that she'd gone off to visit a friend after cooking for them? Viberti had never managed to exchange more than a few words with her.

Mercuri asked him about recent films, concerts, exhibitions; they were the only things he missed from his old life. When curiosity won out over indolence or the needs of his vegetable garden, he rented a film. The last time, he'd seen one that had made him cry. He didn't remember ever crying at the movies. In front of the television, sure, natural disasters, great tragedies had always moved him. On September 11, 2001, he'd cried thinking about the dead and their families. He'd cried thinking about the doctors waiting futilely at the hospitals for the injured. In general he felt like crying even when he saw children in war-torn countries.

But that particular film had moved him in a different way—less routine, more logical.

Viberti asked what he meant by being moved in "a more logical way."

"I know it doesn't make sense . . ."

"What film was it?"

"A film by that Spanish director, *Talk to Her*."

"My God," joked Viberti, who hadn't seen it and was relying on Giulia's opinion, "isn't that about necrophilia?"

"No, no, not at all. It's a love story—about an impossible love, but love nonetheless. And there's a scene where someone sings a melancholy old song, it wouldn't mean anything to you, but it was a song from before the war, 'Cucurrucucú Paloma'; my father used to sing it languidly, with real soulfulness. Listening to it, the main character, Marco, starts crying, and out of sympathy, I started crying too."

There was an awkward silence, then Viberti said, "So you watch a film and you're moved . . ."

"Yes. Although watching a film by yourself makes you a little sad."

"Why by yourself?"

"She doesn't like them," Mercuri said.

"She doesn't like films?"

"She never even watches television, she says she can't understand."

"She's not deaf, though."

Mercuri chuckled. "No, she's not deaf. She says they talk too fast . . . But it's not true, you know, it's that it just doesn't interest her."

What was Mercuri alluding to with that laugh? That his wife was such a simple soul she couldn't even appreciate Italian television? Or that truly simple souls didn't let themselves be contaminated by television? She was his wife, and it was best not to try to figure it out. He'd married her because they shared something—life in that town, the garden, the silence, the bed.

Viberti had drunk three glasses of wine; it was a gorgeous day, the food was excellent and the view fantastic. He wasn't easily moved, no, he'd been brought up not to feel sorry for himself, but at that moment, all of a sudden, he felt a lump in his throat and had to rest his fork on the plate and turn around to face the rooftops of the town that stretched out between them and the sea, pretending to study the Saracen tower that he knew by heart, so that Mercuri wouldn't notice what was happening to him. He pictured Cecilia sitting at the table with them. He imagined taking her there on a proper visit, to introduce her to his old friend. He wished she were there with him.

After a while Mercuri asked about Marta. Viberti would rather discuss her situation calmly over coffee, show him the tests; he didn't want it to become just so much talk—that would make it too easy for the elderly doctor to quickly withdraw into his usual fatalistic mind-set. But Mercuri's influence over him was so strong that Viberti always ended up smoothing the way and making things easy for him, as though for a debt incurred long before and never settled. And so, by turning the conversation toward Giulia's hardline approach, and jokingly using the term "aggressive care," he ended up giving Mercuri what he wanted: the chance to decree that harassing Marta was pointless, there was nothing to be done.

Then, with a drastic though futile gesture, sacrificing the best troops to an enemy who had already won, Viberti pulled the test results out of his briefcase. Mercuri looked at them, asked a few questions. What did the doctor who'd seen her most recently say?

"The geriatrician mentioned only annual checkups, to monitor the rate of decline—for that matter, it's not a given that it will get worse."

They discussed the advisability of mild antidepressants, and Viberti admitted that he hadn't understood (or hadn't wanted to understand) whether the geriatrician was recommending them or not, since in any case it was a matter to address with the psychiatrist, and Marta wasn't necessarily depressed.

Who said she was?

Giulia said so. Because Marta shut herself up in the house, she didn't want to go out.

Mercuri shook his head, muttered something. Instantly his eyes were brimming with tears (he wasn't afraid to show emotion, not him) and, smiling sadly, suddenly showing all of his eighty years, he said: "But maybe it's not the worst ending, you know, not remembering anything anymore." The very words Viberti had dreaded hearing from him that day.

He felt a tinge of anger toward the old man. He immediately repressed it. He had thought about it during the entire train trip and he'd said to himself: "If I prepare him well, if I back him into a corner, he can't brush me off in five minutes." It was important that his mentor not show indifference to their profession, that he not be reluctant to talk about new treatments, new drugs, new developments. It was sad that he didn't care about anything anymore. Still, he cared about Marta, and as Mercuri wiped his eyes Viberti squeezed his arm, placed a hand on his cheek, uncertain whether to extend the gesture into a caress, then put away the folder with the test results.

"Every so often," Mercuri said, "I think back to what she used to say: 'When the end comes, abandon me on the ice pack,' remember? It always made me laugh."

"Yes, and you know why she said it?"

"She always lived in holy terror of Alzheimer's."

"But the idea of the ice pack came from that film we saw, *The Red Tent*."

"Did I see it with you?"

Viberti was fourteen when his father died. The family consisted of three people, but his father worked ten hours a day, and often he didn't return for supper or was off traveling. In the rare moments when he was at home, he was barely noticeable, always sitting in a corner of the couch reading the newspaper, his tie loosened, the cuffs of his white shirt rolled up, a cigarette slowly burning itself out in the ashtray. He wore a black Chinese cap with a silk border, because he claimed that "the tip of his head" felt cold in the house. In general, he always claimed his "extremities" felt cold: "my fingertips are cold," "my ears are cold," even "my chin is cold." Seeing him from behind in the hallway, in a cloud of bluish smoke, with that skullcap of sorts, he seemed out of place, transient, as if in a waiting room.

Yet after his death, the apartment took on an air of bleakness and desolation. In the evening, at the table, Marta and Viberti found themselves caught up in a different kind of solitude, which they couldn't get used to: they weren't expecting anyone, no one would ever come home. At fifty, Marta was a widow with a teenage son even less talkative than his not very talkative peers. Imperturbable, inscrutable, it wasn't clear if his father's death grieved him, it wasn't clear if the mild hostility he'd shown his father when he was alive had become rooted in a deeper resentment. So Marta filled the silence of those first weeks of mourning by telling him everything she knew about her husband's colorful family, scattered throughout the world and therefore rarely if ever seen, a lengthy serial novel that included: a cousin who was a doctor in that town of concertinas and accordions; a recluse aunt who lived in the country (the only time she'd come to visit them, she'd locked the cat in a chicken coop so he wouldn't run away and had returned three days later to find him strangled in the wire mesh, the metal links painstakingly and cleverly spread apart after a struggle lasting several hours); another aunt who had a more or less secret passion for Johnnie Walker; a great-grandfather, a trumpet player, who died of Spanish flu after playing an infected instrument; a grandmother who knew three languages but had never traveled (she carried on an uninterrupted correspondence with perfect strangers around the world for the sole purpose of practicing, and had received two marriage proposals as a result); a great-uncle who died in battle on Mount San Michele in 1915; a cousin in America who had divorced and then remarried the same man years later. Characters whom you could better imagine with animal faces, like in a fable: the grandmother a turtledove, the great-uncle a bear, the cousin a rabbit, the aunts a cat and a fox. But there was no chance of hearing the only story that would have stirred Viberti's interest, the one about the four years his father had spent in a POW camp, in India, during the war. Marta knew almost nothing about those years because her husband had never spoken to her about it (he'd told her only that he'd suffered greatly from the cold: in India?). He hadn't wanted to talk about it, and Viberti deluded himself in thinking that, if he hadn't died, his father would sooner or later have told him more. Under this delusion, he believed that if they'd been adults together his father would not have been able to keep those stories from him, as if adults always told each other everything.

What he especially remembered about his mother's stories was the tone: anxious (Marta worried that her son would forget his father too quickly) and solemn (his father's genealogy evoked to take the place of a living father).

And yet what did Viberti remember about his father? Almost always the same four incidents:

(1) at age five, to impress him, he'd asked Marta which hand was his right one, but before he got to that famous couch, he got confused, and when he raised his left hand, saying, "This is my right hand!" his father, without looking up from the news-paper, absently and rigorously shook his head no;

(2) at age seven, one of the rare times he'd found himself alone with his father, he'd spotted a sign at an intersection that pointed to the airport (they were in the car together and head-ing in that direction) and became afraid his father wouldn't have time to bring him back home, a terror of having to follow him to the ends of the earth;

(3) at age ten, passing a car parked near the house, his father had exclaimed, "Necking!" and his mother, annoyed, had shushed him;

(4) at age eleven, Stefano Mercuri had been to dinner at their house and they'd discussed politics all night (Mercuri was a member of the PCI, the Italian Communist Party, Viberti's father was a liberal); after seeing his friend to the door, his father had returned to the table, poured himself a final glass of wine, and exclaimed: "So, in the end, we protect them, too, from their stupid ideas!"

Other memories occasionally floated to the surface, but were quickly driven back into the depths by time. Those four incidents, however, returned regularly in circumstances related to: (1) mak-ing a bad impression; (2) anxiety; (3) sex; (4) politics. Ostensibly insignificant memory talismans, worn from use but still effective.

In any case, Marta's family stories ended with Mercuri's ar-rival. He'd met them one afternoon as they were leaving a movie theater: they'd been to see *The Red Tent*. Marta had thought that a story about a dirigible at the North Pole would be action packed enough to entertain her son, who, to be sure, would never forget the film for the rest of his life. He specifically recalled the scene where one of the survivors of the disaster stripped down to his woolen underwear and slid into a crack in the ice to end it more quickly.

Marta had apparently let herself go a bit and therefore her hair "was a mess" as she put it; and yet despite that—or perhaps because of it—she was even more attractive. The boy was emaciated, as if he hadn't eaten for weeks, hadn't his mother noticed? Mercuri didn't let on how worried he was and how attracted, but insisted on going home to supper with them, acting like an intrusive friend, as if he were begging them to invite him, as if he were dying of loneliness. Only too happy to have a guest, mother and son welcomed him warmly. It didn't occur to the son that Mercuri was certainly not the type of bachelor to eat a reheated dish alone in front of the television at night; if the mother thought that, she didn't say so to her son.

From that day on, at least three or four times a week, Mercuri would ring the doorbell around seven o'clock: not that he needed an excuse, but one night he began telling them that a patient had given him two pounds of homemade pasta; the following evening it was a salami, then a jar of mustard, even a roast chicken. It became a game, to the point that patients occasionally brought him a full bag of groceries from the supermarket. But Mercuri didn't only stock the pantry. He cooked, and kept mother and son amused with stories about patients and inept, uninformed physicians, a whole catalog of egregious blunders that years later would in fact end up in a joke book. Month after month he was a constant presence in their lives, even on weekends, when he played tennis with Viberti, even during the holidays, when they went skiing together. The dead father became a difficult subject to deal with, and was almost completely set aside. Mercuri, unlike Viberti's father, had a wealth of anecdotes about the war, which he'd taken part in when he was sixteen, fighting on the right side, and which he'd won (so to speak). He was a born storyteller.

———

Antonio had caught them at it. Antonio unpredictably disguised as a dog owner. Summoning up all four memory talismans associated with his father: anxiety ("Cecilia might find out she'd been recognized"); bad impression ("caught going at it in the car like a python"); politics ("I missed the union meeting"); sex ("necking").

Antonio wasn't a dog owner for long; he managed to find a colleague, a cardiologist, who accepted the gift, since he had a house with a yard. He turned up unexpectedly one evening at Viberti's place quite depressed, or at least depressed enough to want his friend to see. And therefore very depressed. Viberti had rented Almodóvar's *Talk to Her* and had just started watching it. Antonio buzzed the intercom and invited Viberti to come and have a drink; Viberti didn't feel like going out and invited him to come up.

Antonio came in, spirits sagging, telling him about the dog and the cardiologist. Then, with a glass of wine in hand, he began complaining about his hopeless situation, perfectly illustrated by the dog's inevitable fate. (A) His ex-wife's brainless parents give their grandsons a Dalmatian puppy, using their mother and father's histrionic, stormy separation as an excuse not to deny the boys anything. (B) His ex-wife refuses to let the dog inside the house and the kids hand it over to him, promising to walk it twice a week. (C) They keep their promise for half a week and don't take care of it on the weekends they spend with him. (D) Antonio has a very serious talk with his sons, who nod and agree that he will give it away to a colleague, because they hadn't expected it to end any differently, because they couldn't care less about the dog, because they're fourteen and thirteen years old and very unfocused. So the dog becomes a symbol of what the children can no longer have, the parents' union, the all-embracing love, the cartoon-like polka-dotted mantle that protects the family, a piece of inane rhetoric. Viberti nodded. Yes, Antonio was *extremely* depressed. He'd never heard him talk that way. He tried to put it in concrete terms, spelling out objective, irrefutable justifications: "How would you take care of a dog, working all day?" But that evening

Antonio wasn't listening to justifications, least of all objective, irrefutable ones.

They sat in silence, staring at the bottom of their wineglasses. Antonio asked him if he was watching a game.

Viberti said no, there were no good matches on, and besides, he'd rented a film.

"I'll stay and watch part of it."

"I'm not sure you'll like it."

"What's it about?"

"A woman in a coma."

"Great."

They often watched soccer together on television. Or they watched separately, calling each other to banter about the results, or after a goal, or even after a goal that had been narrowly missed. They watched with married friends when big games were on, and took in the Tuesday or Wednesday cup matches with Antonio's sons. They watched soccer on other evenings as well, recorded matches, minor teams from the German Bundesliga or the English Premier League or the Spanish Liga.

Viberti restarted the DVD. After a while, Antonio asked if there really wasn't a game. Viberti said he *wanted* to see the film, Mercuri had recommended it to him and it would be courteous on his part to call him and tell him what he thought of it.

"Can't you lie to him?"

They began laughing at the characters' expressions.

Marco, a journalist, was in love with a female bullfighter, Lydia.

"So you're separated," said Lydia.

"I'm single," Marco corrected her.

Maybe it wasn't a good idea to see that particular film that night.

Lydia was gored by a bull and ended up in the hospital, in a coma.

"In your opinion," Viberti said, "did I become a doctor so I could cure my father?"

"How do you mean?"

"Because I felt guilty for not having saved him, as if I were responsible for his death."

"Oh," Antonio said. "Well, even if you did kill him, we're past the statute of limitations by now."

He added that he was beginning to like the film.

Viberti, on the other hand, was bored. He didn't understand what Mercuri had seen in it. Caetano Veloso crooned "Cucurru-cucú Paloma" accompanied by guitar, cello, and double bass. Marco started weeping, though actually, he wept only a single tear and anyway it looked fake. Viberti pictured Mercuri crying as he watched the actor cry.

"I wept when something moved me because I couldn't share it with her," Marco said.

At the hospital Marco met Benigno, a nurse in love with another young woman in a coma (Alicia, a ballet student).

"Alicia and I get along better than a lot of couples," Benigno said.

"You talk to plants, but you don't marry them," Marco pointed out.

Antonio laughed. "This film is pretty interesting."

"Are you kidding?"

"I'm dead serious."

He said that at a certain age men preferred women that way, in a coma.

Viberti felt uneasy. True, maybe it was a good film, but he wasn't in the right mood. His discomfort grew when Benigno ended up in prison, accused of having raped Alicia, and, later, committed suicide. And when Marco realized that Alicia had come out of the coma giving birth to Benigno's (stillborn) child, when Marco saw her, recovered, at the dance school across the street, Viberti felt the same emotion he'd experienced sitting under Mercuri's pergola.

He leaped up, ran into the kitchen, and went out on the balcony through the open French door.

When he didn't come back, Antonio followed him, embarrassed, lingering a few feet away in the kitchen. He asked him what was going on. What was wrong? Did he feel sick?

Viberti couldn't calm down, he couldn't answer. He didn't understand why Cecilia didn't want to be with him. It seemed unbearably unfair.

It lasted a few minutes. Antonio turned halfway around, as if to leave, and stood there staring at the refrigerator. They'd known each other for thirty years, but they'd never found themselves in this kind of situation.

Viberti got the idea of using his mother as an excuse. He said it was terrible to think that a person could vanish like that, into thin air.

Antonio nodded, pretending to believe it.

But that's what a true friend was, Viberti thought later. A true friend pretends there's nothing wrong and believes the first excuse that pops into your head.

After Giulia left the apartment and moved to the third floor, Viberti hadn't replaced the furniture she'd taken with her. They had divided it up as equitably as possible, joking about it: "You get the couch, I get the armchairs." He hadn't even shifted the remaining pieces to disguise the gaps that had been created. The furniture Giulia had chosen or drawn by lot had left behind a paler mark on the walls after its brief stay in that house. Roaming through the apartment, absently entering a room, Viberti sometimes thought he saw those pieces again. A phantom chest of drawers. The skeleton of a wardrobe. The suggestion of a painting.

On many evenings, during the months of June and July, Viberti convinced himself that what had happened in the doctors' lounge and later in the Passat had been a mistake, as Cecilia said, and though he didn't speak to her about the matter again, he let her know (or rather he thought he let her know) that he'd accepted the verdict, however harsh and final.

He never went straight home, and would sometimes linger in his mother's kitchen until ten or so. Lying, he'd tell her he'd already eaten, and he'd listen to Marta's memories as they went further and further back in time, ever more complicated and farfetched, forgetting he was hungry until he crossed the threshold of his own apartment, where he would open the refrigerator in a rush, eat something cold, and go straight to bed. Some evenings, though, he found himself alone, and after supper he would sit out on the balcony in an old wicker chair, watching the courtyards for hours. Evenings when it had rained, evenings when it couldn't make up its mind to rain, oppressive evenings, the sky stainless steel, heat you could cut with a knife, a fresh breeze like an unexpected gift, the light impervious.

On the balcony he often recalled an incident that had occurred during a period when Marta was sad. He used to think it had happened after his father's death, but recently he'd become certain he'd been mistaken. The day after the incident he'd had a fever, he remembered this, too, quite clearly.

She'd locked him out on the balcony by accident, when he went out to get a bottle of mineral water. And she hadn't heard him calling her. Maybe because she'd gone to bed. And stayed in bed all afternoon. She didn't realize she'd locked him out until eleven o'clock that night, when she turned on the light in the kitchen to make herself some herbal tea. He'd been outside on the balcony in just a T-shirt for seven hours, in the middle of winter. He smiled, remembering it. And they'd always laughed about it with each other. But what was so funny? He might have been twelve or thirteen. Out in the cold like a survivor from *The Red Tent*. He'd come down with bronchitis and Mercuri had hurried over to treat him.

Marta! How could he be angry with Marta? Hold a grudge against his mother over such a stupid thing? In fact he didn't hold it against her. He'd even created an alibi for her: his father's death. But in reality (he recalled) it had happened *before*, not after. And then another time she'd left him locked out of the house all afternoon. He kept ringing the doorbell, but Marta was in bed and didn't hear it.

And yet, and yet . . . Two episodes of shirking her motherly responsibilities in eighteen years (if you considered the age of majority as the cutoff). Two incidents of probable blackout due to depression in eighteen years. He didn't recall any others. But perhaps there had been some and he hadn't noticed them or hadn't wanted to notice. Those two he'd had no choice but to notice, Marta had forced him to be more alert. Maybe because usually he paid no attention? Maybe so that he would report the episodes to someone else? His father? Mercuri? Too complex, too convoluted, his mother wasn't that convoluted, no one was that convoluted.

In any case, he didn't hold it against his mother, and his mother had never been seriously depressed. No matter what Giulia thought.

Still, he remembered that afternoon and that frigid evening spent out on the balcony. He hadn't dared break the windowpane, maybe he should have. Huddled against the French door to steal a little warmth, watching the lighted windows of the houses across the way. People moving about in a yellowish, sixty- or seventy-five-watt glow, getting ready to go to bed in that luminous space. Lowering the shutters, as though shutting their eyes and not seeing him. Acts of hostility toward him. If only he'd at least seen a woman undressing.

One evening, toward the end of July, my father moves his armchair outside, prepared to let his gaze wander along the perimeters formed by the dividing walls between the courtyards. Imagining him in that position has a strange effect on me, given that later on I saw him many times, as an old man, observe the same courtyards with a serene expression on his face. I have to erase that serenity and replace it with anxiety and dejection.

The block where Viberti, Marta, and Giulia's apartment house is located is a group of buildings, four or five stories high, almost completely surrounded by walls on all sides, like a fortress. The balconies and windows are draped with rainbow flags against the war in Iraq. Only on the left does a low building break the line of the interior facades: at one time it was an old factory that made pudding molds, now it's a supermarket. The center of the quadrangle is occupied by a garage, now converted into a gym, and a small storehouse with a red-tile roof, nearly falling apart, where generations of cats have lived. The remaining space is divided among the courtyards. The smallest even has a little garden with a very tall pine tree; the others are paved with concrete tiles.

My father knows them well, those tiles. Rough but slippery, awful on the knees and elbows. As a child he spent his afternoons spinning around the yard on his bicycle, leaning in at every curve like a motorcyclist and covering himself with scabs from the inevitable falls. As a boy, when the weather was nice, he liked to study in that wicker chair, watching the cats' antics, the factory workers carrying the aluminum molds, the cars driving up the garage ramp, for hours as he reviewed his lessons. Rather than being a distraction, the courtyards' panorama had become a mnemonic device: he would associate each courtyard with the paragraphs of a certain chapter or the assumptions of a theorem or the phases of a historical event. Now, each time he returns to the balcony, his eyes feel compelled to follow a specific order. Only after he's done so can he let his gaze and his thoughts wander.

At one point he thinks he sees a shadow slip between two chimneys on the roof of the supermarket. The more closely he looks, the more he thinks he knows who it is. It's Giulia's husband. What is he doing on that roof? It's not something that intrigues him or arouses his curiosity. He's never been jealous of Giulia's husband. He's never been as fond of Giulia's son as he's been of Cecilia's son, for example. Then, too, as a general rule, he's always preferred to know as little as possible about other people's business. *As a general rule, it's always best to know as little as possible about other people's business. Not that it's difficult to keep the things you accidentally come to know to yourself and pretend you know nothing. But even if you pretend not to know, you do know, and your life is invaded by the lives of others. You see someone slapping his son as you're walking along the street. Then, each time you see him, you think about how many times he's probably slapped his son in the meantime.* Giulia's husband walks unhurriedly to the storehouse, climbs over the tile roof, disappears on the other side. As if it were no big deal, as if he did it every day. He can even do it twice a day, as far as I'm concerned, Viberti thinks.

Can anyone see *him* on the balcony? Someone from the windows across the way? Someone who, like him, has lived in the same house for forty years and noticed his inconsequential move upstairs, who has realized that the boy on the second floor who was once locked out on the balcony has become the solitary adult on the fifth.

He's angry, he feels let down. He's only forty-three years old, but he feels Cecilia was his last chance to be happy with a woman, and, besides that, his last chance to have a child. He feels his loneliness will have to be filled by friends and other people's families and by his work. He feels he's always known this, that he's always imagined he'd grow old alone and self-sufficient. He feels he will never make love with Cecilia.

The phone rings, it's her. She tells him she was at a pizzeria with some colleagues a few nights ago, the children are away at summer camp, and she felt bad about never wanting to go out with him and she'd like to make up for it and invite him to a restaurant on the river. "All right," Viberti says.

———

At a restaurant for the first time, sitting across from each other at a candlelit table. There's a gentle sound of flowing water, creating silvery eddies along the riverbank. There are mosquitoes that bite only the feet, like fetishists. There is the clink of silverware against plates, the buzz of conversation. It's very hot, but Cecilia is in a good mood and Viberti can't keep up with her stories. She teases him because he's eating normally: "I think I've only seen you with boiled zucchini, potatoes, and spinach." She calls him Dr. Anorexic and Mr. Bulimic. "That's not exactly true," Viberti says defensively, flushing. He'd like to explain his nutritional approach to her, but she's already moved on to something else.

Two nights ago she'd gone out with some colleagues and they'd ended up in a horrible pizzeria near the hospital. Not to celebrate the start of vacation, since, as the chief surgeon pointed out with a wistful expression, "The days when everyone took vacation at the same time are over." When he was young, the city emptied out in August, there were no sick people anymore and legendary soccer tournaments were organized at the hospital. "Good times," a nurse whispered in Cecilia's ear, "when we were in short pants." Cecilia does a perfect imitation of both the pompous head doctor and the Neapolitan nurse and Viberti laughs.

But it's true, only a third of them will start vacation the following Monday, cities don't empty out anymore. So how come they all went out for pizza, then? To say goodbye to a nurse who is leaving: she's taking a year's leave of absence to go work in a village in Mali. At the end the young woman made a short speech with tears in her eyes, and despite the lousy pizza, the subzero air-conditioning, and the unrelenting neon lights, everyone was glad they'd gone to send her off. The chief surgeon hugged her and made a silly joke, loudly, so everyone could hear. The doctors and nurses, exhausted, laughed in unison with a strange sense of liberation.

Viberti, too, keeps laughing; Cecilia's high spirits are contagious. Under the trees, along the river, the heat is almost bearable.

But after dinner, when they get to the street, the asphalt is scorching and steamy.

"If this keeps up, all my little old folks will die of dehydration," Viberti says. He's thinking about the death of letting her leave by herself, the death that is life without her.

He thinks Cecilia is about to say good night and he's prepared for a disappointing kiss on the cheek. He offers to take her to her car.

"I didn't come by car," Cecilia tells him.

"You seem angry," Viberti says, "is it my fault?"

"It's always your fault." She shakes her head with a sad smile.

They get into the Passat without another word, Viberti crosses the bridge and turns left onto the broad, tree-lined drive that runs along the river. He drives in silence, he doesn't exceed thirty miles an hour, Cecilia has her seat belt on and has leaned her head back, closing her eyes. Five traffic lights, red, green, red; at the second-to-last intersection Viberti slows down, hoping the light will turn yellow; at the last he actually stops at a green light. The giant trees form a dark curtain that hides the river and the sweltering city beyond it. Cecilia hasn't opened her eyes, but when they reach the piazza surrounding the large circular church she takes Viberti's hand, resting on the gearshift, and asks him to go back. "Back where," he asks, "to the restaurant?"

She asks him to drive back along the riverfront the way they've come. They cover the same route back and forth twice, as if they've decided to spend the night driving, in the air-conditioned car.

After the third lap, Cecilia opens her eyes, turns to Viberti, and looks at him.

Viberti doesn't ask her to go with him to his apartment, he knows she wouldn't agree. He drives in silence along the broad avenue that runs along the river, until he finds a dark, secluded spot.

READMITTED TO HUMAN SOCIETY

Memory is unfair. The person remembering is now older. She was no longer able to feel what she had once felt for Luca. She remembered clearly the sensation of something that was fading and then the sensation of no longer feeling anything, and later still the anger and regret; she'd lost him forever. She remembered how she'd felt, having loved him in a hazy former time, and realizing that she didn't love him anymore, not at all, at that moment, an instant before, discovering that she hadn't loved him for who knows how long. She'd begun to stop loving him without being aware of it, maybe because it wasn't possible to know it before being ready to admit it and by that time it was too late. And besides, the person remembering is now older and more disillusioned and forgetful than the young, deluded, determined protagonist of her memories. That's why memory is unfair.

She had loved him. It wasn't true that she didn't remember. She'd loved him and she had proof of it. There had been gestures, places, words; they acted as clues, memories that she guarded closely, at times loathing or feeling ashamed of them. Every now and then smiling over them. She'd loved him, a long time ago. Only if she'd loved him could she have done and said and thought certain things. She had told at least two girlfriends that she was completely *infatuated* with him. She'd written "I love you" on a bus ticket and put it in his coat pocket so he'd read the message when he stamped the ticket in the machine (only now did the sexual innuendo of the act occur to her). She didn't know how to iron but sometimes she had to iron a shirt of his, and as she ironed it she thought he'd notice how badly it was ironed and he'd feel the wrinkles on his skin and he'd think of her.

Motionless in bed, sleepless nights. She didn't want to take sleeping pills every night, maybe she should have. But she was so tired that deep down she liked the simple fact of lying there in bed, motionless. And also knowing it. As if knowing that she still had four hours of dark immobility ahead of her were more restful than spending that time unconscious in sleep. She didn't move, didn't turn over, didn't straighten her legs or hug her knees. She lay motionless in one position, facedown on her stomach. And her thoughts weren't necessarily unpleasant thoughts. Her mother's words, after-school arrangements, incidents from the ER. Calm, slow processions, each thought leading another by the hand, or one hand on the shoulder of the thought ahead of it, like the Beagle Boys. Anxious thoughts arose every now and then out of fear and fueled it, but they too moved along unhurriedly.

The first thought always concerned her child. Let the boy be all right, let him continue to eat, let him become more cheerful and spirited, let him grow stronger, let his arms and legs grow sturdier, especially his legs: the thought of her son's scrawny legs was the advance guard sent out by anxiety to reconnoiter. After which she thought and thought about his meals, comparing them, recalling them, summoning up details from recent days, as well as times from previous weeks that had signaled some progress (when he'd asked for a second helping, even a small one, when he'd shown a liking for a certain dish—and then she'd remember, make a mental note of that dish, create variations, use it as a staple to make him eat more) or a minor setback (decipher the cause without him noticing, figure out if he'd eaten too many snacks or heavy foods at school, or if he had any allergies, find out if something had upset him). Overcoming her anxiety, making his terribly skinny figure seem innocuous, driving back the bleakest thoughts by making a list of things to do. First, don't make him feel like he's under observation. Second, forestall his refusals. Third, take your time planning dinners. Fourth, engage him by appearing distracted. Fifth, let him help you set the table. Sixth, don't overdo it when filling his plate. Seventh, don't rush him (don't watch him out of the corner of your eye, don't check on him, don't touch his plate, don't correct his posture or the way he holds his knife and fork). Eighth, let him have a choice. Ninth, accept it when he leaves something, but remember how much he left. Tenth, if he's happy he'll feel hungry. The Ten Commandments, the Covenant of the Dinner Table.

Before and after the first separation, the sleepless nights weren't at all restful. Back then her thoughts raced along swiftly, rising in intensity and then suddenly plummeting in twisted downhill spirals, against a backdrop of catastrophic scenarios.

When she and Luca had shared that bed, she would toss and turn to wake him, irritated that he went on sleeping, unaware, or seemingly unaware, of the intensity of her anger. Angry that he woke up rested and better equipped than she was to face another day of fighting. When he finally left and she had the double bed to herself, she'd tossed about in all directions, kicking and getting it out of her system as she'd never been able to before. But there was no longer anyone to awaken. Those had been nights of nervous gymnastics, of anxiety and fear. Then she'd given in to a sleeping pill.

Mattia had been ill; Luca came back home for a few months

and then left again. Now she saw him once or twice a week, depending on her shifts. Peaceful meetings on the landing, the children entering the house, passed from one warden to another (they had stopped calling it a "prisoner exchange," sarcasm had lost much of its appeal), and him lingering for five minutes of very civil conversation, encouraging and comforting. Whatever the topic of their talk, his words said that they could do it, lots of couples were in their situation, there was nothing dramatic about it. That's what the words said, and she submitted to them without putting up any resistance, neither curbing nor encouraging it, accepting each conversation for what it was. But meanwhile she kept thinking—and it had come to her often, recently, like the refrain of a song—she kept thinking: How strange, I loved this man.

The second time he left, there was no violent wrench. Maybe there'd been no wrench at all, ever. He hadn't been the only one who'd gone, maybe. Both of them had agreed to leave the past behind. If they hadn't gotten back together for those few months, following Mattia's hospitalization that winter, she might not have mislaid the memory of her love. But she wasn't even sure of that. A year ago: How could she remember what she'd been capable of feeling a year ago? A year ago she still felt an attraction. Though she hated him more, she felt a serious sexual attraction toward her future ex-husband. She hated him and she wanted to fuck him. Many nights, during the prisoner exchange, she felt like grabbing him by the tie, pulling him into the house, and taking him to bed. And then throwing him out again. But it was difficult to explain the real difference between sex and love to a man (men were sure they knew it, they thought they knew it). Then, too, what *was* the difference?

A moment ago it had seemed quite clear to her. Maybe she was getting sleepy. When her thoughts became confused and contradictory it meant that she was getting sleepy (thoughts that the next day would seem confused and contradictory). But she wasn't getting sleepy. She was just confused. What she meant was, if they hadn't gotten back together, she would have always nurtured in some corner of her mind the idea that she still loved him or that she could go back to loving him. Instead they'd gotten back together and she'd suddenly lost the impetus of hostility she had toward him. They had an emergency to deal with, their child needed them. She'd begun to see Luca as an old friend who could help her.

She could gladly see that new old friend of hers a couple of times a week without missing him. But when he came back home for a time, they'd again made love as husband and wife. Luca no longer seemed horrified by her, as he'd claimed to be a few months before. When he couldn't touch her. When he said he no longer recognized her. He'd come back home because their child was ill and they'd made love again to conceive him a second time, to have him be reborn with a new, normal appetite. After a while, they'd no longer felt like it. The expression "once the novelty wears off . . ." came to mind. More appropriate in their case was "once the novelty wears off *again* . . ." And instead of feeling angry or bitter over the burst of sarcasm, she laughed alone during her sleepless nights, her face pressed against the pillow.

Luca was trying to take it slow, he was afraid of wounding the child. But she was afraid that if they took their time, he'd never leave again. She felt panicky at the thought that he might want to stay. She spoke to him and suggested they take it step by step, according to a plan. Conspire to avert the children's suspicions, get them used to it little by little, immunize them. She was so worried he might not want to leave again that she'd have been willing to let him have all the furniture—like the sacrifice a lizard makes, leaving its tail behind for its pursuer—all the books, the CDs and DVDs. Luca began to sleep out "for work" a couple of nights a week. By January, the nights away became four, there was a new apartment and the children went there every so often. Everything was going well. Without having to explain (they weren't good at explaining, and in any case there was no need for explanations), it was all working out.

She'd thought the children would no longer react. But one day, out of the blue, Michela told her that she should get a new bed now. Now that their father had *really* gone, she should get a single bed. If she was no longer married she couldn't sleep in a double bed. "Who says I won't get married again?" She didn't say that. You couldn't joke like that, or at least she couldn't. She would have to learn. If she'd had the presence of mind to say, "Maybe I'll get married again, I might need room for another man," with a playful smile on her lips, her daughter might have been less obsessed. Or maybe she'd have become even more insufferable. Or maybe the problem wasn't Michela, and the desire to get a single bed was written on her face; maybe her daughter had simply read it aloud.

Where could she have gotten such an idea—that a mother doesn't have sex? At a certain point, she'd lost the urge. She'd stopped feeling like it during all the fighting three years ago. It had returned during the separation, but maybe it was just anger in another form. It had gone away again. "It comes and goes," that, too, was pretty funny, though not as funny as "once the novelty wears off again . . ." "It comes and goes," patients said that often. The pain comes and goes, not even pain is consistent. Sleep comes and goes. She remembered a woman, sixty years old, who came to the ER accompanied by her husband at three in the morning, dressed in her Sunday best. Written on the triage chart was the notation: *Can't sleep.* She'd gotten scared because she couldn't sleep. It had never happened before.

Between traffic lights, she often thought about the shy, reserved internist. Or she recalled the sleepless nights and the chain of thoughts she had spun out during the night, lying motionless on her stomach in the dark. Later she would relate some of these thoughts or anecdotes to the internist, who would inquire discreetly, subtle and cautious, probing only where he perceived no resistance.

For example: while eating a slice of watermelon, the boy had started laughing over something silly his sister had done, and a small piece got sucked up his nose from his throat. After a while it came out through a nostril and the girl screamed: "Mattia's nose is bleeding watermelon!" The watermelon nose was funny because the boy suffered from frequent epistaxis. Citing harmless disorders was comforting to her as well as to the shy internist listening to her.

If Viberti hadn't encouraged her to tell the story, and hadn't recalled and mentioned it occasionally as a small sign of their closeness, the episode would have faded and then vanished; instead it fed off repetition and over time grew more resilient. The internist was reserved, but curious. He had a nice way of inquiring, without being intrusive, and he didn't get much, because she didn't tell him anything important. But he was omnivorous, interested in any topic, any small incident, maybe just to hear her talk. Or maybe just to see her. There, that's where her morning's rumination had been heading as she drove to the hospital. The shy internist was in love with her.

The idea bloomed in the car like an overpowering perfume (the aftershave or cologne patients doused themselves with before coming to the ER). Too big a car, like the bed she'd left an hour and a half ago without getting back to sleep, a double bed of a car. All the cars moving in a row from one traffic light to another were extensions of beds. People at the wheel or sitting on a bus or waiting to cross the street, their eyes sleepy or worried or absorbed, but she especially noticed the eyes that were irritable, grumpy, like those of children dragged out of bed.

If she had the morning shift she left before the children, who were then taken to school by the housekeeper or their grandmother. It was better for her to go and pick them up, later on; picking them up was the hardest part. The main hitch after school was Michela with her numerous social engagements: there was always a friend to invite or another friend's invitation already accepted, arrangements made with complete disregard for the needs of others.

But before picking the kids up at school, at lunch she would see the shy internist. Who was in love with her. That's what she called him to herself, the shy internist, while in public she called him Viberti. At the hospital everyone spoke in familiar terms, but doctors were addressed by their last names, nurses by their first. For patients first and last names were reversed: Santi Luciano, Rocca Vincenza. Hierarchies. Every now and then, in her own mind, she called him "my sweetheart." She wasn't one hundred percent sure he was in love with her. He was shy so he hid it. There was an eighty percent chance he was, or was ready to fall in love at the first sign of encouragement from her. Encouragement that she intentionally didn't offer, nor did he ask for any. He was content to see her at lunch, and that was hard to understand. A man of forty.

In the early days, when Mattia was hospitalized, the internist couldn't hide his joy at seeing her. Joy, excitement, whatever it was, he was awkward and content. He was extremely happy to see her and didn't hide it; either he couldn't hide it or he didn't want to. About a month, more or less, after their first meeting, something happened, he'd become more cautious. Someone had told him that Luca had come back home. That same someone might have told him that they'd separated again, this time for good. But he hadn't pressured her recently, on the contrary. Should he have? What did she expect from him?

If she expected him to court her more insistently, she should maybe think again, she was likely to be disappointed. Let's suppose that's what she expected. And let's suppose he was merely a decent man, concerned about the child and consequently about the mother, a childless man who had never been interested in children, but who now kept asking about Mattia as if deep down he'd adopted him. Or maybe he was so partial to the table behind the column that he didn't want to give it up at any cost and that's why he continued to show up for lunch with her. Just maybe.

There was an eighty percent chance he was in love with her, but a twenty percent chance that he was fond of the child or the table in the café, whereas she needed to feel desired. In that case it was possible that she needed to be courted and needed to lay herself open to the mute adoration of someone, anyone, like a statue of the Madonna. And it was possible that the realization that Luca no longer desired her (she realized it, somewhat surprised, each time he came to pick up or drop off the children) wasn't at all as liberating as she told herself it was.

The trees along the avenues were sprouting tender little green leaves that didn't yet hide the skeleton of the branches, young trees all skin and bones. She liked the shy internist. Yes, he was a nice man. Nose and mouth were nothing special. But the eyes fooled her. They seemed sad, the sad eyes of a dejected dog. Then all of a sudden they stared at her and they were arresting, full of passion. Serious, committed passion; not a game. A sad dog who could look at you intensely. Making promises that maybe he couldn't keep. Completely different from Luca, or completely different from how Luca was with her. Luca was convinced he had a situation under control, even when he didn't. The internist was so insecure that she often felt like hugging him or patting him encouragingly on the shoulder. So let's suppose she needed to be loved by a man who was insecure. For how long would the insecure man continue to love her in silence, content with her Virgin Mary–like apparitions in the dim café?

She found a parking space. She headed for the ER. An insecure man, in love with her, wouldn't impose conditions on his love. Was that what she was thinking? For example: if she were to tell him the entire story, just as it had happened, he wouldn't think badly of her. Was that what she wanted? Fortunately as soon as she entered the hospital she wouldn't be able to keep thinking; six hours of respite lay before her like a vacation.

The beach seemed bigger, but it was the same as always: white and gray pebbles and darker gravel along the shoreline, a handful of black, shiny rocks on one side and in the center the rusty iron frame of a small pier whose blue wooden planks were still missing. The summer crowd hadn't arrived yet, and there were no rows of umbrellas and lounge chairs to regulate the distribution of families and groups of friends; Mattia had noticed it immediately. It was a long holiday weekend: April 25, Liberation Day, gorgeous weather, the water extremely cold though some were already trying to swim. After months spent cooped up in stuffy rooms with artificial lighting, the brightness and fresh air were overwhelming, all that sky seemed to crush you.

Sitting a few yards from shore, Cecilia and her mother were exchanging remarks in a slow-motion dialogue, while the children had run off down the beach to play. After a moment Mattia had come back excited and out of breath and said, "There are no umbrellas, there are no chairs." They started laughing. "No, there aren't." An excellent opportunity to steer the conversation onto less problematic terrain, to talk about the child without talking about his problems. They hadn't been to the shore at this time of year in three years and he couldn't remember the beach being deserted. "How sweet, he thought it stayed the same all year." "He's intelligent, that boy, he notices things, and he knows his multiplication tables so well, Michela couldn't recite them that well." It didn't take a great deal of intelligence to notice that there were no umbrellas, but the conversation seemed to have set out on the right track.

However, regardless of the starting point, the stations along the way always led in the same direction: Mattia's intelligence, Michela's likability, Michela's temperament, Michela's similarity to Aunt Silvia, Silvia's being alone, Silvia's work problems, Silvia's problems in general, Silvia will never marry. A coworker of Silvia's had called the house a couple of times; Silvia got angry because he was a pain in the neck. Then, one day when they were on the bus with the children, her mother had noticed a young man looking at Silvia. That's just what we need, she thought, someone "normal."

Cecilia laughed. "Since when do you notice men who look at her? Did you do that with me, too?"

When she felt like she was being made fun of, her mother didn't return her smile. "You always had very discreet admirers, I didn't notice them."

"Tell me, did you notice boys watching us even when we were little girls?"

She didn't smile. "You always played with respectable children."

That is, as long as they'd been under her jurisdiction. Cecilia laughed but didn't feel like pushing it. She wanted to feel good, and to feel good she had to make her mother feel good. "Do you also notice when men look at you?"

Finally her mother smiled and told her to quit being silly. She was smiling, she wasn't offended.

Nevertheless she immediately resumed her plaintive litany: she'd made a mess of things, she knew it, she'd made a lot of mistakes with Silvia when she was a child, when she was a girl. "I was too strict, but I wasn't ready for her, you spoiled me."

Cecilia laughed, though she was beginning to get irritated: "Well now, Mama, don't tell me it's my fault." Then she quickly added: "I don't think you were too strict, far from it, you always let her have her way. Still, the truth is I don't remember."

And she really didn't remember. But her tone was the same one she used with certain patients, to deny the obvious: "I don't think you're too fat," as if she were trying to sell a suit.

Now she had to set them off in another direction, to prevent her mother from falling back into the litany of "Silvia single, you divorced, me a widow." A safer course was the latest news of their relatives, old furniture in need of restoration, household chores, fatigue, low blood pressure, quick medical advice, reassurances.

"No, don't worry about SARS. There's no need to wear a protective mask."

It was nice sitting on the beach and chatting with her mother, nice to feel the sun on her face and arms, unbuttoning her blouse so her neck and breasts could tan, nice to take off her shoes and socks and get her feet wet, nice that her sister wouldn't arrive until that evening, not because she didn't want to see her, but because in Silvia's presence her mother became much more difficult to handle. Especially nice to see the children playing in the distance, having fun and yelling excitedly. Even nicer when they ran back to her every now and then, taking turns. But that happened rarely now. At one time, when they were little, those return visits were the most delightful part of a day at the beach. Every twenty or thirty minutes, one of them would race back and collapse on top of her, clinging to her. And she'd pretend she was tired and that they were heavy, all the while smiling as she pretended to be impatient and somewhat irritated. Now she would give anything for one of those appearances, and when it happened she had to contain her joy. They arrived and demanded attention because they were thirsty, because they were hot, because they'd been mistreated, because they had something to tell her or because, like Mattia, they had to complete a thought begun an hour earlier: "But without chairs and umbrellas there's room for fewer people, because they're less orderly." Yes, his grandmother was right, he was a very intelligent child, and she adored him.

As usual, they disappeared when it was time to leave and she had to go looking for them. She couldn't find them. All the other children had gone, where had hers ended up? She began searching near the cabanas; one row was made of stone and so hadn't been dismantled like the wooden ones. She thought they might have gone off with her mother when she went up to the house to prepare lunch. She turned back to the water and saw them behind the rocks. She shouted to them; they didn't hear her. So she walked over to them, approaching from behind. They hadn't yet noticed her. Mattia was sitting cross-legged, facing the rock wall, being punished, at least that's what it looked like. Michela was standing, looking toward the beach, keeping an eye out to make sure no one was coming. She had no idea what they were doing, if they were doing something. She called them. The girl turned to her, startled. Had she surprised them in a secret game? Mattia stood up somewhat wearily and passed his mother without taking his eyes off the rock.

Silvia arrived very late Friday night after the children were already in bed and it was too bad, her mother said, because they'd been waiting all day for her. She explained that she hadn't been able to get away any earlier, and her mother glanced at Cecilia, who avoided meeting her eyes. They spent Saturday morning at the beach, and despite a brisk exchange of repeated provocations, Silvia and her mother did not quarrel. The immense sky and sweeping sea quelled animosity, or maybe the setting had nothing to do with it; at other times the iodine-rich air and scorching sun had fueled their arguments. Michela casually managed to arrange a picnic lunch for Saturday afternoon, taking it upon herself to invite seven children over.

They were staying in a small house divided into four apartments. Their father had bought one of the two ground-floor units with the idea of spending weekends there, though he'd rarely managed to. Together they moved two tables out into the garden and prepared plates of prosciutto sandwiches and slices of pizza and focaccia. The afternoon passed in a flash, what with parents or grandparents dropping off the children, and then parents or grandparents coming back to pick them up. Silvia and her mother were perfect at entertaining guests, and Cecilia was able to retreat to the house and almost take a real nap. She woke up after twenty minutes, but remained stretched out on the bed, staring at the white ceiling. She thought about her father.

He was a man who was always cheerful and optimistic. Why he had married her mother was a mystery, but who was she to judge other people's marriages? Anyway, she didn't think they'd been unhappy together, maybe they didn't have much to say to each other, maybe they'd already said everything there was to say. For Silvia, however, the situation was intolerable. It was intolerable that a man like her father should stay with a woman like her mother. Every two or three days Silvia would call to tell her that their mother was *literally* trying to kill their father. She made his life impossible, she tormented him, she tortured him. But what these torments may have consisted of, aside from the fact that their mother was in general a phenomenal pain in the ass, Cecilia really couldn't say. If they were torments, they were venial ones. But at some point something happened: her father let himself get a tumor. He let himself get it, he got it. "I told you so," Silvia had remarked.

She lacked curiosity where her parents' matrimonial mysteries were concerned. She was moderately more interested in another matter. Their father's roots were in southern Italy and the family never talked about it. For one thing because there were no relatives to go and visit down there, no property. Their grandfather had been a postal worker who moved up north in the early fifties, when their father was nearly a teenager. A typical only child, idolized by his parents and eager to please them. All hopes pinned on him. And he hadn't disappointed them. He'd become an engineer, he'd had a fine career, he'd forgotten he came from the south. There remained a trace of an accent, but you had to know about it to notice it. And his last name, Re, was a masterful camouflage, since it made him seem like he was native to his new area. He'd married a woman from the north, maybe he'd never loved her much or maybe he had quickly stopped loving her, and they'd had two daughters. And this must have seemed a perfectly executed plan to his southern parents who'd spent their lives trying to distinguish themselves from the southerners who had followed them, filling the city's factories.

The thing about her father that she recalled with greatest pleasure was the relationship he'd had with Mattia. He'd been his chief guide, his shaman. They'd had a lot of secrets. Her father adored cartoons, he adored the boy's games, the child sensed it.

Silvia had always been his favorite, Cecilia had never minded. She hardly ever knew what to say to him, and becoming a doctor had resolved the problem: they spoke about his health or her mother's health. She had scarcely any memories of him from when she was a child. It seemed she'd always been with her mother, as a little girl. When she became a teenager, and Silvia was still a child, the change seemed to make her father uncomfortable, and he stopped touching her. At the time she thought it was normal. When a girl grew up and became a woman, her father had to step aside. But then Silvia, too, became a teenager and her close relationship with their father hadn't suffered, apparently.

Her father had spent his free time playing cards with friends and reading science fiction novels (when her mother didn't find something for him to do). Exposing the pretense that lay behind their parents' marriage and verifying the extent of their unhappiness was an irrepressible passion of Silvia's. As Cecilia saw it, her parents hadn't been more unhappy than the average married couple of their generation. And that (taking the average into consideration) almost always ended the discussion. Being overly concerned with their parents' past wasn't a good sign, indeed it was bad, it was unhealthy if not downright sick.

She didn't want to think that Mattia's problems could have distressed her father to the point of leading him to a premature death. It hadn't been the boy's problems, it hadn't been the torments inflicted by his wife, it hadn't been the ongoing discord between Silvia and her mother. He'd died because he died.

Her father had died the same year in which Cecilia's marriage began to fall apart. And those two events were certainly not related. But Cecilia had become accustomed to reading people's minds at the hospital, and in her mother's and sister's minds she read that date, the year of her father's death, as the origin of the misfortune that bonded them.

That evening they went into town for an ice cream; their mother wasn't keen on the idea but Silvia had promised the children. Such a relaxed atmosphere, such carefree children, could only belong to some other person who didn't have her past, or who perhaps had no past. She seemed to see Silvia and her mother from behind thick glass, in a soap opera like the one she used to watch fifteen years ago, every day after lunch before going back to studying. It was a story about three women; two of them didn't get along and the third was always in the middle. Time passed slowly in soap operas but still more quickly than in real life. After ten episodes a newborn baby would be walking; you could observe half a lifetime in the blink of an eye and it always seemed to make sense. For the three women in real life, however, time was scattered and disjointed, like the figures who appeared and disappeared along the seafront promenade, ice cream in hand, moving in and out of the patches of lamplight.

(If you think of them as frames of a film, you can imagine accelerating the projection to see how it ends or continues, if it continues. And in this case it continues: the seafront promenade continues, the strolling along with their ice cream continues. At some point the film slows down and the picture freezes. There I am, striped shirt, short pants, and flip-flops. Strutting along proudly, a little anxious, licking furiously but fighting a futile battle against the strawberry ice cream that melts down the cone and gets my hand sticky. Behind me, my mother and my grandmother, supervising.)

They were leafing through the notebooks, sitting at either end of the couch with their legs tucked up beneath them. Silvia was smaller and more petite, her legs were shorter and could fold more easily, she was more comfortable in the fetal position, in a tent, in the cramped berth of a train, in a bunk bed, around a fire on the beach: more at ease on vacation. They didn't look like two peas in a pod, but you could tell they were sisters. As a child, Cecilia used to think that Silvia was a more compact version of her, not always with affection. Or maybe a part of her, as she thought now, affectionately.

On that couch they'd argued and fought, set things straight and made up, they'd confided to each other and revealed secrets. They'd spent vital moments of their adolescence speaking in low tones so their parents, asleep or sleepless in the bedroom, wouldn't overhear. They'd talked a lot more there than in the city, where they studied in their room or went out in the evening, rarely talking until two in the morning. A beach house smell from the couch's upholstery rose up through the blue-and-white-striped slipcover, a musty smell of dampness and mold that had the power to make them happy. They needed to feel good, and leafing through Mattia's and Michela's notebooks was a way to enjoy their time together, after their walk, after putting the children and their grandmother to bed.

It wasn't the first time they'd looked through the notebooks together; a few years ago they'd accidentally discovered how much fun it was. Silvia, too, helped the children with their homework and she was curious to read the comments the teachers had written, as if they concerned her personally. In one of Mattia's notebooks they found a class survey of sorts that had to do with odors. Beside each odor was the name of the student who had suggested it. They laughed because a certain Tommaso had come up with "breath," "sweat," and "feet." They laughed because Lisa's only contribution had been "fish." Alessandro had mysteriously and poetically offered "tears," and he must have pleaded his case very well. Mattia had written "hospital" and "minestrone."

Cecilia said she had no idea where he'd ever smelled mine-strone; she never made it. So she'd asked him, in part because when it came to food she was always on the alert. And it seemed a strong odor lingered in the lobby and stairways of his father's new house, and the two children had immediately noticed it. Luca had moved to an old building in the historic *centro*, where half the apartments were still in the process of being renovated. The super, according to Luca, spent her days cooking "a disgusting mine-strone" and other tenants had complained about it, but the woman wouldn't be intimidated. When the children told her about it, Cecilia contained her irritation toward Luca: What was wrong with cooking minestrone, and why associate food with negative feelings when he was well aware of his son's history?

"Did you tell him that?" Silvia asked.

No, she hadn't told him, she couldn't afford to pick fights with her ex-husband over these details. But the children, yes, she'd told them: she said she found the smell of minestrone delicious, and if she didn't make it, it was only because they were used to eat-ing pasta. Ready-made packages didn't appeal to her, but if they helped her with the vegetables they could make it together. So one Saturday afternoon all three of them sat down at the kitchen table and peeled, sliced, and diced string beans, zucchini, carrots, pota-toes, onions, celery, white beans, peas, basil, and parsley, and had a lot of fun doing it. It had the very same odor and in the evening they'd eaten it.

"Did they like it?"

No, not too much. They told her she'd better not make it any-more.

Silvia laughed.

"Don't laugh."

"You shouldn't be so touchy."

"Tell me honestly, don't you think it's important? I can't tell anymore."

"I think it's important for you to pay attention to food, but you shouldn't become obsessive."

"But if this isn't something to obsess over, I don't know what is."

"Even if Mattia doesn't like the smell of minestrone, he could still like the smell of food in general. And even if his father says the smell of minestrone is disgusting, Mattia could grow up to love minestrone."

"You should see him holding the spoon, making the beans and carrot pieces cruise around the bowl."

"It seems to me he's started eating better recently."

"Every now and then I think he could become a great chef."

Silvia looked down at the notebook in her lap.

"Don't treat me like there's something wrong with me," Cecilia said.

"I don't think there's something wrong with you, I was thinking about when I used to imagine what I'd be when I grew up. I would never have imagined doing the work I do, simply because I didn't know it existed."

"Just as I shouldn't imagine the work Mattia might do. I'm acting like a child; it's like saying, 'When I grow up I want to be a fireman.'"

"All I meant is that Mattia is fine, it's been a year, in his own way he's a calm little boy."

"I don't keep after him about having to eat, I'm very careful."

"I know you don't keep after him, I'm not criticizing you for anything, I'm saying it for your own sake, I'm telling you you can relax, maybe he'll relax, too."

"No, you're wrong, I'm not anxious around him, I'm very calm, I have no reason to be anxious, maybe I'm not relaxed, but I'm not tense either."

Silvia closed her eyes and was silent for a while. Then she said:

"That thing you do where you tuck your hair behind both ears is uniquely yours, and you don't do it when you're relaxed."

Cecilia waited for her to open her eyes again. She didn't want to get irritated, she didn't want to irritate her sister. Yet she could find nothing more diplomatic to say than "Well, that's a new one. Just the kind of thing Mama always says to me."

Silvia opened her eyes. "A new one?"

"The fact that you and Mama agree."

Silvia threw a cushion at her. "Idiot. I spend a lot of time with your children."

Cecilia smiled. "Yes, and I'm really grateful."

"I owe you."

"You'll pay me back."

"I wasn't talking only about money."

"You'll pay me back for the rest, too."

Silvia shook her head, opened Mattia's notebook again.

"Tell me about this coworker who called," Cecilia said.

"What coworker? There is no coworker . . . Mama really is a shit. A total piece of shit. I know of course I'm shitty to her sometimes. But every so often. Occasionally. She, on the other hand, never quits."

"But you get along pretty well now. Think about how things were a few years ago."

"It's all thanks to me, she doesn't make any effort."

"And this coworker?"

"So: he's just a coworker. I'm definitely not attracted to him, and I'm not even sure he's interested in me. In any case, I'm not interested."

"Sometimes men aren't interesting, at first."

"Sometimes they're more interesting at first. Anyway, I'm not interested in this guy, I don't know why he thought to call me at Mama's house, or rather, I do know, he found the number in the directory, it matched the address where I have proofs sent to me, since Mama has a doorman . . ."

"So he's Mama's invention."

"He's not a complete invention, it's true he calls me, he looks for me."

"Does he bother you?"

"What do you mean? Of course not, he's totally harmless."

"What does he ask you?"

"Do I want to go out, do I want to go to the movies—why do you want to know? Don't you remember how they are?"

"No, I don't remember." Cecilia laughed.

Silvia threw her head back. "Remember that guy who used to call the house, breathe heavily for ten minutes, and then hang up?"

Cecilia felt a shiver down her spine. The memory of it, or she was beginning to feel cold; maybe now she'd feel like going to sleep. "Of course, how could I not remember."

Silvia looked at her wide-eyed. "We thought it was someone who had it in for you."

"I don't know."

"You suspected one of your boyfriends . . ."

"Yes, that's true. But now it seems unlikely. He was kind of a show-off, but he wouldn't have made calls like that."

"You know what occurred to me a while ago? That we had it all wrong."

"Why do you say that?"

"It was meant for Mama, he called to scare Mama."

"Why would he do that?"

Silvia didn't answer.

"That same old story again?" Cecilia asked.

Silvia turned toward the window. Outside it was dark, the glass reflected their two cowering figures.

Cecilia lowered her voice. "Do you really think it's possible that a man like our father could have had someone else?"

Silvia shook her head. "No, you're right. It's not possible."

"Do you think about Papa a lot?"

Silvia nodded. "Don't you?"

"Yes, of course." But it wasn't true. She never thought about him. That afternoon, when she woke up from her nap, she realized that she hadn't thought about him in months. She picked up an illustrated book that Mattia had pulled off the shelves that afternoon; it was called *Animals and Plants of the European Coastal Region*, and was full of drawings of huge blue-green algae.

"It was nice of Mama to offer you Papa's books."

"She didn't know what to do with them."

Their conversations: at the beginning she felt like the big sister, and maybe she treated Silvia a little condescendingly; by the end she became the little sister, as if Silvia always knew better than she did.

"If you had to leave something to your children, what would you choose?"

"The minestrone recipe."

They laughed.

Cecilia rested her cheek on the back of the couch and smelled the beach house odor even more powerfully. "I'd like to choose which memories to leave them. Can I?"

She didn't like driving at night, and even less so in the gray light of dusk. She didn't like driving on the highway, where everyone went at a different speed than she did. Some had something to prove, others had good reasons to delay their return home. You had to pass or get out of the way quickly. She didn't like driving on the highway at night, because it seemed like everyone was aiming their high beams at her, her eyes hurt every time she glanced in the rearview mirror. She didn't like going back to the city on a Sunday evening after such a long weekend, there was too much traffic and everyone was edgy. She was edgy, too, and there was no real reason for it.

They'd had a good time, the weather had been beautiful, her mother and sister hadn't fought, and there were moments when the children seemed to have forgotten everything; she could read it in their eyes. Now they'd fallen asleep—Mattia almost immediately, Michela an hour later, after repeating no less than four times that at twelve she didn't fall asleep in the car like a child anymore. They slept with their heads lolling, supported by the seat belts; she'd always worried they'd be strangled, but Luca had explained that no, there was no danger. Mattia, the only one who never took his T-shirt off at the beach, she and her mother debating whether he was ashamed of being too skinny. Did he know he was skinny? Was he cold, like he said? Then again, she hadn't taken her T-shirt off either. Michela, on the other hand, was worried about keeping her bathing suit top in place, proud of her budding breasts. Silvia knew how to get on her good side. She'd had to leave early; their mother had rolled her eyes. Silvia, still convinced that their father had had a mistress. Of all the possible fixations, the most improbable. The children's party was nice, nine of them in all; that was the secret, always having kids around. Mattia tagging along, playing whatever the other kids played. Funny because when he was alone, he thought up lots of games. But he played them by himself—he had no interest in recruiting others, in winning them over. For example, the fish market game: oleander leaves served as anchovies, hydrangea leaves were sole, pinecones were sea urchins. Luca was on vacation with "friends," but she expected that sooner or later the children would tell her, "Daddy has a girlfriend." Michela would tell her, proud, jealous, delirious. Learn to hide the irritation that delirium caused her.

To distract herself she thought about the emergency room. The spring-summer season was starting. Like the forest, or fashion, the ER changed according to the seasons. In the summer and before vacations people came to drop off their elderly relatives. In the winter, immigrants and the homeless came to sleep in the waiting room or just to spend a few hours in the warmth. During the Christmas holidays, relatives from the south came to visit their families and took advantage of the opportunity to seek medical advice. Then it was deserted during the World Cup. Last time, in two hours, there'd been only one little old woman suffering from depression. At Ramadan medications were a problem; Muslims couldn't take them before sunset. Summer brought the elderly: dehydrated, or with pneumonia from air-conditioning. Winter, influenza. Not to mention the pleasure of unforeseen outbreaks such as SARS. Before the divorce, she would reach the end of her shift and realize she hadn't once, not for a moment, thought about Luca and the children. She'd feel guilty. Now she was thankful that, for six hours, she was forced to think about something else.

She didn't like driving on the highway in the dark, she should have left earlier, but the children hadn't let her. Her mother was staying at the beach house alone for one night, to deal with the ghost. Cars passed her, men alone at the wheel turning their heads slightly to glance at her; did they expect her to wink at them maybe, in the dark, a quickie in the emergency lane? The intrigues in the ER, the intrigues at the hospital, the shy internist. Her children were sleeping. Michela was twelve years old. A teenager, and so you could count on her being argumentative for at least another seven or eight years. How she'd changed: she moved in a different way, as if dancing on pointe, and she was very pretty. Fewer hysterical scenes, though they were perhaps more dramatic. That strange game they'd been playing on the beach. Not as free after Mattia's problem. Forced to act more like an adult. And then, her period. Checking her jeans every now and then, afraid the pad might have shifted. But at the beach she'd become a child again, running around with the others.

Hard to go back to that beach; memories populated a place, and Luca always seemed to be missing. Not always, not in all places—their home, for example, had forgotten him; it was as if Luca had never lived there, the children's clutter covered up the absence of his very orderly things. But the first day, when it was time to leave the beach, she'd had the impression that they all turned toward the sea, that they were about to ask, "Where did Daddy go?" Not just Luca, not just him. "Where did the fathers go?" Two fathers gone within three years. What a shame. She slapped the steering wheel in irritation. She couldn't stand it anymore, the biting sarcasm that still ran under the surface and occasionally emerged.

"Why did you slap the steering wheel?" Michela asked, awake.

"The lights in my eyes bother me."

"They bother me, too," Mattia said, awake.

Both of them awake, she hadn't noticed. And now she had to entertain them.

Michela said, "I fell asleep, we're already at San Pietro," and then she repeated it to Mattia, who didn't say anything because he couldn't remember where San Pietro was and how far it was from home. "We slept for more than an hour!" And again, shrilly: "I didn't realize we were already at San Pietro."

"How much farther?" Mattia asked, not realizing that he was sealing his fate.

"We're almost there!" Michela exclaimed. "Don't you know where San Pietro is?"

When they were younger, she used to sing to them, on car trips without Luca, to make them fall asleep. Sluggish, buckled into their car seats, bothered by car sickness or by the seat belts, the children hardly ever joined in. They stared out the window, and rarely cried. What was wrong with letting them look out the window, with being quiet? She couldn't help it. She had to know what they were thinking, occupy their minds, put them to sleep. She would sing songs from cartoons or songs they were learning in kindergarten. She never abandoned them.

"Let's play a game: tell me your three best memories from the past few days."

Silence.

"Mine are: when we fed the seagull on the pier and the evening we walked to town with Grandma and your aunt, when we put on our shawls."

She was lying: her favorite memories were the first morning at the beach when the children came running back to her every now and then, and Saturday night when she browsed through the notebooks with Silvia.

"That's only two," Mattia said.

"Tell me yours and I'll tell you my third."

She lied out of habit: she imagined that the memory of the seagull might be one of Mattia's favorites (fascinated by their feathers, he'd pull his hair back, flattening it over his head to imitate their sleekness) and that the memory of the walk might be one of Michela's favorites (proud to walk by herself a few steps ahead with her aunt and seem older). She was used to suggesting. Like she did with patients: "Do you also feel a heavy sensation? Does the pain go away after eating?" And the brief satisfaction of confirmation when they replied: "Yes, it goes away after eating." Except for the doubt, later, that she may have influenced them, the doubt that they'd said yes to make her happy.

Michela said, "My favorite memories are: first, how cold the water was, because I really didn't expect it, and second, the walk."

"That's only two," Mattia said.

"And then the scent of pitch pine, which I'd never smelled before."

"Now you have to tell us yours," Cecilia said to Mattia, "come on, don't make us beg."

"The seagull," Mattia said.

"That's only one . . ."

"The head, wings, and orange legs," Cecilia spoke for him.

"No fair helping!" Michela said.

No fair helping, no fair suggesting, no fair knowing other peoples' memories, reading minds. *Now tell me your three favorite memories from when there were four of us*, the questions she would never ask, *and now tell me your most awful memories, tell me all of them.*

She might wake up at two o'clock, three o'clock, four o'clock. But the worst was waking up at five, no hope of losing consciousness again, too late for a pill, too late for a whole chocolate-coconut bar, or two fruit yogurts, or a package of vanilla wafers. "So much the worse for you." To wake up, in the early morning hours, the bed full of scratchy thoughts like cookie crumbs. The dreaded morning hours. From the other side of the house she heard the second bathroom door slap lightly against the jamb every two or three minutes. A faint draft, she had to remember to close the door before going to bed. She didn't feel like getting up right now. The house seemed to be breathing softly.

At the beginning of their separation, three years earlier, she would wake up furious in those dreaded morning hours. Before waking up she'd already be dreaming about being angry with him, and as soon as she opened her eyes she wanted to clobber him. She'd sit cross-legged on the bed and look at him. She had a rolling pin, which wasn't a club and wasn't a mallet and wasn't just a piece of wood. It was a rolling pin, and with that utensil used for rolling out dough, inherited from her grandmother, which her children sometimes used to flatten clay, she wanted to bash him not in the groin, but on the mouth. Whack him on the mouth for what he said when he was awake, but most of all because often, in his sleep, he'd be smiling. Punish him as if he'd done it on purpose, she who couldn't even yell at the children without feeling guilty.

She was pregnant and she was furious. It wasn't planned and it wasn't welcome and she couldn't afford to be and she had no desire to be and she had two children she loved dearly, they were enough for her, and she had made it through the hardest part.

Mattia was in first grade and she had no intention of starting over again with another one. Mattia was a problem child in any case and she wanted to devote herself to him without any distractions, she didn't want to give him a new reason to be jealous and cause problems for him. She'd had the girl when she was twenty-three, even before she got her medical degree, but she'd stayed on track and had soon begun her internship. At twenty-six she was pregnant again, but she hadn't taken more than a two-month leave and had continued on without missing a year. She'd completed her residency with a daughter who was already in school and a three-year-old son who didn't talk much but made you love him. At thirty-two she was working in the ER, it was what she wanted to do and she was doing it. She needed stability, not another child.

After living through nine years like the past nine years. Having gone through her father's illness and death—she'd been the one who diagnosed his tumor. Her father had died two months earlier. Did she really need an unwanted pregnancy to balance the loss? It was what life had handed her, the doctor responsible for her *father*'s diagnosis. Forced to stop and think about what she wanted from life, forced to realize that there was something wrong and sense that it was something quite serious and being tremendously afraid to face it. So instead you become furious.

She wanted to remove the obstacle as if the obstacle were the one and only source of her rage. But if that were the whole story she could have avoided telling Luca. Guessing his reaction, and having no intention of discussing it, she could have lied to him and taken care of it herself. Instead, she'd dug in her heels and crossed her arms, or her legs. Sitting cross-legged on the bed, she watched him smile in his sleep and waited for him to wake up. She told him she was pregnant and, without giving him time to appear surprised or happy or concerned, she added: "I can't keep it." So he was forced to react to the second piece of information; the first had been left behind. The unplanned pregnancy, the possibility of a third child, they'd never talked about it. Saying "I'm pregnant and I can't keep it," she'd dictated the terms of the conversation. "What do you mean you can't keep it?" "I don't want to keep it." He sat up, he was silent, letting the news she'd just thrown down between them settle. "But why?" he finally muttered. And she told him angrily, "Because I don't want to." "It's something we need to talk about calmly, we can't just decide like this." She wanted to say, "*We* can't? I'm the one who'll decide, we're not deciding together," but she kept silent.

There was nothing she could do about it. Or maybe there was, maybe she could have discussed it with him and persuaded him to accept the decision *she*'d made. If she'd cared about him. Only then did she realize that she had no desire to and no intention of sitting down and talking to make the decision easier for him. He had to accept it and that was that. Wasn't it *his business*? Well, it was also his business, he was her husband, how could she deny it? If she didn't want it to be his business, it meant that something had changed and she hadn't noticed, she hadn't wanted to notice. So let's say it was also his business, but she would rather it wasn't. And getting to the point of learning that she was pregnant and realizing that not only didn't she want to be pregnant in general, but that she especially didn't want to be pregnant by *him*—getting to that point made her furious.

What had happened to their love the last few years? It seemed like nothing had really happened, but that wasn't true. Luca had agreed to take on a big client in Rome, he was never home, and on weekends he often shut himself up in his room to work. He'd been very uncertain about whether to take on that responsibility. He'd agreed primarily because she'd told him that they would manage (she was used to saying it, she was programmed to give that response). But at the time she'd said it, she didn't know what she was saying. Or maybe she did, maybe she knew very well and had said it to encourage the dissatisfaction that was beginning to germinate in her to take root and grow stronger.

And as she continued thinking about the death throes of their marriage, she tended to date the beginning of the end further and further back; sooner or later she'd have it coincide with the starting point, in accordance with the principle whereby only the origin is whole and uncorrupted and cells begin dying at birth. Luca's absence had brought out the worst in both of them. Just as she was completing her residency, just when her father fell ill, just as Michela began taking catechism seriously enough to worry them, just when Mattia, who spoke little and poorly at four years of age, had to go to a speech therapist. Instead of bringing them closer together, instead of making her feel she couldn't do without him, Luca's absence had flipped a switch in her head so that when he was around she felt an appalling urge to fight with him. And still she wondered: How could such ordinary things (distance, fatigue, worries about work and the children) have estranged him from her? There had to be something else.

So she went further back. Mattia's birth, imagining that Luca didn't love his son as he loved his daughter, that he didn't want to care for him, imagining that he saw him as a rival. But even that wasn't enough. So she went further back. The fact that she worked, that she'd insisted on continuing to work: despite the fact that he pretended to be proud of her achievements, like all men, Luca would have preferred a wife who was a replica of his mother. No, that still wasn't enough. It was all too insignificant. How could all these insignificant things produce so much? How could nothing produce all that?

"We can't talk about it calmly, it's something I need to decide quickly." Luca looked bewildered, he continued touching her, turning her face toward his, putting his arm around her shoulders, searching her eyes as if he didn't recognize her. "There's something you're not telling me—you've had tests done and there's something wrong with the baby." Always quick to suspect doctors of bad faith, of having black souls, not to be trusted given their innate ability to lie. "There is no baby, so there can't be anything wrong with it. What's wrong is me. I can't keep it." But he wanted time to talk about it calmly. How much time did he need? She wasn't willing to give him any more. Sitting cross-legged on the bed, thinking about a rolling pin bashing in Luca's smiling mouth, she'd already made her decision.

It had been almost three years ago, but she remembered it perfectly. The image she'd had of his shattered mouth, gums and teeth reduced to a bloody pulp. Something she'd seen at the hospital? Of course. Even though emergency surgery was separate and they never saw the injured accident victims when they arrived. But of course, no use denying it, she'd seen a young man whose face had been smashed by a hammer.

And she clearly remembered all the rest as well. She wouldn't forget it, she wasn't asking to forget it. But she'd have liked to talk to someone about it every now and then, not to ease her conscience, but just to talk about it, because if she didn't tell it, the story made no sense. If she didn't tell about the abortion, Luca's reaction didn't make sense, their divorce didn't make sense. Not that the abortion was the cause of their divorce. It was a harbinger, but a cryptic harbinger. She'd aborted her love for him and no one knew it. Not her sister, much less her mother. She was certain that Luca had never told anyone, it was too momentous.

To her this momentous thing was an object with a form and shape, it was tangible and had a substance of its own. It was an object to be examined, observed from a suitable distance. How to talk about it was a mystery to her, as was how to think about it. Should she feel guilty, as Luca wanted her to, as he thought was natural? She couldn't seem to. Should she feel like a monster? She couldn't seem to. At a certain point, so that she could imagine at least a part of herself as readmitted to human society, she would have liked to view the other part as monstrous. Was there something wrong with her? And she'd go over the whole story from the beginning again.

She'd had two children, desired, adored, by a man she loved, children she cherished more than anything. She became pregnant

again by a man she no longer loved (even though she didn't yet
know it at the time) and had had an abortion. Had she done
something sinful? No. Had it been painful, devastating, violent?
Yes, of course, for her, painful, devastating, violent. She still
thought about it, in fact, in those dreaded morning hours. But she
didn't understand. She'd have liked to talk about it, talk to someone about it. When Mattia had been hospitalized, she'd been advised to speak to a psychologist. Therapy for the child wasn't
expected, it was expected for the parents. Luca wouldn't hear of it.
She'd been the one to go. And she'd burst into tears in front of the
young woman who had just gotten her degree and who was five or
six years younger than she. A child with a box of Kleenex ready on
her desk. Prepared. Instead of talking about Mattia, she'd burst
into tears during the first session and told her about the abortion.

Talk to someone about it, she wanted to talk about it. To the
shy internist, naturally, because he knew how to listen. He was
nervous about matters of his own, at that time. Not that he avoided
her, he couldn't, but he was anxious. He was in a state of anxiety
again, like when he'd met her. She'd have liked to tell her whole
life to the shy internist, so she could read it in his eyes. He was an
open book, he wouldn't be able to hide anything from her.

When the day of his declaration came, Cecilia thought about how
blind she'd been, how strongly she wanted everything to remain
as it was, for nothing more to happen in her life, for each day to be
like every other, each action indistinguishable from that of the
day before, for the children to always be children. The shy internist declared his love and she thought about the fact that Michela
would soon have her first boyfriend.

That morning she'd started laughing when a patient looked at
her, standing with a female colleague and a resident, and asked:
"When will the doctor get here?" Later, distracted and preoccupied since the day before, she'd placed the stethoscope on a

patient's back and said, "ER," as if answering the phone. All three women had had to leave the examining room so they wouldn't be seen having a laughing fit. What was she doing now in that café, fortunately deserted, why hadn't she come up with some excuse? She knew very well the reason for the meeting, and she'd gone to face the music without trying to avoid it. Before leaving the hospital she was about to quip to her colleague: "I'm heading out, there's a guy who wants to hook up with me." She'd stopped herself just in time, it wouldn't have been nice to make fun of him like that.

If she'd asked him to postpone the talk, maybe he would have changed his mind, afraid of losing what they were able to share, he might have backed off. Instead, there he was in front of her, stammering. He said he'd kept quiet for a year, thinking everything would work itself out; he talked about it as if it were a health issue. For a year he'd been coming to look for her in that café, as if the fault of having dragged things out to that point were his alone, as if she had always ended up there against her will. For a while she wasn't able to react, crushed by the weight of yet another mistake. Her life studded with mistakes that sparkled like the Virgin's halo, the Virgin Mary, who for a year had appeared to the shy internist in the steamy café. "Holy Virgin Mary, you know I didn't tell a lie," Michela wept during her mystical crises. Under the illusion that she never made mistakes, she'd made another mistake.

Without doing anything to discourage him, she had soaked up that silent worship, had fed on his ever-deepening love. So when he seemed to have exhausted his speech (if it had been prepared, it was badly prepared and even more poorly delivered) Cecilia thought: What have I done? But given that she'd made a mistake, and that she was used to correcting her mistakes quickly, she thought that by this time it was too late to play the part of the innocent virgin, and also too late to play a virgin indifferent to the attentions and attractions of others, and that if she didn't want to be a *complete shit* she had to save their friendship, or rather transform that relationship into friendship. She didn't want to lose the man who sat in front of her, whatever he was to her. She felt the blood return to her face, she must have turned pale, she felt like she was blushing, but it was because she was recovering.

She thought lying was the lesser of two evils and told him she truly hadn't been expecting it, that she'd been going through a difficult time and was worn out, maybe that's why she hadn't realized it (it wasn't true that she'd been going through a difficult time, it was the most stress-free time in three years). She said she'd never thought of him in that way, but that she thought about him a lot. That little word game, which she would have been proud of on another occasion, seemed completely fatuous to her and sapped her of the strength to go on talking. She imagined standing up and saying, "I have to go now," she thought of escaping. Instead she remained seated and started confessing part of the truth. She told him how important those lunches were to her. And gradually the tension melted. They started talking as they never had before, with a pleasure and connection discovered at that moment. For that reason, when the time came to leave, Cecilia had the distinct feeling that she'd manage not to lose the shy internist's friendship; in fact she thought she'd already managed it.

For a few days they talked a lot. Cecilia even told him something about the divorce. She was amazed at how everyone was used to those kinds of stories and no one seemed incredulous when they heard the predictable reasons which, for her, had constituted such an ordeal ("We started fighting"). Even adults accepted the excuse that had worked with the children, which the children hadn't even dreamed of challenging, because in fact it was terrible enough to be acceptable: Mama and Papa don't get along anymore, they still love each other but they can't live together any longer. In the end everything was entirely plausible and she was the only one who thought about the *real* reason, who thought that was actually the root cause of all the consequences, rather than just a consequence like any other.

She was also amazed to find herself talking to Viberti about something she really never thought about: how her children judged her, what they thought of her, what they thought of the divorce. Maybe it was so she could find out what *he* thought of her and her divorce. But Viberti was too guarded to let anything slip.

Viberti talked about his mother, he talked about his ex-wife, and he talked about himself as though he were a prisoner in his apartment building. When he said to her one day, "You're the first person who hasn't immediately asked me 'Why don't you move?' because though I actually should, maybe, I don't like having everyone remind me of it," she was so touched she felt like kissing him.

After their trip back on the highway, Mattia made up a new game. He lined his toy cars up along the hallway in the house and made them pass one by one through a barrier he'd built with Lego bricks, a tollbooth. Cecilia watched him as she went from the kitchen to the bedroom and stopped to listen to him from behind the partly closed door. Mattia mimicked the metallic voice of the automatic toll-taker: "Insert ticket," "Insert card," "Thank you, have a good trip." He also said "Ticket expired" or "Card over the limit" or "Watch out for fog," "Fasten children's seat belts," "If you're tired, pull over and take a nap."

He went on playing the game for more than two weeks, handing out tickets to speeders caught on the monitoring camera and stopping trucks with suspicious loads, stolen television sets or cats for vivisectioning. For a few days Cecilia pretended she hadn't noticed, then she asked him: "What's the name of that game?" Mattia shrugged without looking up and mumbled: "Tollbooth." He didn't just imitate the recorded voice of the automatic toll collector, he also made up conversations inside the cars. "Daddy, when are we going to get there?" a child complained. "I didn't expect this backup" (a lower voice, the father's). "Yes, there's a lot of traffic" (the mother, a little irritable). "I want to go home," the boy persisted. "Everybody wants to go home," the father snapped.

Overnight the lineup of toy cars disappeared from the hallway. Cecilia thought Mattia must have gotten tired of the game and removed them on his own. Those were the days following the declaration and she had other things on her mind: the shy internist, his words, the complex feelings they'd aroused in her. So it was almost a week before it occurred to her to wonder what had happened, why had he tired of the game? She was curious, and, as usual, rather than ask him a direct question, worried about not worrying him, all she said was: "I noticed the traffic has cleared up in the hallway." With a slight smile on her lips, waiting and hoping he'd know he should smile back. But the boy didn't react; he busied himself looking for a notebook in his backpack and pretended he hadn't heard. He had to finish his homework for Monday and Cecilia might have been better off letting it go, but she couldn't help herself. "Hey, I asked you a question," she said, no longer smiling, and the child stopped, taken aback, unsure whether to keep pretending he hadn't heard, uncertain about the question he'd been asked, since *in fact* he hadn't been asked a question.

"How come you don't play Tollbooth anymore?" Cecilia asked, pulling him to her.

"It made a mess."

"It made a mess? No, that's not true. Who told you it made a mess? You can play in the hallway as much as you want. Sometimes it's fun to be messy."

"Michela said that you said it made a mess."

"Michela? Are you sure?"

"Yes, Michela said so. But it's true, it made a mess."

She told him to open his notebook and start his math exercises. Then she stood and walked out, her steps measured so as not to seem rushed, so she could slow down and have time to stop, if she decided to stop, if she hadn't decided instead to go and find

Michela, who was lying on the couch in the living room, studying her history book. She closed the door behind her, took a few steps toward her daughter, and before she could think rationally and restrain herself, gave her a slap on the head that landed between her forehead and her eye. She realized an instant later the enormity of what she had done, but her rage had not subsided. The girl put her hands to her head, incredulous; her book had fallen to the floor. She didn't cry and she didn't say anything because she still didn't know what had happened. "Don't you ever dare give your brother orders," Cecilia hissed without raising her voice, "and don't make up things I never said. If he wants to play in the hallway with his toy cars, he can, do you understand?"

The girl started sobbing and Cecilia collapsed on the couch, her legs trembling. She hugged Michela, who hugged her back as if the woman who'd slapped her a moment ago weren't the same one who was now comforting her. There was a glazed earthenware pot on the cabinet behind the sofa. The writing said HÔTEL DES TILLEULS; they'd gotten it as a gift during a vacation in the South of France. On the way back they'd stopped at that aquarium, on the Côte d'Azur. In the depths of a tank, which visitors could view from underground, two dolphins had been mating in a frenzy of splashing. The children hadn't understood, Luca had squeezed her hand, smiling. All this centuries ago, in another life, which would never return.

Despite the sound of Michela's desperate weeping in her ears, she heard a creaking, and out of the corner of her eye she saw the door open and Mattia standing in the doorway.

There was no need to get over the incident or cause the children to see it as an incident or offer reasons that might excuse her action. There was no need to go back and talk about it or to ignore it. She was certain the children wouldn't forget in any case, and she was equally certain that they didn't want to talk about it anymore and that they were actually able to not think about it anymore, except unintentionally, briefly, quickly suppressing the thought. She was certain of it because that's what she'd done as a child when faced with something disturbing or incomprehensible or violent.

Despite this certainty, she spoke to them. During supper, she explained that she had lost her temper because she didn't want them being spiteful to each other (the offense reduced to "spiteful-ness"). Smiling, she asked Michela if seeing her mother angry had scared her, and Michela nodded, not at all sure it was something to smile about. Meanwhile, Cecilia checked Mattia's plate with-out letting him notice. Worried that he might not eat that night, she hadn't filled it as much, but there were no immediate conse-quences. For long-term ones, she'd have to wait and see.

Meanwhile, however, when she went to pick the kids up at Luca's after his turn with them on Sunday, her husband came out on the landing, pulling the door closed behind him, and asked her what had happened, if it was true that she'd slapped Michela. He asked her, but not angrily; it was as if she had been the one slapped, with the solidarity of one parent talking over a problem with the other, in order to solve it. She nearly started crying, she was so moved; on the dimly lit landing, surrounded by the smell of minestrone, they were once again a couple, albeit part-time. She confessed that she'd lost her head because she liked to see the boy play and she was disappointed that he'd stopped—the row of toy cars like a ray of hope, a matter of waiting and then the traffic jam would clear up.

Luca said: "Every now and then Michela deserves a slap. And we never gave her any."

"Do you think I've became a violent parent?"

Luca hesitated, it was inevitable, and she regretted the question, even when he replied with a smile: "No, I really don't think so."

———

She thought often about the shy internist's declaration. It must have cost him a lot, he must have thought about it for months, but perhaps he hadn't expected a different result. So why declare himself? To free himself of an obsession, he'd stammered something like that. In fact, afterward, after delivering his little speech, it seemed like a great weight had been lifted off his shoulders. But within a couple of weeks all the benefits disappeared and their lunches became more strained. If there'd been any momentary relief, it soured quickly, like certain perishable substances delivered to the hospital. Expired, ineffective, it wasn't an honest-to-goodness, effective relief, maybe because the underlying intention hadn't been to free himself of that weight. She thought and thought about this possibility, and felt that the shy internist had inadvertently managed to find one of her weak points, a soft spot where she was easily moved. Yes, she'd been moved because that forty-year-old man had not only declared himself, but had begged her (almost immediately, anxiously) to discourage him, as if he himself were afraid of his own feelings. How hopelessly incompetent.

She thought and thought about his constancy and his commitment, about the extraordinary attachment the man had for their table at the café. She went so far as to think that probably no one had ever loved her so much, but she immediately had second thoughts. It was ridiculous for two reasons: first, someone else had loved her, and second, an undeclared love doesn't count. It counted only from the time of the declaration, before that it was mute adoration, infatuation. To worship someone for a year without telling her—it took constancy, but it was sheer madness. If he was mad, the internist's madness was concentrated in a single symptom: her. Yet this was a further sign of absolute commitment.

She thought and thought about the declaration while she had the children do their homework. Mattia had to reconstruct the chronological order of a newspaper article that the textbook authors had divided into six segments and mixed up.

They left their dog alone on the balcony and went off while the summer heat hung over the city with a temperature of over 100 degrees.

Whatever idea she may have formed about Viberti, he didn't seem to her to be either an abandoned dog or the victim of a cruel master.

Firemen quickly arrived on the scene and thanks to their vehicle, equipped with a ladder, they went up to the balcony and carried the dog to safety.

It was a strange association of ideas: when the conversation became less strained, he'd said he sometimes felt like a dog and told her that she reminded him of a cat.

The neighbors reported that it wasn't the first time the dog had been left alone on the balcony for days.

While the boy read the jumbled parts of the story, she imagined holding the shy internist on a leash.

They then transported him to a veterinary clinic where he was examined and treated.

But she had no intention of being his mistress.

The dog owners were ultimately charged with cruelty to animals and the dog was turned over to the municipal dog pound.

So maybe she would speak to him and tell him that he was wasting his time, that she was still getting over the divorce and too busy with the children to get involved in a relationship, that even if she could, it didn't necessarily mean she wanted to.

It happened yesterday, on one of the hottest days of the year. An anonymous caller alerted the volunteers of ENPA, the National Board for Animal Protection, who immediately went to the scene and called the fire department.

She'd tell him that she was fond of him, but nothing more. She had to have the courage to give him up, not mislead him into thinking that something might happen in the future. After the declaration she'd been scared, because she didn't want to give up their lunches, but now she had to do it quickly.

Mattia dashed off the correct order of the segments, 1-6-2-4-3-5, and started closing his notebook.

Cecilia insisted on checking, and it was right.

She told him he'd done well and quickly, too. The child looked at her then shook his head, dismissing the compliment: "It was a breeze, Mama."

She wanted to talk to him, but she didn't have the nerve. The next day she saw him at lunch and they spoke for an hour about the hospital administrator's absurd, dangerous, unconstitutional initiatives, the chief surgeon's stupidity, and a patient with malaria, the first of her career. She didn't feel guilty and didn't think she was leading him on. Claudio Viberti was not an inept bumbler, he was a forty-year-old doctor, in love with her, true, but old enough to make his own decisions without being led on a leash.

One afternoon, however, while she was trying to remember where she had parked her car, she saw him turn a corner and walk down the other side of the street. He hadn't noticed her, and his curved back and hunched shoulders, the downcast eyes staring at the sidewalk, made her feel dejected again, as if his sadness were her fault.

She didn't mean to spy, but her eyes couldn't help following him. He was headed to a café that was not their usual one. She ran after him and caught up with him inside. She teased him a little for betraying their table so lightly, he accused her good-naturedly of having followed him. It occurred to her to ask him about his father; she'd thought about it one night, tracing back a thread of associations. It had started with the words of a patient who, shaking his head, had said that "to be a doctor you have to really be cut out for it." Being cut out made her think of being scarred, and looking back, she hadn't been able to find any suitable traumas in the first eighteen years of her life. She kept thinking she'd fallen into medicine by accident, yet the profession captivated her. Yes, she was cut out for the job, but maybe she was well suited for any job in which she had to constantly prove she was the best in the class and win the professors' praise. The shy internist, on the other hand, had compelling reasons: a father who'd died of a malignant lymphogranuloma when he was a boy.

Viberti didn't buy the explanation, and he seemed quite embarrassed to have to disappoint and contradict her. But the explanation he gave was exactly the same, though in disguise: there was a father figure involved, a well-known doctor (Cecilia had seen his name in a journal) who'd taken his father's place, and who had inspired him. She thought of pointing out that the two interpretations were perfectly compatible, but she was afraid to stick her nose into matters that didn't concern her. She was tempted to tell him about her own father's illness and death, although that certainly didn't explain anything—she'd actually already gotten her residency—so she dropped it. As soon as they parted, however, she felt a stab of longing in her chest, a feeling she'd never felt for him and that she hadn't felt in a long time for any man, except her son. It was the wrench in her heart she felt in the morning when she watched Mattia go into school. She wanted to take Viberti by the hand and walk with him through his day. Maybe she wanted to hold him, too. For the first time since she'd known him, she thought she should invite him home some evening, let him see Mattia again; the boy might hardly remember him, but who knows.

The next night she began thinking about the shy internist and for four nights her sleepless hours were filled by images of sisterly embraces, innocent walks hand in hand, films watched together on an imaginary couch, her head resting on his shoulder. So it was a great surprise to her when, arriving at the café on Monday and finding Viberti already sitting there waiting for her—his skin sunburned, his hair a little disheveled, his white shirtsleeves rolled up—she realized she was actually attracted to the man, wanted to put her arms around him and kiss him and probably make love to him. She ate almost nothing while he told her about his weekend with the elderly Mercuri, about a walk in the countryside, amid the vegetable gardens, about a world in which you felt strange and far away from everything. She felt strange and too close to him, after a quarter of an hour she told him she had to go. She was worried she had bungled something in the ER, she wanted to go back and check.

Viberti suggested she call, and in fact it would have been the most sensible thing to do.

"I'd rather go see," she said briefly, already on her feet.

"You shouldn't take it so seriously," Viberti said.

And how! Of course I should! she thought coming out of the café. She was going down the ambulance ramp by the time she remembered she didn't really need to go back to the ER. Was she hoping someone would keep her there for another six hours? But if she hadn't bungled anything, why had she gone back? She pretended she'd forgotten her cell phone, though it was safely in her handbag, and as she searched around, as a colleague helped her look for it, she imagined it ringing and making her look like a fool. So she fled from the ER, too, and as soon as she got outside she called her sister and asked her to go pick up Mattia and bring him to his grandmother's, she had an emergency at the hospital. A specialist in emergency medicine, a specialist in emergencies, she didn't want her children to see her in that state.

At that hour of the afternoon, in the park along the river, you met mothers out jogging with high-tech, three-wheeled strollers that in her day hadn't existed. Not that she'd ever had time to go jogging with the stroller, she'd had to study. There were children two or three years old convinced they were in full control of their tricycles, actually guided by nannies through rear handlebars as long as exhaust pipes. You met elderly retirees who looked bewildered and men of various ages who sprang out of the bushes like the wolf in the fairy tale. You met dogs merrily running around and panting owners trying to catch them.

The trees bursting with leaves seemed immense, and she stopped and threw her head back to see how tall they were—how come she'd never noticed? How come she'd never noticed the heightened rustle of leaves stirred by a light breeze? She perceived everything more intensely, saw the colors as brighter and more brilliant, and in the park's silence the slightest sound seemed to call to her. She saw the streetlamps stretching ahead of her and kept on walking as though she'd decided to return home on foot and wouldn't sooner or later have to go back and retrieve her car. She walked for half an hour and sat down on a bench, she was tired and wanted to sit awhile. But a couple of old men began loitering nearby. Unless they'd figured out she was a doctor and wanted to ask her advice about their prostatectomy?

She walked back toward the hospital exhausted by the heat and by a sense of futility; she'd wasted two hours and also wasted her sister's time, and Silvia would probably have to work until three in the morning to make up for it. But it was too late now to call her and change the plan. She went into the supermarket across from the hospital even though she had no urgent need to do any shopping; she loaded a cart to give some meaning to the day. Coffee was on sale, buy two, get a third one free. There were egg noodles at home and though it was the children's favorite pasta, they weren't about to run out. The tomatoes didn't look particularly good, but she took a pound just the same. Aluminum foil would always come in handy.

With no more energy left, she dragged herself to the car, put the shopping bags in the trunk, opened all four windows, and waited in the shade until the temperature in the car came down a few degrees. All of a sudden it struck her that she had bungled something after all, because that morning she'd forgotten to fill out a report for a suspected TB case. Couldn't she call? Yes, but she might as well go back inside.

It was much cooler in the hospital's basement, even though there was no air-conditioning. She filled out the form while her colleagues asked her why she had come back, why she hadn't called. By the time she left the ER, her legs were moving of their own volition and they certainly weren't headed out the hospital's door. She didn't want to stop, but even if she had wanted to, it was too late, because the moment she stepped out of the elevator and the moment she reached Pediatrics and the moment she knocked at the door, she knew very well that the doctors' lounge was the place she wanted to go, to be, to stay. The shy internist was waiting for her, without knowing it, he never knew anything, that man, blessed in his innocence.

She awoke in the night seized by the darkest anxiety; she wasn't in love with the shy internist, she didn't want to begin a relationship, being with him that afternoon, kissing him, letting herself be undressed in the car like a teenager had been a mistake, a terribly selfish outburst, she was an irresponsible fool and instead of discouraging him, as she should have, she had led him on. Even more distressing because she knew very well that she'd enjoyed it. She couldn't sleep anymore, sitting cross-legged in the middle of the bed; she got up an hour before the alarm went off, paced back and forth in the kitchen so as not to wake the children. She ate two packets of mascarpone spread on rice cakes.

The anxiety continued throughout the morning, even working didn't help, even throwing herself into examining patients, with a full waiting room and not a single moment to think. If a day like that didn't do the trick, not even opium would save her. When she was able to speak with Viberti at lunch, as she apologized and told him there was no justification for it, as she asked him to forgive her and explained that it had been inexcusable, she felt a slight relief that consoled her until the afternoon. Later she pretended to be exhausted, putting on a little performance for her mother and the children. Her exhaustion was nothing new, even when she didn't complain about it they could read it in her eyes.

She went to bed early, and after dozing for less than an hour she woke up and began crying softly. Almost immediately, retracing the day's events, she found a deep, dark well that swallowed her up. She remembered sitting on a bench, while wandering through the park like a sleepwalker. Sitting alone on a park bench was perhaps one of the saddest things a human being could do. She remembered thinking, as she sat on the bench, that if she continued walking along the river in the same direction, she would come to the circular clearing where, three years ago, she and Luca used to go when they needed privacy so they could argue, isolating their resentment and anger so it wouldn't infect the children. She recalled Luca's words to her, those expressing horror and contempt. She recalled them one by one. The way he shouted them at her. Then she took pity on herself and fell asleep.

(It's nice to imagine her every now and then sunk in a deep, dreamless sleep. To imagine her in a state of unconsciousness, oblivious to herself, relaxed. Before resuming the story I'll lower the volume of the outside world to a minimum, shut everything out, draw the curtains. Because Cecilia is always lit up, and she dazzles me.)

She remembered every detail, the birth, the first days, the first months, and the memories were hers alone, no one would ever steal them from her. She was watching their heads close together, as they lay on their bellies in front of the TV, who knows what they were saying, they were giggling. She had seen those heads come out of her own belly (maybe she thought she'd seen them, maybe she had felt them so intensely that she was able to see them with every cell in her body, if not with her eyes), and she remembered every detail, and no one could ever erase those memories. The girl hadn't had any hair, the boy a lot of dark fuzz which he'd lost in the first few months, but the heads were their heads and they had passed through her, how she didn't know, they'd had to stitch her up. That's how living things passed from one condition to another, that's how living things split apart and one thing gave birth to another. Memories that were hers alone, that she preserved, even those that were ridiculous, grotesque, shameful. Why had she been so ashamed? While she was giving birth, she wasn't at all ashamed to have the nurses and doctors see her vagina, but the fact that she felt like shitting and might really have shit in the labor room, that certainly was embarrassing. She'd said, "I'm very sorry," and they'd all smiled reassuringly. She'd never spoken to Luca about it; during the birth he'd stood nearby, apparently nervous, but never on the verge of fainting. She didn't say "apparently" nervous to be mean—all she remembered of him was a figure there by the bed, and she knew very well that the presence of a figure was important enough. Then she remembered him afterward, very happy, beaming.

Fathers can afford to beam after the birth; mothers are a bit spent, though still happy about the baby and greatly relieved. That wasn't being mean either; the fact that fathers don't have to experience the pain of childbirth is written in the natural order of things. Because of this, the shy internist, for instance, would have fathered ten children if he could have. And that, on the other hand, really was being mean.

But she wasn't angry with him. It wasn't Viberti's fault that what had happened had happened. The fault was hers alone. She was glad she'd realized it right away and had told him so. She'd been the one to go looking for him, she'd turned him on, and that was inexcusable. She was extremely ashamed of what she'd done. She'd done it because she was unprepared, taken by surprise, she'd never wanted to admit to herself that she was attracted to him. On the whole, in those months, it hadn't been easy to admit that she needed the opposite sex, or sex itself (the odd moments when she happened to think about it). She'd needed to believe that she should and could do without it. Moments of that hour spent with Viberti came back to her that evening as well, sitting on the couch, watching the children watch a DVD. She'd lost control, she'd been attracted to him, but it wasn't a solution to her problems. She cared about Viberti, she didn't want to lose him, but they had to be just friends. If she had liked him a lot or if she had been crazy about him, or if he'd swept her off her feet—then there would be no question about it. That meant she wasn't in love with him. She was attracted to him and was fond of him. Better to drop it.

"How many months have you lived since you came on earth?"

Michela giggled. "Listen to him! The expression is 'come into the world.'"

"Since you came into the world."

"Or 'were born.'"

"How many months?"

"That's easy," Cecilia cut in, "just multiply twelve by twelve."

"A hundred and forty-four," Mattia said instantly.

"You already knew the answer," Michela said.

"No, it's a trick, they taught it to us today. You have to think of the numbers as squares and rectangles."

She recalled every detail, especially the growing reasons to be proud, the gallery of maternal trophies. The smile when they recognized you. Holding their head erect. When their reflexes proved to be functioning (she'd tried out what she learned from books on them, the Moro reflex, the sucking reflex, the triple retraction). Having the pediatrician pronounce her healthy, pronounce him healthy (and before that, the rating at the moment of birth—she remembered a father who protested because his son hadn't gotten 10/10—a 9/10 for Mattia and Michela, the perfect score, because in life there must always be room for improvement). Not fitful, sleeping at night (but if they wake up at night, calling out without being demanding, in a polite voice). In the early months, small feats: how the dog goes, bowwow; clapping their hands; playing peekaboo. And nodding yes and no, even if they have no idea what it means. And then, later on, managing to get dressed by themselves (but still needing a little help). Starting to remember things they've done with you, remembering things that you don't remember but that for him or for her were important. Asking you to repeat stories always using the same words. And besides that, learning the text of *Matilda the Fast Turtle* by heart and surprising you one day by reciting it perfectly, pretending they've learned to read.

But she also remembered the isolation of the assembly line, the continuous cycle of suckling-pooping-sleeping. She remembered the sudden feeling of not being able to be free of it. Half asleep one day, ears pricked for the slightest whimper, a senseless thought had occurred to her: "When the baby leaves home." She'd repeated reassuring phrases such as "Once this phase is over . . ." without ever adding the second part: ". . . there will be another." In the first three months she'd never left Michela, and even while resting, even when she lowered her eyelids, she saw the baby's face, like in an old negative. She could still hear the explosive bursts of her wailing. She'd tried to breast-feed the child, she had a lot of milk in the first weeks. Michela devoured her nipples, excruciatingly painful. She'd had to buy nipple shields. She'd bought a breast pump to feed her later with a baby bottle. Luca wasn't happy that the baby could no longer suck her breast. He'd never particularly loved her tits, even when they'd swelled up during pregnancy. But he'd had a fit of anger one evening when she abruptly tore the child away because of the pain. "What the hell are you doing," he yelled, "can't you see she's crying?" Later he apologized and they laughed about it. Protect and feed the young, an ancient coding in his genetic makeup, his wife's sore nipples didn't worry him. One of the first things the shy internist had done, on the other hand, was to suck her nipples with great gusto; if she'd let him he'd have slurped her all up.

Mattia got up and went into the kitchen, while on the screen Harry Potter flew astride a broom. He came back from the kitchen with a package of cookies and gave it to his sister, who started eating them. He'd gotten up to get the cookies for her from the kitchen. They weren't for him. Cecilia hadn't noticed Michela asking him for them, she must have whispered it, without even turning her head. She'd rather not see these things. Michela was telling her brother that her religion teacher had said that Harry Potter's life was inspired by Jesus's. The year before, the same teacher had said that *Lord of the Rings* was inspired by the Bible.

Five years ago (it seemed like ancient history), when Cecilia had completed her residency and diagnosed her father's tumor, Michela's brief mystical crises had reached their high point. They'd sent her to catechism because Luca, or Luca's parents, felt it was important, even though Luca wasn't religious, or if he was, he'd never said anything, and in any case he was nonpracticing (unlike his parents). They'd been married in the church because it was customary, but Cecilia hadn't viewed it as an obligation. Her thinking wasn't clear on this either, and although her upbringing had been decidedly secular, she had made her First Communion. So why deny it to Michela? Sending her to catechism had seemed reasonable, especially since all the other children in her class went. The mystical crises, however, had scared even Luca, and they'd decided to postpone her Confirmation until she was of age. Mattia, on the other hand, had gone through catechism during the year of their first separation, skipping a number of classes and barely learning the names of the four evangelists. He didn't attend his First Communion ceremony, because he was in the hospital. The priest gave it to him two months later, a First Communion especially for him, and at least he'd eaten the host (maybe).

But what did Michela's mystical crises consist of? When she was around seven or eight, her temper tantrums took on a religious tenor. She couldn't stand to be restricted or controlled in any way. Cecilia and Luca had called them "mystical crises," a kind of private joke they could laugh about together. For a while Michela had casually lied about various subjects. Homework, how many hours of TV she watched at her grandmother's, brushing her teeth at night. When caught, she'd begin crying and screaming, pacing back and forth like a penitent, thumping her notebook on her head and intoning: "Holy Virgin Mary, you know I didn't do anything wrong, I beg you, stand up for me, make Mama and Papa see the truth." She prayed aloud in her room at night, kneeling before a creased picture of Our Lady of Fatima. She prayed loudly to make sure everybody in the house could hear her and said things like "Please Holy Mother Mary, protect everyone in my family, my father who often flies, don't let the plane crash, and my mother who treats sick people, don't let her catch an incurable disease, and my little brother who doesn't talk properly, please don't let him be retarded." She was very precise in her use of words, a little monster who spoke like an adult. "You're my incurable disease," Luca would say, cuddling her on the couch as they watched TV, while Cecilia and the boy observed them out of the corner of their eyes. She prayed for ten minutes, leaving her parents to either laugh at or worry about it, depending on their mood. When Luca or Cecilia went back to her room to look in on her and tell her that she had prayed enough and that it was time to go to bed now, she joined her hands one last time and, without looking at them, still facing Our Lady of Fatima, said: "And please, Holy Mother, forgive those who don't believe in you."

"It's all simulated, I told you, done on the computer," she said to her brother now.

Cecilia couldn't hear Mattia's replies.

"No, it's impossible, flying brooms don't exist, I know it!"

But Mattia, his voice low, insistent, was adamant.

In those sweltering June days, her two sweethearts were going through a difficult time. The shy internist was gloomy and confused, but she didn't know how to help him. The child, too, was rather gloomy and confused. They had suggested he go to summer camp for two weeks. The place was an hour's drive from the city, and if need be they could go and bring him back at any time. His best friends, three classmates of his, went there and had insisted that Mattia join them. It was an "adventure and discovery" camp. And the boy really wanted to go, but he wasn't sure.

"I'm not sure," he kept saying.

"About wanting to go?" Cecilia asked.

"No, I'm sure about wanting to go."

"So you want to."

"Yes, I want to."

"Then what aren't you sure about?"

Was he not sure he could do it, maybe, was he not sure it was a good idea, was he afraid it would be too hard or that they would force him to eat? She and Luca had decided to neither push him nor discourage him. They agreed to adopt this strategy: play down the difficulties, emphasize the fun, respect the child's decision. If he didn't feel like going, it was fine. The boy decided he felt like going, maybe because he didn't want to disappoint his friends. And so they started getting ready.

Just the two of them were left at home; Michela was already at a "tennis and English" camp, two weeks at the shore. They went out one afternoon to buy a sleeping bag to use at the main camp, on the bunk bed, and for when they would sleep in a tent for a couple of nights. The boy was wearing blue shorts with lots of pockets, and the pockets were full of chestnuts and cypress cones and Magic cards and corks and rocks that he never parted with. Usually it wasn't noticeable, because he kept his treasures in his backpack, but on weekends and in the summer he looked like a duck, with his skinny shins sticking out from his bulging thighs.

Cecilia often saw him rummaging in the baggy side pockets and pulling out the small cypress cones, his favorites. He'd told her (or confessed at her insistence) that he gathered them at the foot of a tree in the schoolyard. Cecilia had said that they smelled like cypress, so they'd looked for them on the Internet together and found their real name: not cones, not berries, but *galbuli* or *coccole*, cypress "berries." Cecilia smiled. "*Coccole*, what a nice name," since the word also meant "cuddles." The child made a face, a little irritated. When they dried out, the cones (or *galbuli* or "berries") opened up, releasing the seeds that Cecilia found when she turned his pockets inside out before putting the pants in the washing machine. On the inside, the "berries" revealed a delicate, very symmetrical structure, with compact scales attached to a central axis by slender stalks.

She didn't dare ask him what those amulets were for, whether they were amulets, or prompts or mementos or pieces in a secret game. The Magic cards were the most predictable items in the collection. She didn't want to be a nosy mother, but one day she asked him if it was really necessary to always carry everything around with him, wasn't there a chance he might lose something? He shrugged, as if the objects weren't as precious as his mother thought. And she found herself in the no-win situation in which the child often left her, not knowing whether to be more concerned about the fact that her son went around with all that stuff or about the fact that he didn't seem to value it enough. Michela, who seemed more complex, was an infinitely simpler child. She neglected her things, left them around and lost them, became inconsolable, and acted like a pain in the neck until her mother gave in and bought her new ones. When she wanted something, she wanted it.

In the car she made the boy get into the front seat, even though the seat belt came up too high, too close to his throat. He seemed proud to ride in an adult's seat. He swam in it, looking even skinnier, shrunk by too hot a wash cycle along with his T-shirt. He'd always been thin. He had never been eager to eat, he'd never had an appetite.

When he had started not eating a year and a half earlier, or

eating only certain things (yogurt, creamy cheeses, mashed potatoes) and in very small quantities, she and Luca had reacted differently, at different times. Having the boy with her every day,
she'd been slower to see it and hadn't wanted to become alarmed.
There were already too many alarms sounding loudly; she was
somewhat dazed. She had probed cautiously, buying time, in other
words, hoping that the crisis would pass and the child would start
eating again. Maybe it didn't seem alarming to her because the
boy didn't do anything to hide it; he left the food on his plate and
didn't even pick up his spoon or fork. He lied halfheartedly. If she
suggested "Did you maybe fill up when you had an afternoon snack
at your grandmother's?" he nodded. His grandmother couldn't
remember how much the children ate at snack time. But at some
point Silvia had asked her briefly: "Your son doesn't eat a thing, is
that normal?" Because she was the doctor and everyone thought
she should be the first to notice.

How long had their collective blindness lasted, how long had
they ignored the evidence? Three weeks, a month. Hence the need
for hospitalization, later. Luca had gone to find her in the ER to
have a face-to-face talk. He'd said to her: "Let's forget everything
else." Luca had been keeping an eye on the child for some time.
Since he no longer saw him every day, maybe he had a better
chance of noticing it, his eye sharpened by discord, anger, and
resentment. The contentious scrutiny of the children, in search of
signs of neglect. But no, it wasn't that, and even if it were, it didn't
matter.

He'd been the first to notice and had purposely gone to look
for her in the ER because he had to do something that would
break their routine of tension, silences, and recriminating looks.

"Let's forget everything else, there's a problem here now." He
said that what scared him the most was the child's remoteness. As
if the son were checking on the father and not vice versa.

"When you ask him why he doesn't eat, is he the one checking
on you?"

Yes, the child was checking that he was still doing his job as a father, it was obvious.

Cecilia shook her head, she still didn't want to face it. Only when she spoke with the pediatricians, when she saw the test results, did she begin to admit the truth. At that point she was no longer a mother, maybe, she was a doctor in familiar territory.

All of these things (and others as well) had come out with the child psychologist, the one with the Kleenex. To whom Luca, however, hadn't wanted to go. Curiously, he, too, like the psychologist, considered it a given that the child didn't eat in order to force them to talk to each other and face the problem together. But the child psychologist claimed it was something else as well. "You haven't had any deaths in the family, recently, have you?" Cecilia said no. Then she corrected herself. "Well, two years ago, my father. Mattia was very close to his grandfather. But he can't be reacting two years later." "Does he ever talk about his grandfather?" "Oh, yes, he talks about him a lot. But not as often as he used to. When my father died," she said, smiling, proud as usual to tell stories that showed her son's intelligence and sensitivity, "Mattia was only six years old, but he said something I thought was remarkable: I don't want to grow anymore, because when you grow up, then you die."

The child psychologist nodded without smiling and murmured: "A child who doesn't eat is in no danger of growing." She wasn't heartless, but she'd already adopted the insufferable attitude of psychologists who think they can read your thoughts. No, her father's death had nothing to do with it, or maybe it did for the sole reason that it anticipated her and Luca's separation. The separation was the incurable disease that the child wanted to cure.

Besides, hadn't they gotten back together in the following months, to show him that they understood, that he was right, that he had won? But she'd never believed it, she didn't believe it would last and it didn't last. She did her best to see that it wouldn't last but that it would end better than the first time. If he had wanted to make them separate in a different way, the child had succeeded. But what if that weren't enough for him? What if he'd wanted to bring them together forever?

In the sporting goods store, amid two hundred different kinds of hiking boots and two hundred different kinds of backpacks, there were only two sleeping bag models, a very heavy one and a very light one. The day was too stifling to leave the air-conditioned store empty-handed and go in search of another, so the question had to be resolved then and there. Cecilia said the sleeping bag fit for a polar expedition was definitely better, if he was hot he could keep it open. Maybe she was afraid he'd feel colder than the others; maybe the child understood that but had to come to terms with his fears. Mattia preferred the lighter one because two of his friends had the same one. Cecilia didn't believe him—he was so distracted, how could he have noticed the brand of sleeping bag? She insisted a little, but Mattia seemed very sure and determined.

"I won't go to camp with this one," he said.

So she lost her patience, took her cell phone out of her purse and called the mother of one of his friends (the one who seemed more sympathetic and who would maybe understand her since she, too, was divorced). She asked her if the brand and model of the lighter sleeping bag really matched her child's. The mother was sympathetic, but she confirmed that yes, they matched.

The child said: "I told you." He didn't seem annoyed, though. Cecilia had to smile, a good mood spread through her like a stain on white linen. There was nothing to worry about, the real child was wiser and more mature than the imaginary child who lived in his mother's head.

"Try getting into it," she told him.

The boy smiled: "You don't try on sleeping bags."

"Go on, try it."

"It's not allowed." He pointed to a sign she hadn't noticed: TRYING OUT DISPLAY MERCHANDISE NOT PERMITTED. "It'll be fine for me, for sure," he said.

"I was afraid you wouldn't fit in it," she smiled, ruffling his hair.

They headed for the checkout counter carrying the sleeping bag, and halfway there Cecilia stopped to look at a collection of small aluminum flashlights in a glass display case. She remembered that the child had really wanted one of those flashlights; his father had one, she remembered the colorful metal and the grainy handle. She called him back and showed them to him.

"If you want I'll buy you a present."

The boy shook his head. "I don't need one. They give them to us at camp, for hikes in the woods at night."

"Yes, but this will be yours. You really wanted one."

"I don't remember, when?"

"Can I buy it for you as a gift?"

"I don't need one."

"Yes, but can I give it to you as a gift?"

He nodded. "Sure, okay."

They reached the checkout counter and paid. She pictured Mattia turning the flashlight on at night, inside the sleeping bag, so he could inspect his amulets or read a comic book.

"You really don't remember how much you wanted one?"

The boy shook his head.

As soon as they got into the car, however, she saw him take it out of the bag and put it in his pocket, rearranging his things a little, as if to make room for it, to welcome it to the family. And that gesture cheered her up.

She missed the children a lot. She missed Michela, when she'd sit next to her on the couch in the evening and start telling stories about her classmates, stories about other parents; she had a gift for seeing the most comical side of people, she could imitate them perfectly. She was delightful, not always, but she missed her, even in her less-likable moods. She'd driven her to the shore and during the trip they'd talked about a friend of hers.

"Laura's parents don't speak to each other."

"Who told you that?"

"Laura."

"They never speak to each other?"

"When she's there, no, they never speak to each other. Maybe they talk when she's not there."

"Well, they must say something to each other now and then."

"Better off separating, then."

"Every family is different."

"You and Papa talk to each other."

"Of course."

"Did you ever fight?"

"Oh, sure, we fought a lot."

"Laura's parents don't speak, because if they spoke they would fight."

"Who told you that?"

"Laura. She's not sure. She thinks they don't speak so they won't fight."

Pause.

"When do you two fight?"

"Now we get along pretty well. But in the past we fought."

"That's why you separated."

Her daughter knew the difference between separation and divorce.

"Yes, that's why."

"And then you'll get divorced."

"Yes."

"But I didn't see you."

"You didn't see us what?"

"I didn't see you fight."

"We tried not to fight in front of you."

"Oh."

Pause.

"You could have though. I wouldn't have gotten upset. Mattia would have, maybe."

What she missed about Mattia was their conversations. Without being aware of it, she talked of little else, she told everyone about their phone calls in great detail. Only her sister proved to be loving or cruel enough to tell her she was overdoing it.

"Take advantage of this time to get out," she said. "We can go to a movie, there are outdoor concerts, or let's go have a drink, that way you can see people."

"It's too hot."

"Is the heat wave dangerous?"

"No, you just have to drink a lot of water."

To show Silvia that she wasn't cut off from the world, she'd have liked to tell her about her relationship with Viberti, if it was a relationship, but she didn't feel like it. Better to talk about the children, stick to the predictable, the predictable was more satisfying. She told her she'd spoken with two counselors at Mattia's camp. They assured her that the child was fine and was eating well, in fact "heartily."

"They used that word? 'Heartily'?"

"Yes, 'heartily.' Did you ever think you'd hear them say that about your nephew?"

"Well, sure, why not?"

"So isn't it awful that as soon as he leaves home he starts eating?"

Without thinking, Silvia said she thought it was perfectly normal. Then she saw the expression on her sister's face, as if she had stabbed her in the back, and tried to remedy things:

"Lots of kids are more willing to eat away from home."

But Cecilia was still upset.

"Besides, you think so, too, you've told me a hundred times. Didn't the psychologist say the same thing? Didn't she say that it's his way of reacting to what's happened?"

Then Cecilia asked, "What reaction did Michela have, in your opinion?"

Silvia thought for a moment, then said: "She's not as carefree as she used to be."

"I still think she's over the top no matter what."

"Yes, but not like before."

"She's grown up."

"That's true."

"And you haven't noticed anything unusual?"

"What should I have noticed?"

"Her relationship with her brother . . ."

"What about her relationship with her brother?"

Cecilia sighed, she didn't know if she wanted to talk about it at all, she didn't know if she wanted to talk to her sister about it.

"Is something wrong?" Silvia asked. "It seems to me their relationship hasn't changed . . . They get along all right together, they have fun, they fight, like all kids. Or they ignore each other."

Cecilia told her about a few incidents, including the one with the toy cars in the hallway.

Silvia shook her head. "Don't do this, please."

Maybe she should listen to her sister and stop. Maybe, by voicing certain thoughts she might conjure them.

"Do you think it's possible that Michela, in some way . . . don't ask me how . . . encourages Mattia to not eat . . ."

Silvia stood up and held her hands out in front of her with a frightened look.

". . . or actually compels him, that she has such influence over him . . ."

"Please, that's enough, please," Silvia said.

Cecilia stopped and bowed her head. "All right. I know I'm scaring you, and I know you're right, I'm sorry, but telling you helps me stop thinking about it."

"Right, promise me you won't think about it anymore, promise me."

"I can't promise you, how can you promise not to think about something? But I promise that when it pops into my head I'll remember the expression you have now and I'll ignore the thought."

She went out with the shy internist one evening because her sister had told her to take advantage of the children's being away to have a little fun, or maybe because Mattia was doing well and the future looked less bleak than the past, or maybe because she felt guilty for having made Viberti fall in love with her, or because for some nights she'd been imagining him in scenes that were no longer merely fraternal, hand in hand, head on his shoulder.

She hadn't dreamed up such detailed fantasies since she was seventeen or eighteen, as if her curiosity had returned, as if the *novelty* had never worn off. For instance, she wanted to suck his lips as she'd done that afternoon in early June, she wanted to slide her tongue over his eyelids. She wanted to squeeze his cock, feel the blood throbbing, feel its firmness. She wanted him to grab her between her legs as if he wanted to rip her open. She wanted to bite him.

She came, and her eyes flew open in the dark. Dear God, she really wanted to bite him. But of course she wouldn't do it. She got up to check the anatomy book to see what one of the carpal bones was called. If the children had been home she would never have masturbated and she would never have gotten up in the middle of the night, turning on all the lights, to go and look for a huge anatomy textbook that she hadn't opened in who knows how many years, to reread the morphology of the hand bones, sitting at the kitchen table: there, that was it, the *pisiform bone*, an unmistakable shape.

At the restaurant she talked for two hours, inundating the shy internist with a torrent of dumb stories, she, too, like Michela, *over the top*, in fact, she worst of all, the original. Throughout the entire dinner she kept talking and thinking that she wanted to fuck Viberti but that she wouldn't because it was better that way. She stopped talking only when they were outside in the close, muggy air, under the dark masses of trees that reminded her of the walk a month ago, the dense fog in which she'd felt enveloped.

She should have immediately called a taxi and gone home, but she went to the parking lot with Viberti as if she'd also driven there. She didn't say a word until the shy internist stopped looking around for the Scénic and turned to look at her. Then she was forced to admit that she hadn't come by car and he offered her a ride. She shouldn't have accepted, but she got into the Passat, where she'd ended up a month ago after wandering around like a sleepwalker. She kept silent, because if she spoke it would break the spell. She knew what she shouldn't do and she was doing it. Frozen in her seat, her eyes closed, she let Viberti drive up and down the avenue along the river.

Against the black screen of her eyelids she saw the children running toward her. She had the feeling, vague as a distant memory, that she'd left them at the parking lot so she could go and have a good time. Instead, it was the children who were having a good time without her. Was she jealous? Did it bother her that they were so happy? Child neglect, or children neglecting their parent? Mattia had stopped drawing parking spaces, fortunately. They drove up and down the avenue waiting for her to be ready, like in a waiting room, waiting for a decision to be delivered. Waiting room, waiting lane. Which specialist should they see? Each had become the other's specialist.

The seat belt was crushing a nipple, she loosened it. That touch was enough to rouse her from her torpor. Although a part of her was absent, another part was present and excited, and when her excitement found an opportunity to emerge, Cecilia opened her eyes and looked at Viberti. He no longer seemed so shy, this internist. It had happened too quickly. And it was about to happen again. Viberti stopped the car in a dark side street and she climbed astride him without even waiting for him to unzip.

And regretting it this time was easier and more abrupt. All she had to do was ignore the phone calls and messages, wait for the children to return from their summer camps, load kids and luggage in the car and join her mother at the shore. Nowhere in the rules was it written that she owed him an explanation, and a period of silence would do them both good.

PART III

(2004)

THE TEA CEREMONY

In his memory the child's face had become more and more blurry. He tried to remember back to the days when the boy had been hospitalized, two years before, and found details he thought he'd forgotten almost intact: the notebook with the parking lot sketches, the blue pajamas, the *Supercars* book, the cover of *Pinocchio*. He could see certain images again, like the skinny wrist peeking out of the pajama sleeve, or the feet tucked into the blue slippers, or the upward-curving wisps of brown hair falling over his ears, so that his head looked like a pagoda. He remembered images that he couldn't have seen, the child biting into an apple and leaving two parallel marks on the fruit, as if he were still missing his front incisors (they weren't missing).

And after a while he realized that he was transforming him, or had already transformed him. His face had become a child's version of Cecilia's face. Now he wasn't so sure that Mattia resembled her all that much. And maybe he'd never see him again. In two years he must have changed a lot. He was ten now, he might be unrecognizable. No, maybe not unrecognizable, but certainly changed. So in that sense he was right: he would never see the child from two years ago again. He didn't have the courage to ask Cecilia for a picture of the boy. It seemed like a strange thing to do. Then, too, he didn't want to make her have to look through photos from that time. He tried to remember, but every attempt was hopeless.

It happened one morning in mid-February, at winter's coldest point, a day that lacked the decency to slip by without leaving a trace; not only was it a Monday, not only was it bitterly cold, but the sky was an intense, bright blue swept clean by the wind. Not one of those gray skies that swaddle the city like a tightly tucked flannel blanket. On days like that, according to Marta, a headache lay in wait, that's why they called it "high pressure."

At ten Viberti was to start examining the fifteen patients admitted to the ward. While waiting for the nurse to let him know she'd finished her rounds of the beds, he quickly calculated their average age: seventy-five (one sixty-year-old lowered it). When the average age of the patients was higher than the national average life expectancy it was a bad sign—one devoid of any scientific basis, but bad nevertheless.

He had just turned forty-four, and if he were to have a child in a year, he'd be fifty-five when the child turned ten, when the child turned eighteen he'd be sixty-three. He'd have to stay in shape to be able to play tennis at that age.

He was joking with two residents. He advised them to always tell the family that the situation was difficult; if the patient later recovered, they could then recite the magic formula, "he has a strong constitution," which made everything all right. A strong constitution that could be passed along genetically was a guarantee that shone brightly on the future of children and grandchildren. A strong constitution made everyone feel better. The nurse came to call them; she overheard his remark and gave him a stern look.

In some rooms, the shutters were lowered halfway due to the

brutal light, but the sun came through the cracks, blades of light on the floor, refracting against the walls. Even in semidarkness, the rooms were full of smothered light. The first patient was a chronic bronchitis relapse. Viberti listened to his back and told the two residents they could reduce the steroids.

In the bottom of his coat pocket his cell phone began to vibrate against the patient's side, scaring him and then making him laugh. It was an unknown number. He went out into the hall to answer, he heard Cecilia's agitated voice and ducked into the deserted dispensary where he could talk quietly. The room was on the other side of the building, and, before his eyes could adjust to the dimness, with the door closed behind him, he thought night had fallen over the world. It was the first time Cecilia was calling him from home. She absolutely had to see him, not at lunch, not in two hours, but that very moment, as soon as possible, she had something to tell him that couldn't wait.

Just the idea of her summoning him put him on the alert; it was a call that had to be answered. Not to would mean to break a fragile stability and risk losing what he both feared and desired losing. Calls from people like his mother or Cecilia had to be answered, regardless of fears or desires. Especially calls from Cecilia, with whom he was in love, or at least assuming he was in love with her, as he was in the habit of doing.

"Has something happened to Mattia?"

"Nothing happened."

"Can't it wait until lunchtime?"

"I'm not coming to lunch, I have the evening shift."

"I can't get away before an hour or so."

But she kept insisting and Viberti promised to be at the usual café within forty minutes.

"Not the usual café." She asked him to please meet her at a playground halfway between the hospital and her house.

"I don't know where it is, wouldn't it be better to meet in a place I know?"

She had to go pay the children's dentist near the playground, then go back home right away. "Please, please."

Viberti agreed.

He completed his rounds in fifty minutes and ran down the stairs. Why was he running? Because he hated being late. "Am I running because I want to see her or only because I hate being late?" He remembered a taxi stand in front of a side entrance to the hospital: if he went out through the main entry, passing the locker room to get his coat first, it would take him more than half an hour.

He went out into the harsh light and biting cold huddled in his white coat; he counted on jumping straight into a taxi, but the stand was empty. It was so cold that the street seemed wider, the houses cowering back, snuggled against one another. Viberti pulled out his cell phone to call a taxi, gave the address to the dispatcher, then dashed into a café to wait. He called Cecilia to let her know he'd be late—he stopped just inside the glass door plastered with stickers for food coupons, brands of ice cream, and images of the Madonna of Medjugorje, turning his back to the room—but Cecilia's phone was turned off or out of range. He looked up, he'd thought he'd gone unnoticed, but there were only two customers in the café and the barista was staring at him.

He wasn't familiar with the places on that side of the hospital, he'd never been in that café. He approached the counter and chose a package of candy. The barista looked suspicious or irritated, as if he knew that Viberti hadn't really come in to buy candy, as if he considered him a parasite who'd come into his café to keep warm while waiting for a taxi. Viberti had never been able to ask to use the toilet without at least ordering a cup of coffee. He walked to the door to leave, at which point the barista asked him if he was a doctor by any chance. His son had a varicocele and the doctors (he made a vague gesture to indicate *other* doctors, present company excluded) weren't able to help him. Did he know a good specialist? Out of the corner of his eye Viberti saw the taxi stop in front of the café. He told the man the name of a colleague, then mentioned another. The barista didn't seem satisfied. So Viberti took the café's card from the counter and said, "I might come up with another one, I'll call you later, I promise."

In the taxi he pictured Cecilia waiting for him in the cold, sitting on a swing; he tried to imagine what could have happened—it was the first time she'd asked to see him with such urgency. Nothing could have happened, it was crazy, it made no sense to respond so promptly to calls like that without probing further, without demanding answers. He closed his eyes. Since the time he was a child he'd found sunlight refracted through the windows of a car extremely grating, and in a few minutes he felt nauseous. It was the thought of that light that made him feel sick, he didn't get carsick. He remembered once when he had to wait for his mother in the car, he'd locked himself in and was so bothered by the light that he wrapped his head in a scarf. Marta got angry when she came back, she told him he could have *hung* himself (hard to hang yourself in a truck, impossible in a car).

After a while, the taxi driver asked him if by chance he was a doctor. Viberti diagnosed an irritable bowel syndrome, paid, and got out. The playground was between the avenue and the river, behind a local police station where he'd paid a few fines in the past. There was the standard equipment found in all modern playgrounds, things he would have gone crazy for as a child. Even now he was intrigued by features like the spongy flooring, a great way to protect children from falls. *Then, too, what fascinates me are the small improvements, because they make me believe that everything can be improved, always, little by little, and that we mustn't lose hope. Take the blender, somehow, for some reason, one day it occurred to someone not to have it rotate in one direction only. Press it once: clockwise. Press it again: counterclockwise. That way it juices better.* No trace of Cecilia, she must have left already. He took out the phone to call her and apologize for being late and saw that he had received a text ten minutes ago; he hadn't heard it: *I'm on my way*. If he'd arrived on time he would have been waiting half an hour for her in the icy cold.

He blew his nose. The whole thing didn't make sense anymore. He'd been telling himself that for weeks now. After returning from vacation there had been a "relapse," and another relapse in December. He'd started calling them relapses to make her smile, so they could laugh about it together, because their relationship was a recurring illness, because they were doctors unable to cure it, but now it was no longer funny. The idea of relapses wasn't funny, the idea of a serial killer wasn't funny (a bizarre serial killer who always struck the same victim). And so, freezing to death, he sat down on a big spring rider with a red, blue, and yellow flower-shaped seat and asked himself again: Did I race over here because I wanted to see her, and I couldn't stand not seeing her, and I'm in love with her, or because I didn't want to say no, and I was afraid I would regret it, and I'm afraid of being alone forever, and for some time a ridiculous idea has been stuck in my head, that it's too late, that this is my last chance?

He was angry, with Cecilia, with himself. After the last relapse, when, for the fourth time, the scene of repentance had repeated itself, when for the fourth time she'd told him, I'm sorry but I can't do this, he'd remarked: "So it's all over." Cecilia had gotten offended, she hadn't appreciated his sarcasm, and had retorted, "Though maybe it never began." At which point he had gotten offended. They hadn't spoken to each other for two weeks, until Christmas, then they'd made up. He looked at the pairs of swings, motionless in the cold. He imagined sitting on the swing with Cecilia and talking, swinging up and down. By synchronizing their movements they could easily converse. But even without synchronizing them, even if they got out of synch, they would still meet at least once each swing.

He decided to wait another ten minutes. After ten minutes he decided to wait another five. A homeless man shuffled along slowly, pushing a shopping cart with all his worldly goods. His home. The man stopped to stare at him. And Viberti saw himself through the homeless man's eyes: a man in a white coat sitting on a big spring rider, in a playground painted strictly in primary colors. Should he go? Stay? Return the look? And what a look! Impossible to stare at someone with such intensity, a gaze that was blurry and at the same time sharp.

After an interminable time the homeless man came up to him. He must be full of pathologies! A whole cross-section of samples. For a moment he thought the man actually wanted to ask him if he was a doctor. Instead he asked for a cigarette. Viberti smiled. "Asking a doctor for a cigarette? Ridiculous." The homeless man wasn't smiling. Viberti pulled out the candy and started to offer him one. The man took the whole package and went away without thanking him.

Like the homeless man, I, too, observe my father sitting on the flower-shaped spring rider, shivering in the icy February chill. It's an image that should be read in its entirety, like a sign. The cold is a damp cold that goes straight through you. In the playground along the river, the internist Viberti is rigid, frozen in place, he seems chained to the flower, a prisoner. But we mustn't forget that he's sitting on a spring, like James Bond's passenger in the Aston Martin, and at any moment he might be ejected.

He might fall down with me on the playground's spongy floor. I'm very familiar with that rubbery material, I can almost feel it under my feet as I fall from above, bouncing with my friends. My father bounces with me in my mind, in reality he's sitting on a bench nearby, reading a newspaper. Whole afternoons, when the weather was nice.

When she arrives, Cecilia's face looks very tired. Viberti is freezing and would like to forgive her for everything, but he can't, because there's nothing to forgive, and the blame, if there is any blame, is distributed equally between them. There is no blame, why should there be blame?

Cecilia wants to walk along the river, Viberti implores her to go to a café he spotted on the street. They sit at a small table in the back. Cecilia talks about the children, Mattia has a cough, maybe he's caught the flu, she sent him to school but she's already sorry. And when he's sick, it's even more difficult to get him to eat.

"But you didn't call me here to talk about that," Viberti says curtly.

"No, but don't be mean to me," she replies, her voice cracking.

"I'm sorry, but try to understand, I have to get back to the hospital, I thought something serious had happened."

She tells him she hasn't been sleeping well at night, she's so tired she collapses at ten, right after turning off the light in the children's rooms, then she wakes up at two or three and starts tossing and turning in bed. She doesn't want to start in again with the sleepless nights she had the year before. Every now and then she gets up to check on the children, to see if they're breathing. "Can you imagine? Something you do with newborns."

Viberti sighs, takes her hand, squeezes it tightly. He expects she'll try to break free immediately, because she doesn't usually welcome signs of affection in public, instead she pulls him to her and gives him a kiss on the cheek. This is why she called him so far away from the hospital, so they could behave normally, for once at least, without being afraid that someone might see them.

"I'm getting to it, okay? I'm getting to it."

And Viberti thinks she intends to tell him that they mustn't see each other any longer, that she's as tired as he is of that friendship which is not only friendship, that there's no place in her life for such a waste of emotion.

Instead Cecilia says: "When I have to think about something wonderful and good I think of you, at night I think of you and I calm down and fall asleep."

"Well, better me than a benzodiazepine."

Cecilia ignores him and continues: "So I said to myself that maybe I'm in love with you. I don't know. I'm asking you: Do you think I'm in love with you?"

Viberti lowers his eyes. How should he react to that question? By throwing his arms around her, weeping, shouting for joy? But the very fact that he asks himself this question means he doesn't want to react in any way, it means he doesn't believe what Cecilia has said, doesn't believe that she's really in love with him. He believes she's very confused, and confused people confuse him, he doesn't know how to act.

"You don't seem thrilled," she says.

He can't speak, he can't find anything sensible to say.

"Please, say something."

He shakes his head.

After a seemingly interminable time he says: "Of course you're in love with me. I'm in love with you, too."

Cecilia nods.

"But being together isn't easy, is it?"

"No, it's not easy."

"Not after what you went through."

"Not after what I went through. What I'm still going through." She squeezes his hand again. "You see. You understand me. You understand me right away."

Viberti thinks: Why don't we try? Why don't we try being together?

It's not what she wants. Is it what *he* wants?

He's seized by a sudden fit of anger. He doesn't know why Cecilia lets herself go like that: old, scruffy loafers, a missing button at the neck of her blouse, that shabby backpack.

"What are you thinking about?"

"Nothing. I'm sorry you're feeling miserable. I'd like to help you, but I don't know how."

"But you do help me, you help me a lot." Her eyes glisten with tears. "If you weren't here, I don't know what I'd do."

"If I weren't here."

"Yes," Cecilia says.

"But I am here."

They remain silent, holding hands, studying the brown ring of coffee left in the bottom of the cups. Cecilia concentrates on trying not to cry. Viberti is startled to have said "I'm sorry you're feeling miserable." He'd never realized how miserable she felt, "to feel miserable" means feeling *very* miserable, otherwise he would have said "I'm sorry you're not happy." And even more startled because she didn't deny feeling miserable (therefore *very* miserable). She's aware of it and doesn't deny it, and she doesn't talk about it, because it's too painful to talk about.

He glances around to see if anyone is watching them. A love story that has taken place entirely in cafés. One table among many. A tiny table on which to uncomfortably rest your elbows. The looks of strangers who embroider a wedding canopy around you, the paper place mat acting as the bridal veil, a small bottle of mineral water for the toast.

Then Cecilia perked up and asked him to tell her the story. Viberti didn't know what she was talking about.

"The story your mother told you, which had a Cecilia in it, you said it was a scandalous story . . . I thought about it last night and couldn't forgive myself for never having asked you about it."

"The scandalous story . . . I'm not sure I remember it anymore. Why are you interested?"

"I don't know, because it has to do with you. I'm interested in everything that has to do with you. And it has to do with me, too, you told me about it the first time."

"The first time?"

"When you gave me that solemn speech."

"The solemn speech . . . Oh yes, the solemn speech, I remember."

He couldn't tell her he didn't feel like it. He didn't want to tell her that he couldn't take it anymore. To cheer her up, to cheer himself up, he tried to reconstruct the story he had heard from Marta nine months ago, but he quickly realized that he wasn't capable of telling it with his mother's same rambling pace, her words rich with euphemisms and allusions. He went too fast, often forgetting an important detail, forced to go back and fill in the gap. Right off the bat he forgot a critically important detail. He began telling it halfheartedly and continued halfheartedly. He told the story to finish things in a hurry so he could get back to the hospital.

His narration made it really seem like something an elderly, sick person would make up. Halfway through he felt guilty; Marta didn't deserve to have her story dishonored that way. Or maybe the story gripped him as it hadn't the evening he'd heard it, stole the scene and used him as a puppet. He recalled that at one point his mother had said something that made him laugh, and he recited the line as if it were his own: "And now you have to imagine one of those movie scenes with a dying man on his deathbed." As if the two of them never saw any dying men. Cecilia laughed and said, "Oh sure, I can imagine."

Now he felt a different urge to tell it, the story no longer seemed so improbable, he was no longer sorry to have told it but he was sorry to be coming to the end. He managed to make Cecilia laugh again, imitating the glowering face of a watchmaker wearing a monocle.

Because at the heart of it all was a pocket watch, locked away in a jewelry box in the drawer of an enormous dresser in the room of a man who is slowly dying. The man has been a widower for ten years, he is no longer able to walk, never leaves the house, and has trouble speaking. His daughter, Cecilia, cares for him with absolute devotion; though she's only twenty, she spends her days with him and lives as a recluse in a house full of furniture and bric-a-brac, not far from the bank where her father worked before his sudden illness. One day the old man takes a turn for the worse, doesn't get out of bed, can no longer speak, and must be spoon-fed and washed when he soils himself, like a child. Cecilia prays that he won't suffer much, but she can't bring herself to hope that he will die quickly. She watches over him till late, sleeps in an armchair beside the bed, is always ready to serve him.

One evening her father asks her to get the claret-colored velvet jewelry box from the drawer. Cecilia is familiar with the jewelry box, she knows it contains some of her mother's keepsakes, she thinks her father wants to give them to her. But there's also a pocket watch in the jewelry box that doesn't seem to be of much value. The old man raises his head from the pillow with an enormous effort, his forehead beaded with sweat, and mumbles something, he wants to speak but he can't. Cecilia puts a pencil in his hand, supporting him so he can write on the first page of a book. He prints some letters in a shaky, somewhat lopsided hand. Cecilia recognizes the last name of the watchmaker who repaired the old grandfather clock at their home a couple of times. She thinks her father is asking her to take the pocket watch to be fixed. She thinks he's delirious, she doesn't take him seriously. That night her father dies.

Several months go by; Cecilia gets over it. She decides to straighten up the house. She comes upon the watch again. She weeps, thinking about her father. And it occurs to her that maybe she should respect his last wishes, absurd though they may be, and take the old "turnip" to the watchmaker. A considerate gesture, a way of remembering him. Would visiting the cemetery and placing fresh flowers on the grave be any different? So she makes her way across the entire city, in a horse-drawn tram, the watch wrapped up and tucked in the purse she holds tightly on her lap. She arrives at the watchmaker's place. She's never been in the shop; the watchmaker has always come to their house, where he'd take the clock apart on the floor and arrange the pieces carefully on a white cloth. The small shop is very simple, the sign unassuming. Cecilia enters and the tinkle of the bell announces the arrival of a customer, but the watchmaker is bent over his workbench, wearing his monocle, and seems not to have heard. From the back, pulling aside a red drape, a young man has appeared; he looks into Cecilia's eyes and she knows that this is the man for her. The young man looks just like Cecilia's father when he was twenty, in a sepia photo, wearing a Cavalry uniform.

"Then what?"

"Then they got engaged, they got married."

"So where's the scandal?"

"They were brother and sister! Didn't you get it?"

"No, how can that be? Wasn't he the watchmaker's son?"

"He was the son of the girl's father, who had gotten the maid pregnant. The watchmaker married her afterward. And the girl's father helped them, he set up the shop, he sent his son to school."

"Well, okay, you didn't tell me about the maid."

Viberti smiled. "I forgot . . . but it wasn't that hard to figure out."

"But, come on, how come his father, that is, the watchmaker, knew and how come he didn't object—the mother, too, the maid, she knew her son was the other man's child, how come she . . ."

The story had had the desired effect, it had taken her mind off things. She was smiling contentedly, murmuring to herself: "Really *quite* a story," and she squeezed his hand as if by telling it to her, he had given her a gift.

Thinking about his mother, however, had made Viberti strangely melancholy. Thinking about his mother, who remembered reading or thought she remembered reading that story. That story: like a mistaken diagnosis, the death of a neglected patient. The confession long in coming, deferred until fully delirious. The old man must have loved that boy more than anything, but who can say if he meant to have him marry his daughter. Maybe he merely wanted her to know of that brother's existence. And if the character wasn't in a story by Chekhov or Maupassant or Tarchetti, who could the author be?

They spoke about a scandal that had hit the hospital: the arrest of the hospital administrator on charges of corruption. Then Viberti stood up, saying he had to find a good urologist.

Cecilia misheard "neurologist," she thought he was talking about his mother and said, "It won't get any worse, you'll see."

Viberti wondered how she could know about the barista's son, he didn't think he'd told her about him. He gave her a kiss on the cheek and left.

Nothing changed, nothing had to change, though if someone had overheard their conversation without knowing the story of the months leading up to it, he would have thought that everything was about to change, because Cecilia had never opened up as she had that day and Viberti had never opened up as he had that day. Two nights later they made love in the car and then everything went on as before; they saw each other because Cecilia needed to and because Viberti didn't have the courage to tell her that it was better if they didn't see each other anymore. Besides, it's impossible to pull the plug on hope.

A total inability to read people: the art of semiotics, fundamental in medicine, never learned. *Certain things, for example, you learn only through experience. When I was forty I found that if you open the left rear window a little, the air that comes in through the left front window doesn't create a draft but cools your car. Because it's immediately sucked out, channeled, see? It's one of those things that nobody can teach you.*

Every now and then Viberti thought that Cecilia might one day come to him and say that, yes, she wanted to try, she wanted to start a new life. But he thought that only occasionally; usually he was sure it would never happen. He was struck by the absolute skepticism with which he'd reacted to that confession of sorts: "So I said to myself that maybe I'm in love with you." Not only had he not believed her, not only did he think she was saying exactly the opposite, it was as if she were asking him to put a period on the story and start a new paragraph, as if she were telling him: "So I said to myself that maybe I'll never be in love with you." And in fact she came up with the story Marta had told, to close the circle.

He couldn't get it out of his head, the idea that he'd appeared too soon in Cecilia's life. She and her husband had just separated, the wounds hadn't yet healed, in a couple of years she would be ready for another relationship and he would always be remembered as a transitional episode.

But something Cecilia had said stuck in his mind and refused to be dismissed, indeed it rose to the forefront as the only noteworthy thing that had been said that morning: "Not after what I went through. What I'm still going through." What was she still going through, exactly? Why after all those months of friendship with relapses hadn't he thought to ask her: "So how is your relationship with your husband now?"

And why hadn't he ever had the urge to follow her? And see with his own eyes where she lived? Who she went out with at night, if she went out, since she wouldn't go out with him? So he decided he would do it, he would station himself near her house, in the parking lot behind the church, to spy on her. It seemed like a perfectly reasonable decision, and until he acted on it the infinite sadness of the plan didn't occur to him.

He took up his post the first time, saw her return home after an afternoon shift, at half past eight. Nothing happened, there was nothing to see. After an hour he got fed up and went home.

Another time he waited from six to nine and didn't see anyone who even remotely resembled her husband or ex-husband appear.

He followed her out of the hospital one afternoon then lost her in traffic, and instead of going straight home he continued driving down a very long road, almost leaving the city, and began wandering through the northeastern outskirts. Huge shopping malls had sprung up there, replacing abandoned factories, along with new buildings that architects tried to make less depressing by painting the roofs blue or the shutters pink; here and there, the empty shells of the old factories still stood, each carrying the weight of its entire history like the homeless man he'd met at the playground.

One day, instead of lurking around to spy on her, he stopped under the trees where they'd kissed for the first time that late afternoon in June, and another evening he looked for the exact spot where he had parked when they made love in the car. He stayed there thinking for an hour; that, too, was a way of spying on her; that, too, was a pathetic way to spend his time. He thought of all the times he had masturbated thinking about making love with Cecilia in the car. Their relationship was still in transit, maybe it would never reach port, and he couldn't allow himself to think beyond fantasies of car sex. At most, he imagined doing it in the comfort of the backseat.

He stationed himself one last time and saw Cecilia take the child to someone, maybe his father. All the boy had with him was his schoolbag. Was it his father's house or that of a classmate? He stood waiting for Cecilia to come back down, imagining her with her ex-husband. And there, in that place that told him nothing, in that neighborhood that wasn't his, at that address which he'd never wanted to know, he thought that maybe he didn't care about Cecilia anymore; maybe he wasn't just fed up with that strange friendship-with-relapses, maybe he didn't love her as he thought he did, maybe he no longer loved her or maybe he had never loved her, and it was just the fear that she might be his last chance playing a nasty trick on him.

He started the Passat and drove away, instantly feeling a sense of relief. Enough is enough. He was letting go, he had let go. The moment when you can finally say it's over comes just like that, out of the blue. Even with relationships that seem never to end (maybe because they never began).

Nevertheless, he continues to see her. For two years, lunch has been their time together and it's difficult to end the habit overnight. It's equally difficult to come up with credible excuses when Viberti decides not to show up one day and the next day Cecilia asks why he didn't come. Then again he has to eat in any case and he might easily be spotted if he went to one of the other cafés across from the hospital, so all through the month of March Viberti some-times uses the side door and goes to eat his boiled vegetables in the café that he's renamed "the urologist's." But he's not at ease as he eats, he feels like she's going to surprise him at any moment.

One day, coming around the column that conceals their table, for a moment he thinks Cecilia has brought her thirteen-year-old daughter to lunch. The young woman sitting with her looks famil-iar, even though Viberti is certain he's never seen her before. He would remember the wide black headband in her hair and her in-timidating look. Too late to retreat: Cecilia invites him to sit with them: "This is Silvia, my sister."

Viberti sits down and says hello. "You never told me you had a sister," he murmurs, gets up again, starts to sit down a second time, and then decides to get up and go order the plate of boiled vegeta-bles and a glass of mineral water. All he has to do is go around the column, lean over the counter, and order his plate from the barista, but what he'd like to do is leave, go out the door, and eat by himself at another café. He mistook her for Cecilia's daughter because the idea of meeting the young girl frightens him.

He returns to his seat. He's petrified, like marble, and he thinks it shows, as if blue veins had appeared on his skin. He has no desire to make conversation; he hadn't wanted to have lunch with Cecilia, let alone with Cecilia and her sister. This Silvia seems less interesting than Cecilia, not as tall, less attractive. He doesn't know how it could have happened—in two years not a hint about the existence of a sister. He'd like to insist and say again "You never told me you had a sister," to punish Cecilia, but it wouldn't be polite. He feels rigid, like the column behind him. In fact, he *is* the column, he's turned into a column so he can stay in that café forever, ignored by everyone, in mute adoration of the woman sitting at the table.

"Claudio always eats boiled vegetables for lunch," Cecilia says. If she'd wanted to put him at ease she could have come up with a different opening. He feels like refusing to speak for the entire lunch so that Cecilia will realize how offended he is. But it's hard to say absolutely nothing. If you don't talk, you're saying you don't want to talk. Instead you have to be able to talk without saying anything: his mother was a master at this.

Cecilia persists: "Silvia, too, used to eat boiled vegetables for lunch and dinner . . . years ago. Remember, Silvia?"

"Were you on a diet?" Viberti asks.

Silvia is painstakingly chewing a bite of her sandwich and can't answer, she taps her lips delicately with her fingertips, a gesture that Cecilia often makes, as if to say, "Wait, I'll tell you."

But Viberti can't wait, he's embarrassed at having put her on the spot. "Sorry, I didn't mean to intrude. You liked boiled vegetables, that's reason enough for me."

Silvia finally swallows. "I've never been on a diet in my life."

It's strange being a threesome for the first time, as if the last time for the two of them alone had already passed. And it's strange that it's never happened before; could it be that in two years not one coworker or friend had come into that café? And could it be that no one, seeing them, sat down at their table? The table is hidden away, that's why Viberti had chosen it. And he certainly wouldn't bring a friend or a coworker there on his own; he has no brothers or sisters, and he never wanted to share Cecilia with anyone. Nor has Cecilia ever done so before today. There must be a reason for it.

"I like boiled vegetables," Sylvia adds, "but back then I ate them because I had a plan."

Cecilia nods. "A plan . . . of course, it was a *plan*."

"I had to eat the same dish for a whole week. One dish a week for four weeks and then I would decide what made me feel best."

Viberti smiles. He was supposed to be irritated and offended throughout lunch and instead he finds the story amusing. He asks what the dishes were.

"I remember the first one was boiled potatoes and boiled fish. Another was poached eggs, carrots, and zucchini. Then rice, peas, and chicken. I don't remember the fourth. Midway through the rice, peas, and chicken I got fed up and dropped it all. Still, I should remember the fourth. Mozzarella, tomatoes, and figs? What do you think, Ceci? It seems to me there were figs and also asparagus. No, that's impossible, they're not in season at the same time. I remember artichokes, too, but I could be wrong about the artichokes, I've never been a fan of artichokes. Once I pricked myself with an artichoke. No—there was mozzarella in the fourth dish, there was tomato, but I don't remember the third ingredient."

"And you didn't eat anything else?"

"Ah, I knew this story would intrigue you," Cecilia says, her sarcasm plain. She's edgy, he hadn't noticed. He'd been so irritated about the fact that she'd kept the existence of her sister hidden from him that he hadn't detected the dark look on her face. She's upset or angry, or very tired. Something must have happened in the ER, or to the child.

"In the morning I had yogurt and cereal for breakfast," Sylvia says, "and in the evening I also ate fruit. Not just any kind of fruit. Bananas, for instance, are disgusting. Our mother always told us not to say that a food was disgusting, but there's no better way to describe bananas. Remember, Ceci? No bananas. And mind you, bananas are very good for you. The potassium. Take allergies, for example. I read somewhere that bananas are great for allergies. Pears, apples, plums. I ate them all. But not bananas. But then again, who knows if these things you read are true? You doctors, when you read these things, do you believe them? I always suspect it's the banana growers who pay the journalists."

"So, in the end what foods made you feel best?"

"Maybe the eggs with carrots and zucchini. After three days of rice, peas, and chicken I was desperate."

"But how did you come up with the idea?"

"I don't know, at the time I was obsessed with food. I had gone to a lecture, a Swiss guy—he wasn't a doctor or a dietitian—had come to give a talk at the university. I remember going to it by chance, a friend had dragged me along." She turned to Cecilia, "Enrico Fermi," then turned back to Viberti: "An old friend of mine, his name was Enrico but I called him Enrico Fermi because in a debate once he had defended nuclear power and we'd almost lynched him, plus he had red hair . . ."

Cecilia was getting up. "Enrico Fermi had very red hair, yes."

"Are you going already . . ." Viberti says.

"Will you call me?" Silvia asks.

Viberti rises, Cecilia has quickly slipped on her jacket and says, "Ciao, see you," smiling and touching his arm.

Silvia repeats: "Will you call me later?"

Cecilia nods, and the next moment she's gone.

Viberti sits back down. He's at a café with a stranger, somehow, for some reason. He can't afford to be late either, he has appointments. He could have remained standing and said goodbye, then left immediately. But he can't help it, he has to cover up the awkwardness. Because Cecilia's headlong flight has made both of them feel uncomfortable, it doesn't take much to see that. And Silvia does nothing to ease the situation. She keeps staring in the direction in which her sister disappeared.

"You were telling me about this Swiss lecturer . . . who was he?"

Silvia lowers her eyes. "Yes. Well, he was from Switzerland. I don't remember his name, something like Fletcher or Frecher. I'm not sure—I had gone by chance with this friend, I mean, I had absolutely no interest in the man's philosophy."

"Philosophy?"

"I don't remember it all that well. It was all based on ritual, he aid that nutrition must observe a ritual, that you should only eat raw foods or boiled stuff, otherwise the foods are *injured*, you know, by being fried or grilled. I don't understand why boiling things would be any better, he was a bit of a charlatan—oh, and then he had this idea about a soup bowl . . ." Silvia takes a sip of tea.

"A soup bowl?"

"According to him you should always eat out of a soup bowl, because the food must be *held*, it must be *embraced*, like this—" Her hands form the shape of a shell.

Viberti smiles. Silvia smiles, too.

"Yet later he convinced you."

"He convinced me?"

"The philosopher."

"Yes, he was quite fascinating, the way he spoke, the way he described it all. And I got the urge to try it, because among other things he advocated the principle of the one single dish."

"And did he also tell you to drink tea at meals?"

"No, that's a habit that I fell into afterward."

And she starts talking about her passion for green tea, about how difficult it is to find good Japanese tea in Italy (stuff about the product's perishability and temperature changes during transport), she says that green tea is much more delicate than black tea. She talks about properties that are good for the heart and circulation, others that prevent virtually all types of cancers. "I'll have to send you the link to a great site, you'll see, you'll be converted, too."

Viberti listens to her. It's funny how this woman is similar to yet unlike her sister. Then he remembers that he has to get back. But he makes no move to get up. He looks at the sandwich that Cecilia left untouched on the table. Was that all she had for lunch?

"The way you're looking at that sandwich . . ." Silvia says.

"How am I looking at it?"

"Like it did something wrong."

It's a mortadella sandwich. The pink-and-white slices peek out from the edges of the bread like small naughty tongues. "No," Viberti says, "I would never eat it, but I don't resent it. I respect it. It lives in its world and I in mine."

Silvia laughs. "There's a fantastic novel you should read, it was one of my father's favorites, it's called *The Cook*. I'll lend it to you, if you'd like. I'll give it to Cecilia. It's about a chef who seduces, or influences, or deceives—in short, who *manipulates* people with his recipes."

Viberti stares at her, bewildered, why on earth would that book interest him?

Suddenly Silvia is standing up and putting on her jacket. "Now I really have to go. Write down your e-mail." She puts a blue clothbound notebook under his nose, hands him a pen.

Instead of writing, Viberti reads a note that jumps out in the center of the blank page, *I want her to like me*, and is left dazed, staring at the underlined words. Then he looks up.

"Your e-mail," Silvia repeats, "write it down there. You do have an e-mail address, don't you?"

Viberti nods, writes down the address, hands back the notebook.

And at that point he, too, can finally stand up, say goodbye, and quickly leave the café.

———

He was waiting for Giulia and Marta outside the main entrance and was surprised by the smiling crowd that seemed to drift aimlessly around the hospital, not a forlorn crowd—people with real or imaginary ailments, patients' families, doctors, vendors peddling useless first aid kits—but the kind of festive weekend crowd you'd find at an amusement park. Giulia had made another geriatric appointment for Marta.

The hospital had been built in the thirties and the prosthetic wings added after the war stuck out from the decrepit body of the original core. The past always in plain sight yet invisible to everyone, like certain traits fathers pass down to their children, similarities you don't want to see, the past that doesn't pass away. *What did I really teach you? Did I teach you anything useful? Anything concrete? Did I teach you how to tie your shoelaces or how to knot your tie? See, these are the things you get from a parent that stay with you later. No, I'm not kidding. Every time I pack a suitcase I remember the day my mother taught me how to fold a jacket. You spread it out on the bed. You fold one sleeve over and then the other. Then you fold the lower half of the jacket over the upper half. I'll never forget her graceful gestures.*

When Giulia and Marta appeared at the end of the driveway, Viberti saw that his ex-wife was talking while his mother prudently stayed silent. Giulia wasn't being cruel, and she didn't need further confirmation of her mother-in-law's memory loss; Giulia spoke out of compassion because, unlike Viberti, she wasn't used to being silent. For years she had talked with Marta, for more than ten years they had told each other everything, and it was inconceivable that silence should now descend on them—she had to revive the dialogue, recite the lines for the both of them. Every so often he imagined himself hospitalized in Giulia's ward, stuck in bed, helpless, forced to listen to her talk.

The parked cars and all the commotion disturbed Marta, who stopped and turned around every few steps, though once they'd passed through the gate Giulia had taken her by the arm, dragging her along. Viberti walked down the entry steps, uncertain whether to go and meet them. He didn't want to complicate things further. What was his mother afraid of? The ambulances, taxis, motorbikes she heard coming up behind her. Maybe she didn't remember where to go.

"Here we are!" Giulia chirped with the satisfaction of a mother at her child's first steps.

"You look very elegant, Mama," Viberti said, and it was true. Marta's tastes were simple but refined: that day she wore a charcoal-gray knit suit and a cream-colored blouse; she certainly didn't look eighty-three years old.

"But it's not a doctor visit, right?" she asked.

Giulia shook her head. "We just talked about this."

"Even if it were, Mama, you're perfect, with you we won't make a bad impression," Viberti said, taking her arm and squeezing it, then immediately letting go, worried that he might break a bone.

"We were taught from an early age that for a doctor's visit . . ." Marta began telling them.

"But it isn't," Giulia interrupted her.

"It isn't, you won't have to undress, you won't have to let everyone see your undies," Viberti teased her.

"Silly, that wasn't the reason, I'm spotless, what do you think . . . Where's the entrance? Has it always been here?"

Giulia said goodbye when they reached the first corridor and was swallowed up by the crowd of patients in gowns and slippers and visitors shouting into their cell phones. Viberti led Marta, who was increasingly confused, to a side staircase past a vending machine that dispensed coffee and hot chocolate. A small elevator reserved for staff waited behind a frosted-glass door. From his coat pocket he pulled out a key that he'd had a nurse give him (he'd lost his) and inserted it into a lock that stood in place of a button.

Marta observed him: "You look very elegant, too, in that white coat."

"Thank you, Mama."

You look very elegant, too: she hadn't forgotten the compliment he'd paid her earlier and wanted to return it.

Giulia had arranged everything so that they wouldn't spend even a minute in the waiting room. As soon as they reached Geriatrics a nurse recognized Viberti and introduced herself warmly to Marta before leading her into the examining room. "Take care," Viberti said. Marta disappeared behind the door without answering.

His phone rang immediately. It was Giulia.

"Did you see how frightened she was?"

"I saw."

"I told you, she's afraid to leave the house. I realized it this winter, when she insisted it was too cold to go out, and you know that's a clear sign."

"Maybe for an elderly person being afraid to go out is normal. If they snatch your purse and you end up on the ground . . ."

"Don't be silly."

"What is she afraid of, then?"

"Of not finding her way home!"

"Keep your voice down."

"All right, we'll talk about it later, but I promise you we'll talk about it."

"And what's your solution?"

"She needs someone full time."

"There's Angélica."

"Three full days and three mornings, but from Saturday afternoon to Monday morning Marta is alone. Not counting the time that Angélica is at your place. Couldn't you have found another housekeeper? Did you have to take your mother's?"

"She's said over and over that she doesn't want her at night."

"You're her son, you're a doctor, order her to! It's not all that hard: you say, 'Listen, Mama, you have to have this person in your house . . .'"

"I'll think about it, we'll see how the examination goes."

"The examination won't tell us anything."

"Then why are we doing it?"

"To make her see she needs help."

As if a light had abruptly been turned off. "We'll talk about it later," he murmured, and hung up.

After twenty years at the hospital he still wasn't used to people's stares, to the effect the white coat had on nameless patients. He would have liked to hang a sign around his neck: I'M SORRY, I CAN'T HELP YOU. And he would feel the same way his whole life. I remember him nearing retirement, going around the hospital with that furtive, guilty look. In self-defense he kept his eyes lowered to the ground, specifically the bottom of the wall where the baseboard curved down and smoothly joined the floor. He thought about other things. Every now and then he got so absorbed that he walked right past the door or hallway he'd been heading toward. *If you get lost in the woods, the first thing to remember is this: don't give in to fear and panic instead of trying to find the way out, or you'll make the situation even worse. What you should do is sit down, take a few deep breaths, and calmly attempt to mentally reconstruct the way you came, then get up and try to retrace the steps you took. Everyone leaves a trace, no one can make himself truly invisible, not even accidentally, even the prehistoric man who fell into a glacier was discovered eventually.*

Cecilia hadn't told him she had a sister, she had kept silent about the existence of a sister, she had treated him like a stranger. Not only had she kept him out of her life, not only had she kept him away from her children. He would have liked to see Mattia again; for two years he'd been wanting to see the boy again and she'd never let him see him. He would have liked to buy him another garage, at Christmas. He'd seen it in a toy store, a two-story garage with a gas pump and a lift for raising cars, that one was definitely suitable for a child her son's age. But Cecilia had said that Mattia was too big for that kind of toy.

He went into the locker room to change before going back to get his mother and take her home.

"You see," Marta said to him as they rode down in the elevator, "I always got a twenty-nine at the university, I was never good enough for a thirty, or maybe the professors were tougher than they are now, but here it's an excellent mark, you know."

"You scored a twenty-nine again on the Mini mental test? Really?"

"Does that seem so incredible to you? I'm not a moron, I just have memory issues."

"Of course, Mama, I didn't mean you're a moron."

Later he was supposed to have dinner with the whole family at Giulia's place, but as soon as he got out of the shower he heard the doorbell ring. Through the peephole he saw a caricature of Giulia, an enormous head and an inverted cone for a body, even more irritable and mad at the world than she looked a moment later, in the flesh, once he'd opened the door.

She said she'd come up to speak with him alone and Viberti didn't dare ask for even two minutes to get dressed; instead, he invited her into his spartan kitchen and sat down with her, his hair wet, in his bathrobe. She'd found someone to stay the night with Marta, she was Peruvian, a cousin of Angélica's, or a friend, or niece, or goddaughter, "with these people you never know where the family begins and where it ends." The same observation could be made about *their* family, but Viberti had no intention of pointing that out to her. Angélica's cousin, Maria, could start right away, but they had to hire her at once, maybe give her an advance, not pass up the opportunity, start out with daytime assistance.

Marta was against it, she'd said it a thousand times, she didn't want strangers in the house at night, she wouldn't be able to sleep peacefully. One night in January, however, around three a.m., she had shown up at Giulia's door wearing a coat with a fur collar and a woolen hat pulled down on her head, with a crocodile handbag dug out of the bottom of her closet: "I don't know why Angélica hasn't arrived yet, can you let her know that I had to go out on an errand?" Her clock had stopped at 9:20 the night before and not only hadn't she noticed that the hands had not moved from that position, but she wasn't even surprised to see that it was still pitch-dark outside. She thought it was nine in the morning. Which was more troubling: the fact that she didn't remember being afraid to leave the house, or that she wanted to go visit her sister in the hospital, the sister who'd died ten years ago? The following evening Marta had laughed about it with Viberti. "Just think, last night I was sure your aunt Bruna was still alive. How silly."

Viberti admitted that things were getting worse, even if the symptoms were contradictory. There had been no more serious incidents, but Giulia tended to view any sign of deterioration as irreversible. Viberti argued that with Angélica doing the house-work and cooking, Marta was self-sufficient. For most of the day she didn't seem at all forgetful and she hadn't scored any lower in the Mini mental test. One morning, however, Giulia had found her cooking with three burners turned on and two pots full of vege-tables boiling on the stove. "I had nothing ready for Claudio," she said. Giulia seemed even more angry when maternal feelings and instincts floated up through her mother-in-law's senile dementia.

"Unfortunately, every now and then women find themselves having to deal with senile mothers and menopause at the same time," Antonio had said to Viberti.

"But Giulia is forty years old and Marta isn't her mother."

"Premature menopause."

Recently Giulia had gotten into the habit of sitting at the table with her chair turned at a ninety-degree angle. She couldn't man-age to put her legs under the table, as if her legs suffered from claustrophobia. Viberti, wisely sitting across from her, saw her in profile and she almost always faced the French doors as she spoke, turning every so often to meet his eyes.

"Fine, let's sign her up, let's hire her," Viberti said.

"Fine, my ass," Giulia said, "don't think you can get out of it just like that. You have to be the one to tell her."

"All right, I'll tell her."

"And if she says no?"

"I'll persuade her."

Giulia stared at him. She raised her voice: "Don't think it'll be easy. Don't start out with the idea that it'll be easy, because if you can't persuade her I can't guarantee anything. It's not as if you can find good people who are willing and able on every street corner."

"You're right," Viberti said, "if I can't persuade her I solemnly swear to find someone else within two weeks."

"Like hell you will," Giulia said, shaking her head.

It had been a long day, and it wasn't over yet. Viberti said he absolutely had to dry his hair, he'd be back in a sec. That day he'd received an e-mail from Silvia Re. He hadn't responded yet, he'd printed out the message and put it in his coat pocket to remind himself to reply in his own good time that evening or the next day. Every so often he found it in his hand again, didn't remember what it was, and reread it. He'd reread it a few times during the day and read it again when he found it near the sink, then he left it on the stool nearby.

Not turning off the handdryer, he looked in the mirror and said aloud: "I'll speak to her tonight. She'll say yes. You'll see."

He returned to the kitchen, found Giulia in the same position.

"I'll speak to her tonight. She'll say yes. You'll see."

He stretched, extending his arms, and rubbed his eyes. When he reopened them, Giulia was looking at him. He drew the flaps of his bathrobe closed, trying not to make it too obvious, hiding the little patch of bare chest he had unintentionally shown.

"You were always modest."

"There's not much to see."

Yet for a while after the separation, three or four times a year, even after she'd remarried, Giulia would climb the two flights of stairs and go back to him. They, too, had had their relapses.

After a brief hesitation Giulia nodded: "She'll say yes to you. She never says no to you."

Then she stood and told him not to come down in his bathrobe, that in fact he wasn't much to look at.

Dinner nearly turned into a disaster. Viberti spoke with Marta in Giulia's study; he told her that Angélica had a cousin who was looking for work and that they'd promised to help her. Marta, with a surprising lucidity, replied that she'd expected as much, she knew they would keep trying to bring someone into the house, and she didn't think badly of them, for heaven's sake, "I know you want to do it for my own good," but she didn't need anyone. Viberti suggested a trial period, but Marta took him by the hand and led him out of the study. "Dinner is ready, you must be famished, and in any case you won't be able to persuade me." In fact, Viberti was starving.

At the table Giulia launched into a tirade against the obsession with diets. Marta said that at one time people were thinner because there wasn't so much stuff to eat. Everyone smiled. Viberti said: "Do you remember how skinny I was as a kid, Mama?"

Marta said that Viberti had always been rather plump. In fact, she'd been afraid he had inherited his diabetic great-uncle's body.

Viberti began fidgeting in his chair. "Plump? No, Mama, you're confused. I was thin as a rail."

"Come on! We called you Fatty—"

"*Fatty?*"

The others burst out laughing, but Viberti wasn't taking it well. Giulia signaled to him to let it go, for once she was the one ready to forgive Marta's confusion, and Marta pressed her advantage.

"I always thought your getting fat like that was a reaction to your father's death. Luckily, Stefano Mercuri came along and took you out to play a little tennis."

Viberti shook his head. Giulia's husband passed him the pasta bowl: "Some more tagliatelle, Fatty?" They all laughed.

After dinner he had an idea. Maybe Marta had already forgotten his previous attempt, maybe he could try again as if he were asking her for the first time. He joined her in the living room, where she sat playing cards with Giulia's child, and repeated the same speech. In fact, his mother didn't seem to remember that, an hour ago, her son had already asked her to take a Peruvian caregiver into the house overnight, though she demonstrated exemplary consistency: her response was the same.

Times past and forgotten flowed out of Marta's mind like the genie from the lamp and settled around Viberti, who, not knowing what else to say, glanced toward the dark corridor and saw Giulia's shadow go by. Eavesdropping?

Maybe Marta had *pretended* not to remember. It occurred to him that her senile dementia was making everyone demented. He'd repeated his speech as if he didn't remember having already said it, his mother had replied not remembering that she'd already replied, or had remembered it and was pretending to reply for the first time, *like* the first time. Dementia was spreading through people and things, dictating a new order.

He leaned forward, took his mother's bony hand into his own, the skin thin and spotted, unconsciously he felt her pulse, bradycardic.

"I know you don't need anyone. It's for our peace of mind, you see? We'd like to stay with you, but we can't. Do it for us, take this person. I'm asking you as a favor."

Marta seemed distraught. She stared at Viberti and her beautiful blue eyes glistened with tears. Suddenly she said, "All right, I agree."

"You agree?"

"If it's to do you a favor, yes. You could have told me sooner that I had to do it for all of you. Because I really don't need her. I'm just losing my memory."

Viberti enfolded her in a hug—she was small and slight, easy to enfold—and gave her a kiss. Then he asked: "But is it true you called me Fatty?"

Two days later he came home in the afternoon with a gardenia he'd bought from the kids at the rehab who had a stand outside the hospital; he set it among the other pots on the balcony and sat down in the wicker chair to gaze out at the courtyards. His eyes followed the walls separating the yards, their edges, the shards of glass, the climbing vine, the window of the gym, and the roof of the storehouse. After a bright shiny day, a dull patina had settled over things, the morning's promises betrayed or forgotten, as if the colors of the world had always been spent, or slowly fading. He could have remained in that chair for hours, he would have if he hadn't needed to go to the bathroom. Afterward he washed his hands and, on the floor, under a stool, he spotted the slip of paper with Silvia Re's e-mail, damp and wrinkled like an old parchment. He had no intention of reading a novel in which a cook manipulated people, whatever the verb "manipulate" might mean in this case (Viberti suspected it meant "cooked"). Still, he wanted to thank her, because she was Cecilia's sister, because it was kind of her.

Before he could think twice about it, or at least before he could think more clearly about it—and imagine how the call might go—he dialed the cell phone number that Silvia had included in her e-mail and a moment later, unprepared and regretful, he was listening to an account of the extraordinarily bizarre circumstances in which the book, hidden in the recesses of her mother's attic, had turned up while Silvia was looking for a volume she needed for work, the very day after their meeting. "So it was fate." Claudio said again that she had been very kind to write to him, that the book sounded interesting though he was very busy with work just then and didn't have time to read, maybe as summer reading, who knows, he might use it to avoid overeating while on vacation.

"I always lose weight on vacation," she interrupted him, "how can you gain weight on vacation?"

He said he didn't know, maybe he ate more, maybe he ate things that were fattening.

"Like what?"

"I eat a lot of pasta."

"Yes, it's true, on vacation there's always someone who knows how to prepare a special sauce."

Viberti said that even without special sauces pasta was the fastest thing to cook.

"One time I ate pasta without sauce. Awful. What about desserts? It's desserts that are fattening."

"I don't eat many desserts."

"You don't eat desserts on vacation?"

"I don't know, I don't think so."

He began to feel the weight of that idiotic conversation; their first interaction had been fun, but he shouldn't take a chance by repeating it. A second time would turn Cecilia's eccentric sister into a loquacious babbler.

Silvia seemed to sense his impatience and said she wasn't using the book in any case, she would lend it to him or maybe give it to him, would he rather have Cecilia bring it to him at the hospital or did he want to stop by and pick it up? Come to think of it, there was no need for them to agree on a time, she could leave it in her mailbox, it was a paperback, small as a prayer book, the mailbox was big enough to hold it and it was always unlocked, so even if she wasn't home Viberti could pick it up at any time, or even if she *was* home and he was in a hurry and had left his car double-parked, he could dash in quickly and grab the book from the mailbox, any day that week or the next, she would put it in the mailbox the next morning, because she wasn't planning to go out that night.

"Yes," Viberti said, "let's do that."

Maybe it was impossible to reach some baseline of clarity with that woman, who was vague in a way that was opposite yet complementary to her sister. Cecilia was more reticent than vague. But, all in all, in the end the effect was the same.

"Which?" she asked, not letting it go.

"I'll come and pick it up in the next few days, where do you live?"

And so Viberti discovered that Silvia lived in an area north of the city center that wasn't more than half an hour on foot from his neighborhood, an area he was familiar with because Stefano Mercuri had lived there for forty years before finally moving to the coast. A half hour's walk when he was in his twenties. Viberti often met Mercuri at his house and from there they went to the tennis courts at a nearby club together. He would leave home in shorts and a T-shirt, his tennis shoes caked with red clay, the racket slung over his shoulder like a rifle.

"I know the area well, a family friend used to live there, it's not far from my house," he said.

They talked some more about the two adjoining neighborhoods. Silvia also had a friend who lived in Viberti's area; she, too, was amazed at the coincidence and said so two or three times, until Viberti was certain that there was really nothing extraordinary about it, it wasn't a sign, it meant nothing.

But the minute he hung up he genuinely dreaded the thought of the lonely night that lay ahead of him; he thought about the mild evening and the nice fresh air, he thought about the walk he used to take twenty years ago, proud to have people look at him, and also a bit worried that they might stop him and steal his racket or shoes (because in those years thefts of motorbikes and jackets and wallets were common). Now no one would notice a guy walking down the street in tennis clothes anymore, but at one time it had been different, in fact, his mother always used to say to him: "Are you going around dressed like that? Aren't you ashamed?" It didn't sound like a reproach, she was honestly surprised that her son wasn't ashamed to go around in shorts (her son was ashamed of the fact that tennis wasn't a sport of the Left since he'd decided to be a leftist like Mercuri, who on the other hand didn't think twice about playing tennis).

He had everything he needed for dinner; he didn't have to go out. He didn't feel like cooking, however, and sitting alone at the table, and spending the evening on the balcony watching the courtyards until it got dark and then trying to find some game on television. He put on his tennis shoes, a green Lacoste polo shirt, and a pair of blue shorts. They weren't as short as those he used to go out in when he was sixteen, no one wore those anymore. He took his keys, wallet, and phone and squeezed them uncomfortably into the less-than-roomy pockets. He went out hoping not to run into Giulia or his mother or one of her helpers on the stairs. The late-afternoon air was fresh and the temperature mild—things weren't covered with a gray patina after all but seemed mellow and inviting instead, edges softened and lines blurred, as if everything were clothed in velvet or terry cloth, or a special rubber that would cushion the day's falls.

Leaving the house with his shoes caked with red clay put him in a good mood. Not only that, he felt like laughing; he would have liked to laugh with Cecilia, dragging her along on that nostalgic stroll, happy together, down the crowded streets, then under the trees lining the boulevards, around the piazza with the equestrian statue, once streaked with bird droppings and now black and shiny, and then under more trees, dense with foliage and tapered clusters of white flowers, not yet weary of being so laden. March-April: they put out leaves; April-May: they put out more leaves; May-June, they put out too many leaves, or maybe the ones they put out got bigger, and you could tell they couldn't handle it anymore, they went from florid to obese in just a few days. Right now, though, the trees weren't yet corpulent, now, at the end of May, they were in full bloom, tall, sound and vigorous, some heavier, others more slender, and walking beneath their still young canopies, through clouds of downy pollen wafting in the air, Viberti reached Mercuri's old neighborhood.

He turned onto a street where there'd been an old movie theater, now demolished, where he'd seen many films with his friend: on Saturday and Sunday afternoons, on rainy days or after playing tennis, agreeing to take a chance, as one normally did then, without discussing what they were going to see, because they weren't actually going to see *that movie*, but whatever film happened to be playing in *that theater*. Viberti couldn't think about that theater without remembering a movie rated unsuitable for those fourteen and under, his first R-rated film (and he was fifteen at the time). Mercuri hadn't realized it was R-rated, he just took it for granted that they only showed films for everyone there, because that's how it had always been. And he thought it was a mystery, "I thought it was an Agatha Christie–type mystery," he later explained to Marta. "You seem upset, was there something upsetting?" his mother had asked him. Viberti replied that, yes, the part about reincarnation had scared him a little, but then he realized it was all a dream, and Mercuri had confirmed it. What had disturbed him (though he hadn't told Marta) was the reason the film had been rated R: some rather explicit sex scenes (or so they'd seemed to him). He'd never seen a man and a woman making love, though even in the film you didn't see their genitals, just two naked lovers embracing and moaning and panting like animals. Viberti was almost more embarrassed by Mercuri's embarrassment, which he could easily sense from the man's nervous fidgeting in the seat beside him. Emerging into the afternoon light, they hadn't mentioned those scenes. Mercuri shook his head and repeated, mortified: "What a terrible movie. I thought it was a mystery because it's called *The Mystery of* . . ."

In the movie there was a young man who kept dreaming about being someone else and being killed, struck with an oar by a woman in the middle of a lake. The woman was on a boat, dressed, while the man in the dream had dived naked into the dark, oily waters of the lake and was laughing, maybe inviting the woman to join him in the water, a challenging laugh rather than a cheerful one, the woman's face cold and indecipherable, or perhaps upset and furious (actually Viberti didn't remember the woman's face, he only remembered the man's laughter). The young man convinced himself that the dream had really happened; he began searching for the house on the lake that he'd seen in his dream and he found it. The same woman in the dream, forty years older, lived in the house with her daughter. The young man fell in love with the daughter and slept with her, and the mother, realizing that the husband she'd killed forty years ago had been reincarnated as that stranger, killed him too. *Quite* a story, Cecilia would have said.

All he had to do was turn the corner to find himself in front of Mercuri's old house, incredible that his name no longer appeared on the intercom. And after two more blocks all he had to do was turn left again to find the apartment where Silvia lived. SILVIA K. RE read the name on the intercom. Well, whatever it meant, that K. seemed to go along with the headband that made her appear more imposing.

Now that Viberti had arrived he had no desire to go in. The book might not be in the mailbox yet; was Silvia home or had she gone out? The truth was he hadn't been listening to her. He pictured her out to dinner with Cecilia. He imagined them having a spirited discussion, the kind they would have had the day he'd surprised them together, judging by Cecilia's mood afterward. So pressing the intercom button wasn't too much of a commitment, Silvia probably wasn't home.

Instead she answered immediately, asked him what he was doing there, told him to come up, buzzed open the door. Viberti thought of an excuse to justify his sudden appearance; after saying he had no time to read he certainly couldn't pretend he was eager to get the book. The interior of the house was similar to the one in which Mercuri had lived, late nineteenth-century buildings, solid old houses for artisans and clerks and, later on, railway personnel; the station wasn't far away. The old houses were still solid, though somewhat grimy and a bit moldy, with a dank smell and the reek of vinegary wine rising up from the cellars, the walls saturated with the odors of life spent cooking or washing or smoking a cigarette on the landing. Would-be "vintage homes," awaiting gentrification. Pointless to make up excuses, he would say he was curious to see the neighborhood again.

The elevator went only as far as the fourth floor; for the fifth there were the stairs. Attics converted into studios or two-room apartments. A door painted bright red, like a fire exit, opened the moment he set foot on the landing. Silvia was wearing a very loose black tank over another top, a gray T-shirt, and a pair of black jeans with white stitching that seemed brand new. She didn't have the black headband on, and her hair stuck out wildly in all directions. She was bent forward a bit, massaging her thighs. She said she wanted to stretch the jeans out, they were too stiff and tight. She rarely found clothes that fit her well the first time, she didn't wear a standard size, either she was abnormal or everyone else was.

Viberti stood there smiling idiotically. He'd taken a good look at her when they first met and thought she wasn't as attractive as Cecilia, and maybe that was true, she wasn't as attractive as Cecilia, but she looked a lot like her. Not only her facial features, but the way she carried herself and the way she moved her hands and her head; he hadn't noticed it the first time or he hadn't wanted to see it, and now the resemblance troubled him.

Silvia lived in a two-room efficiency: the room they were in had a kitchenette, a sofa and TV, an office area with a desk and computer, and an entryway, but all the areas looked alike because every piece of furniture and every inch of wall space was covered in rows of books.

"Have you read them all?" were Viberti's first words.

"Were you playing tennis?" Silvia asked, ignoring the question.

"Cecilia told me you work for a publishing house," he said without answering.

"For three publishing houses." She waved at the stacks of paper on the desk, as if to say: *Go on, get lost.*

"You correct the mistakes."

"Basically, yes," she said, and handed him the chef's book.

Viberti took it and thanked her. He leafed through it seeing nothing but yellowed pages, not even one illustration.

Silvia said she didn't know if it would really interest him— on the phone it had seemed like he couldn't care less and then suddenly there he was.

Viberti smiled absurdly, saying "No, no," and turned to a poster hanging behind the door; he asked where it was from. The writing was Chinese or Japanese, and the poster depicted several small pieces of fish: red, orange, white.

"It's a memorial plaque," Silvia said.

Viberti didn't understand, but he was used to not asking too many questions when patients said nonsensical things, so instead he said: "I've never eaten sushi in my life."

"You've never eaten sushi? I can't believe it!"

"I've never been to a Japanese restaurant."

"So you've never been to Japan."

"Should I have?"

"There are two good Japanese restaurants in the area, I'll send you the addresses."

Viberti was about to say that they could go there some evening with Cecilia, then it seemed like a dumb idea and he murmured, "I don't want to take up any more of your time."

Silvia said he wasn't disturbing her, she wasn't planning on doing any more work that evening. She didn't say anything else but meanwhile she moved slightly toward the door.

Viberti followed her. Then Silvia opened the door. So Viberti crossed the threshold and stepped out onto the landing.

He turned and thanked her again, holding up the book: "I'll let you know."

They said goodbye almost in a whisper, as if they were both embarrassed at not having shown a little more interest in each other. Viberti took the stairs to the ground floor without using the elevator again, wondering if he'd said something wrong, or if he'd done something wrong by not saying anything else.

But when he got outside he stopped thinking about Silvia and set out walking slowly, lost in thought, toward the neighborhood's busiest streets, where the market was held on weekday mornings and where restaurants and grocery stores were still open. He could buy something for dinner, even though he didn't need anything. He passed an old *latteria* and was surprised that the dairy shop still existed. Through the store windows he saw people inside hurrying to make last-minute purchases, waving the numbers that ensured their place in line. *Every so often along the street I see someone who strikes me and I think: In five minutes I'll have forgotten him. And then right afterward I feel a sort of panic, oh God, I think, now I'll never forget him. But with patients it's different: some cases you can't help remembering, they get under your skin like thorns, and they don't cause infection, and they won't come out, they stay there and then they become part of you.* Eating alone as he often did didn't kill his appetite. He would gladly have eaten the marinated cutlets and Easter pie and potato salad with swirls of mayonnaise and those prosciutto roulades in aspic and the meatballs in tomato and mint sauce that he'd just seen in a shop window. He strolled down the street, unable to make up his mind to turn around and head home.

Going home was impossible that night, too depressing. Maybe he'd be better off eating in a restaurant. But how could he, dressed the way he was. He was afraid he'd run into an old patient who, out of gratitude, might invite him to dinner. Or that seventy-two-year-old son, the only child, who'd accused him of negligence, and who sent him a letter every year, on the anniversary of his mother's death, announcing in an increasingly sprawling script that he would never forget.

He recalled clearly now the sense of security he'd felt as a boy when he would stroll around the neighborhood with Mercuri, dressed in tennis clothes, rackets on their shoulders. The peace of mind that Mercuri's regular presence had given him, and the peace of mind it had given Marta. She no longer felt alone, abandoned with a child to raise; in an emergency there would be that old friend, and the old friend had always been there, he'd never left them. He'd moved away only much later, after retiring at seventy-two. "Well, well, now, don't tell me you feel betrayed by Mercuri," Viberti chuckled, "don't tell me the old man shouldn't have gone to live on the coast."

There was a Marian shrine nearby where Mercuri had dragged him many times, on their way back from tennis, to show him the ex-votos that adorned the chapels. Mercuri wasn't a believer, but he loved the votive offerings, the stories behind them. He told him that in the summer, returning home from the hospital, he'd go into the cool darkness of the church to find a bit of relief and there he would play a little game: he'd imagine a different life, someone else's life, a dramatic event, an accident, a narrow escape, gratitude to the Madonna, and the idea for the small painting or statuette. Viberti had never felt at ease in the church, obviously because of the shorts. Or because of the danger that always lurked at the end of their tennis matches, the chance that Mercuri would insist on going up to their apartment and would find Marta lethargic.

I'd like to continue imagining my father's languid stroll as he slowly made his way home, submerged by the rising tide of memories. But it would mean imagining another man, with a tolerance for melancholy even greater than his. It's a strange thought, a strange desire. I don't think it's a self-destructive impulse, on my part. I think it's a desire for symmetry, for simplification, just as things start to get complicated, and the unexpected lies in wait. So I continue creating my ex-voto.

Thinking about Mercuri, Viberti finds himself in front of a place that unless he's greatly mistaken is a Japanese restaurant. What a coincidence, he thinks. He tries reading the menu posted outside, but it's a text for the initiated and he can't understand much. Why hadn't he invited Silvia to eat with him? There wouldn't have been anything wrong with that. "What's the harm?" he wonders aloud. He pictures telling Cecilia that he had dinner with her sister, he pictures her surprise and amusement.

He takes the phone from his pocket and calls Silvia. He asks her if one of the Japanese restaurants she mentioned to him is called Hasaki, because if that's its name, he's found it. But that's not its name, it would be too easy. Hasaki is a *fake* Japanese restaurant, the owners are actually Chinese. Not a *bad* restaurant, but not a *real* Japanese restaurant.

Viberti says: "I was rude, I didn't ask if you wanted to eat something, I'm sorry."

Silvia is silent, then she says, "Are you inviting me to dinner?"

"Yes, actually, I am," Viberti says.

Silvia says, "Well, then I'll be there in five minutes."

A moment later she calls him back: "Go in and ask for two seats at the counter."

A moment later she calls back again: "Can I come in jeans?"

What will he say all evening to this crazy woman? Viberti enters the restaurant almost hoping that it will be full, but while the dining room is full, there's no one at the counter. A Chinese host comes to meet him. Chinese, Japanese, Korean, who can tell. He shows him to a seat. Viberti takes out *The Cook*, but doesn't read a single line of it; instead, he watches the real chefs on the other side of the glass, who are cutting the fish with strokes at first slow and cautious, then suddenly swift and brutal, and he doesn't take his eyes off the spectacle until Silvia arrives.

She's put on a green skirt in the same creased cotton as the tank top and T-shirt. "I changed after all," she announces. She's also put the headband back in her hair.

This woman, Viberti thinks, this woman knows no shame.

She never shuts up. She wants to explain the menu to him. Viberti's discomfort is physical, as he struggles to get a word in every now and then to show that he's paying attention. Sitting at the counter is easier, however—he doesn't have to face his dinner companion and so can keep his eyes on the Chinese cooks, who, pretending to be Japanese, brandish their knives with dexterity, as if the course of the planets and the stars depended on their movements.

"You order for me, let me sample the main dishes," he says to stem the tide of words.

Silvia orders, and out of the blue, without warning, she's talking about Cecilia. She says they're very close, she doesn't know what she would have done, at certain times in her life, if it weren't for Cecilia. She isn't just a sister and she's not a friend in the traditional sense of the word. She didn't try to mother her, Silvia wouldn't have stood for that. She has some issues with the idea of maternity, in particular with the idea of maternal authority. Not with the idea of authority in general. The idea of maternity implies an authority exercised through affection, through the exploitation of affection, which is a paradox. Maybe she was exaggerating, certainly that's not always the case, and it doesn't apply to all mothers, of course. Was she exaggerating?

"I see what you mean," Viberti says, "yes, it seems a bit of an exaggeration. You were saying that Cecilia wasn't like that, though. How many years are there between you?"

Five, enough not to step on each other's toes. Cecilia serves as a counterweight, she balances her relationship with her mother. When Cecilia got married and left home, in fact, it was a problem for her. She stuck it out until she got her degree and then got out of there.

"At a certain point it's time to go," Viberti says. This is where his monologue would fit in, about the building he's lived in all his life, but that evening, with that woman, he doesn't feel like reciting it. He'd told Cecilia the first time they met at the café, so it's no wonder.

Silvia says that Cecilia is an excellent mother, considering the example they had. Considering the difficulty of the divorce, considering the problems with the boy.

As soon as she says the word "boy" she stops suddenly and looks at Viberti, who wasn't expecting such an abrupt break or that look; he reddens, thinking that Silvia has read something in his expression.

"Am I talking too much?" Silvia asks.

Viberti smiles. "No, of course not."

"No, I mean, you know these things, don't you? You know my sister well . . ."

He shakes his head and thinks he's shaking it correctly, with the naturalness and credibility of a consummate actor. "I can't say I know her well, but I know about the divorce and I met the child, when he was hospitalized. Cecilia tells me things every now and then, but most of the time we talk about work."

Silvia shakes her head in turn, she says that Cecilia actually doesn't tell her anything. It's not a matter of discretion, of privacy—it's genuine reticence. And this, for her, is her sister's only fault. Cecilia doesn't open up as much as she would like, she doesn't open up enough. But this fault may be what allows them to have a close relationship: she says too much about everything, Cecilia says nothing or almost nothing about everything.

She looks at him again: "What is Ceci like at work?"

"How do you mean?"

"Tense, nervous?"

"She's a very good doctor."

"Every so often I think it's too stressful for her."

Luckily the sushi arrives; Silvia appears to completely forget about her sister and begins explaining the names and characteristics of the fish, piece by piece, as if the poster hanging behind her door were there in front of her. Though Viberti doesn't ask how she knows all these things, she tells him about a boyfriend who made her fall in love with sushi and green tea. He went to Japan a lot on business; she's never been there, it's too expensive, but she dreams of being able to afford it one day—though really it's like she's been there, like she's visited it through her boyfriend's stories, since he talked about it constantly, describing in detail the streets, the buildings, the parks, the shops and restaurants, especially the restaurants, the endless business lunches in Tokyo, Osaka, and Hiroshima, in restaurants that she'd be able to find with her eyes closed, almost—and in any case she has the map of Tokyo, for instance, imprinted in her brain, and she associates the areas with the photos that her boyfriend sent her and that she still uses as screen savers even now, images of neighborhoods that have become so familiar that they appear to her in her dreams, not just as exotic backdrops but as three-dimensional spaces full of life, including people talking and the noises of the city—or rather almost excluding them, because her boyfriend told her an incredible fact, that absolute silence reigns in Japan's megalopolises, in the streets, on the subways, in the supermarkets, even the cars seem to make less noise, and the children don't cry.

"The children never cry?" Viberti asks smiling.

"Never."

They laugh. When she laughs, Silvia looks more like Cecilia. The two sisters are very much alike though there's no real physical resemblance; what unites them is what Silvia can still be and what Cecilia will never again be, as if the younger one were a more carefree version of the older sister: a person who can still be happy.

Silvia stops abruptly and looks at Viberti: "I don't believe it, I can't believe you've never eaten sushi," she says.

"It's true."

"I might know someone who's never eaten pizza, but sushi, no, it's not possible."

Viberti smiles. He loves the hot sake, it seems like one of those things, like cider, on which it's impossible to get drunk. "I swear."

"I don't believe it."

"Take your sister," Viberti says, "has she ever eaten sushi?"

"Of course, here, in this same restaurant. We came here a bunch of times, especially after the affair with the Japanese guy ended."

"He was Japanese? I didn't realize that."

"His mother was Japanese, but he had always lived in Italy. I called him the Japanese guy. At one point he went back there."

"And afterward, did you still feel like eating this stuff?"

"By then his memories were mine, and I didn't want to give them back, it wasn't right, and besides, raw fish is one of the few things that I can always digest, even at times of intense anxiety. For example, I would have starved to death when my father died, but Cecilia came here and bought sushi and brought it home to me."

Viberti looks at her: "When did your father die?"

"Four years ago."

"Of what?"

"A tumor."

"A tumor?"

"Yes, why?"

Viberti takes a gulp of sake.

"It's odd. We talked about my father, Cecilia and I. He died of a lymphogranuloma, many years ago. I don't know. If she had mentioned her father's illness, it would have been natural for me to tell her about my own father's, I guess."

"I told you, she doesn't open up about *anything*, it's awful."

Well, maybe she's reticent by nature, but maybe especially so with him. As if he were a stranger. But he doesn't want Silvia to notice how his mood has changed.

"Were you very close to your father?" he asks, hoping to set off another monologue that will give him time to recover.

But Silvia just nods.

Viberti continues drinking hot sake, maybe that way he'll manage to get a little drunk, at least. He feels a long surge of melancholy about to wash over him. All evening he'd tried to avoid it, coming up with that unlikely dinner with Cecilia's long-winded sister, but sadness has caught up with him, it's suddenly in front of him, around him, inside him. He sees the world as it truly is, and it's the disorder of Silvia's impossibly small house, the sheer volume of paper per square foot; it's the deep, dark, cold lake in the film about reincarnation. He's never liked lakes.

Poor Silvia starts talking again, telling him about a friend who lives in Barcelona. Behind that merciless conversational capacity, Viberti thinks, lies a heart more human than her sister's unfathomable one.

At some point it's clear to both of them that Viberti isn't going to open his mouth again for the rest of the evening. Silvia says they'd better go, wait for her a moment, she'll make a quick trip to the ladies' room and be right back. The restaurant is still full, the Chinese cooks are cutting up the fish with the same flourish, but they seem less fascinating now that he's been watching them for an hour. Viberti pays and goes out to the sidewalk. The evening air is not enough to restore him. He realizes that he's had too much to drink, after all. He looks at his tennis shoes, his hairy calves, and smiles wistfully, not for the boy he was at fifteen, but for the ingenuous, enthusiastic man of a few hours ago. He has two options, to laugh or to cry. Start crying and confess to Silvia that he's hopelessly (*hopelessly*) in love with Cecilia, tell her the whole story, disclose everything. And finally shut her up! Well, that would do it. He'd leave her speechless. He smiles. He chuckles to himself.

"So you're not sad," Silvia says, joining him outside. "I thought talking about my father had upset you, I'm sorry, I'm an idiot, I always notice things too late."

Viberti shakes his head. "I drank too much," he says, as he goes on chuckling.

Silvia smiles. "Are you drunk?" As if it were good news. "Then I'll tell you something: when it's time to pay the check I always get the urge to pee. By now it's a Pavlovian reflex, you know? Because for years I used it as a trick not to pay, because I never had any money."

"Now you do?"

"Have money? No, of course not."

"So you didn't want to pay. You went to the bathroom to avoid paying."

They laugh uproariously. A Chinese man comes out of the place to see what's going on.

And they go on like that, Viberti pretending or exaggerating his drunkenness to make Silvia laugh, Silvia pretending to believe that he's drunk or drunker than he really is, while worrying about how he is and how he'll make it home safe and sound. And so, when they get to her house it seems like the most natural thing in the world to both of them for Silvia to invite him to come up.

The excuse is to drink a cup of tea with cherry blossoms, *sakura*, to revive Viberti a little, but when they enter the small apartment Silvia says she wants to go through the whole tea ceremony with him. She boils water in the kitchenette and sets out a flower-shaped tray with a teapot and two hand-painted cups. Picking one up, Viberti recognizes Papa Smurf in his village of cheerful mushroom cottages and starts laughing again. "Now I'll explain how it's done," says Silvia, taking the cup out of his hand. She spreads two rectangular straw mats between the sofa area and the work area, makes Viberti kneel down. "We'll skip the preparation stage," she says, "maybe another time I'll tell you about that, too. Not that it isn't interesting, but it's rather long."

"Sure, let's smurf it up," Viberti says.

"Hey, don't joke around. This is serious."

"Okay, okay."

Silvia kneels down at Viberti's left, pours the tea into the cups. "Let's pretend we are both guests and the person offering us tea is sitting here with us." She turns to Viberti, bows slightly, and says, "*Oshōban itashimasu.*"

Viberti giggles. "I don't know what to say," he whispers.

Silvia smiles slightly. "You don't have to say anything. It's the opening phrase. I said, Please, allow me to share tea with you."

"All right. I allow you. Let's move on to the second stage."

"Don't be in such a hurry."

Silvia bows to the nonexistent host and says: "*Otemae chōdai itashimasu.*" Then she whispers to Viberti: "I told him that it pleases me to drink his tea."

"Well," he says, "tell him I said so, too."

"Pick up the cup, the *chawan*, with your right hand and place it on your left palm. Hold it firmly by placing your right thumb on the rim of the cup. Make a slight bow."

Viberti does what she says, even though his hand is shaky.

"Now take hold of the rim of the cup with your index finger and the thumb of your right hand and turn the cup ninety degrees clockwise. Take a sip and make a comment about the tea."

"Mmm. It tastes like cherry."

"No, the comment has to be more positive."

"Oh. Well then, excellent."

"Between sips rest the fingertips of your right hand on the mat in front of you. At the last sip you must make a slurping sound against your palate."

"I've never been good at making slurping sounds."

"Try it."

He emits a kind of cluck, then starts giggling again.

"Now wipe the rim of the cup with your right thumb and index finger. Turn the cup counterclockwise on your palm to return it to its original position. Set the cup down outside the edge of your mat and admire it. You can make comments."

"About the cup?"

"It's not mandatory."

"But can't I talk about something else?"

"No, not really. What did you want to say?"

"That I like being here with you."

Silvia smiles, leans over, and kisses him. A moment later they're lying down, embracing. Viberti is excited, even though he can't stop thinking about Cecilia. Going to bed with her sister is not the best strategy to win her, but at that point it's impossible to stop, as if he were no longer himself, as if he were the reincarnation of the Japanese boyfriend.

Later, back home, he tried to understand why he had done it. It was all very complicated. Made worse by a raging headache. He did it because he felt like it, because he was confused and frustrated; even though he'd enjoyed it, it didn't mean anything, he was in love with Cecilia. He would tell Silvia that he couldn't keep doing it, he would ask her to please not say anything to her sister.

Over the next four days, however, he perfected the tea ceremony with her two more times. They set a fourth date, but Viberti didn't show up. He sent a text to say he wasn't feeling well. Silvia asked him if he needed anything, then said she hoped he'd feel better soon. It wasn't like him to lie like that and in fact he hadn't thought it was possible to do so with such ease. It was necessary, however, because if he continued to see her, the mess he'd gotten himself into would be impossible to clean up. Maybe it already was, maybe Silvia had already told her sister everything. He felt a great tenderness and yearning for Cecilia and finally understood the state of mind in which she found herself after being with him. He would have liked to call Silvia now and tell her: "It's not possible, I can't keep doing this anymore." But in the days that followed he did not call, and it became progressively more difficult to break the silence.

He didn't see either sister for ten days, until Antonio phoned him late one Monday morning to tell him that Cecilia Re's son had been admitted to the hospital after he'd fainted at school. It didn't seem to be anything serious, and his father was with him. Viberti climbed the stairs with his heart in his mouth.

The boy had grown, he looked fine, he was much better, he wouldn't have recognized him. Or maybe he would, maybe he would have recognized him, even though he was much more confident, bolder and more cheerful. His bond with his father, at whom the child glanced repeatedly as though seeking confirmation and permission, made Viberti jealous. This ex-husband of Cecilia seemed like an easygoing person, decent, pleasant. He was afraid of running into Cecilia. Besides, his visit was over. He had nothing to say to the boy, he felt like a stranger. He said goodbye to him, shaking his hand, and told him to have a good time on vacation.

In the afternoon he called Silvia. He apologized, he shouldn't have disappeared like that, but he was confused, he didn't know what to do and maybe it would be best if they didn't see each other anymore. "I wouldn't want you to think I'm a shit," he said.

Silvia said she absolutely didn't think that, and she agreed, it made no sense to go on seeing each other. She thanked him for calling her.

Sitting in an armchair in Marta's living room, Viberti is leafing through a monthly travel magazine that Giulia buys regularly, even though she never goes farther than Bocca di Magra, and then passes on to her mother-in-law, who almost never leaves the house anymore. The usual beaches and monuments and sunsets, but between the lines the fear that people will give up vacations once and for all. An excess of enthusiasm, unsolicited reassurances, petrified smiles. *At one point I started to keep a notebook in which I recorded all my vacations, weekends and short trips, New Year's and*

birthday celebrations, whom I'd spent them with, where I had gone,
but then I got tired of it, and if I forget them, so be it. I started because
one day someone asked me where I had spent New Year's 1986 or 1987.
I couldn't answer and I felt disoriented.

Windows open, the beginning of June, it already feels like
summer. Marta has fallen asleep in the armchair next to Viberti,
her head lolling, her mouth partly open. The TV is on, there's the
news, but as soon as he saw his mother dozing off, Viberti turned
off the sound. They'd eaten together, Giulia had dropped by to say
hello, and now Angélica is tidying up in the kitchen.

It could be a peaceful evening, he could wait another ten minutes and then get up and wake his mother with a kiss on the forehead, and offer to take her to bed (it's not good for her to sleep in
a chair). Or he could ask her if she feels like venturing out for a
stroll around the block, the weather is so mild. He could also leave
the living room quietly and ask Angélica to wake his mother in
ten minutes, run off without saying goodbye since his mother
wouldn't notice his absence in any case. He could go up to his
apartment and listen to some music, straighten up the house and
his head, think calmly about the situation he's created with Cecilia, make some decisions before submitting, as usual, to those of
others. He could, but the phone in his pocket starts ringing.

Cecilia's name flashes on the display. Viberti answers, speaking softly even though his mother can't hear him.

Cecilia's voice is pained, though she's not crying, she's not
frantic. She says she heard about Viberti's meeting with the child,
they're back home now, she asks him how he thought he was.
Viberti replies that he thought he was doing just fine, that Mattia
absolutely remembered him, even if he thought he was a cook. "I
don't know if he was teasing me, but I don't think so, I think he
really thought I was one of the cooks on the ward, because two
years ago I always showed up at lunchtime." Cecilia pretends to be
amused and pleased, she talks to him with the familiarity, affec-

tion, and intimacy with which you talk to an old friend, a person you rely on and from whom you expect support. And Viberti feels a chasm open up in his chest, in place of his heart there's a black hole that is collapsing, swallowing up the universe around him, because he realizes that Cecilia knows everything.

"This time it turned out well, but I don't know how much more I can take, I'm falling apart physically, yesterday I couldn't stand up, my legs were shaky."

"My legs were shaky today, too."

"I don't know what to do and I feel like there's no one I can ask for help."

"I'm here, I'll help you."

"No, you're not there either."

"Why would you say I'm not here? You can call me anytime—where are you now? Do you want to meet me?"

"You're not there."

"Cecilia, I want to help you, all I want to do is be there for you."

"That's not true. It's not true."

"It *is* true. Where are you? Listen, tell me where you are. I want to come to you."

"Why are you seeing Silvia? What's going on with Silvia?"

Now, maybe, she's crying. Hard to know. Viberti remains silent. He's been caught unprepared, but he knew it. He has no idea what to say. The chasm in the center of his chest has closed up, something is squeezing the pit of his stomach, a rigid, bony hand like that of his mother, who is asleep in front of him.

"Why are you seeing her?"

Viberti doesn't answer.

"Claudio?"

"I'm here," he says finally.

"Why are you seeing her?"

"I don't know, I really don't know. I can't explain it to you."

They're both silent.

"Have you been with her? You've barely met . . . Have you been with her?"

Viberti doesn't answer. Cecilia's voice is uncertain, she stumbles over the words; despite the inquisitorial tone or maybe because of it, she goes from anger to entreaty in the space of a question.

"I saw her one night. We went out to dinner."

"Are you in love with her?"

As if she'd slapped him. His head snaps back. He gets up, paces up and down the room with the phone pressed against his ear. He's faced with the facts, with his own life reflected back at him, and yes, it's really him.

"God, Cecilia, what kind of question is that?"

"I'm asking you a simple question, I need a simple answer."

"No, I'm not in love with her."

"Are you sleeping with her? Do you spend the night with her? How many ways do I have to ask the question?"

"You shouldn't ask!" Viberti intensifies his words while continuing to speak softly; what comes out is a hoarse whisper that is more likely to wake his mother than if he were speaking normally. He's heard them often, the people who whisper on the phone, the ones who threaten. At the hospital, for example, turn the corner of a corridor and there's a woman saying: "Are you sleeping with her? Do you spend the night with her? How many ways do I have to ask the question?"—she looks at you but she's not talking to you, she's talking to her cell phone. Now he's the one on the other end, now it's his turn.

"Wasn't there something between us?" Cecilia asks.

Viberti looks at his mother. Her head is still lolling, but maybe on the other side.

"Was there something between us?" Cecilia repeats.

"Is that a question or a statement?"

"It's a question."

"Yes, of course, there was something between us. What are you getting at?"

"I'm not getting at anything. I just asked if there was something between us."

"Yes, there was something between us. But you've always been very clear about it."

"Do I seem to you like a person who is very clear?"

"Very clear, very firm. I thought you knew what you wanted."

"Don't change the subject. Tell me how it happened, how did you end up with Silvia. She's my sister."

"Cecilia, you can't make a scene and act jealous, you can't, you have no right!" Now he's really raising his voice, he leaves the room and runs into Angélica in the corridor, who, alarmed, has come to see what's going on. Viberti slips into the kitchen and steps out on the balcony. Before him, the courtyards: this is his earliest view, that of his childhood, of his adolescence. This is the balcony where he got locked out that evening, where he's still locked out today.

"No, I have no right. But you were in love with me, weren't you? You always told me you were in love. Or maybe you didn't tell me, maybe you led me to think you were, and so maybe I misunderstood you."

Viberti is at a loss, backed into a corner.

He murmurs: "No, you didn't misunderstand me. I am in love with you. I've been in love with you since the first day I saw you."

Cecilia is crying on the other end of the line, there's no doubt about it now, she's crying.

"You're in love with me, but you're fucking Silvia. Was that what it was? Did you need to get laid?"

"Please, Cecilia, don't be like that."

"You're right. I have no right to. I'm not allowed. I'll hang up now, you probably have to go out. Goodbye."

"Cecilia, wait . . . Cecilia? Cecilia?"

He tries to call her back. Her phone is turned off.

For a moment, holding the phone away from his ear, checking the display to see if he's locked the keyboard, his strength fails him. His legs give way, the phone slips out of his hand, bounces off the balcony, and shoots off one of the concrete pillars; it's pretty much dead by the time it lands in the courtyard.

Marta is leafing through the travel magazine. When Viberti apologizes for having raised his voice, she looks at him blankly.

As she does more and more often lately, she starts talking by continuing a conversation that she was perhaps having in her head. She says she should have traveled more, that she hasn't seen anything of the world, that she let her husband travel around without going with him; occasionally she had the opportunity—he insisted that she leave the child with her sister, but she didn't feel right about it, or maybe she didn't want to go, silly fears, being afraid to fly, or being afraid she wouldn't find anything to eat.

"Anything to eat?"

"Yes, in Hong Kong, for example, nothing that I'd like . . . or in Brazil. What do people eat in Brazil?"

Viberti runs a hand through his hair; he's plunged back into the absurd, or maybe he never left it. "I don't know, Mama, I've never been there either."

"But you should travel, listen, if I may give you a word of advice, you should travel while you're young. Don't wait until you retire. I should have traveled more with your father, you know, he always insisted that I go with him, but I didn't feel like it, maybe I was afraid I wouldn't find anything to eat."

"All right, Mama, I'll travel. Where do you think I should go?"

"One place is as good as any. The important thing is to go."

Viberti nods. He clings to the arms of the chair, he needs a mooring so he won't be swept away, a harness so he won't nosedive, he needs to be securely tied down. Tied? No, no, no ties, maybe a punch in the face that will leave him stunned or unconscious on the ground, or maybe a drink would do it, stop or at least slow his racing thoughts, a glass of wine, some port, some rum, but here there isn't anything, he has to get back home as soon as possible. He has to interrupt Marta, say good night to her.

"You should travel more, like your father did. Traveling is very instructive. But I can't blame you—in fact it's the opposite, I think I'm the one who passed my fears on to you."

"Don't be silly, Mama, I'm not afraid of traveling, besides, it's not like I never go anywhere."

"I never liked it, partly because I was afraid of flying and partly because I thought I couldn't leave a young child."

"Okay, I'll try to travel more."

"Well, you should, you haven't set foot out of this house. You're a homebody, that's what you are."

"What do you mean?"

"You've always lived in this building, haven't you?"

"Yes, Mama, I've always lived here. Always," and he starts to get up.

"Because in the end who's really lived?" his mother says, setting the magazine down beside her on the sofa.

Viberti looks at her blankly, sits back down on the edge of the chair.

"Yes, in the end who's really lived? Think about my grandparents, or even my parents, did they live any less because they didn't see certain places, because they didn't have certain experiences? I've always wondered, because as a young girl, you know, I was fascinated by hermits"—she gives an amused little laugh—"never going anywhere, seeing the same things each day, the same scenery, going without television," which is turned off, Viberti notices only now; did she turn it off? Did she think the voice that was out of control was coming from the TV? Or was she aware of everything? Had she really been asleep? "By now we're used to seeing everything like that."

He'd like to ask her "What do you mean 'like that'? How are

we used to seeing things?" Instead he smiles and says: "I can't picture you as a hermit. In the old photos you seemed like a girl who was full of energy, who wanted to have a good time."

"Well, let's not exaggerate: having a good time is a tall order. If I'd wanted that, I wouldn't have married your father!"

They laugh. Marta is worried about the confession that came to her so impulsively. "Did I say something bad?" she asks, blushing.

She had been a beautiful girl, but maybe she didn't know it. Or at least Viberti has always thought his mother belonged to that class of women: unaware of and indifferent to her beauty. A woman who doesn't know how to use her beauty, who has no interest in taking advantage of it. When he was little, and his father was away from home for weeks on end, they would sometimes go out to a restaurant. When they entered the room, the child noticed the men's glances as they turned around to admire his mother, a young woman, beautiful and vital, and he thought they were all friends of his father, inhabitants of his father's world, a world he and his mother were excluded from, messengers who had to deliver letters, bring news.

"Did I ever tell you about the trip to Trieste? For the Giochi Littoriali, the swimming competitions. I had such fun! But I didn't like to travel, not even then. I remember there was a border with guards, and I was scared. And later a girl I met there wrote to me and drew a big gun in her letter, because each time the starting gun went off, it scared me! How silly . . ."

"You've had a wonderful life. Do you feel like you haven't really lived?"

"Me? I've lived maybe too long! Remember Chekhov's *The Cherry Orchard*? When you were in high school we had a theater subscription, once a month . . . you were so bored!"

Yes, Viberti remembers Chekhov, he'd been struck by the fact that he was a doctor, like Mercuri. But what does Chekhov have to do with anything now? Why the hell did he pop into her head?

For a moment he'd been distracted and had stopped thinking about Cecilia and Silvia and now he has no desire to think about cherries, about *sakura*, about Japanese cuisine.

"There was that character, a nostalgic old man who was always whining, remember?"

"No, Mama, I don't remember him."

"Because he hadn't lived enough, you know? He complained that he hadn't lived enough. And I always thought he was such an idiot!"

He doesn't remember, he doesn't care. He stands up and says, "Mama, are we sure you have a memory problem? It seems to me you remember everything clearly."

Marta reaches out her arm, as if to introduce herself, extends her open hand. Viberti shakes it. He will continue shaking hands with her as long as she lives, she clinging to him, and he clinging to her, in her few remaining years, until the day comes when, seeing a close-up of the Pope on television, she'll ask softly: "Why is he looking at me?" until the day she scratches out people's eyes in the old family photos, until she becomes convinced that her caregivers want to kill her, until she hurls insults at him, calling him a "little toad" because she doesn't want him to give her an injection, until she no longer gets out of bed and she widens her blue eyes without speaking, and stares into his.

Some months ago Viberti had dreamed about Mercuri uttering the word "hypocomist." No one answered him, nothing else happened. There was that word on Mercuri's lips, and in the dream Viberti thought it was a synonym for "anesthetist" and was put out and amazed that he hadn't learned it or even encountered it in his twenty-five years of medicine, from university to hospital. A brief dream, just before waking up, no anxiety or distress. It consisted almost entirely of amazement, of the resentful feeling of never being able to measure up to his role, of never being able to measure up to Mercuri (the idea that the doctors of the past were less specialized, but more capable). For a while, after opening his eyes, he continued to be certain that the word had a meaning and that it was precisely the one in the dream, then he woke up completely and admitted to himself that it didn't mean anything. It was the first time he'd dreamed about a word.

"Hypocomist" bore no resemblance whatsoever to "anesthetist"; instead it made him think of someone who was hypo-communist, "not communist enough." Or someone who ate too little (*"Vamos a comer,"* Angélica said to Marta). It could mean that Mercuri was asking him about an anesthetist, so as not to suffer too much when his time came, or it could mean that Mercuri was criticizing himself by saying, "I wasn't communist enough." Both made sense but it didn't make sense for Mercuri to be accusing him of not eating enough.

He thought about it again when he went to visit Mercuri at the coast, on the third weekend in June. He hadn't seen him in two months, and each time before he arrived he wondered: Will I find him changed? One day I'll suddenly find him older, and resigned to old age, acquiescent and pliable. Mercuri immediately went to take his bag from him and Viberti said, "I'll carry it. You always want to prove you're in better shape than I am."

"Around here, the day you're no longer in perfect shape they take you up the hill and leave you there to wait," Mercuri said, smiling.

The cemetery clung to the sides of the mountain, and each time Viberti visited, the old man found a way to make that joke, alluding to a family that convinces a dying relative to start up the hill on his own two feet, "Come on, the air is better up there," both out of laziness—so they won't have to carry a heavy coffin on their shoulders—and to save themselves the expense of a funeral; and *that*, the tightfistedness of the Ligurians, was certainly the main point of Mercuri's irony. The repetition was a message from the older man to the younger one ("I have death on my mind"), but also a sign of senility, one of the few that Mercuri let slip.

"If you ask me, you'll make a diagnosis and go there on your own, when you decide it's time."

By now Mercuri no longer bothered to explain his wife's absence during Viberti's visits; the house was, in any case, ready to welcome twelve guests. Eating under the trellised pergola they spoke almost exclusively of recent developments regarding Marta's dementia. Compared with last year, Mercuri's concern revealed no emotion, it was one doctor getting another's advice. Viberti responded point by point, reporting even the smallest detail.

Bringing the coffee to the table, Mercuri said, "Stop looking at the sea like that."

Viberti smiled. "How was I looking at it?"

"Ah well, I wish I were still your age."

"I don't believe it."

"When it comes to women, I would. That's the only thing."

"Was I thinking about a woman?"

"Two, at least."

He was irritated that the old man had guessed the truth with a simple remark. In the last ten days Viberti hadn't seen or heard from either Cecilia or Silvia. Cecilia didn't answer the phone, she no longer showed up at their usual café. He didn't have the courage to go and look for her in the ER. Maybe he'd come to see Mercuri to borrow some courage from him. But he would never talk to him about his romantic affairs, and he thought he knew why.

He didn't want to see Silvia again. He wished it had never happened. In the past few months he'd convinced himself that he was no longer in love with Cecilia and now that he knew he still was, that he'd never stopped being in love with her, he was bewildered. How could he have fooled himself like that? Suddenly he seemed to remember exactly how he'd felt, at sixteen or twenty, when falling in love meant complete, unconditional surrender.

Thinking constantly and exclusively about a person, feeling that that person opened the door onto a new season, gave birth to a new life.

Mercuri went to take a nap and Viberti stretched out on the iron bed in the guest room and stared at the white ceiling. He didn't think he would fall asleep, but the exhaustion that had been building up weighed on his eyes like a firm, gentle hand. He sank deeper and deeper into sleep and awoke an hour later, disoriented and afraid of falling. He felt along the edges of the bed with his hands to make sure he wasn't in any danger. At what age did you learn not to fall out of bed anymore? It didn't mean you couldn't lose that skill when you got old. Old people were always falling out of bed in the hospital; a sense of balance was merely part of a transitional phase.

Absurd thoughts; he never slept in the afternoon. When Mercuri came to call him for their usual walk to the vegetable garden, he was ready to go out and stretch his legs, get good and tired, be exhausted by nightfall. It took more than an hour's walk inland to get to San Giorgio, twelve uninhabited stone houses where generations of Ligurian farmers had lived for centuries. The gardens were divided by dry-stone walls and they were all cultivated, all perfectly cared for. Voices could be heard from time to time; a head of white hair would peep out from the rows of tomatoes and an arm would pop up to wave hello. It looked like ghosts were tending the land.

"Have you ever stayed and slept out here?"

"Are you crazy?"

There was a green wooden chair in front of the toolshed (inside was a cot, in case anyone needed a nap), and Viberti usually sat there, as though outside a café, and spoke with Mercuri, who immediately disappeared among the plants. He talked, and the old man mumbled confused, clipped phrases, partly because he was distracted by his work, partly because he was out of breath from the exertion. Would Viberti be able to carry him back down if he collapsed? But Mercuri didn't collapse.

Viberti, however, got bored after ten or twenty minutes and announced he was going for a walk. He continued climbing up the mountain until his legs hurt. Then he stopped, sat down on the rocks along the trail, amid the oaks and chestnut trees, and tried to empty his mind. Black or reddish rocks, natural steps or shaped over hundreds of years, polished and carved by footsteps.

Suddenly he remembered an incident or a conversation that he'd meant to tell Mercuri and returned to the garden, bounding down the slope. There was a young boy in his building, fourteen or fifteen years old, who always wore a belt with the words MANY ENEMIES, MUCH HONOR and the colors of a soccer team. The boy might not know that the phrase was Mussolini's, but what about his parents: How could his parents let him wear that? At the end of the story, Mercuri raised his sweaty forehead from the row of tomatoes he was tying up, and said: "They must be Fascists." As if it didn't worry him that there were still Fascists around.

"They're not Fascists, and that's worse."

Compared to Mercuri he felt like a hypocomist—confused, inept and superficial—but Mercuri was more of a hypocomist than he was. Did he have some justification that Viberti wasn't entitled to? He was no longer able to engage Mercuri in discussion, and he felt he was to blame for that, too.

It turned out that Mercuri had never been a Communist. Viberti told him about an area where shopping centers, multiplexes, and university buildings had replaced the old abandoned industrial plants. In the sixties Mercuri had worked in a tire factory and continued to talk about how gloomy and dismal those places had been back then.

"But you did it because you were passionate about it, didn't you?"

"A doctor in a factory because he's passionate about it? Not likely, I'd say."

"You told me it was difficult to give it up, in the end there was a feeling of great change in the air."

"A great disaster."

"Yes, but exciting."

"Maybe. An office was better, though."

"An office?"

"I left so I could open an office and set up a private practice."

"You told me they were making life impossible for you because you were a leftist, they accused you of covering for the habitual absentees."

"Could be. But I left to open an office." He smiled. "I probably told you they fired me so I could brag about being persecuted by the bosses."

That summer afternoon, sitting on the chair in the garden, watching the old man hold up *miraculous* specimens of various kinds of vegetables as if he were trying to sell them to him, Viberti thought that you had to be Mercuri to grow old like Mercuri and that he himself would have preferred a life like that.

That Monday, he sat down on a bench not far from the ER, like a patient waiting for a doctor. Cecilia would pass by, she couldn't help but come that way and all he needed were a few seconds to let her know that nothing had changed, that they should resume their long, interrupted conversation. For a while all he saw were colleagues who recognized him and asked him, smiling, what he was doing sitting on that bench. He replied that he was waiting for Cecilia. A cardiologist pointed to him and said, "You're waiting for Cecilia!" without even stopping. Because everyone knew they were friends. And there was no need to hide anything, there was nothing to hide anymore. He wasn't completely at ease, sitting on the bench, for various reasons—people expected a doctor to always be on his feet, always on the run. To avoid their stares he took off his white coat, folded it, and set it beside him on the bench. He wasn't really uncomfortable, he knew that everything would be fine as soon as the doctor he was waiting for appeared and examined him and reassured him by saying: "You're in excellent health."

And at the end of her shift Cecilia appeared outside the doors of the emergency room. She saw him, waved and smiled, forlorn and hurt, but not hostile, not guarded. She went over to him, said hello, and Viberti asked if he could walk her to the locker room. "All right, walk with me," she said. They went up two flights of stairs in silence and in silence walked down a hallway. Then Viberti asked her how the boy was and Cecilia said he was fine.

"I really enjoyed seeing him again, I didn't think he'd remember me."

Cecilia smiled. They stopped outside the locker room door, in front of the window from which Viberti had watched her, two years ago.

"Once I saw you from here, down there in the parking lot, the car key kept slipping out of your hand."

Cecilia put a hand over her mouth: "I remember! They had just released Mattia . . . What was I doing?"

"You were bending down to pick it up and then it dropped again."

"And it was all muddy, it must have rained . . ."

"Yes, it had rained."

"More than two years ago. And how long did you stay and watch me?"

"Until you left."

Cecilia nodded. The courtyard was full of parked cars, but the saplings hid them and it was hard to remember exactly where the car had been parked, which way Mattia had come with his father; the leaves obstructed the view and the foliage had perhaps grown more dense. Still, in their memory they saw the same scene again, Viberti the way he had seen her, Cecilia imagining what he had seen from that angle.

After a while Viberti said, "I have to tell you something. I'm not the man you think I am. I'm a very boring, self-centered person.

I'm a man who lives alone. I've lived alone for years and I don't think it's by chance. Often, when I'm alone, I don't think about anything. Nothing comes to me and so I sit on the balcony and look out at the courtyards."

Cecilia raised a hand to her mouth again, then moved it to cover his mouth, shook her head to make him stop. "Ssh . . . Don't."

She stroked his cheek. "You're not self-centered, you're not boring. Don't say anything more."

They stood in silence, lowering their eyes then glancing at each other briefly. Then Cecilia asked him: "Will you eat with me tomorrow?"

Ten days go by and as Viberti comes out of the hospital he sees Silvia standing near a newsstand. I'd rather not have to describe her again with that black headband that makes her hair puff out like a mushroom, but I fear I have no choice. I could assume it's a given, I know it isn't nice to keep repeating it. Should I be more tactful, should I have more respect and reserve, or should I be indelicate? After all, I only said it makes her head look like a mushroom (there, I said it again).

At that moment, Silvia has her back to the entrance, and she's facing across the street, but it's her for sure. She can't have seen him. Without stopping to think, Viberti finds himself running down the sidewalk in the opposite direction. Taking the long way around, he finally reaches the parked Passat and sits behind the wheel, feeling ashamed at having run away like that. But he couldn't help it, his legs started moving before he could consider whether fleeing was the most sensible thing to do. The most sensible thing now would be to go back and look for her and talk to her. He doesn't know why he's running away. He only knows that he doesn't want to see her. He sits in the car, not moving, until he realizes that he's sweating profusely; the car was in the sun all day, it's a furnace.

He opens the windows. He's better off going home, calling her and arranging to see her. He's better off calling her later on.

He approaches his house and as he looks for a parking space he sees her in front of his building; this time he's certain that she, too, has spotted him. He caught her look of surprise, her face brightening as she decided to get his attention. In the rearview mirror he thinks she started to raise her arm. How did she manage to get there before him? She must have taken a taxi, but when? She must have taken a taxi because she saw him running away in front of the hospital, it's the only explanation. How shameful. So shameful, Viberti thinks, and without even deciding that he doesn't want to see her, he remembers a way through the courtyards that will allow him to enter the building without going through the front door. To escape again? To prove that he was already home and therefore wasn't the one who ran away in front of the hospital, in front of his building?

He parks down the block and hastily slips into the driveway that leads to the old garage that's been converted into a gym. For twenty yards he hurries along the glass walls in sight of people running in place on treadmills, in the cool air-conditioning. He knows a little metal door that was never locked when he was a child, there might be a padlock on it now, it might also be walled up, it must be thirty years since he's used it. But in the wall at the end of the courtyard the magic little door appears before him as in a fairy tale, intact, still unlocked, maybe a little creaky on its rusty hinges, maybe identical to his recollection.

Sweaty and euphoric, having made it through a narrow walkway between two vine-covered, redbrick walls, he comes out in the courtyard of his building. In a second he's in the cool shade of the stairs. He presses the elevator button and hears voices on the first or second floor. There's a woman's voice, then another woman's voice with a Spanish accent, and then a third woman's voice, which is his mother's voice. He can't understand what they're saying, but it's not hard to figure out what's happened. Silvia buzzed his mother, the other VIBERTI on the intercom. She went up to her apartment! What does she think she's doing? Is she planning on camping out in front of his door?

And for the third time, instead of deciding to see Silvia and invite her up to his apartment to find out why she's looking for him, he goes back to the courtyard and cuts across it diagonally, no longer headed toward the magic door but toward a ladder leaning against the wall in the opposite corner, the ladder that he's seen Giulia's husband use a couple of times to climb up to the roof of the supermarket. As soon as he reaches the roof, he turns around to glance at the building's internal facade, an instinctive gesture to make sure no one is watching him. But then his gaze lingers and focuses on his empty balcony. There, on the wicker chair, a ghost returns his look and, astonished, seems to say: *You went down to the courtyard; you used to be a spectator, now you've become the leading man, what's gotten into you? And you didn't even jump off the balcony, you didn't shatter on the brick pavement. You went down to run, leap, scale the wall, scramble up. What do you think you're doing?* He looks toward his mother's balcony, Giulia's balcony, but the apartments on the left side of the building don't have a good view of this area. That's why Giulia's husband climbs that slightly sloping, red-tiled roof and goes back down the other side. Looking for what? The warehouse roof juts out from the flat roof of the gym and creates a space in which you can hide, a kind of small urban cave for part-time hermits.

He crouches, taking cover in the shadows; he wants to think and prepare what he's going to say, he wants to face Silvia—but right away he starts thinking about Giulia's husband; what does he come down there to do? It's certainly not a comfortable place, you're sitting on the tarred roof of an old garage that's been converted into a gym. Viberti remembers when, perhaps thirty-five years ago, workers had laid down black rolls of tar paper, securing them with molten tar, sealing the joints and stinking up all the houses on the block with noxious fumes. How odd to now see up close the material that he often imagined stepping on; he thought it would be gummier. The warehouse wall is peeling in many places, the bricks are pecking out beneath the plaster and between the bricks there are cracks two fingers wide where a small tin of Dutch cigars and a lighter can easily be stored.

So simple, so predictable, no mystery. Giulia's husband doesn't come here to phone a lover in privacy or enjoy half an hour of autistic solitude. He comes to smoke a cigar on the sly, like a boy of thirteen, because Giulia has forbidden it. So simple, so ridiculous. How he manages to hide the stink afterward, that's a different story; smoke, tar, stink, and again Viberti thinks it's none of his business.

His business is Silvia right now and that's the business he has to focus on. He ran away, he made a bad impression, but it's not serious, it can be remedied. He'll leave the cave and go home now, and if Silvia really is camped outside his door, he'll let her in and find a way to explain that he didn't mean to run away, and find a way to listen to what she has to say.

Silvia must want to tell him that she found out about his relationship with Cecilia, and doesn't understand how he could have slept with her.

That's what made him run away, that's what he was ashamed of.

He starts to get up then, but it occurs to him that he'd like to smoke first, he'd like to stink a little, too. It's been twenty years since he's smoked a cigarette and he wants to inhale and feel the effect of tobacco in his lungs again. He takes the box—Giulia's husband won't notice if one cigar is missing. He lights up, inhales deeply. He coughs, but he doesn't choke. He feels his throat burning. He takes another puff. He's never understood why people smoke. He persists, turns the cigar between his fingers, coughs, goes through the motions so that the ash drops from the tip. Halfway through he stubs it out.

From the courtyard he reenters the lobby of the building, takes the elevator. Silvia is not waiting for him on the fifth-floor land-ing. He'll call her later, for one thing because the moment he steps into the house he notices that his head is spinning and that he's beginning to feel nauseated. He feels a little idiotic. The intercom buzzes. Who could it be? He doesn't answer. Feeling queasy, he peeks out the window and sees Silvia in front of the building. She's still here, why doesn't she go away? What does she want from him? A crazy lady, a maniac, why doesn't she give up, why doesn't she go away? Why isn't she put off, doesn't she understand that she should be put off? There are some patients like that, people who are unwilling to understand, who won't resign themselves to the worst. The nausea is almost turning into an urge to vomit; how can one small cigar cause such distress? He swallows two Plasil tablets and lies facedown on the bed, monitoring his distress. The inter-com buzzes again. Maybe it will buzz again and again, that woman will never get it. He spends the evening drifting from bed to couch, the TV on and off, now at the kitchen table, now pacing back and forth in the hallway like a prisoner in the rec yard. The intercom doesn't buzz again.

He woke up in the middle of the night. The open window framed a square of vertical and diagonal lines, flickering like the screen of an old television that needs tuning. It was pouring, pounding on the rooftops, rushing through the gutters; it smelled like rain; the storm outside was torrential. The fogs of the past were gone, and now instead of just rain there were monsoons. The nausea had passed, his mouth was sour. He went into the bathroom and brushed his teeth, scrubbing furiously until his gums bled, then undressed, leaving his clothes scattered in the bathroom and hall-way. In the bedroom, he put on his pajamas and started to close the window. He opened it again, and looked out at the deserted street; for a moment he thought he saw her through a watery film of rain. He decided it was a shadow, that he'd dreamed her up. Then he glimpsed her again and now he was certain he'd seen her.

She sat huddled in the recess of a small doorway across the street, facing his building. From up there it was impossible for him to tell if she was alive, if she was sleeping, if she was keeping an eye on the street in her obsessive, paranoid way, if she was a madwoman who wanted to kill him. He tried going to bed and turning off the light, as if by ignoring her he could make her disappear, but his motions lacked conviction; he knew he was bluffing. He listened to the pounding rain for another ten minutes, then got up, put on the clothes he'd just taken off, drank a glass of water, took an umbrella and the car keys, and went down to the street.

But Silvia wasn't there—either she was no longer there or she'd never been there. He crossed the street without opening the umbrella, getting drenched even though the rain was now letting up somewhat, and took cover in the doorway where he thought he'd seen her. He crouched down and in the faint glow of a streetlamp studied that patch of sidewalk as if he might find traces of Silvia's former presence on the stone and concrete. He sat on the step and looked around. The rain had stopped, the temperature had fallen. The facade of the building was dark and dismal, no lights in the windows, just the streetlamp casting a dim glow from below. The fifth floor was enveloped by wispy trails of mist. It looked like pieces of cloth were flying out the windows of his house, like someone was tossing out garments, rags, sheets. Like the house was reaching its arms out to the night to seek help and refuge and protection. "That's the house I've lived in all my life," he said to himself, and heard the words with some irritation, as if it were an old uncle talking, telling a family story for the hundredth time. He sat on the step awhile longer, then went back upstairs.

The house empty, lights turned on, windows open, the air smelling of rain. He put his pajamas back on, but instead of going to bed, he sat down to write a letter to Cecilia. He hadn't written

a letter to a woman in twenty years, it had never been his specialty, but the style wasn't important; there were things to say and
they should be said. In the final version he copied from the rough
draft more than an hour later, he told her that she was the first
and only woman he had ever truly loved, because he had never
loved anyone the way he loved her, and before he met her he had
never known a love so great. He got tangled up in that adjective,
"great," for two or three paragraphs, and tried to modify it; great
because it was fulfilling and great because it was mature. Laugh-
able, because seen from outside their relationship didn't seem at
all fulfilling, let alone mature. But he wasn't talking about the
duration of the relationship or the type of rapport—it was the intensity and the quality that made it feel great. And never before
had Viberti imagined that he could love with that intensity and
that quality. Everything he wanted was bound up in her, coin-
cided with her, the happiness he dreamed of enjoying he dreamed
of enjoying with her, the trips he dreamed of taking (the ones
Marta had urged him to take) he dreamed of taking with her, the
house he dreamed of having he dreamed of having with her (he
did not mention a child). The tone was softened so as to make it
more credible, and Viberti ended by saying that he still didn't understand why he had fallen so deeply in love with her, what was
special about her. Well, this was one more reason to spend the
remaining days of his life with her, to discover the basis for that
love. *I never talked with anyone like I have with you. No one has ever
talked to me the way you have. Maybe we haven't been together in the
traditional sense of the word, but talking to you and listening to you has
been the most wonderful love story of my life.* He sealed the letter in a
white envelope and wrote *Cecilia* on it. He left it on the desk and
went to the bathroom. Before going to bed he picked it up again
and stared at the name in the center of the white rectangle. He
underlined it with his pen.

———

The following afternoon, the women who looked after his mother called him because Marta was upset; she wanted to leave, she was already packing her bags and had phoned a travel agent. Talking over each other excitedly, the two Peruvians tore the phone out of each other's hands to add further alarming details: the *signora* had found an old ID card belonging to her dead sister, a sister who had died young, and realized that she had never visited her grave, she was determined to set off for the cemetery. Viberti told them to give her one of the tranquilizers that were on the credenza, marked with a note written by Giulia, but he saw that they were in a panic, that for some reason they couldn't handle the situation and needed him to come home as soon as possible.

When he got there he found Marta in her robe in front of the closets, which were all open; for half an hour she'd been giving instructions to the two women, who were shifting clothes and blankets from one section to another. The emergency had faded. "Good for you, Mama," he said, resting an arm around her shoulders, "every so often you have to straighten things up," and he kissed her on the forehead. On the bed lay an open suitcase, still empty and perhaps forgotten. Leaving the room, the women told him about the ID card found accidentally in the bottom of a drawer during one of the general clean-ups that for some time had become Marta's chief occupation. Angélica showed Viberti the document, pointing out the name, "Maria Rita," and Signora Marta's extraordinary resemblance to the woman in the black-and-white photo. It wasn't a passport photo, but a real portrait shot in a studio where a photographer had taken pains to pose his model, looking for the best angle and the best lighting, completely unnecessarily since the forty-year-old woman was beautiful regardless.

Viberti explained that Maria Rita was Marta's real name, which she had always hated; all her life she had insisted on being called by that diminutive of sorts (which was also a real name). *"Así que no es su hermana,"* Angélica said, suddenly understanding. *"Niente hermana,"* no, not her sister. Viberti shook his head. The new twist was that Marta hadn't remembered the name recorded on her birth certificate and was convinced she'd found a sister's ID. "Wait," Viberti said, "let's do a test."

He went back to his mother and told her he'd found her old ID card in the house: "See, it has your real name, Maria Rita." Marta took the document as if seeing it for the first time and exclaimed emphatically: "I always hated that name!" Then she immediately marveled at how young she was in the photograph, and shook her head, laughing; no one knew why she found it so funny.

They sat in the kitchen and drank iced tea, Marta still chuckling to herself, looking at the photograph. Viberti wondered if Cecilia had yet read the letter, which he'd slipped through a crack in her locker. He was almost sure the envelope had been firmly inserted in the locker's frame and that when she opened the door, Cecilia wouldn't be able to miss it, but he continued to imagine possible mishaps, scenarios in which the letter might have fallen to the bottom of the locker and gotten buried among old sandals and schedules from past shifts in the ER.

"I remember perfectly when I had this photo taken," Marta said. "I remember perfectly" had become one of her favorite expressions and Giulia never failed to point it out to him. "The photographer's studio was downtown and I'd never been there before; he was a shady-looking little hunchback who infuriated me by making me stay in that pose for an hour, taking me by the chin to turn my face from side to side and putting his hands on me to arrange the folds of my dress. When I told Stefano about it he got really angry and wanted to go there and make a scene." *The eccentric uncles everyone used to have, and the friends who were a little crazy or disabled or hunchbacked, but unique and unforgettable, don't exist anymore. Among my mother's girlfriends there wasn't one who was normal. And my father had a whole tribe of protégés and dependents, who continued to seek protection and charity even after his death. My friends and I, on the other hand, are apparently normal people, forgettable and interchangeable, our disabilities concealed, our humps internal.*

Viberti smiled at the idea of his father causing a scene, ignoring the fact that his mother had called him Stefano. But Marta added: "He had just finished playing tennis and said he'd smash the racket over his head." She laughed happily, quite content, and Viberti made an effort to laugh with her. Instead of stopping to think twice and deciding to let it go, he said: "I didn't know Papa was so jealous."

"Oh, no, no, I really did mean Stefano Mercuri. Your father wasn't at all jealous. Stefano, on the other hand, made such scenes . . ." She laughed again, maybe only because she was happy to have shown her son that she could still remember something. She didn't seem at all concerned or aware of what her words implied. And Viberti knew he shouldn't attach any importance to that strange, unintentional confession. How many times had he thought to himself that there was something between Mercuri and his mother? How many times, as a boy, had he hoped that Mercuri and his mother would get married? Hoped or feared.

To escape the awkward situation, he stood up and went out on the balcony, glancing around the courtyards, noting that from that side of the building the part-time hermit's cave truly was well protected and hidden. It was entirely possible that Marta had been raving deliriously. But wait a minute, he thought, they'd been talking about a time when his father was still alive and well, a period, in fact, when his parents had been married only a few years and he was little. Maybe Marta wasn't raving, and Mercuri had been her lover before and after she married. But Viberti didn't look anything like him. Then again he didn't look like his father either. He looked a lot like Marta.

As soon as he left his mother he went to look for Giulia on the third floor. She had just returned from the hospital, she didn't know anything about the mix-up with the ID card. They talked a bit about Marta's new anxiety attacks, which worried them both, and discussed the best dosage for her sleeping pills and tranquilizers. Then Viberti, smiling with feigned nonchalance, told Giulia about Marta's mistake, how she had attributed to Mercuri the jealousy of a husband.

Giulia shrugged. "You've always thought that, too, haven't you?"

Viberti's smile immediately faded. "Well, but we're talking about the sixties here."

"I see," said Giulia.

Viberti kept his irritation in check.

"I have to go," he said, and left before Giulia could add anything else.

He did not try to call Silvia Re that night or the next day. Silvia left him messages but he didn't call her back. It was Friday, and on Saturday morning he would take Marta and the two caregivers to the house in the mountains, where his mother would spend the rest of the summer away from the sweltering city. He wouldn't be able to see Silvia over the weekend, so he might as well put off calling her until Monday. Maybe he should call to tell her, but he kept putting that off, too. All he could think about was how Cecilia would react to his letter. He hadn't heard from her, hadn't seen her at the hospital or at the café. Maybe the letter really had fallen to the bottom of the locker and disappeared forever. Maybe Cecilia had read it, had liked it or hadn't liked it, but since it didn't change anything, since it didn't solve the issues that kept them apart, she thought she'd talk to him about it later.

By five in the afternoon Viberti was tempted to go back to his wicker chair and watch the courtyards from up there, but something held him back, as if it were no longer possible. Still, the temptation was strong. Watching the courtyards he'd be able to think about the affair between his mother and Mercuri, about how bitter and sad it made him feel.

Soon after, Cecilia called him. She sounded excited, happy. She'd read the letter, she'd found it very moving, she wanted to get another one just like it that very instant. Then she said she wanted to have dinner with him that evening, she recalled that one day, months ago, Viberti had told her about making a pasta with a special sauce.

"Yes," he said, "I can make it again anytime," and she laughed. "Then you're inviting me to dinner? When can I come?"

"Whenever you like, I'll be waiting for you."

"I'll be there around eight."

He hurried to take a shower, but when he was undressed, instead of getting under the stream of water, he ran naked into the kitchen and started pulling the ingredients for the sauce out of the fridge, setting the table with a nice white tablecloth and some elegant dishes, never used, that had been left to him after he and Giulia had divvied up the wedding gifts. The sauce was simmering, a bottle of white wine was in the refrigerator, he already had what he needed for a special salad, but there was no bread, he had to dash down and buy it. He realized that he was naked, that the French door was wide open, and glanced at the buildings across the way: no one was interested in an exhibitionist cook at that hour on a Friday in July.

He showered, changed his shirt, and ran out to buy bread. He bought several kinds of bread: whole wheat, raisin, sesame, small rolls to go with the salad. Two salads, he decided, one wouldn't be enough: valerian lettuce with walnuts and parmesan cheese and fennel with oranges and anchovies, even though oranges weren't in season, grapefruit might be better, where do citrus fruits come from in July? *Remember the saying "You are what you eat"? That threat of sorts reminds me of another expression, "One day all this will be yours": as a child I didn't really understand it and thought the phrase was "One day all this will be you," and I figured that sooner or later my father would take me aside and tell me, word by word, who I would become, as if he could know beforehand, as if his dreams could become my memories.* He ran from the bakery to the fruit-and-vegetable stand and on the way he stopped to buy ice cream; Cecilia might bring something, wine or ice cream, it didn't matter, better to have a spare in the refrigerator. When he returned home he prepared the salads and a fruit cocktail and in addition decided to make an omelet with marjoram, mint, and St. Peter's herb. He showered again and threw on another shirt. He looked at his watch: it was just seven.

Cecilia appeared at the door at half past eight with a large bouquet of red roses. Viberti was speechless, breathless, without a vase to put the flowers in. He rummaged through the house, opening and closing cabinets, knowing full well he wouldn't find anything appropriate. No one had ever given him flowers, he'd never bought himself any, the vases had probably ended up at Giulia's. In the end Cecilia found an oval skillet, used for frying fish, in the pots and pans cabinet: it had been left to him, for some reason. She filled it with water and arranged the roses in it with their vermilion heads resting on the edge and the stems soaking. Back in the kitchen, Viberti didn't ask her how she'd managed to find the cabinet with the pots and pans so quickly; he suspected it wasn't a very intelligent question, and instead stared at the roses lying there in their voluptuous abandon, picturing Cecilia naked in his bathtub.

"Are we expecting anyone else?" she asked with a smile, pointing to all the food Viberti had laid out on the table, in addition to the pasta that he'd tossed into the boiling water as soon as he heard the intercom buzz. "Were you worried I'd starve to death?"

"I was worried, yes," Viberti mumbled.

"Don't tell me my sister is coming?" Cecilia added, laughing.

Viberti looked dismayed and she hugged him to cheer him up; she was only joking.

While the pasta was cooking, Cecilia asked to see the house, and the balcony overlooking the courtyards she'd heard so much about. Viberti had been hoping they'd sit down and sip the white wine that he had already poured into two glasses, but Cecilia picked hers up and went into the hallway.

The blue five-seat sofa sat in the center of the living room, facing the television. There were no armchairs, no table and chairs. There was a tall breakfront with lots of drawers, never organized, which held ten years of bills, receipts, tax returns, certificates, and other documents.

"What if you have guests, if you want someone to sit down?"

"We all face the same way, and the worst seat is the middle one."

"And a table?"

"I eat in the kitchen."

In the first bedroom the double bed had been left behind. One of the two nightstands was wrapped in protective padding, as if they'd decided to leave it at the last minute. A lamp and a stack of newspapers stood on its black marble top, the only part that had been unwrapped. The doors to a large, half-empty wardrobe were missing.

"She had them painted by a friend, a huge landscape with hills, trees, flowers, cars. I don't know if I cared for it. In any case, she took them with her."

Another room with no furniture, full of old magazines piled on the floor, against the walls. In a corner, a toy garage bought by mistake two years ago. "The children's room." Spoken without irony.

The study: a desk with a computer, a swivel chair, a stand with a printer, a stereo.

The bathroom, at least, didn't lack for anything.

A room with a washing machine. Underwear hung out to dry.

Cecilia didn't say a word, she didn't ask why he hadn't replaced the furniture, didn't ask why he hadn't bought new doors for the wardrobe, instead she held Viberti's hand tightly throughout the tour, as if she were the one guiding him. They went out on the balcony. The balcony looked like a jungle, Cecilia said, it was crammed with plants and flowers, how did he find the time to care for them?

"I don't, in fact, every week one of them dies, but I buy another one immediately."

"You admit it."

"Yes," he laughed, "it's a kind of terminal ward."

"Silvia says we doctors are unbearably cynical."

Viberti lowered his eyes. There was a silence.

"Okay, we won't talk about her again," Cecilia said.

A light breeze cooled the air.

"Why don't we eat out here?"

"Out here? But what would we lean on?"

"We don't need to lean on anything, come on. You sit here, on the stool, and I'll take the wicker chair."

Viberti looked at her, smiling.

"I want to sit in your chair."

"All right. I'll go drain the pasta."

They ate with their plates on their laps, setting the glasses on the floor. Cecilia told him about some phone calls to the children, they were fine, they were big now and independent and they no longer needed her. She was struck by the fact that, for the first time, both of them had asked her, "And how are you, Mama?" She smiled. Then she said she didn't like it when people said that Mattia was really okay now, she was afraid that talking about it would bring the problem on again. Then she said they would return from their summer camps tanned and in great shape and that they would spend some time with their grandmother. They were used to having everything planned so they wouldn't get bored.

"Did you get bored?"

"As a boy? I went to the school of boredom."

"They're always saying, 'What should we do now?' Every now and then even my mother calls to ask me, 'What should they do now?' when the children are with her." They laughed. Cecilia asked if he used to sit in the wicker chair and watch the court-yards when he got bored as a child.

No, Viberti said, the chair went back to high school and, espe-cially, his university days, when he would study out on the balcony. He told her about the mnemonic system he'd used to remember the elements of a subject, assigning each to different areas of the courtyard. They talked about the various methods they'd used to memorize the more difficult subject matters; Cecilia had filled notebook after notebook with keywords. They talked about the anatomy exam, because all doctors sooner or later start talking about the anatomy exam. They talked about the mental foramen, the infraspinatous fossa, the round pronator and Penfield's homun-culus. And Viberti was able to name all the bones of the hand.

Then Cecilia stared at him with a serious expression, and Vi-berti slid the stool away, knelt down and began kissing her. A long, passionate kiss. A few pauses to take a breath; he went on kissing her for ten minutes, even though his knees hurt.

Then she told him to sit back on the stool, she had something to tell him.

"I'm not saying it's the reason we separated, Luca and I, but it's something that happened, four years ago, and you should know about it."

She told him she'd been expecting a third child, that she didn't want it, she didn't want another child and she didn't want one with Luca, so she'd had an abortion. She told him in a few words and then fell silent and looked out over the rooftops of the houses across the way, toward the hill.

Viberti took her chapped, red hands, kissed them, rested his head on them like a pillow.

"What do you think of me?"

Viberti said he didn't think anything; it must have been terri-ble for her, but he didn't feel he could judge her, he didn't know enough about it.

"You don't think I'm a monster?"

He looked at her, confused. No, he didn't think she was a monster.

"What if I did it to you. If I decided to abort your child."

What troubled him the most was the way Cecilia spoke to him, with that contained anger.

"Why would you do that?"

"To hurt you."

Viberti shook his head. For a moment he was afraid he hadn't understood. Because in fact he hadn't understood a thing, up until that moment. But it was possible that he had no hope of understanding, ever, not even when faced with the evidence. "Then I'd be worried about that, that you would want to hurt me. Did you want to hurt your husband? What did he do to you?"

"Nothing. Absolutely nothing."

They remained silent. Then Cecilia added: "I didn't love him anymore. Maybe I wanted to punish him for that."

Viberti kissed her hands again, he told her she'd had a few difficult years, but they were behind her now and it would all be better.

"Why would it get any better?"

But the question was too complicated and maybe Cecilia regretted it as soon as she said it, and told him it didn't matter, he didn't have to answer. She stood up, took him by the hand, said "Let's go in now," and led him inside.

The next day Viberti woke up very early and found himself on the left side of the bed. He lay there watching Cecilia for half an hour; during the night she'd wrapped herself in the sheet. He, too, had felt cold and woken up a couple of times, gone to the bathroom and come back to bed with his bathrobe. His pajamas were trapped under the pillow Cecilia was using. He studied the skin of Cecilia's shoulder and arm closely, the downy blond fuzz, the constellations of moles. All those stars. If only he'd seen some flaw in her, if only falling in love hadn't blinded him. But maybe it wasn't falling in love that blinded him, maybe he'd been blind since birth and Cecilia was teaching him to see. It was the second time in a couple of days that he'd had occasion to change his perspective, looking up at the balcony from the courtyard, looking at the right side of the bed from the left, and he didn't yet know if he liked all those changes, or whether he felt threatened by them. He got up to make coffee, but as soon as he set the pot on the burner he went back to the bedroom to look at her. He didn't want to wake her. He drank the coffee in the kitchen, getting up every so often to gaze at her. That night they'd made love in a bed, and it didn't seem real to him yet. Their first night together. Whereas before Cecilia's body had been revealed in partial installments, he had now seen it whole, its parts reassembled. It was a lovely body. He went back to the kitchen where the two salads, the herb omelet, and the fruit cocktail had been left overnight, untouched, like sacrificial offerings. He began cleaning up without making any noise. He knew she was there, asleep in his bed, in his house, and it was a luxury, a gift, a privilege. It was like that film with the woman in a coma, in a sense. But it was better, because Cecilia would wake up. Even though there was a chance that when she woke up she might again tell him she'd made a mistake. In fact, not just a chance, a certainty: she would tell him it was all over, yet again.

THE DESIRE TO BE WITH HIM
THE NEXT DAY, TOO

They say memory plays tricks, but memory doesn't play tricks, it always knows what it's doing. She remembered the moment she'd read about it in the newspaper. It happened in January after her first night on duty, back from a week's vacation. A busy night, but without incident. She wasn't tired despite the fact that the emergency room was full of stretchers thanks to the official start of flu season; she'd seen about forty people. In a period of uneventful calm, between six and seven, one of the paramedics had come inside bringing with him a blast of cold air, brioches, and a newspaper. She'd found the paper in front of her, and though she hardly ever read it, sitting at a desk, head propped on her hand, she started leafing through the pages as she answered questions from a colleague who was filling out the last case chart.

The headline CHILD STARVED TO DEATH was a flashing alarm, a wailing siren. She shouldn't have paused to read the article. After a few lines, it became impossible to get it out of her mind. (Was it inevitable that she spot it? I went to see where it appeared. Bottom of the page, inconspicuous, competing with a story about a building destroyed by a gas leak. No, it wasn't inevitable.)

Every day, from then on, she followed the story of the mother who had let her three-year-old son starve to death. At first there was only the child's corpse at the morgue, along with a man, the mother's partner, who had brought the child to the emergency room. The couple—the woman twenty-three years old, the man forty-five—lived in one room with two other children, without potable water or electricity. The woman was out of work and the man had a criminal record for selling heroin. Eight years before, when she was only fifteen, they'd tried to elope, but her family had opposed the marriage and kept them apart.

The third or fourth day, the results of the autopsy were released, detailing the appallingly emaciated state of the child's body, traces of ecchymosis and probable assault. Then it came out that the other two kids living with the couple, a boy of six and a girl of five, weren't the woman's children, but those of the man's former lover. Those two children were in good health (good *physical* health, that is). It was also discovered that though the one room lacked electricity they had access to power through a pirated connection, and that the couple had air-conditioning and satellite TV, but often no money to eat.

And finally the story of the woman and the child's biological father was revealed. After the failed elopement, the woman had endured her patriarchal, violent family for two more years; at seventeen she fled and went into hiding in a nearby town, where she supported herself through prostitution. A client (a well-to-do businessman, married with three children) fell in love with her and for a year kept her in an apartment, promising to marry her, but then abandoned her soon after learning he'd gotten her pregnant. At nineteen she was homeless, unemployed, and expecting a child. She sought help from her old lover, who had never forgotten her and took her back. The baby was born. The mother and her lover hated him because as he grew up he looked more and more like her old client. They fed him only when the other children left something.

She would remember the details of that story forever. What

did she learn from it? That you shouldn't let children starve to death. That you shouldn't nurture your own fears. That it's better not to read the newspaper. That memory serves, among other things, to fill sleepless nights with troublesome thoughts. That you have to defend yourself against memory. That natural selection among memories is unpredictable. Beautiful memories survive, and they comfort and cheer us, and the reason is clear. And, of course, savage, harsh, merciless memories also survive, memories with bloodshot eyes, trained to snarl and bite (even if you try to tame them).

Stock phrases to reprimand them. *Don't make me repeat myself.* But they wanted to hear her say it again, and ultimately she wanted to repeat herself—the day when all she had to do was ask or decree or forbid just once in order to be obeyed (or ignored, or obeyed and then ignored), they would be adults and the pleasure of repetition would find other outlets. *Don't make me repeat myself* to the boy who should start doing his homework, *Don't make me repeat myself* to the girl who should clean up her room. She thought they got along very well, they'd become friends. But putting it that way didn't get the idea across; they had always pretty much gotten along. Now, though, they were friends in a different way. She noticed it because she felt excluded, she no longer had to mediate. Or maybe Michela had decided to change her attitude toward her brother. Because she'd grown up. Or because she was the one who gave the orders in any case. Though Cecilia didn't actually believe it, the paranoid fear that it had been Michela who caused Mattia to stop eating continued to suggest itself. She was so afraid it would strike her unexpectedly that she led all her thoughts back to that particular thought so she could think about it and then stop thinking about it. *Stop it.* Now they usually stopped. But when they were younger they tested her endurance. *Stop it, I said.* And they persisted, looking straight at her and smiling defiantly (when they were very little) or looking sidelong at her to judge how angry she was (when they'd grown up a little). *Are you going to stop it?* She'd stopped buying the newspaper. The story of the child who'd died of starvation had vanished completely, relegated to general oblivion on the one hand and to her personal memory on the other.

Now, however, she searched the Internet for similar stories. There was little material on the subject, whereas murderous mothers, along with all kinds of discussions about them, abounded. Mothers in forums who wrote: "A mother who kills her own children deserves to die." Mothers terrified of being tempted to kill their insufferable children. But the murderous mother was almost always a violent killer, it isn't every day you come across the kind of cold-bloodedness or ignorance or stupidity that lets a child starve to death. She remembered the cat who pushed away the puniest kitten when she suckled. She found pages and pages on male hamsters who killed their young so that the females would be ready to mate immediately. They didn't just kill them, they devoured them, leaving only the heads on the plate (so to speak). She turned off the computer, unplugging it. The air was sucked up by the dark screen, for a moment she couldn't breathe.

Don't make me mad. When she said it she was already pretty mad, on the way to getting good and mad. *Don't make me mad* was a bad sign for the kids and worked much better than *Stop it*. She'd been sure she was a good mother, too permissive a mother, but one day, in third or fourth grade, Michela had come home with an essay in which she'd written: "When we're good my mother is like a beautiful angel, but if we make her mad she swoops down on us like a crow." Dr. Angel and Mother Crow. *Swoops down on us.* In the long run, the fear of being regarded as a creature with a long beak and long glossy feathers who punishes naughty children gave way to the fear of being viewed as a pure, angelic being with white, gauzy feathers, who protects and cares for good children *only.*

She remembered the shy internist's dismay and rebellion, the day of the infamous declaration of love, at hearing himself described as a fine person and a good friend, a decent, amiable man. She also recalled his irritation at being called Dr. Anorexic and Mr. Bulimic. If anyone was incapable of having a split personality it was him. Instead of telling her to go to hell, he was stuck in his mute worship like a broken record. And she was in big trouble. *Otherwise there'll be trouble.* There was trouble already. For a couple of months she'd been resisting the temptation to make love to him. She knew resisting was the right thing to do, she wanted to find out whether the attraction was really serious, whether it wasn't just pent-up desire. Or rather, she thought it was pent-up desire and wanted to prove to herself that if she could just hold out, the attraction would go away. *Serious trouble.* The attraction wasn't going away, and besides still wanting to make love with him (especially on sleepless nights, when the children were at their father's and she found herself alone in the house), she felt a tightness in her chest. A tight chest wasn't one of the known cardiological symptoms, nevertheless it existed, as the patients in the ER knew. It didn't matter if it was a nervous contraction of the muscles at the pit of the stomach. In fact, with a tight chest you were never hungry. *To bed without supper!* The threat she could never use with her children.

Moments when she found herself alone in the house in the middle of the day, free because she'd finished her shift or free because she hadn't yet started it. She'd close the door behind her and immediately be tempted to go back to bed. Instead she started straightening up. The deserted, silent house, even when it showed signs of the children's presence, seemed like someone else's. For some reason they had learned to put the milk back in the refrigerator. They didn't put anything else back where it belonged, their rooms were a mess, yet they put the milk carton back. The house always needed straightening up and it was a more relaxing activity than hiding under the covers, provided that it was ultimately productive.

One morning Luca called to let her know about a business trip: three weeks in Rome and Sicily, he wouldn't be back for the weekends.

"Almost a month away, how come?" she asked, surprised by her frightened tone, even before realizing that his departure really did frighten her.

"I know, I know, I'm sorry, if you want, when I get back I'll take the kids two Sundays in a row, but I can't do anything about this."

She told him it wasn't about the weekends, it was about the children, they would miss him.

"Well . . ." He seemed embarrassed. "It's very sweet of you to tell me that, I'll bring them back a nice gift, I'll find a way to make them forgive me and, listen, if you need anything, there are always my parents."

Cecilia giggled nervously and told him she hadn't meant to be sweet, she'd only said the truth, the children adored him. They fell silent. The times when he used to insult her were so long ago. One day he'd told her that she was *obviously* in *no position* to raise children. How distant, that violence.

Then Luca suggested planning a dinner at his place before he left.

When she hung up, Cecilia thought she had every reason to be worried; she could solve the logistical problems without him, but his absence would have consequences for the children. She wondered if she was jealous: two weekends away, maybe it meant that Luca had someone else. But she decided that no, she wasn't jealous, she never had been. Besides, if there *was* someone else, better that she was in another city.

They tried to make up for the distance with lengthy phone calls. During the first week Luca called every night. Michela described her days to him in detail, and because her father could never remember the previous installments, she yelled at him and made him listen to an even longer rundown of the news of the day. As she talked, she ran through her whole assortment of funny faces and expressions; listening to her, Cecilia and Mattia laughed and exchanged meaningful glances, though they'd already heard the stories. When it was his turn, Mattia answered in monosyllables. After a few days Michela completely dominated the conversation, while the boy ran off to the bathroom the moment it was time to take the phone and talk to his father. On Saturday, Luca phoned twice and the second time spoke with Michela for thirty minutes. The call took place in the kitchen, where Michela talked while looking out the glass door, one foot resting on top of the other, balancing. Seeing her come back to the living room, Cecilia assumed she was bringing the cordless phone with her to pass it to Mattia, but she had already hung up. "Papa says hello," she told her brother. Cecilia kept silent on the couch, arms tightly folded, moving her eyes from the TV screen to the back of Mattia's neck, as he lay motionless on the floor in front of her. She didn't want to notice these things, but the boy's indifference frightened her.

That night she began to think that Luca was making a mistake. She would tell him so. He should talk to Mattia when he called, and even if Mattia didn't seem interested in talking, he shouldn't fall into the trap. Above all, he shouldn't delegate his communication with Mattia to Michela, as if there were a pecking order between them. She began to think that the child would become one of those people who do nothing to bridge distances. The distance that separated him from his father existed, she wasn't dreaming it up. He would always insist that others make the effort. He wanted to be loved for what he was. He was a perfect cat, an obese, furry cat in the body of an undernourished child, more catlike even than she was, and that's why he beguiled and bewitched the shy internist. The whole world was captivated by the child's silent power; everything always seemed to revolve around him (even Michela, of course, even Michela, precisely because she believed she controlled him).

The shy internist had been very fond of the child, then he'd become very fond of the child's mother. And the child's mother was very fond of the shy internist. She was enormously fond of him. She reached under the covers to her left and to her right, wondering how it would feel to hear someone asleep beside her again, breathing quietly or snoring loudly. And the thought flashed through her mind: maybe she was in love with Viberti, maybe those fantasies were a sign that she was no longer able to interpret. She had to talk to him, she had to make up her mind. The idea was disturbing, and to stop thinking about it she got up, with the excuse of checking to see if the children were tucked in.

She took the pasta that Mattia hadn't eaten out of the refrigerator. She never knew what to do with leftovers, often she threw them out and sometimes she saved them. It was easier to throw away larger amounts, she saved the smaller, less-risky portions, in case anyone wanted to check. She heated the pasta in the microwave, added a little oil, and ate it quickly.

The next day she was on the evening shift, four hours from eight to midnight. She took the children to school, did a little shopping, and prepared for the prospect of a whole day off ahead of her. At home she hung the wash out to dry, one of the household chores that made her by far the most irritable, or, in some cases, determined. She'd always hated extracting that intestine-like skein of clothes from the belly of the washing machine, the coils immediately unwinding as though contact with the air caused an instantaneous necrosis of the tissue. She hated the smell of laundry. She scattered socks and underwear from the bathroom to the drying rack in the room down the hall (since she always forgot to take the basket with her). After a while there was no more room on the drying rack, maybe she didn't make the best use of it, or maybe she didn't feel like rearranging the pieces that had already been hung. Often she abandoned a last tangle of clothes, hoping that someone (the housekeeper or Luca) would see to it. Since Luca no longer lived with them the loads to be washed had gotten smaller, his countless shirts, all identical, had disappeared, and there was always room on the rack now, and still the laundry wasn't arranged properly.

Luca had always been better at loading the dishwasher, hanging clothes, and packing the trunk of the car. She had a vague idea of the reasons for this shortcoming of hers, something that had to do with being methodical, something that men seriously took to heart, that women didn't have time to take to heart, or even (let's admit it) something that women's minds weren't suited for. Who cares. Think of Viberti's obsession with rules. She thought of asking him to write out rules for loading the dishwasher and rules for hanging the wash. She thought he would do it for her. She thought that no matter what she thought about, Viberti popped into her head. And it was too bad she didn't have the courage to tell him so.

She would never have the courage.

She wasn't brave, she was timid and cowardly. Fear of being left alone drove her to delude a man who asked nothing of her and who loved her. She had to tell him that she loved him, too, and that it was best they not see each other anymore. *That* was what she urgently had to tell him.

A damp tablecloth fell out of her hand, went plop on the floor. She left the laundry half-hung and went out into the hallway, not knowing where she was going. She found herself in the living room, sitting on the couch with her back straight, her legs together, her hands on her knees, like at a job interview. The moment she realized that she was frozen in that rigid, ridiculous position, she slumped back against the sofa. The living room was a mess from the night before: newspapers on the floor, games left unfinished, videos and DVDs scattered around, the battlefield after the surrender and after the children had agreed to go to bed. She felt like she was suffocating, but she wasn't upset. Well, maybe she was. She wanted to talk to Viberti. Tell him over the phone? No. Wait until the next day? No. She pictured them at the café. Announcing that they should no longer see each other in the same café where he had confessed to being in love was pointlessly cruel. Among other things, she wasn't sure he would agree not to see her anymore. He might insist. Was she hoping he would insist?

She called him. He was at the hospital, she told him she had to see him at once. Right away, immediately. She couldn't go too far from home because the boy was sick, and it wasn't a complete lie, he'd been coughing for three days. Referring to Mattia continued to be a trump card with Viberti. She told him she had to go to pay the dentist and asked him to meet her halfway. Why it was so important to lie each time, she couldn't say.

The fact that Viberti agreed to all her conditions made her feel better. She went into the bedroom and instead of getting ready she slipped under the covers, dressed. She imagined what she would say to him, she imagined him nodding in silence. She couldn't make herself move from the bed until five minutes before they were supposed to meet.

Viberti's cheeks were red from the cold and he looked a little comical; who knows why he'd left the hospital in his white coat. He looked very anxious, he had a solemn, regretful air, as if he had some bad news for her. Seeing him, sad or cheerful, serene or gloomy, put Cecilia in a good mood. They retreated to a café; it was their destiny. Instead of telling him they shouldn't see each other anymore, she told him that she thought about him often and that maybe she was in love with him. He remained silent, waiting for the follow-up to those words (there was no follow-up), as if he hoped or feared that she had something more to say. But the admission, whether true or false, had drained her, the effort at sincerity or at imagination was exhausted. If their relationship had become a problem, she didn't have any solutions. After a while she realized that she was clutching his hand like a fifteen-year-old girl (the age Michela would be in two years), but she didn't loosen her grip. She confessed that she got up at night "to go and see if the children are breathing," and to make sure they were covered by their blankets. Now she was the one who was uncovered, but Viberti wasn't skillful enough to take advantage of it. He hadn't had a sister to argue with, a mother to try to control.

He didn't know how to exploit other people's moments of weakness. What relationship had he had with his mother? She imagined a cold, proud woman, who spoke little.

She asked him to tell her the story that his mother had told him, the one with the protagonist named Cecilia. And as he was speaking, an idea occurred to her. Keep the children apart from time to time. Now, for example, with the excuse of Mattia's cough. Now that Luca was away. Take Michela to her grandmother's. See how Mattia does without his sister around. Or take her to Silvia's. The girl would be fine at Silvia's. How to explain it? She didn't need to. Mattia's cough was justification enough. She was the doctor, everyone would believe her. She felt a sudden joy, the urge to give it a try, right away. Could it really work? Will it really work? she wondered.

Viberti finished telling the story and she told him she couldn't picture what kind of woman his mother was. "She's elegant," he said with a sweet, sad smile. Cecilia, however, understood him to say "She's arrogant" and without knowing exactly what he meant, sensed it was something that would require a lengthy explanation. She remained silent.

The boy proved to be a perfect accomplice. Leaving school, his eyes were feverish and he complained, "I'm tired." Cecilia placed her lips on his forehead and said he felt hot. She took him by the hand and walked off hoping that none of the mothers would stop her as they made their way through the small crowd of children and parents. As if they could read the sick intention in her eyes, the desire to separate the children, and might try to dissuade her.

She left Mattia at her mother's house and went to pick up Michela. She told her that her brother was sick and that he was going to sleep over at their grandmother's.

The girl nodded. "He was coughing this morning." She'd just left her piano lesson and was drumming on her knees, humming softly.

That's always the secret, Cecilia thought: children are like that, you have to present things as facts and they're not surprised.

"Do you want to hear how the new science teacher talks?"

"How?"

"And nooow take out your booooks and ooopen them to paaage six."

She said it was a family defect.

"A family defect? What does that mean?"

"Her sister is an Italian teacher and she speaks the same way."

"Yes, but you don't say family defect. You say speech defect. But it isn't, in this case. It must be an accent from somewhere. She speaks like that, you speak differently. It's not important."

Michela nodded.

"Try to imitate me."

"Huh?"

"Imitate the way I talk."

"You talk normally."

"You've never done an imitation of me."

Michela made faces, glowering, then wide-eyed and frightened, then cross again, then scared again.

Cecilia laughed. It was possible that the teacher came from a town not far from her father's birthplace, which in turn wouldn't be far from the town where the child who was starved to death had lived his brief life. And this, certainly, had upset her, though for a few days she hadn't admitted it to herself. Because it didn't actually mean anything. She sighed.

And later on, sighing, she told Silvia that she had left Mattia to sleep over at their mother's house.

"She insisted so much that I couldn't say no."

"Sure, I get it, when she acts like that she's unbearable," Silvia said, also somewhat distracted, also ready to be fooled by Cecilia's smokescreens.

"Listen, do you want me to bring Michela to sleep at my house for a night? I never offered, because I thought you might not like to be away from them, but if it might help you a little . . ."

It seemed like her mother and sister were reading her mind, in which case there were two possibilities: maybe they could read only part of her thoughts, her anxiety and fatigue, and sincerely wanted to help her; or maybe they could read everything, including her intention to separate the children, and would rather not oppose her.

At the start of her shift, at eight, she sent a text message to Viberti saying that she was at the hospital without a car and that she got off at midnight. The internist replied that he would be waiting for her outside the main gate. They went to the same area where they'd parked the last time and made love. Until she'd felt the urge to see him and sent the text message, she hadn't thought of him for almost twenty-four hours. If someone had said, "Tonight you're going to have sex with Viberti," she'd have replied, "It's more likely I'll go to the moon." As for the rest, it was just like the other times: she enjoyed it a lot and immediately afterward she was positive she would never do it again.

The next day, she asked Silvia to go and pick Michela up from volleyball at six and keep her for another night.

When her shift ended she stopped by her mother's to pick up Mattia and brought him back home. For a moment, as she opened the door, she pictured the dark, deserted interior of the house, the shadowy corridor that seemed cushioned with thick, soft felt padding. She turned on the lights in the hall and without taking off her coat walked into the kitchen, turned on the light, went into the living room and turned on the light, and went into the bedrooms and turned on the lights. She returned to the door and saw the boy standing in the doorway, watching her.

For the first time in three days Mattia asked where Michela was.

"Have you missed her?" Cecilia asked.

Mattia nodded, but as usual it wasn't clear what his true feelings were.

The house didn't seem to have missed them. Beds made, rooms neat, the kitchen clean and even the dishwasher emptied. Each time she came home after a short absence it occurred to her that maybe she should get out of that place, move like Luca had done, because the apartment would never forget their past life together.

The child, however, was happy to retrieve his playthings; he immediately started rummaging in a box, looking for a toy car. They would be able to enjoy an evening by themselves. It had taken two days of long-distance discussions and phone calls and car trips from one house to another and talking about contingency plans to create that opportunity and get to that moment, even if the moment didn't seem like anything special. Sitting at the table with Mattia, she wondered what she had hoped to achieve. He ate with his normal listless air, he had no more appetite than usual, he looked neither happier nor more unhappy. Despite Cecilia's attempts to entertain him, he went back with stubborn determination to the one topic that seemed to matter to him: going to school the next day, not missing another day. He had phoned a classmate from his grandmother's house to get the assignments from him.

They had studied simple sentences, subject and verb. "Like: the cow moos, the dog barks, the lion roars."

"Only animal sounds?"

"Mama!"

He couldn't stand her being silly.

"Not just animal sounds. For example: the plane flies, the thief steals, the father works."

"For example: the boy finishes what he has on his plate."

"No! That's not a simple sentence."

"The boy eats."

Finally he smiled, too, and took a forkful of pasta.

Then Cecilia told him that it was fine, if he felt like it he could go back to school the next day.

They watched television until ten, then Mattia got his schoolbag ready and went to bed. Cecilia took the cordless phone into her room, closed the door and phoned Silvia so she could talk to Michela.

The girl was already in bed. "She was sleepy, she was exhausted when she came from volleyball."

"Was she hurt that I hadn't called her?"

"No, I don't think so."

Cecilia said that when Mattia got sick, she always lost track. She assured her, however, that she would definitely bring Michela home the next day.

Silvia told her not to worry, she hadn't lost track, nothing awful had happened.

But something awful had happened, Cecilia thought, she'd made love with Viberti again. She knew it wasn't right, but she couldn't remember why.

She had never cheated on Luca, now she felt like she was cheating on the children. But cheating on the children was a weird idea. She fell asleep, not knowing what it meant.

Between late winter and early spring Michela's nights at her aunt's house became habitual, which perhaps only made her grandmother jealous. Cecilia remained alone with the boy more often, though he didn't seem to notice his sister's absence; he seemed to know that it was only one night every once in a while. He ate the way he'd become used to eating by then, enough not to worry his parents, without ever showing a particular appetite or any particular preference for one food or another. Eating was like doing homework. His teachers said he was polite, respectful, too proud to ask for help, and though he did only the bare minimum, it wasn't because he was lazy, but because he lacked the energy. They thought all he needed was encouragement. Encouragement to make it through, to become an adult who was distant and aloof and indifferent? Cecilia didn't agree and continued to try to cheer him up with her jokes, hoping he'd become a little more animated, more spirited, that he would learn to laugh or at least smile sometimes.

One day Silvia showed up in the ER, toward the end of the morning shift. Having a family member turn up at the hospital was one of Cecilia's recurring nightmares. She imagined it would happen like this, or something like it: She'd be examining a patient who had chest pain and a negative EKG; she would be asking if the pain was localized or radiating, like a pinch or like something pressing, if it stayed in one place or traveled up to the neck. She'd be concentrating on making her questions understood and concentrating on understanding the responses, when a colleague would come up and touch her arm: "Come with me, there's a patient in Room Two you have to see." "Right away," she'd say, perhaps irritated by the "you have to," and she'd ask the nurse to draw a blood sample to check the enzyme levels, still focused on the case in front of her. Beyond the door of Room Two, on the gurney, she would find Mattia unconscious or Michela crying or her mother with fear in her eyes. But mostly the boy, nine times out of ten it was the boy in the examining room. The malnourished boy, the boy who was starving to death while she wasn't paying attention. Lying there defenseless and gaping, like an open mouth. The food he was waiting for was her.

Silvia was fine though, she'd come to pick her up so they could go and get something to eat together.

"Did we make a date to do that?" She was afraid she'd forgotten.

But no, they hadn't planned on lunch. Silvia had come unexpectedly because until the last minute she didn't know if she really wanted to speak to her.

"Is there something wrong? Are you all right? Is Mama all right?"

Silvia patted her hand, told her not to get excited, everyone was all right.

"Do you need money?"

Silvia smiled slightly, shook her head. She wanted to talk to her about Michela, about something Michela had told her in confidence. But they should find a quiet place to sit.

"Does she have a boyfriend?"

"Is there someplace else where we can talk?"

It was only one fifteen, but Cecilia asked her colleagues if she could leave early; the waiting room was empty and there were no ambulances on the way.

When they were seated at the table behind the column, her sister told her that Michela had started crying one night. They were watching a two-part film about the life of Mother Teresa, "Awful," Silvia said, but they agreed that they would watch only a half hour of it, because a teacher had talked about it and Michela had found out that she was the only one in the class who hadn't seen the first part.

Cecilia snorted: "She's the one who always decides what we watch in the evening, Mattia and I, we can never have a say. Besides, I thought that problem at least . . ."

Silvia said: "If you're thinking about how for a while she wanted to become a saint, I don't think that has anything to do with it. She just wanted to see it so she could talk about it. It wasn't the film that made her cry."

It irritated her to no end when Silvia read her mind.

"Then why was she crying?"

Usually there was no need to insist in order to hear Michela's thoughts, even her most secret ones. But this time she'd covered her face with her hands and didn't want to talk, while Silvia stroked her hair and whispered not to worry. She'd started crying without warning; she wasn't anxious or upset, she hadn't been sad or troubled when they got home. At dinner they'd talked about school and Michela seemed like the same sunny child she always was.

Finally the girl calmed down, and said, "Mama can't stand me."

Cecilia looked down at the sandwich she hadn't yet touched, a slice of mortadella peeking out between the slices of bread like a patch of bare skin revealed by an undone button or a lowered zipper.

"Look, I'm not telling you this to make you feel bad," Silvia said. "I thought about it for two weeks and I couldn't figure out what to do."

Make her feel bad? But she didn't feel bad at all, and she was afraid that if she raised her eyes from the sandwich, her sister would realize it. Or maybe she did feel bad, but not in the way Silvia meant.

In any case, she looked up and saw that Silvia was feeling much worse. She took her hand, she seemed to be trembling, but maybe it was she who was trembling, her gaze wavered and she saw the table and the glass and the bottle of orangeade and the cup and teapot and the prosciutto sandwich and the mortadella sandwich waver, too. "I don't think you're telling me to make me feel bad. Not at all. Then what did she say?"

"She told me she knows you can't stand her, but she doesn't know what to say to make you happy."

Cecilia lowered her eyes again. She knew she should at least be moved at that point, and if she'd been able to fake emotion she would have. To put an end to the matter, to put an end to their lunch.

"Don't look like that, don't make me feel like a piece of shit."

"You did the right thing by telling me, really. But did she say anything about Mattia?"

"She said you're so worried about him you don't notice anything else. She repeated that she can sense it, she senses that she annoys you."

"But that's not true. You're with us a lot: Does it seem to you I treat her as if I'm annoyed with her?"

"No, in fact I told her: Mama always listens to you, and she likes listening to you, and the next day she tells me what you've talked about. But she was adamant."

"And what do you think? Aside from what you told Michela, do you think I only act like I'm annoyed and irritated with her?"

"It's true, though: she exasperates you."

"Yes, children are exasperating, that's nothing new."

"But no, I don't think you only act like that with her."

"Good. Because that's true. I don't only act exasperated and irritated. I'm pretty sure I let her know how much I love her."

"Don't get angry."

"I'm not angry."

They fell silent. Cecilia thought that maybe everything was settled, that they could talk about something else now. The two women at the neighboring table, doctors or clerical staff or relatives of patients—all presented less-risky topics of conversation. Instead Silvia resumed the discussion.

"Maybe, but . . ."

"But what?"

"That talk you had with me, when you thought she might be influencing Mattia in some way . . ."

"I was beside myself, I wasn't serious. You were right then when you told me to cut it out."

"Yes. But she might have overheard something."

"She heard what she says she heard, that I'm very concerned about Mattia. And it's true: I'm more concerned about Mattia than about her. I think she'll get by very well in life. I don't think she needs me as much."

"You're wrong. She's thirteen years old. She needs you very much."

"I know she's thirteen, if you didn't remind me, she would, she tells me all the time, she talks to me a lot and I talk to her, it's not like she's all by herself."

"Don't get angry."

"I'm not angry."

"I told you about it because she was really crying. I don't think she was putting it on to make an impression on me."

"She's a born actress."

"She wasn't acting. She said it was something she's felt for a long time. She didn't know how to make you like her. She used those very words: *I want her to like me.*"

Maybe the only way to end that discussion and get out of that café was to actually get angry. Start shouting, ask Silvia if she realized what she'd been through the past several years, tell her it was easy for her to talk, having no responsibilities, knowing there was always someone to cover for her. Get angry and be unfair. Say something obnoxious and apologize a moment later. Get up from the table and walk out of the café. Getting angry would make her feel better and afterward it would make her feel worse.

It was at this point in the discussion that the shy internist appeared from behind the column. Cecilia grasped at his arrival; in an act of desperation she invited him to sit with them, and when Viberti got up to go and order his usual plate of boiled vegetables she whispered to her sister that she'd forgotten she had arranged to meet her coworker, that she couldn't send him away, and that they could pick up their conversation later on. If she thought Silvia would get up and leave them alone she was sorely mistaken. Not only did she remain seated and start eating her sandwich and sipping her tea, but she began chatting amiably with the internist. Poor Viberti was more uncomfortable than usual and tried as hard as he could to get a polite, normal conversation going with Silvia. But it was impossible to speak normally with Silvia, the conversation veered off in all directions. *Like a cat on fire*, her father used to say (she suddenly remembered the summer when her father had made up that expression after reading in the newspaper that pyromaniacs were drenching stray cats with gasoline, setting them on fire, and tossing them into the woods so they would spread the flames as they dashed madly from one bush to another, crazed with pain). For a while she thought she could stay in her seat and observe the scene and maybe even eat the sandwich that she hadn't yet touched. Instead, she grew increasingly edgy, her chest felt tight and her stomach clamped, and after ten minutes the anger and pain made her leap up like a spring. Silvia had referred to her perennial boyfriend using the old name she'd stuck him with, Enrico Fermi, and among the many things about her sister that rubbed her the wrong way, her obsession with nicknames was particularly annoying. Partly because she was afraid it would rub off—when she called Viberti "the shy internist," for example. And when she was finally outside, her eyes filled with tears at the thought of her daughter crying and saying, "I want her to like me." Heels pounding the sidewalk as if to punish the pavement as she strode along, she reached the car, parked in the sun as usual, and too far away.

(An update on settings: the hospital has been largely decentralized, the oldest buildings demolished, my father's section no longer exists; the Emergency wing was torn down, set up elsewhere, razed, completely rebuilt; Cecilia's house was sold and divided into two smaller apartments; my father's house hasn't changed; their café is still there, and this is what amazes me the most, after all these years they've replaced the furnishings, naturally, but the column, the column is still standing, "like an ancient ruin," Silvia would have said.)

A few days later, all of a sudden, she found herself thinking about how hateful her sister could be. She thought of how she had protected Silvia when their father was ill. She'd made sure she didn't see him fall to pieces. She'd arranged her sister's visits so that he'd seem like a retired old general, rather than a cancer victim. At the hospital one night, her father had ripped out the IV drip; they'd found him half-naked in the hallway pushing a wheelchair, he no longer knew which ward he'd run away from, he was convinced he was at the supermarket. When he returned home he'd confided to her that he was afraid of seeing Silvia alone, and she advised him to always take a Xanax before seeing her. It was odd to discover that her father behaved like all other human beings, that he ran away, and cried, and felt hopeless because he was afraid of dying.

The day the boy returned to the hospital, he wasn't starving to death in an examining room in the ER, but was waiting for her in the outpatients' department in Pediatrics. It was Antonio Lorenzi who called her and, in a light, playful tone that Cecilia didn't care for, told her that her son had come to see her, with Luca, as a surprise.

"What happened?"

"Nothing serious, he had a little fainting spell at school, but he's fine."

She felt like she was going to die.

"Come on up and we'll tell you all about it," Lorenzi added.

Her heart was in her throat and her legs were unsteady and two flights of stairs were unthinkable in that state, so she got into an elevator with two male nurses pushing an empty gurney. The elevator started and then immediately jolted to a stop; the nurses tried pressing a few buttons at random but nothing happened, they were stuck.

"Are we stuck?" they asked each other. "Are we stuck?" they asked her, but she was too frightened to reply. "Well, what the heck's going on?" one of them asked. "I'm a little claustrophobic," the other man said, though he seemed very calm.

The first one leaned toward the control panel, sounded the alarm, spoke into the microphone alerting someone of the situation.

A voice crackled from the microphone: "I'll check."

"Nothing we can do but wait," the two men said, looking at her again.

Cecilia lowered her eyes to hide her panic.

"Are you claustrophobic, Doctor?" they asked her indifferently, with no hint of irony.

"No, thank you," she replied mechanically.

The two exchanged glances. Another crazy lady, they thought. Or: There's not one normal person in this place. They tried pressing the buttons some more and the elevator suddenly started moving again. When it stopped at the first floor, the doors opened and the two nurses got out without saying goodbye. "You see, it all worked out," one said to the other.

She stayed in the corner, leaning against the metal wall, stuck in place, because her legs refused to respond to her commands, and her commands were uncertain and confused.

Then the same voice as before crackled from the microphone: "So, tell me exactly what the problem is."

Cecilia leaped forward, got out of the elevator, and took the stairs.

The first person who came up to her was Luca and she took refuge in his arms, unable to speak. Luca kept repeating "Everything's okay," stroking her hair, and they stayed like that, holding tight to each other as they hadn't done in years. He told her that the child had fainted at school, that the teachers hadn't been able to reach her (her cell phone was dead), and the ER's number was always busy, so they called him.

They drew apart only when Lorenzi came out of the outpatients' ward and walked over to them and said to her, "You're white as a sheet, wait, you can't go in to see him like that," and he led them into the doctors' lounge. This time the shy internist wasn't there waiting for her.

Lorenzi made her sit down, meanwhile reassuring her, it was a simple fainting spell, no need to worry, everything seemed all right, they would do a CAT scan but it was clear that there was nothing. Then he said: "Hey, I hadn't seen him in two years, but I thought he was in great shape," and Cecilia was grateful to him, it was an acknowledgment of her as a mother, not a compliment from one doctor to another.

Luca said something but she wasn't listening. Lorenzi cited a similar case. She, too, thought of one. After ten minutes, without finishing a sentence, she said she felt better and they stood up to go to the ward.

Mattia was sitting on the gurney with his back to the door, his legs dangling and his head tilted back. He was looking up at a louvered window. Cecilia wondered how long he'd been in that position, how long he'd been looking at the window from that angle. He could see only the sky so there was nothing to look at as he sat there thinking his thoughts with the blue in his eyes.

"I'm okay, I want to go home," he said, shrugging off his mother's hug. He sounded like an angry teenager, complaining to his parents about not being allowed to go out at night.

She explained that it was best for him to spend a night in the hospital: it wasn't anything serious, but it was safer to remain under observation and have a little checkup the next day.

The boy shook his head and said he was fine, he wanted to go home right away.

"I'll sleep here with you, tomorrow morning I'll take you around the hospital and in the afternoon we'll go home, I promise."

"I can't stay here for a month, vacation is coming up soon and I have to go to summer camp."

"You won't be here for a month."

Finally, Luca and Lorenzi intervened, seeing perhaps how defenseless she was, that she lacked the strength to persuade or force him.

"You'll go to camp, I promise," Cecilia added at the end. She prayed the boy wouldn't start crying, though it was much more likely that she would be the one to burst into tears.

Later she returned to the ER to trade shifts so she could be free for a day. Then she phoned her mother to go to pick up Michela; she didn't want to ask Silvia because she'd noticed that she seemed tired lately, up nights working to meet a deadline. Nevertheless she called her, too, and asked her to stop by the house to pick up a pair of pajamas and a toothbrush for the boy. Silvia assured her that she would go get them a bit later.

Mattia wouldn't eat, but he was fine, he was lying on the bed looking out the window, still angry but now resigned to spending a night in the hospital. Being there with him in those circumstances was difficult; Cecilia felt she was annoying him, so she came up with things to do. She went to buy a small bottle of mineral water to put on the bedside table, a large sketchbook, and an Asterix comic book, and then went looking for a towel. She spoke with Lorenzi, she spoke with another pediatrician, she spoke with the head nurse and another nurse, each time she went back to see Mattia and told him what everyone was saying, that it was nothing, that the next day they would do a fun test with a huge doughnut that would go around his head, and draw a perfect map of his brain. Mattia nodded, but wouldn't talk. At some point, thankfully, he began reading *Asterix in Britain*.

Cecilia went to wait for Silvia in the hallway and sat down on one of the iron benches just outside the glass doors. She tried looking up at the sky to see what kind of thoughts the prolonged observation of that color in that exact shade could induce and concluded that they couldn't be too bad, the child was just sulking to express himself and she happened to be the closest person handy.

"What happened?" she asked him once they were alone.

"I don't know," he said.

"But where were you?"

"In class."

"And what were you doing?"

"Listening to the teacher; Miss Elisa told us she's going to India."

"Then what?"

"Then all I saw was black. When I opened my eyes I was lying on the floor and I saw faces all around me and the teacher said to stand back, that I needed air, but I was breathing okay."

"All you saw was black?"

"Yes."

"Was it awful?"

He thought a moment and then replied: "No, because I wasn't conscious of it."

"And then you were okay?"

"Yes, but the teacher insisted on calling Papa. I mean, first she called you and you didn't answer, and I told her again that I was okay, and she called Papa."

"My phone was dead," Cecilia said guiltily, as though confessing a terrible sin.

In front of the elevators two colleagues were talking with a tall, thin man who wasn't wearing a doctor's coat. Ever since the hospital administrator had been arrested, any man in a suit and tie who didn't look like a doctor or a patient was assumed to be a plainclothes revenue officer. She recognized one of the two, she'd taken a CPR course with him in which they simulated chest compression and ventilation with an Ambu bag on a life-size mannequin. The mannequin's name had been Ken, but she'd forgotten the name of that coworker. During the coffee break, he'd told her all about his daughter, who in the first five years of her life had been bitten by a dog, a rabbit, and a mouse (they lived in the country, and the little girl had walked into the dining room where the family was gathered, waving the index finger to which a small gray mouse was tenaciously clinging), had swallowed a coin and a battery from a Swatch (they discovered the battery before stitching up the dog bite, when they did a chest X-ray), drank a few gulps of dish detergent, was nearly drowned (pushed from a pier by a younger child), and had broken her arm flying off a swing. According to her colleague, some children couldn't help it, it was as if they were born without whatever gene urged caution, as if they lacked the innate ability to recognize danger. Now his daughter was sixteen and had learned to be careful. But they'd gone through five years of terror. (As her coworker said that, he was smiling, he wasn't terrified in the least, that wasn't *real* terror.) Five years of terror, Cecilia thought; maybe years of terror are never more than five, maybe there's a rule or a law that establishes the maximum number of consecutive years of terror. The small group broke up, and she went back to the boy, who in the meantime had fallen asleep. She returned to the hall and noticed that the sky was a warmer shade of blue, a color that would continue to fill her with positive thoughts, thoughts tinged with joy, in fact, like those dreams in which nothing happens yet you experience an intense feeling of happiness.

Silvia's silhouette appeared as she approached from down the corridor, walking along an imaginary diagonal line, veering to the left, then pushed back to the shady side of the hall by the light pouring through the windows. Cecilia didn't move and Silvia noticed her presence at the last minute, maybe because she didn't expect to find her sitting out there, maybe because she was preoccupied. She seemed preoccupied as she hugged Cecilia and asked for the latest update, distant and certainly less talkative than usual. Cecilia thought her sister must be upset, like she herself had been a few hours ago (like she still was); she thought Silvia, too, might be afraid that it was starting all over again, just when it seemed to be behind them. She didn't have an exclusive on terror.

Silvia hugged and kissed and cuddled Mattia, then pulled his pajamas out of her bag, first the top and then the bottoms, and laid them out on the bed next to him, shaping them into a full-length figure. Cecilia and the child watched her, not knowing what she was doing. When she realized it, she took the pajamas and folded them again, then handed them to Cecilia, saying, "Here you are." She seemed ill at ease. She began joking, saying that if you asked her, Mattia had pretended to faint because he was sick and tired of being in school. Suddenly she went back to being the boisterous sister, chatty as ever. She insisted on a detailed description of the fainting scene, and without letting Mattia finish, told them about how she'd passed out once in college. She had ended up stretched out in front of the lectern with professors all around her, as if she were the subject of an examination. The boy laughed.

When it was time to go, outside the room, Silvia asked if Cecilia had been frightened.

Cecilia said yes, very much so. "And you?"

Silvia didn't understand.

"I mean: Were you frightened, too?"

"Oh, yes, very much so, me, too."

"Did you have an argument with Mama?"

"Me? No, absolutely not."

"You seem strange."

"I haven't even talked to her."

"Do you think she's worried?"

"I'll stop by and see her, then I'll call you or send you a text. Do you want me to bring Michela to spend the night?"

"No, it doesn't matter."

They said goodbye.

Mattia had started reading the Asterix comic book again. She should find something to say to him, but she couldn't think of anything. Someone had put a sticker on the closet door. It was very high up, she couldn't read the inscription around the Madonna's face, Lourdes or Czestochowa, Fatima or Medjugorje. She took off her shoes and climbed onto the bed next to Mattia's, but before she got a chance to read the words she saw Silvia reappear in the doorway.

"I forgot something," Silvia said without asking what she was doing standing on the bed, and motioned for her to come outside.

They went back out to the hall.

"I didn't know if I should tell you, but then I decided to tell you because I'm afraid of complicating things for you."

"What is it?"

"That coworker of yours, the one you introduced me to that day . . ."

"Viberti?"

"Claudio Viberti, right. You know what a screwup I am, I . . ." She paused, not knowing how to continue.

"Did you say something to him about me?"

"About you? No, of course not. But we saw each other again and . . . I don't know how it happened. We saw each other two or three times."

Cecilia froze, her entire body felt icy cold.

"So?" she asked with a smile, though she didn't feel like smiling.

"We're not a couple, I don't think we'll ever be, I don't know what he wants but I'm very confused and . . ."

Cecilia shook her head, maybe too vigorously. "But you shouldn't worry about me, he's just a coworker, why should I be angry?"

"No, actually, I didn't think you'd be *angry*. I thought I might embarrass you, because I'm the usual screwup, and who knows what your coworker will think of me."

"He won't think badly of you, but I don't know him very well,

I'm not sure, right now I'm a little upset about this thing with Mattia."

Silvia nodded, maybe too vigorously. "Of course, I'm sorry, I mentioned it because I didn't want you to hear about it from him, or from someone else, and think I'm just being an idiot as usual."

Cecilia smiled, pretending to be understanding. "I'm certainly not going to judge you." She wasn't judging her, but she wished she'd disappear instantly, before the mask she was wearing crumbled. She told her not to worry.

Silvia muttered that it was destiny: "With you it's my destiny to always be the child; you will always be my big sister."

"Well, I certainly can't suddenly become your little sister."

Silvia forced a smile and finally left.

Viberti had gone to bed with her *sister*, he was attracted to her *sister*, he was falling in love or had already fallen in love with her *sister*. How could he *do it*, how could he even *think of doing it* before he did it? And how did he think he was going to *tell her about it* now? Show up at their table one day and announce the good news? "I started seeing Silvia, and well, she's not you, but at least she's in the family."

The ward was half empty, she'd managed to arrange for Mattia to have a room with two beds with the intention of sleeping there with him. He slept and she paced up and down the corridor, unable to find peace. She pretended to be talking on the phone whenever she glimpsed a silhouette behind the glass doors. They looked like murky ghosts, growing more and more distinct as they approached, until the door opened abruptly and someone appeared in the flesh and looked straight at her.

For an hour she kept the phone in her hand, holding it to her ear whenever a colleague or nurse passed by. Like a crazy woman. So she wouldn't have to make conversation. Cell phone to her ear, she thought Viberti must have wanted to get even, yet that was impossible because he wasn't a vindictive type, and so he must have *unconsciously* wanted to get even because she had frustrated him, keeping him tied to her while giving him almost nothing. She also thought that he was free to do whatever he wanted, that she had never asked him for an exclusive relationship and that given their situation she couldn't very well demand that he be faithful to her, the very word "faithful" made no sense, so what he did was his business.

But not with her sister! That much she could certainly ask, even demand, of him. Not with her sister and possibly not even with a coworker in the ER and possibly not even with anyone from any other department in the hospital. And she thought back to when Silvia had told her: the icy chill she'd felt was very different from feeling a tightness in her chest; at that moment her heart had turned into a vast, frozen arctic sea. At that moment she'd felt nothing, no pain or sorrow, no anger or resentment, not toward Viberti or toward Silvia or toward herself. She just wanted Silvia to go away, as if her reappearance in the doorway had been a mistake in the chronology that drags us all forward, as if by stitching together the moment she'd left the first time with the moment she'd left the second time, that ridiculous confession could be eliminated.

Why had she felt the need to tell her? Why hadn't she kept her mouth shut? Why was she always so childish and stupid?

An hour earlier, playing cards with Mattia, making all the wrong moves while the boy protested, thinking she was letting him win, she'd begun to doubt whether her sister had actually confessed to sleeping with Viberti. She hadn't said that, she hadn't said they'd *fucked*, maybe they went out a couple of times, maybe they'd kissed in the car. But Silvia would never have been so hysterical over a kiss, if it had been only a kiss she probably wouldn't have felt compelled to confess anything, so it had to be a really shameful thing, that's the only way it made sense.

At that point she was no longer so sure she didn't feel anything:

certainly she felt incredulity and confusion, she'd thought she knew the internist quite well and it turned out she didn't know him at all (she'd never again be able to call him "shy"!), she'd deceived herself and deceived him, she didn't know what she wanted, or she was even less sure of it than before. Even the anger she felt pacing up and down the hall, even there she wasn't sure with whom she was angry: Viberti, Silvia, herself. But she was sure she felt angry, now. So sure that she was afraid it showed and that pretending to talk on her cell phone wasn't enough to hide it.

To take cover she went back to the child. The room was in shadow, no one had lowered the blinds, they thought she'd do it. The cars on the avenue in the summer twilight already had their lights on. Some drove around the traffic circle and continued on, others crossed the bridge and disappeared, followed by a train of double red taillights, into the tree-lined area where she and Viberti had sought seclusion the first time, as if hiding in the woods. She was very angry, but also very sad. The whole thing was unbearably sad. But not meaningless, not pointless.

The point was that she had to atone for her wrong in any case. Whatever she'd done, it was wrong and she had to pay for it. The point was that the atonement was ongoing, a lesser purgatory of minor, vindictive retributions such as Mattia's fainting, and deceitful, grotesque punishments such as Viberti's betrayal, which technically wasn't even a betrayal. Mattia was fine, but it was a reminder that it could have been worse; Viberti had cheated on her and she didn't even have the right to get angry. Of all the women in the world, her sister. If she hadn't brought Silvia to their table, they wouldn't have even met. Ridiculous and very sad. She didn't want to be part of that sad, sad story. The story wasn't supposed to end that way. The chapter of the story that had begun. Maybe it had to end somehow, but not like that.

For the first time since Silvia left she was tempted to call Viberti. Telling Silvia everything wasn't possible, talking to him was. She lowered the blinds. She lay down on the bed without even taking off her white coat. Mattia was sleeping all curled up. He was fine, that was the important thing. She would tell Viberti that she'd heard about it or had a feeling about it. It was hard to keep her composure, even just the thought of talking to him and asking "Is it true?" was upsetting. *How much* of it was true? *What* had actually happened? More than anything she felt like crying.

Only now did she feel like crying, lying across from Mattia, as she thought about it and imagined a conversation with Viberti. Maybe because for the first time she pictured Viberti in front of her, ready to listen. She imagined him as indifferent and maybe argumentative, and in the end hostile.

"Let's try to be adults, we didn't have a future, you and I, our relationship perhaps never even began, we kept seeing each other because we were afraid of being alone, so this somewhat abrupt, surprise ending is for the best, there's a part of you in your sister, and it's as if I'd courted you for two years to get to her, with her there's no need for courtship, let's say . . . not only because she's more decisive than you, more *uninhibited*, but because I've already moved on from that stage; and it's not like it's an ending for you, either, it's a beginning—you can devote yourself to your children, and in time you will certainly find someone and fall in love, probably with a man who's different from me, he won't be so insecure and introverted, he'll be someone more like your husband, but different, better, less self-centered—was your husband self-centered? You'll find someone who isn't, your children will be grown and you'll no longer be afraid of betraying them, you'll make a new life for yourself. And you know what the best thing about it will be? That we'll keep seeing each other! Of course, because, after some initial tension, you and Silvia will patch things up and become close again, and given how much you care about Silvia, you'll care for me as well, and you'll forgive me for what happened."

A sarcastic, offensive, brash, long-winded Viberti. Effusive like Silvia. As if he'd been infected by sleeping with Silvia (he'd done it *for sure*) and now he, too, talked like a cat on fire.

But all in all this new internist was improbable, no, she didn't believe it, he couldn't have changed so radically in two weeks. A silent Viberti was a more likely Viberti. Speechless, mortified, ashamed, unable to justify himself. Faced with the more probable internist, she would have to be the one to speak.

"I'm trying to be an adult," she would say, "I'm trying to understand and not judge. But I don't understand, and even though I'm not judging you, I'm just asking myself: How was it possible? What got into you? Wasn't there something between us? Wouldn't it have been better to wait and clarify things with me? I know I have no right. I can't accuse you of anything, let alone of having behaved incorrectly, but I have to ask you: Wasn't there something between us?"

Mattia was breathing peacefully in his sleep, the faulty blinds projected bands of light onto the ceiling. Eyes open in the dark, Cecilia thought she should start off with that question, a compelling question: "Wasn't there something between us?" or better yet as a positive: "Was there something between us?" Any other questions would then follow naturally. Why my sister? Do you hate me that much? What did I do to you? Were you trying to get even? Did you think I didn't love you? And if I told you that I love you, now, what would you do?

What would Viberti do if she told him she loved him? Probably nothing. Like when she *had* told him, a few months ago, in the café beside the river. Better to speak to him by phone, better to just ask, "Has there been something between us, these past two years?" And hear what he had to say. His version. Unless he remained silent, overcome by shame. The coward, the hopeless incompetent.

———

The next day, when Luca came to relieve her, they stood talking in the doctors' lounge and she told him the result of the tests they'd done that morning, going on at length with various reassuring details. For once things were looking good and it wasn't enough to say "everything is fine." She exaggerated to store up a little good news, provisions in case things got worse.

Suddenly Luca stopped her and said: "There's something I have to confess, I thought about it yesterday, but I'd had it on my mind for who knows how long . . . our son scares me. Not always, I'm not saying I'm *always* afraid to be with him, or that the thought of being with him scares me, but sometimes, when we're together, I'm afraid of what he thinks of me and of what he could do."

Cecilia smiled. "What could he do?"

Returning the smile, to lessen the absurdity or the sting of what he was about to say, Luca said: "Don't you think that some-day, maybe when he's grown, when he's old, he might decide to make me pay for it?"

Encouraged by his smile, determined not to take him seriously, she said: "No, I don't think that. Make you pay for what?"

Luca went on smiling, no, he wasn't serious, just a little: "Okay, he won't make me pay for it, but still, I'm afraid of him, of what he thinks, of what he feels . . ."

"Me, too, he scares me, too," Cecilia said to comfort him.

Sharing that fear lifted her spirits. Driving home, she found that she could think about the matter of Silvia and Viberti more calmly, curiously examining her jealousy toward Silvia. She thought: I've never been jealous of her and I never thought I'd have reason to be, especially over Viberti. But she wasn't telling the truth.

True, she had never been jealous of Silvia as an adult and true, she had never felt jealous of her because of a man. The men Silvia liked usually got on her nerves. She had, however, been jealous of her sister when they were children. Being jealous of a sister was a predictable, commonplace thing, inevitable, infantile, and

self-centered. Overcoming that kind of feeling was part of becoming an adult.

Still, she remembered clearly, as if it were that very moment,
how she'd felt as a child when Silvia entered the room, screaming
and laughing, and a spark lit up her father's eyes. She remembered
the satisfaction of watching her mother scold her, whenever Silvia
was punished. But over time she had trained herself not to be jealous anymore, to feel important and more *grown-up* since she had
to protect her. She'd stopped feeling jealous of the special bond
that Silvia had with their father, she was sure of that, and Silvia's
constant bickering with their mother didn't concern her. Or else
she had learned to deceive herself almost entirely.

And she was sure she could never talk to her about it. She could
never call Silvia and tell her about her relationship with Viberti.
Never, ever. She had to try to resolve the matter with him. That
morning, while she was taking Mattia from the CT scan in Radiology to Pediatrics, she'd gotten three calls from the internist,
which she hadn't answered because she didn't feel ready yet. But
she had to talk to him and ask him what his intentions were, and
also ask him for a favor: not to ever say anything about them to
Silvia. The thought that Silvia might feel threatened by her terrified her.

After sleeping very little or not at all, she nearly fell asleep in
the shower, sitting with her legs drawn up and her forehead resting on her knees, the spray of water hitting the back of her neck.
She'd thought all night about Silvia and Viberti and ultimately
imagined them making love, imagining Viberti making love as he
had with her and imagining Silvia making love in a way that she,
Cecilia, had never been able to: imagining her more practiced and
more skilled, imagining Viberti rapt in ecstasy and overcome by
desire. Viberti, who maybe for a moment, as he was making love
with Silvia, had thought about how strange life was, to fall in love
with a woman and worship her for two years only to discover that

she was concealing a more delightful, more passionate version of herself (more *compact*).

So she wouldn't start thinking about it again, she got out of the shower and went into the kitchen to look for something to eat. There was a bowl of leftover rice salad, she lifted the plastic wrap and ate a few forkfuls standing in front of the open refrigerator, its chill encircling her. She caught herself picking out the tastiest toppings without eating the rice, a thing she always scolded the children for. She put the fork in the sink and took some water from the fridge; the frosty bottle reminded her of one of her first deaths, one that had the uncanny ability to summarize them all, because afterward she'd learned to forget them. She could take her time, but if she stopped she wasn't sure she'd be able to get moving again. So she hung the robe in the bathroom, walked down the hall naked and, seeing herself in the full-length mirror in the bedroom, felt a sharp pang of desire for Viberti, the bastard.

In Pediatrics, Lorenzi told her that the internist had stopped by during the lunch break to see the boy.

Cecilia hadn't imagined he would show up in the ward without being asked, as if he now considered himself part of the family, as if he weren't at all concerned about her reaction—or more likely didn't yet know she knew—and thought he could act as if nothing had happened, believed he could put on an act in front of her when she knew him so well. He'd come by, but Lorenzi didn't know what he'd done. He must have spoken with Luca. And with the child, of course. What had the boy said to him, had he recognized him, had he remembered him? She pictured the internist's pleasure, but she no longer felt the tenderness that her son's friendship with that solitary, childless man had once aroused in her. At least trying to imagine him with the child kept her from imagining him with Silvia.

Once they left the hospital, the boy cheerful and in good health, and got to his grandmother's house, thinking was no longer an issue: Michela had two days' worth of stories saved up, and was eager and excited to see her brother again. In the car she'd started talking at breakneck speed; twice she used the expression "we were so worried," turning to look at Mattia, who sat quietly and contentedly in the backseat.

Cecilia cut her short: "Everything's fine, it happens, Mattia is growing." She was the doctor and people believed her, even when she spoke in clichés, indeed, when she spoke in clichés they believed her all the more because they *understood* what she was saying. Michela went on chattering, and to shut her up Cecilia announced that they would be allowed to eat in front of the TV to celebrate the homecoming.

At the end of the meal, however, when she got up from the couch to clean up, Michela followed her into the kitchen, shuffling along in the turtle slippers her aunt had given her. She began talking about a classmate who pestered her by acting like a jerk and about how relieved she was that school was almost over and she wouldn't have to see him for a few months.

"What does he do to pester you?"

"He gives me really ugly presents."

"Presents?"

"He gives me little toys from Kinder Surprise eggs, he gives me old stickers, you know, for those albums where you have to put together a scene with a few pictures, and sometimes he gives me sets that don't match, I don't stick them on anyway, but . . ."

"I don't think he's doing anything wrong."

"Because you've never seen him, he's an idiot."

"I'll tell you a secret, the best thing is to ignore him."

"But I do ignore him."

"How were things between you before he started acting that way, were you friends?"

"No, not friends, but he does so badly in school, he's terrible, he never studies, he says he doesn't have time because he has to work in his parents' store, so I felt sorry for him and a couple of times last year I went over his science and history lessons with him, and he got decent grades and was very happy."

"That's so nice, Michi, you never told me that. That's a lovely thing you did, helping him like that. So it's understandable that he's taken a liking to you, there's nothing wrong with that."

"But it's not my idea, it's the teacher who teams us up."

"Oh, yes, teamwork, I think it's a good idea."

Michela wasn't at all convinced and lingered in the kitchen to talk until Cecilia returned to the living room where Mattia was still watching *Harry Potter*.

Now she had to call Viberti, she couldn't put it off any longer, if she didn't call him she'd spend another sleepless night, though she might still spend a sleepless night even if she did call him, unless venting her anger allowed her to recover her peace of mind and get to sleep. She decided to mentally recap what she wanted to say to him and prepare a list of topics so she wouldn't sound like she was a raving lunatic. The only words that came to her, clear and conclusive, were "Was there something between us?" but she couldn't figure out when to say it. Beginning that way didn't seem possible, not for her, anyway. It would come up as they spoke. And maybe she could put it off, maybe she shouldn't impose on the half hour before the kids went to sleep. She could call Viberti after ten. She might find the cell phone turned off, though, she might not find anyone home. She stood up, torn by anxiety. She wanted to call him immediately and settle the matter. The children were stretched out in front of the TV, they wouldn't follow her.

She locked herself in the bedroom. She phoned Viberti. As soon as she heard his voice she felt like crying. She tried to stay calm and talked about the children in sober tones. Then, rather quickly, the phone call fell apart, nothing that was said made sense anymore, it was as if they were competing to see who was more unhappy. She started crying. The questions formulated themselves and were one single question that she managed to voice after several attempts: Had he slept with Silvia? The answers weren't answers, Viberti was in a panic, Cecilia sensed it and understood and in the end she was ashamed of having asked so insistently, as if that were the point. That wasn't the point, and she resurrected the only question that she remembered having prepared: "Was there something between us?" But she didn't want to punish him anymore, she just wanted to end the call. She didn't understand his stammered apologies, if they were apologies, she didn't understand anything anymore, she sobbed into the cell phone, crouched on the floor with her back against the bed, her head nearly under the nightstand so the children wouldn't hear her. She wanted the call to end immediately, she hung up and turned the phone off.

On her knees beside the bed, as if preparing to say her evening prayers, she buried her face in the pillow to wipe her tears and took a deep breath; before going back to the children she wanted to go to the bathroom and wash her face.

As soon as she opened the bedroom door, she saw Michela's shadow, standing in the dark hallway for who knows how long, sneaking around, eavesdropping, maybe alerted by her crying.

"What's wrong?" Cecilia asked, more frightened than irritated.

Michela didn't answer and Cecilia realized that she, too, was crying.

She took her in her arms and whispered, "What is it?"

She hugged her.

The girl was crying.

Cecilia took her into the bedroom, hoping that Mattia was still watching the movie, that he hadn't been affected by their grief; she closed the door, a watertight compartment preventing the deluge from flooding the whole house.

She led Michela to the bed. "Are you crying because of your

classmate who pesters you?" Her daughter was crying like a little girl, she was a little girl. They lay down on the bed, their backs against the raised cushions, Cecilia made her rest her head on her breast. She asked again, "What's wrong, Michi?"

Michela didn't answer right away, but after a while, when her mother was about to ask a second time if she was still upset because of that stupid kid who was infatuated with her, the girl spoke: "It's not my fault, I swear, it's not my fault."

"What's not your fault? What are you talking about?"

"If Mattia isn't well it's not my fault."

"But Mattia is fine."

"I heard you crying, I could hear that you were crying."

"Because I'm so worn out, and I had a scare, but the tests went well and Mattia is healthy as a horse. Do you believe me?"

Michela didn't answer.

"And I don't think it's your fault, it's not a matter of fault, it's no one's fault."

She went on comforting and reassuring her, losing track of time, hugging her daughter, who hugged her back, exhausted. She remembered a ridiculous phone call from Silvia, she couldn't say when, five or six years ago. Her friend Stefania had been in a panic because her cat had been diagnosed with feline hepatic lipidosis and was in danger of dying. The cat was obese and hadn't eaten in two days. "The cat is consuming himself," Silvia had screamed into the phone, "don't you see? He's devouring himself!" That was her sister. And she never told anyone to go to hell.

She must have closed her eyes at some point, because only when she sensed his presence beside the bed did she realize that Mattia was standing there.

He was watching them curiously. "The movie is over," he announced in his bored, solemn tone.

———

After the phone call she felt better, bruised but still intact, or rather, the more bruised she was, the more intact. She didn't see Viberti for almost two weeks.

Silvia brought him up only once, at the end of a long, complicated story about her work, saying it was a difficult time, that she was facing a lot of problems, not personal problems, though, because the situation she had mentioned to her had ended quickly and she wasn't sorry about it. Had she caused her any trouble?

"No, I already told you," Cecilia replied.

"Do you still see him?"

"Sure, every so often I run into him," she lied.

"And he hasn't said anything to you?"

"Of course not."

She was very composed. She didn't try to figure out where that composure was coming from.

She understood, however, ten days later, when she found Viberti waiting for her outside the ER. He had his usual beaten-dog look. He *was* a beaten dog. As usual (not to say that it meant anything important), seeing him raised her spirits. He didn't talk much, he didn't know what to say, and Cecilia took pleasure in his embarrassment and his silence. They talked about the boy, then they stopped at the window opposite the locker room and the internist told her about watching her through that window two years ago, on the day Mattia was discharged after his first hospitalization. What Viberti remembered about that scene (which she remembered vividly), the way he spoke about it, touched her deeply. Two years had passed; they seemed like twenty. Then the internist began a sad, confused confession, a kind of self-accusation like at a people's court, and she stopped him before he could scourge himself too severely, told him not to say anything more.

They began seeing each other at lunchtime again as if nothing had happened. They didn't mention Silvia, and they didn't talk about their future. For two weeks they ate together as they'd always done, enjoying each other's company, talking about the usual things, the hospital, Marta's condition, the children. The children were on vacation.

If she had the afternoon shift, Cecilia spent the morning in the house, which was still cool, lying on the bed in her bra and panties reading old Maigret and Poirot mysteries. Or she took out the folders with the children's drawings: serene cats and anxious dogs, scurrying clouds, graceful blades of grass endlessly repeated, hysterical suns and somewhat demented moons, cheerful redbrick cottages. Or she leafed through the books they'd looked at together for years, every night: books by Richard Scarry, with those tiny little creatures that filled the white pages, the big red double-decker elephant-bus with Big Ben in the background and the distracted bunny who crosses the street and is sent sprawling by the rhinoceros-taxi, while the bunnies on the sidewalk despair. Or she would start watching television: reruns of a popular cooking show from last season. She watched an hour-long episode in which professionals and amateurs discussed a thousand ways to prepare *carbonara*: bacon or pancetta, pecorino or Parmesan cheese, whole egg or just the yolk, toss in a pan or pour onto the plate. A few months ago she might have gotten restless, but now she watched it straight through, relaxed and serene.

If she had the morning shift, she left the hospital at two and walked to the pool, braving the sweltering heat in the shade of the chestnut trees, swam for an hour and a half, and then went to spend the evening at her mother's. They ate together in front of the open kitchen window, longing for a breath of air. Since the internist had confessed to watching the deserted courtyards for hours, not thinking about anything, she often moved a chair out to her mother's balcony and did the same thing. At home the interior windows looked out onto a dark shaft where there was nothing to see. Picturing Viberti in that melancholy pose, putting herself in his place, she no longer felt sad; instead, she felt like laughing and patting his ghost sitting next to her. Her mother sometimes caught her with a big smile on her face, and said it was nice to see her smile like that again. And she nodded, letting her believe she was thinking of Mattia, about the scares she'd had. But in fact, during that time she was learning not to think about her children as incessantly as she once used to. Not because they'd grown up; as if she had grown up.

She hardly ever saw Silvia. She was closeted at home, finishing up an assignment. Cecilia wasn't jealous of her anymore, if she ever had been. On the contrary, one day it occurred to her that her sister had helped her. And apart from everything else, she now had an excellent excuse to keep her relationship with Viberti a secret for a little while longer. Above all, it eased her mind about keeping it hidden from the children. All of those thoughts, which she considered as she lay diagonally across her bed, naked or in a bra and panties, were thoughts detached from reality, given that she and Viberti had become friends again, not lovers.

The day before going to pick up Mattia at summer camp, when she opened the locker in the dressing room she saw a white enve-lope fall to the floor. She opened it; it was a letter from Viberti. Could he have copied it from a novel? she wondered. She smiled, imagining the internist bent over the kitchen table writing her a love letter. She added a huge dictionary to the scene and thought that maybe she really was in love. She was even envious. How had he managed to write such a beautiful letter? He must have copied it. The fraud. Who did he think he was fooling. She would tell him so as soon as she saw him, and she wanted to see him right away.

She left the locker room and called him. When she heard his voice she knew that she would tell him everything that night. She walked unhurriedly beneath the trees along the avenue, looking for her car. The idea no longer made her anxious, telling the (now shy again) internist everything would be the easiest thing in the world.

(And this is her moment of perfect happiness, a moment that will never come again, in which she walks alone on a summer afternoon and feels lighthearted, like another woman. And even if it's paradoxical, because *it isn't her*, that's how I like to remember her.)

Before falling asleep in Viberti's arms, she thought she wouldn't be able to sleep. She thought she would keep waking up and would lie there with her eyes open, staring at the ceiling in that unfamiliar room. She imagined she would leave at five or six, at the crack of dawn, and get a couple of hours' sleep in her own bed. She would say goodbye to him with a kiss, while he still dozed, avoiding any morning-after conversation. But that daybreak fantasy did not materialize. She fell into a deep sleep and woke up only once during the night: the window had been left partly open. She got up, closed it completely, and went back to bed, wrapping the sheet around her. She still felt cold, it seemed the draft wasn't coming from the window that was now closed, but from the wardrobe without doors, impossible to close. Only then did she realize that Viberti wasn't moving, wasn't breathing or snoring, he was motionless as a mannequin, naked as a jaybird. She touched his arm lightly, still warm, he couldn't be dead. She smiled. She would tease that man for the rest of her life, and that would make her happy.

When she woke up the second time she thought it was very late, but it was only eight o'clock. Viberti was wearing an elegant blue bathrobe and was sitting beside the bed. He was looking at her the way one looks at a sleeping infant or a woman who has just given birth. She didn't want to be heartless, now that she was sure she really loved him. But you could read it so clearly in his face, the desire to be a father, to have a family, children, at least one child, and to make a woman a mother. And that would be a problem, but not a troubling one. They would talk about it quietly, on the balcony, she sitting in the wicker chair and he kneeling on the ground, like the night before, surrounded by those white wedding flowers.

"Why are you sitting there looking at me?"

"Because you're beautiful."

She burst out laughing. "I really doubt it, at this hour," she said, and covered her head with the sheet. "Why were you looking at me?" she asked again, looking for his shadow through the weave of the fabric.

"I brainwashed you."

"At most, you could wash out my stomach with a stomach pump."

But Viberti was dead serious as only he could be. He said that as a child he had watched a TV series that had really scared him. There was a man who entered houses at night, knelt at the foot of the beds as if saying his prayers, and stared at the people sleeping, telepathically planting the seed of a thought in their heads. Usually an evil thought.

"Like what?"

"Like thoughts that turned people into killers."

"Where were your parents, why did they let you watch those shows? This is at least the third show you've told me about that you saw as a child, that changed your life."

"Every so often my mother would sleep for days on end, I don't know what was wrong with her, but I pretty much did what I wanted. In fact, if I have a son I'll let him watch all the television he wants, I'm living proof that it doesn't do any harm."

"So then, living proof, what seed were you trying to plant in my brain?"

"The desire to be with me the next day, too."

She pulled the sheet off her head slowly, cautiously, and looked at him, serious.

"Did it work?" he asked, serious.

"Maybe."

Then he joined her under the sheet.

Where had that man learned to make love like that? It seemed unlikely that he had really spent the last ten years alone. And if it were true? What if she had aroused passion and skill? He knew where to touch her because he loved her: Could it be?

Afterward she said: "I didn't change my mind the day after, though. I was just confused." He nodded.

For the first time in months, maybe years, she felt she had done the right thing. The road to Mattia's summer camp was straight and monotonous, the landscape nondescript. Chandelier factories on one side, faucets and medical supplies on the other, kitchens on display, tiles, a chapel swallowed up by brambles, an abandoned farmhouse, and more bathrooms and sofas in genuine leather. The internist's half-empty apartment: after ten years he hadn't replaced the furniture that his former wife had taken with her, not even the doors to the wardrobe. Should she be worried? Were they signs of a repressed depression, ready to erupt? She didn't need that confirmation to know that Viberti was a melancholy type, she'd read it in his eyes the day they'd met and maybe that was one of the reasons she liked him. So she shouldn't be alarmed. And his mania for watching the courtyards for hours on end wasn't really troubling either. Nothing was troubling or serious or irredeemable. That morning everything seemed curable, there was a remedy for everything. She was melancholy, too, and such optimism frightened her, but it wasn't true optimism, she was far from knowing the genuine, blithe, vigorous optimism of the truly carefree. That morning she simply felt better because pessimism had loosened its grip a little. She would help him choose new furniture, they would play at setting up house together. Two armchairs for the living room, she knew where to buy them. A carpenter for the wardrobe doors, she would recommend one. A recommendation is always welcome.

The cell phone rang. It was Silvia. She hesitated before answering, not because she was driving, but because she was afraid her sister would be able to tell from her voice what had happened.

Silvia seemed to be in a hurry, she was breathless. "I need to talk to that coworker of yours, you know the one I told you about, I can't reach him on his cell phone. Or else he's not answering me, who knows," she said with a sarcastic little laugh. "He forgot something at my house and I want to give it back to him. I can't reach him, do you know if he's out of town by any chance?"

There was nothing wrong with Silvia and Viberti seeing each other, in fact, it was best if the matter ended as civilly as possible.

"Yes, I think he took his mother to the country or to the mountains, I'm not sure. You'll find him for sure on Monday."

They talked about the children and then hung up.

Soon afterward Cecilia came to an intersection, and leaving the provincial road, found herself lined up in a small caravan of parents headed, like her, to pick up their kids. The cars behind and in front of her were carrying fathers and mothers, in pairs or alone. Those who came alone weren't necessarily divorced. Or alone. They drove along, skirting the wooded hillsides that shaded the road, until they came to a colorful sign indicating the final turnoff for the camp. The shade became denser as they entered the woods and the road, now a dirt track, began to climb. After a few curves the rough terrain forced them to park. They would have to cover the last few hairpin turns on foot.

She recognized a mother she'd seen two weeks ago. She'd stayed away from her more or less intentionally. She was carrying an infant in a baby sling. She'd often thought of the woman in the days that followed, thinking she'd had no reason not to speak to her. So this time she went up to her immediately. The baby girl was a delight. She talked about the experience of being a parent for a second time after ten years; the baby hadn't let her and her husband get any sleep that night but now she was dozing blissfully. Cecilia had a clear recollection of that fatigue, what it meant not to sleep a wink because of a baby; she remembered having the urge to suffocate Michela to make her shut up. She hadn't *really* wanted to, she'd just understood how someone might be driven to it. The exhaustion was very different from that following a night spent in the ER. Mattia, on the other hand, had been an angel, he hadn't woken her even once during the night.

They emerged from the woods and came to the lodge, just below the top of the hill. The kids' bags were already waiting in the yard, but the children barely greeted them; they went on playing, their attention elsewhere, as if they were staying at camp for another two months. They'd made a whole bunch of projects, displayed on the porch in front of the main building: plaster casts of leaves, wooden slingshots, antistress balls filled with flour.

It took half an hour to get Mattia away from his remaining companions and persuade him to leave. After the first sharp bend on the way down he let her hug and kiss him and started talking.

He was proud that he hadn't been afraid during the night hike in the woods this time, not at all.

"Of course you're not afraid anymore, you're ten years old now," Cecilia said.

She waved to the infant's parents, who had picked up their other child and were driving off. She stopped next to the car to look for the keys and as she rummaged through the backpack she thought of Silvia, imagining what Viberti might have left there, and she felt a chill.

But it was only for an instant. She opened the door for the child, kissed him again, ignoring his protests, and said: "Now tell me everything from the beginning."

THE UNEXPECTED

Memory is a room that's jam-packed. Four years ago but it seems like ten, her niece's First Communion at Cecilia's house, her father dead for three months; she'd lost four pounds, her mother had quickly assumed the widow's role, in a sense she'd been a widow for years, and this should be probed and exposed, but no, it remains inevitably mysterious (how her father felt about her mother, how her mother felt about her father, what went on in bed, as long as they shared a bed, etc.). That day, the three women in the family, like fragments that will never again form a coherent whole, are making their first public appearance since the funeral, and it is Silvia's personal opinion that they should avoid seeming unnecessarily grief-stricken, the manifestation of extreme, prolonged sorrow is ridiculous, she pointed this out to her mother, who got offended and nearly started crying. She didn't press the issue, she stayed away from her mother so she wouldn't spoil the party for Cecilia. But what could spoil the party for her sister? With broad, resounding steps, Cecilia strides down the hallway between the kitchen and the living room carrying bowls of potato salad, tuna and prosciutto mousse, minicutlets, caprese salad, gnocchi alla romana, lasagna, enough food for a legion of relatives, looking like a person possessed, a person determined to get through it at all costs. Sometimes, often, her sister frightens her: she could run over anyone in her way.

So then, memory is a living room flooded with light and full of smiling faces, mouths all talking at once, and she and Cecilia and their mother, assisted by an occasional woman from Luca's family, see to the food, while Luca uncorks bottles of wine for the adults and pours sugary drinks into colorful plastic cups for the children. Her sister doesn't simply walk down the hallway, she *advances* with a quick, vibrant gait; her mother has one shoulder lower than the other as if she were trying to shrink and disappear, her head tilted like the pointer on a scale to indicate to everyone the weight of her grief, and she actually looks like a servant, a maid who doesn't want to be noticed. Silvia has survived her father's death and she feels like standing on a chair and saying to everyone with great dignity: "Your attention, please: I wanted to let you know that I'm here with you thanks to the good heart of my sister who fed me for four weeks, otherwise I would have starved to death. I came through it, though, and now I'm stronger."

She's not so sure that's true. For a few days now her hands have been trembling, maybe she has a degenerative disease. But who cares, she's the black sheep of the family. Unless even the likelihood of being thought the black sheep is exaggerated. For instance, she always did well in school. Let's just say she's not as perfect as Cecilia, period. On the other hand, who'd want to be as perfect as Cecilia?

Memory is all those eyes that don't see her, and if they do look at her, before really even seeing her they judge her through the lens of sincere compassion or distrust or indifference. Then all of a sudden a pair of eyes, Luca's eyes, stare at her in a way they never have before, and because they're looking for the black sheep in her, because they recognize her fragility and instability, and think they can find understanding and counsel, they lock on to hers for the first time in many years, maybe ever. Luca looks at her in that new, frightened way, and as she places a tray of minipizzas on the table, already half empty after the children rushed her in the hallway, he approaches and whispers, "I have to talk to you," and his eyes are those of a desperate man, a man who is asking for help and who can't be Luca. Eyes like that? They're not like him. So Silvia smiles incredulously. Asking her for help? It doesn't make sense. "I need to talk to someone."

The strangeness of that look: Luca hopes to be seen, but can't see her, he's a black-and-white image on the monitor of an intercom, sad, frightened, unsure of finding her home. Or he's Princess Leia: a very tiny hologram who launches his cry for help, and dissolves. Whenever her father rewatched all the *Star Wars* movies, which was at least once a year, Silvia was the one who kept him company in front of the television. She never had the heart to tell him she thought the story was trite if not downright dumb. Still, she identified quite a bit with the princess and years before had considered showing up for a film history exam with two large "cinnamon bun" coils on either side of her head, although her hair hadn't been quite long enough. She should be the one to launch messages of alarm and requests for help, but instead in this film it's Luke Skywalker, who seems elsewhere, yet is finally within reach; in another galaxy, but in the end a brother.

Memory is therefore a crowded room, a pair of eyes, a look, a feeling that something isn't right, that something has been derailed: Luca and Cecilia's life together was a silent, punctual train, pull the handle only in case of emergency, and things that seem like they would never emerge come to the surface, and the moment the tray is placed on the table, Silvia says, "Of course, whenever you want, but what's happened?"

"Later. Don't say anything to Cecilia." And he walks off. Silvia smiles, still incredulous. Then she thinks: He has someone else, he's going to leave Cecilia. And immediately afterward: Impossible. The look was her own fabrication, he wasn't desperate at all. She's desperate and she's projecting her desperation onto other people's eyes. Luca meant it as a joke: Save me, I can't take any more of this, the house full of people, the screaming, rowdy kids.

Meanwhile Cecilia advances down the hall and her mother slips among the relatives like a servant. The kids scream and chase one another through the rooms. Memory is also the genuine silent panic that grips her in the midst of their noisy, make-believe panic. Despite the occasional temptation to grab one of them and hug him, the temptation, for a few seconds, to be a mother. Michela still hasn't taken off her long white dress and is acting like a bride, even turning her back and tossing a bunch of flowers as if it were a bouquet, a surprising development since until recently she'd played the part of a novice on the eve of her vows.

Not just three forsaken women, in fact, but four. Michela has passed her rite of initiation and enters that caste, enters the family and enters mourning.

Other characters? No. The boy, for example, is absent, in the background as always, unseen. Everyone talks about how much he suffered over his grandfather's death (not caring about how much *she* suffered), but if he really had suffered, he didn't show it.

And Luca's look, for those ten seconds, a look from a black-and-white monitor, or from a futuristic hologram from the seventies.

Then there's another recollection, distinct from the other but contiguous, a scene that took place at another time, which memory continues to associate with Michela's First Communion. It's a different room, crowded with silent presences, Cecilia and Luca's bedroom with the metal stand where all the guests' coats are hung, neat and tidy and silent while their owners, standing in the living room, talk and laugh with a plate and a glass in their hands. And for Silvia, of course, better the company of the coats. (At a family celebration a few years ago, she stole a fifty-thousand-lira note from a coat.)

There's a girl with her, a relative of Luca's who followed her in there despite numerous futile attempts to shake her, and now she won't leave her alone. So instead of Luca asking to talk, recognizing that even a black sheep can be useful every now and then, there's this idiot who won't stop asking questions about her work and showers her with exclamations of infinite admiration. Difficult to admire her work, unless you've completely misunderstood it. Impossible to admire her.

Why does her mind continue to orbit around these two memories? The first might have some reasons to justify its gravitational pull: the intersection of past and present, the first party without her father, a herald of Luca's revelation, a sign of trouble in her sister's marriage (until then perfectly concealed), the end of the glorious era in which she was the black sheep of the family and the beginning of a period of dormancy or cryopreservation that shows no signs of ending. But the second memory, why does it keep coming back with such insistence? A parasitic memory, a rough draft of the first, from which the cloying taste of narcissism emanates; unjustified admiration is almost worse than unjustified disapproval. Only her father was entitled to admire her, only her mother was entitled to criticize her.

"You don't get along with Grandma," Michela suddenly says, as if confiding a great adult secret.

For some time, Michela has been sleeping at Silvia's place at least once a week. It started by accident, Mattia's flu compounded by Luca's absence compounded by the usual problems created by Cecilia's night shifts. It had been natural for Silvia to suggest that Michela stay with her. She was surprised at having suggested it so easily, almost joyfully. She's so used to living alone, proud and protective of the independence she's achieved. And she'd amply repaid her debts to her sister, even if she hadn't technically settled them. So she didn't suggest it because she feels indebted to her or because she feels lonely. Nor did she suggest it to usurp one of her mother's privileges (for years now she had declared a unilateral truce with her mother), though her mother made it known that she was jealous. She wanted to help Cecilia.

But then two things happened.

The first is that Cecilia started behaving strangely, as if she wanted to keep Michela away from home. And this worried Silvia, because the year before, she'd told her a confused story about Michela's alleged negative influence on Mattia's appetite. As long as it's just one night a week, she told herself, it was best to humor her sister's paranoia. She pictured Cecilia and the boy having supper, like two secret lovers, her adoring, him distant and apathetic.

The second is that having Michela at her house made her happier than she'd been in years, maybe happier than she'd ever been. As happy as she'd dreamed of being when she still believed that sooner or later she'd be happy. As she may have been for brief periods on vacation with her girlfriends—except then she would always get into some argument or feel terribly restless or bored to death, and would be even happier to get back home.

She likes Michela. She's always been the last adult to give in when confronted with the girl's exuberance, on vacation or during the holidays. She would put up with it for hours before finally admitting that Michela was capable of being almost unbearable at times. She thinks she's precocious, intelligent, and sensitive. Funny, outgoing. Too impulsive and generous to come up with complex strategies to annihilate her brother. Who, for that matter, is the type to annihilate himself.

Silvia is cooking; she thought Michela was finishing a literature assignment. "What did you say?" she asks, even though she understood her clearly.

"I noticed . . . that you don't get along with Grandma."

She searches for a suitable answer without raising her eyes from the minced onion she's sautéing in olive oil.

"We have very different personalities."

"Meaning?"

"Meaning . . . I don't know . . . you know how your grand-mother is . . . she's very orderly, her house is perfect, all neat and clean . . ."

Michela seems confused: "Your house is clean, too."

"I mean . . . you see what a mess there is in here, I don't care if something sits on the table for weeks, or if that stack of news-papers stays on the floor, or if the remote control is left between the couch cushions . . ."

"You're *messier*."

"Right, that's it."

"Did she yell at you a lot when you were little?"

"I'll say . . . yeah, she was strict."

"Mama is strict, too."

"Oh, no." She smiles. "You don't know what a strict mother is."

"Why, what did Grandma do to you?"

"I was always being punished."

"What did you do?"

"I told her lots of lies, I disobeyed."

"Why?"

"I was a little wild."

Michela smiles. "Even when you got older?"

"Especially then."

"You didn't tell her where you were going?"

"I didn't tell her *whom* I was going with."

"With boys?"

Silvia laughs. "You sure are curious!"

"Tell me, come on . . ."

"I was a little rebellious, but your grandmother was wrong, because she used to lock me in my room."

"She locked you in?!"

"Once she locked me out on the balcony!"

"Then what?"

"Your grandfather immediately came to let me back in. We both screamed and yelled and then we sat down at the table as if nothing had happened."

"And what did my mother say?"

"She stood up for me. But she had other things to do, she had to study, then she got married, you were born."

"Mama always has something else to do."

Silvia pauses, looks at her: "Don't say that. It's not true."

Michela blushes, lowers her eyes. She seems embarrassed.

And as if she hadn't said it, she starts talking about a friend who goes shopping with her grandmother and makes her buy her whatever she wants. "She takes advantage of her, you know?"

Convenient, changing the subject. Period, new paragraph, full of energy and hope, she's talking at the top of her lungs again, as if she has to be heard from across the street; she describes things as if they are happening for the first time in human history, as if her experiences were unique and unparalleled, and her friends one of a kind and exceptional; you can believe that only at that age. A few more years, and then the marks left by words and events fade more slowly each time, like bruises.

Later she thinks back to that time, and wonders how she could have missed the fact that the girl was asking her to do something. During those weeks Michela is always talking about her mother, even when she's talking about school, even when she's talking about her grandmother, especially when she talks about her brother. And since she's not very eager to do what the child is asking of her, for weeks she refuses to understand, smiling about her mood swings and childish chatter. Because Michela is almost always in high spirits, or at least lets her think so, and she falls for it, she *wants* to believe it.

After supper they usually watch the game show *Deal or No Deal*. The girl tells her: "I like coming to your house, Aunt Silvia,

because we watch *dumb* programs that Mama won't let me see."
One evening Michela says they absolutely have to watch at least half
an hour of a serialized drama about Mother Teresa of Calcutta.
She already missed the first part, if she doesn't see it tonight she's
in trouble, it's essential for a history and geography project. What
does Mother Teresa have to do with history and geography?

"Because it's set in India."

Silvia has never liked India. On top of that, she's now revising
the translation of a book on Hindu mythology that is incredibly
tedious. It's a gigantic tome in which gods with immoderate
appetites engage in interminable acts of sexual intercourse for
eons. Japanese elegance is a thousand times superior.

She tells Michela it's okay, as long as she's in bed by ten. They
finish eating and sit on the couch in front of the television. Right
away she thinks she's seen the actress playing Mother Teresa
before, though she can't remember where. She's a young actress
whom they've aged by adding some wrinkles here and there, or
else she's the older sister of a young actress whom she's seen in
another film. She takes her laptop and opens it up on her knees, and
does a Google search for the actress's name; she finds it, it's Olivia
Hussey, and she discovers or rediscovers that she played Mary in
Jesus of Nazareth (Jesus was really hot in that movie, with his hollow cheeks, prominent eyes, and oiled hair), and so, of course, the
choice has a certain logic, the veil suits her. But Hussey was also
in *Romeo and Juliet*, and this is less understandable; or is it?

She starts to tell Michela about her discovery, she turns and
sees that the girl is weeping silently, she hadn't noticed. She weeps
furtively, not making a sound, wiping her tears with a handker-
chief balled up in her hand. Silvia pretends she hasn't seen, she
turns back to the computer screen. What's wrong? What should
she do? The film seemed so insipid, she can't imagine that Mother
Teresa bent over a dying man could upset the girl.

Maybe, deep down, Michela still wants to become a saint.
Maybe she's just learned to hide her earlier mystical crises.

"Hey, is something wrong?"

Michela shakes her head.

"Is it upsetting you?"

She shrugs. "Of course not."

"Want me to turn it off?"

"Yes, it's so boring."

Silvia laughs, relieved, tells her she thought she was crying because of the film. Though actually it's much worse if she's crying for some other reason.

Michela thinks so, too; taking a pillow and pressing it to her face, she begins to sob, letting out everything she's been holding in until then.

Silvia hugs her. They stay on the couch until half past eleven.

At first there's an endless list of trivial events that seem totally unrelated. Not to Michela, who fits them together like Lego bricks.

In between there's a story about a slap Cecilia gave her a year ago, a scrupulous explanation of its dynamics and motivation, and the admission that she hadn't been nice to her brother, but she didn't mean anything by it. And the slap is the only thing Silvia remembers later on, because she didn't think Cecilia ever hit the children, and she can't imagine it.

Finally there's the shattering conclusion that her mother can't stand her, she can sense it, she knows she doesn't like her whereas she wants so much to make her happy.

Silvia reassures her, strokes her, holds her tight.

In the end the girl gives up, exhausted, even though her aunt's reassurances haven't convinced her. How could they? They don't even convince her aunt.

I wonder if I'm not giving too much importance to sofas, it seems I want everything to happen around them. Silvia's is definitely too big for the room it's in. Silvia salvaged it from the family of a friend who wanted to throw it out. It has enormous arms and perpetually sagging cushions that droop to one side; it's covered with a large Indian print cotton spread to hide the stains and cigarette burns on the Prussian-blue velvet upholstery. It's massive, but really only two can sit comfortably there; if you try to put a third person in the middle, after a while the unfortunate soul ends up being squashed by the two on either side, who slowly but inevitably cave in on him. When I think of Silvia, that's how I see her: a piece of furniture too big for the room that contains her.

As soon as Michela falls asleep, Silvia returns to the living room and carefully writes down her niece's words. What's wrong, what should she do? She's not eager to talk to her sister. She doesn't know if she has a choice.

She wants to be a good surrogate mother, and she can understand Cecilia, who surely wants to be a good mother. At one point, during the most difficult period of the divorce, Cecilia was afraid to go and talk to the teachers at school: afraid they might say that the boy was malnourished, neglected, tired, dirty. That the fault, glaringly obvious, was hers.

Anything, but don't act like a teacher. She lies down on the couch, lets her eyes trace the contours of the shadows on the ceiling. Michela arouses something more than simple tenderness in her. To start crying like that, out of the blue! To carry so much anguish inside, hold it in with clenched teeth, and then let it all out with someone she feels she can talk to. To have an inner life and feelings and not be satisfied with living in a state of dormancy.

Cecilia had been the one to tell her that their father was ill. She'd told her in person and without their mother present (whom she'd told the same way, without their father present). Cecilia, the family's protector and guardian. Healer as well, though not capable of miracles. Cecilia stopped by to see her the day of the diagnosis and told her: she said he could be treated, the recovery rates were high, that there was no reason to panic and think their father's case was terminal. Silvia felt like she was going to die, she couldn't breathe. Ceci gave her a sedative. Then she made her promise not to make a scene in front of their father. She promised, but the next day she went to see her parents and burst into tears. And told her mother to go to hell. She did everything she shouldn't have done. But wasn't that what everyone expected from her anyway, that she do what she wasn't supposed to do, what was better and more reasonable for her not to do?

She wept in front of her sister, wept in front of their father, told her mother to go to hell when she asked her to take it easy and not make things worse (on the other hand she, too, was crying, so what the hell did she expect). Their father got up and withdrew to his room; he'd spent the last ten years mediating, he'd just been diagnosed with intestinal cancer (his other daughter had diagnosed it; when she was little she'd been a wonderful child, always so serious), he didn't have the strength to intervene that night, he had a right to a little respite. Silvia and her mother suddenly found themselves alone, wept a little longer, in silence, each to herself, then Silvia got up and left her parents' house without another word. The next day her father called to comfort her; you'd think she was the one who had cancer, that she was the one who needed to be consoled. Her father repeated Cecilia's lies as if he believed them, maybe he did believe them, maybe they weren't lies, he didn't believe them but he was used to believing what he forced himself to believe and so in the end he believed it, yes, he believed it, he believed he would be cured.

At times of sinking self-esteem she feels like a cleaning lady venturing into other people's pages. If you're not familiar with the house, it's more difficult at first, you don't know where the dirt is hiding. Your presence shouldn't be evident. Anyone who comes across the perfect page, after you've cleaned it up, shouldn't be aware of your role, he should think the page was that way to begin with. Pages have a center, sentences a barycenter, they mustn't lean to one side or the other. You have to dust, straighten, shift, and put things in order. You have to know a lot of graphic marks to show where the corrections should be inserted—a pair of legs, raised arms, heads upright or inverted—and in more pressing cases make up new ones—crowned heads, hands with elephantiasis, the male reproductive organs. And to cancel a correction, the most beautiful mark of all: STET! But it's a dying art: in a few years she, too, like everyone else, will be editing electronically.

Alternately, when she's a little less depressed, she pictures herself as a loving mother entering her kids' room (she has to think of them as little kids and they have to be sweet, otherwise it doesn't work). Every toy they haven't put away, every notebook left open, facedown on the floor, every sock tossed in a corner. She has to think about their excited or inept or distracted acts, correct them, and smile. And feel a pang and love them despite the mess they manage to make.

But since in reality these writers and translators are neither children nor grandchildren, when she starts getting irritated she feels like slapping them. How dare they? What were they thinking? What makes them think that someone should come and straighten up for them? Do they think I'm their *servant*? She often talks to the author or translator as she works, addressing the computer screen as if it were HAL 9000's red eye, and tells them to go to hell. People with whom, in person, she has an excellent relationship.

She works alone, no one supervises her. If she doesn't supervise herself, she's lost. When she gets distracted and loses her focus and rhythm, she storms out slamming the door behind her and goes shopping. If she doesn't need to shop, she takes a walk around the block. She returns to her desk ten minutes later and quickly picks up the thread. But if she loses it again she's in serious trouble. She gets up, looks out the window: a lady with a dog is walking down the street. No obligations, a life that lets you take the dog out at eleven o'clock in the morning, immoral, it's immoral, it shouldn't be allowed, it disturbs those who are working, with or without a dog.

What's bothering her? She broods over the question for a few days and finally decides that she has no choice, she must talk to her sister about what her niece told her. It's a Monday in late May, she spends hours at the stupidest job in the world, she checks to see that she's made all the revisions, spelling the words out on the screen, tapping them out, as if she were knocking to find out who's behind them. In the evening she goes out with two of her best friends (the third is living in exile in Barcelona, unless in the end it turns out that they're the ones living in exile).

Her friend Carla has a boyfriend and a child, and that night she's wearing a very elegant black dress, with a stunning neckline. Silvia and Stefania, who live alone and are dressed any old way, notice it and tease her about it. They go to a bar, drink mojitos, and munch on two-day-old canapés, dried-up, shriveled little pizzas, and tasteless jumbo olives. They're well aware that the canapés are stale, and the fervor they put into chewing goes along with their excitement as they laugh and talk, interrupting one another, discussing the fate of their absent friend Francesca. Sometimes Silvia, Stefania, and Francesca discuss Carla's fate, and other times Silvia, Francesca, and Carla discuss Stefania's fate, so it is very likely that Stefania, Carla, and Francesca have discussed Silvia's fate. What on earth would they have to say about her for hours on end? She recalls many shameful things her friends have told her, but she isn't sure she remembers all the shameful things she's told them about herself. They laugh, but they're really not joking, because the questions that fascinate them are questions of life and death: a life they're afraid they won't live, a life that hasn't begun, a love life, a professional life. They fear the lack of strong, passionate feelings and exciting, long-lasting careers, or an excess of tenuous feelings and precarious careers. An absence of life that is fear of death; that is always there.

Silvia, who laughs and talks loudly and chews like the others, can't manage to forget Michela's weeping. They're thirty-two years old. All three are petite, with dark hair, brown eyes. They know they have a lot in common, but they would never admit they look alike. They laugh and talk very loudly and chew the stale canapés and drink three mojitos but pay for only two because they know the bartender. His name is Rumi, he's Australian, what kind of a name is Rumi? It sounds like a dog's name. Rumi, come! They laugh. They sink their molars into the plump olives and all that squirts out is sour liquid. They switch from mojitos to a white wine—*still*, please, Rumi, not *fizzy*—and from the shriveled little pizzas to hot pizzas that are much better. New faces provide material to fill any gaps in the conversation (look at how that one is dressed) and after an hour of talking about Francesca's fate there's not much left to talk about, or better yet, Francesca's fate has lost its distinctive features and coincides more and more with their own.

Silvia remembers when, a few years ago, she'd told them laughingly about Michela's so-called mystical crises. Then she regretted making fun of her with her friends, she felt like a piece of shit and had suddenly turned very serious. Now she doesn't know if she should tell them what Michela said to her. Still, she can't help it. Stefania is talking about how companies replace women on maternity leave with temp workers, how suspicious the system makes her, about what a jungle the labor market is, topics she can go on about forever. So when Silvia announces that she needs some advice, Carla displays what might be excessive enthusiasm.

They talk about Michela for an hour, and Silvia listens to them explain what she already knows: it's absolutely essential that she tell Cecilia what her daughter said. Not just for Michela's sake, not just for Cecilia. For her sake: she can't live with that anguish.

"Am I wrong to call it anguish?"

"Call it whatever you want, but go talk to her."

Then Carla has to get back to her son and leaves them, followed by a trail of desirous, hopeless stares. All that, the dress, for nothing, unless it's for when she gets back home. Silvia and Stefania find themselves alone; Stefi points out some people they met a few months ago, Silvia turns out to be in a bad mood and says she doesn't feel like saying hello to them, Stefi insists, Silvia unfairly says something terrible and uncalled-for to her (whether she'd like to entertain them by talking about temp workers), and Stefi gets up and stalks off. It all happens in a few seconds, no time to reflect and avoid it. On top of everything, the song that's playing just then is "In Between Days" by the Cure, which reminds her of Enrico Fermi and makes her sad. She dashes out, sends Stefania a text message that says: *sorry sorry sorry I'll call you tomorrow.*

When her father got sick, she imagined spending time with him, reading him novels by Philip K. Dick or Ursula K. Le Guin or any other science fiction writer with the middle initial K. She imagined the scene bathed in a sweet, melancholy light, her father immobilized in bed.

But during the months of chemotherapy, her father was no longer the same. He was no longer the same with her. He no longer felt like talking. He seemed to be eager to listen, but it was a ruse. She went to see him every two or three days, her mother always left them alone. Her explanation was that she "took advantage of it to go out," but in fact she used it as an excuse for not staying with them, so she wouldn't have to read her husband's love for his younger daughter in his eyes.

Her father made an effort to chat. His objective in any conversation had always been to avoid talking about himself. Usually he would adopt a diversionary tactic: he'd talk about colleagues, old friends, people he'd met, places he'd seen; he was able to recall entire books. Now he'd become a kind of gentle cop, a kindly but relentless interrogator. He never stopped asking questions and was never satisfied with easy answers.

The window was partly open and the smell of rain or the scent of spring drifted in from outside, the trees along the avenue had finally put out their first leaves, the light in the room took on the same shade of pale green. When she arrived she found him in an armchair, in the living room, a room where they never spoke in the past, it was too subject to her mother's supervision. The TV off, the closed book beside him—always the same novels in those months, *The Left Hand of Darkness* or *The Moon Is a Harsh Mistress* or *Ubik*, the bookmark always at the same point (which maybe wasn't the point, maybe the point was to pick up the book and open it when her mother appeared, to encourage her to disappear again).

It wasn't warm enough yet to have the window open, it wasn't open by accident, just as it was no accident that the armchair was farther away than usual from the couch, and it was no accident that her father's complexion was sallow and his breath unbearable. Cecilia had told her their father was afraid he smelled bad, that he stank of illness and therefore death; he didn't want to cause any discomfort or create unpleasant memories. Silvia sat on the couch, far away from him, looking out, saying, "The sunlight's so beautiful on the trees, the rain's so beautiful on the window panes." It was more beautiful—more incredible—however, to see her mother approach her father as she'd never done, at least not in front of their daughters, to help him up from the chair.

Every now and then she would have liked to take her father to the doctor, to the hospital, without her mother always in tow. She would have liked to spend time with her father, to have him confide in her. Any kind of confidence. She was a little jealous of Cecilia during those months. Her sister had never competed for their father's affection, but in recent years she'd had a formidable weapon: his health. Even before his illness, Cecilia knew things about their father, *intimate things*—cholesterol numbers, SED rate, prostate size—about which Silvia was in the dark. They had topics to discuss—diets, recommendations, dosages—which interested her father more and more as he got older. She saw it in his eyes, she saw it in their looks. The sight of Cecilia reassured him. For a time, when Cecilia had decided to get married, they had stopped speaking to each other. Too young, he'd said, not out loud; for a few months he kept muttering that maybe they could wait. Later he was the first to admit that he'd been wrong; besides, when grandchildren arrive, everything changes, of course. When he gives you a grandson, even the man who is fucking your daughter becomes likable.

When she starts thinking such awful, unfair things, she knows she's hit the rock bottom of her depression. She can't imagine herself being any more depressed than this. Usually her specialties are panic, anxiety, agitation, and worry. But when that odious depression comes over her, the only remedy is to shut herself in and work.

She counts the number of pages remaining in the tome of Hindu mythology. She seems to have spent a lifetime counting pages. Even in college she used to count the pages that remained. To count, she subtracts. She takes the last page, takes the page she's up to, subtracts. But it's not exact. There are pages with illustrations, pages only partially full, blank pages, pages crammed with footnotes that she can ignore because they're just bibliographical references that others will check. Then she comes up with an estimate of these phantom pages and deducts it from the result of the first subtraction. Over the years she's even extended the counting of pages to the books she reads in her spare time. Sometimes when she saw her father holding one of his hefty volumes of science fiction, she would ask him how many pages he still had left. He never had any idea, or rather he was always "more or less half-

way through" (her father was more or less halfway through everything, he was an unfinished man, though that wasn't his fault). In
her work she now comes across texts composed of different-sized
characters, she encounters tourist guides with text boxes and side-
bars that complicate the calculation, illustrations whose space she
must take into account. Counting the pages, guessing the final
number of printed pages: she loves doing that. The editors at the
publishing houses she works for admire her precision. She belongs
to a well-defined category that can immediately be identified: a
valuable employee who has moments of unreliability. Every now
and then she receives a phone call for apparently no reason and
only after a day or so does she realize that they were checking to
make sure the work was going along as it should.

She can't put it off any longer, so she goes to talk to Cecilia. Talking to Cecilia scares her. She gets to the ER entrance and her legs
refuse to go down the ramp, so she continues walking along the
sidewalk to the corner of the street. Then, very slowly, she manages to retrace her steps; she finds herself in front of the reception
desk and asks for her sister.

Cecilia reacts predictably, showering her with her anxiety; she
becomes rigid and digs in her heels, so that Silvia suddenly remembers an expression her father used to describe a certain stance
his older daughter displayed: "Tugging on the leash." Certainly it's
hardly the time or place to recall those words. Cecilia has to be
reassured: everyone is fine, nothing awful has happened, "I just
want to talk to you about Michela." Cecilia doesn't believe her,
but she realizes that she has no choice and leads her to a café
across from the hospital, where they can talk and actually hear each
other.

But when they are sitting face-to-face, they seem glued to their
chairs, she speaking as if someone were twisting her arm behind
her back, her sister gradually leaning farther and farther over the

table, like she's laying her head on the block to await the blade. Then Silvia starts trembling.

Cecilia notices it and now she's the one reassuring her, she squeezes her hand, strokes it. Talking is good for you, God is it ever good. Silvia tells her everything, and the more she tells her the better she feels, until she almost feels good. She's able to tell her everything! She even reminds Cecilia about the paranoid idea she had last summer. She's so pleased with herself that she feels hungry.

Then something unexpected happens: a coworker Cecilia had agreed to meet shows up and sits down to eat with them. A nondescript type, quiet, the kind of man who as a doctor infuriated her, one of those for whom your little bellyache is just a nuisance. But his arrival isn't a problem. She's said what she had to say. I'll finish my sandwich and go, she thinks. But it seems her sister is trying to encourage her to make conversation with this Claudio Viberti, she can sense it; soon Cecilia will utter the fateful phrase, "Silvia works in publishing."

But no, what comes out instead is a very old story, which she'd nearly forgotten, the awful diet she'd come up with in her last year of high school, a kind of self-flagellation. Much better than talking about her work, however, and as she talks about it she's almost happy, as if the earlier anguish had never been.

She recalls a Swiss philosopher's lecture she'd attended with Enrico Fermi. And it's just at that point that Cecilia leaps up and announces that she has to leave. What's wrong?

She doesn't have time to figure it out, her sister has already left the café. Even the nondescript Viberti seems surprised by the scene. They remain speechless. She let herself be fooled yet again. Cecilia is too shrewd for her. She let her think she wasn't angry, she assured her she wasn't mad at her. She seemed only mildly irritated with Michela. Instead, she was upset. She realized it the moment Cecilia grabbed her jacket, the way she put it on.

But the oddest thing is that the nondescript Viberti continues the conversation, as if her bizarre diet and the Swiss lecturer really interested him. Given the fact that it's a bunch of crap and not at all interesting, there must be something to it. He seems about to make a confession. Or a pass. Maybe this man interests her after all.

And as she writes the script and directs this film in her head, she describes the virtues of green tea to amuse the nondescript Viberti, and then the plot of a novel she read centuries ago, one of her father's books, though not exactly science fiction. She manages to get his e-mail address, with a promise to find the novel, and at that point, finally, the lunch can come to an end.

When a relationship ends badly people say it was *wrong* to begin with. They use phrases such as "the right man" and "the wrong man." She's the queen of correction, but her relationships are always wrong. The men are never the right ones. Correcting men and her relationships: impossible.

In the end, her one great love, Enrico Fermi, was also the man who came closest to becoming the right man. If nothing else, by accretion: they broke up and got back together six times. The earliest Enrico Fermi, age seventeen, is part of ancient history, he's become a myth, all the rancor softened into a mellifluous memory. The more recent Enrico Fermis are the worst from this standpoint, the wounds still raw and painful. As a gesture of love, or compassion, to salvage him or to salvage herself, to salvage the time they've spent together, when she speaks to someone about him she makes up alternative biographies: Enrico Fermi the archaeologist, Enrico Fermi the rare tea expert, Enrico Fermi part Japanese.

She thinks back every so often to a particular time. The last Enrico Fermi had lasted one year; they'd been back together for a couple of months and had hit their first bad patch and she told him that maybe it was best to forget it. She'd told him that just before he left to accompany a class on a school trip (a little shitty of her). Then he came back and started to tell her about the trip.

Enrico Fermi was a math teacher (he still is a math teacher). There was an awful kid in the group, not an idiot exactly, kind of a rowdy troublemaker, that's what they would have called him once, the kind who jumped up on his desk in class, took off his T-shirt and waved it around (though maybe in the end there actually was something off about him), spoke loudly and insulted him, yelled "Communist, worthless do-nothing" at him . . . Who knows why he'd targeted him for harassment. He chased him through the halls of the hotel, throwing sopping wet toilet paper at him. He shouted: "You stink." On the last day, Enrico Fermi's tormentor had poured half a can of Red Bull in his shoe, while they were eating lunch at a fast-food place.

"Oh my God, how did he do that?"

Sneaking under the table behind his back. From the beginning the kid had made fun of his blue Clarks, Communist shoes, his ankles, too thin, and his pants, too short. And he'd gone around all afternoon with a wet foot. Then the kids had wanted to go to a music megastore. The other teachers took refuge in the café, while he holed up in the jazz section because it was the only area in the store that was completely deserted and he knew no one would follow him. He took off his shoe. A glass wall separated him from the other departments, the music was at an acceptable level, everything was suffused with a sense of great peace, and suddenly he was certain that she was in that room, hidden among the shelves, waiting for him.

"I wasn't there, trust me."

But something of her was there. And he'd felt much better. Soon afterward, he realized that he was not alone.

"Because my spirit was hovering in the room."

No, there was a sales clerk. An elderly man, diminutive, a little hunchbacked, with thick glasses and a thatch of white hair. Bent over the shelves of CDs, he flipped through them with a swift flick of his fingers, like an obsessive-compulsive squirrel looking over its hoard of nuts. Now and then the clicking stopped and the clerk pulled out a case, studied it, put it back. Every so often he took a block of CDs from a plastic trolley and added them to the row. Aside from the clicking of the CDs knocking against one another and the whisper of the trolley's wheels, he made no other sound.

Enrico Fermi relaxed, looking at the CD covers. He was in no hurry to leave the jazz section, he knew that outside he would be plunged back into a nightmare of persecution. And he wanted to let his foot dry. Besides the sense of peace, besides the impression of being safe, he suspected that he had finally arrived in the foreign country where he naïvely thought he'd already landed three days ago, at Gatwick.

"Foreign country?"

"Far away from everything. It's the same sensation I get when I'm with you."

And that idea made her very, very happy. To be the foreign country where someone could take refuge and seek political asylum. The foreign country someone comes to after a long journey, to rebuild a life. Telling a woman with whom you've reconciled for the sixth time that she's like a foreign country, well, there was something inspired about it.

Enrico Fermi was silent for a while, then he resumed his story. He didn't know what had come over him, he had to talk with the clerk, as if the little man held some secret. So he made up a story about having to buy a gift to cheer up a sick friend. And the clerk didn't bat an eye; making recommendations was his job. He went straight to a shelf, chose a CD, and put it in his hand. With that one he couldn't go wrong, he said, because the heart and soul of jazz was in that recording. It was a concert at which five of the best musicians of all time had played, brought together that night—by chance for the one and only time, brought together despite the fact that they hated one another and barely spoke to one another, that they were quite drunk and more interested in following a boxing match on the radio, and that the saxophone player had hocked his instrument at a pawn shop to buy heroin and was forced to play with a plastic sax. The magic of the music came about by chance, and as it unfolded the players hadn't seemed to pay the slightest attention to it. Then, without another word, the clerk bowed slightly and went back to his work.

"It was Yoda. You met Yoda."

"Yoda?"

"The one from *Star Wars*, the tiny, wrinkled old wise man."

"I brought you a present."

Enrico Fermi pulled out the CD of that concert.

"I don't like jazz."

"It's just the thought. It was the only time I found myself alone. I thought of you."

"I see. Thank you."

Enrico Fermi could no longer recognize a good sign. The appearance of Yoda was a fantastic sign.

That time they'd made it through the bad patch. But instead of continuing to tell her Zen stories, or funny stories, or stories of any kind, instead of understanding how to win her, in time Enrico Fermi had begun acting like a teddy bear, like a stupid Ewok from the Forest Moon of Endor. When he was in trouble he tried to move her by telling her about his problems, as if other people didn't have any, until eventually she just felt pity for him. And anger, a lot of anger.

When she goes to look for Harry Kressing's *The Cook* in her parents' attic, with the idea of using it to reconnect with Viberti, she experiences the surefire, mysterious satisfaction that always accompanies the rediscovery of a book. It happens with books she has at home as well, books she's sure she owns, when she hasn't touched them for some time, as if they might have escaped, as if someone might have stolen them. They have no legs and no one is interested in them, so the joy she feels is all the more inexplicable.

As long as her books don't disappear, as long as her books continue to reappear, like spirits invoked on Walpurgis Night, nothing bad will happen to her.

She hasn't been in that attic since the summer four years ago, the year her father died. She'd had a duplicate key made. At one point she had so many duplicates (building key, apartment key, key to the attic, basement key, key to the garage) that she could no longer remember which key opened which door.

Before going down to her mother's place, she opens the big plastic bag she's brought with her. She takes out three ceramic items wrapped in yellowed tissue paper and slips them into the only open carton, on which her mother had written NONNA RE'S CHINA SET with a ballpoint pen, puncturing the cardboard in several places. The tape has been torn off haphazardly and is hanging down the side of the box, like a loose shoulder strap. She strips it off altogether and seals the cardboard flaps with a fresh piece.

She takes the book, goes down three flights of stairs, and stands in front of the door. She hesitates, then rings the bell. No sound filters from inside. Then a light step and the door opens. Surprised, her mother gives a little start and takes a small step back. She was expecting the visit, but seeing her younger daughter makes her anxious every time. The daughter, on the other hand, finds that her mother has aged, even though she saw her just a few days ago. This, too, is a customary reaction.

She says she stopped by the attic (unconcerned that her mother might wonder where she got the key), shows her the book, "It's for one of Cecilia's coworkers, one of Papa's books, see?" Her mother shakes her head slightly, perhaps unconsciously. Too much information, difficult to put it all together, and at the same time of almost zero interest. Why the attic? Why that book and not another one? Why one of Cecilia's coworkers? Silly questions about things that don't matter, Silvia will only disappoint her.

But the days when being disappointed infuriated her are gone for good, and gone forever are the days when being disappointed really irritated her, and perhaps the days when being disappointed made her feel bitter were on their way out as well. Now her younger daughter disappoints her and that's that. "Would you like to come in? I've just made coffee."

They settle in the kitchen, sitting on opposite sides of the table. "Are there still a lot of your father's books in the attic? I haven't been up there in a while." Probably no one has been up there since she was last there, four years ago. Her mother, maybe, is afraid of the attic.

"No, all that's left are the *Urania* volumes and some other paperbacks . . . but Papa loved this one, I remember."

"Why don't you take them all with you? Why leave them up there, collecting dust?"

She tells her she saw the carton with her grandmother's china.

"Oh, that's right, I'd forgotten I'd put it up there. Take it, you and Cecilia. It's not doing any good there."

Silvia sips the coffee. It's very good. She'd like to inherit her mother's coffeemaker, that's for sure.

She smiles. "I remember when Nonna Re didn't know what was what toward the end and was mean to you."

Her mother frowns at her. But then she, too, smiles, because it was so many years ago, because it's funny, and even though her mother-in-law could never stand her, what does it matter now.

"What was it she said to you?" Laughing, she mimics her grandmother's regional pronunciation: "'Get out of this house and leave my son alone.'"

"Poor thing, she was completely demented. If I reach ninety like she did, I'll get like that, too, you never know . . ."

"Or maybe she said: 'I don't like my son bringing home a woman like you.'"

Her mother snorts. "As it happened, I was one of the people she no longer recognized. The only thing left was hostility, and *that* she was finally able to express."

"Papa used to laugh . . ."

"I don't remember him laughing. It seems odd. He was afraid I'd be offended."

"Your mother didn't lose her mind, why should you?"

"My mother died at sixty-five, she didn't have time to lose her mind."

"If you do, you'll tell the whole truth then."

Her mother's expression doesn't change, as if she hasn't heard the remark. After a moment she gets up, takes the empty cups, puts them in the sink, and begins rinsing them.

Back at home, Silvia writes an e-mail to the nondescript Viberti. She tells him she found the book she'd mentioned to him, quickly reread it, and remembered the reasons why she was so enthusiastic about it: it's a fantastic story, both in that it's improbable and in that it's fabulous—the cook of the title transforms the members of the family he goes to work for into servants, the father into a butler, the mother into a maid, and the son into a cook, then he marries the daughter and lets them support him and serve him happily ever after. The plot isn't even the most important thing, it's not a mystery, so she's not spoiling anything by revealing how it ends. It's a book worth reading. And the ending is still surprising, *colossal*.

She includes her cell phone number as well. She thinks she's done everything appropriately, she's been kind and she's tossed out the bait.

Then she plunges back into the book on Hindu mythology, picking up from where Agni reenters Prajapati, who has just given birth to him, Prajapati lying empty and disjointed, Agni filling him and restoring him to life and vigor, re-creating his creator. And so on.

Occasionally, during the months when he was better, between one chemo treatment and another, her father arranged to see her at a nearby café. He would go out to buy a newspaper, he never ventured farther than the newsstand on the avenue. Silvia told him about a small publisher she'd begun working with, a publisher whose books were a little weird. Her father, amused, pretended to be concerned: weird *in what sense?* No, she replied, not obscene weird: strange weird, New Age weird. Like books about witches and shamans, or books on alternative medicine, prophecies, the Templars, or ethnic cookbooks. She didn't tell her father that she'd read about an herbal treatment for cancer in one of those books, and that when she told Cecilia about it, her sister had given her a withering look, muttering, "Oh, please, give me a break." She'd felt like an idiot.

During that period she was editing the translation of a book that taught you how to use mushrooms to drug yourself. More or less. It was serious stuff. Initiates who took part in the Eleusinian Mysteries ritual drank a potion in which a hallucinogenic mushroom was dissolved. The mushrooms had names like *Amanita muscaria* or *Psilocybe semilanceata*. For a short time she knew all about *Claviceps purpurea*. She could talk about it for hours, her father nodding quietly, pretending to be interested. The important thing was to talk about something *other*. Something other than what?

She took him back home. They sat in their usual places in the living room. Silvia waited for a question that would restart the conversation, but she knew that at some point her mother would appear and her father would start to get up, saying: "I'll just go lie down for a bit." She would try to help him, but he would rely on her mother, out of habit. Or else, to get rid of her, he would send her to look for an old *Urania* volume in the attic: Remember the story where Walt Disney was resurrected in the future? Or he would send her to buy batteries for the Walkman that he used to listen to hits from the sixties on cassettes given away by the newspaper: "If I Lose You Too," "The Boy from Gluck Street," "I Can't Stay with You Any Longer."

———

In the last October of the millennium, the tests revealed that the cancer had returned. Her father underwent a second operation. Opened and closed, said Cecilia, who when she spoke as a doctor did not resort to euphemisms. Though maybe opened and closed actually was a euphemism. You open and close a closet, because it seems like a good idea to straighten things up, but then you can't do it. You open a file and close it again, because in the end you don't feel like working. You open and close a kitchen cabinet, because you're not hungry anymore. You open and close your wallet and tell the salesclerk you'll come back later because you realize you don't have any money and maybe what you wanted to buy wasn't really so essential. You open your mouth to smile and close it again because as you get closer the face of a friend turns out to be that of a stranger. You open and close the buttons on your blouse because maybe you don't feel like having sex after all. You open and close the door of your parents' old apartment because you don't have the heart to go in and see your father dying, and you open and close the front door of the building and thank the heavens above that you're outside, in the open air, alive, even if it's snowing, even if you're crying.

Her father was rushed to the ER and hospitalized at the end of January and died the following morning, unconscious because Ceci had made them pump him full of morphine.

She wasn't able to say goodbye to him.

She had managed to argue with her mother even on the day of the funeral (she ordered her not to touch her father's things, her father's things didn't belong only to her). So much snow had fallen in the small cemetery at the foot of the mountains that getting to the grave site was impossible, an arctic coating of fresh ice covered the tombstones. On top of everything else, she got her period that night, a few days late (this often happened to her, but she'd still thought she might be pregnant, she'd thought Enrico Fermi's son might come to relieve his father). Her mother had moaned all the way, how awful to leave him in the columbarium with people who were strangers. "It's just until spring," Cecilia said, squeezing Silvia's hand tight, out of grief, or to keep from harshly telling their mother to shut up, or to keep her from doing the same. At a certain point Silvia asked her to let go because she was literally digging her nails into her skin. Later on, she thought about the incident with the nails to try to pinpoint the precise moment when her sister had started to fall apart.

When the nondescript Viberti calls her two days later, thanking her for her e-mail, she's not just surprised: she'd truly forgotten all about *The Cook* and Viberti himself. Surprised and at the same time mildly disappointed, because from the internist's tone it's clear that the phone call is a courtesy call and that he'll never come to pick up the book. In fact he says he'll think about it, *maybe*; he'll stop by, *maybe*.

But she's even more surprised and astounded an hour later, when the buzzer sounds and it's Viberti. He must be crazy. She doesn't even have time to change, she welcomes him in her battle fatigues. The most ridiculous thing is that despite having come all that way and making it upstairs and into her house, Viberti seems no more interested in the book or in making conversation or in anything else than he was on the phone shortly before. He doesn't seem interested in anything. He's wearing tennis clothes, is he on his way to play? Apparently not. He came all the way there on foot. He leaves right away, with the book about the cook under his arm.

Silvia follows him from the window as he moves away down the sidewalk. A weirdo, not that she considers herself normal. Not that weirdos don't interest her or that they frighten her, or that she doesn't want anything to do with them. She attracts weirdos like honey draws bees. She attracts them and drives them away, evidently, because this one fled quickly.

She slumps down on the couch. It's late by now, she no longer feels like going back to work. She stares at the dark TV screen and for half an hour lets her thoughts transport her through places in the distant past, populated by her own personal gallery of weirdos. First among them, Enrico Fermi. Or maybe not? Is it possible that Enrico Fermi wasn't at all a weirdo, but the most normal and conventional of men? His dream, after all, was to spend his evenings at home watching old DVDs.

Then the phone rings again and Viberti invites her to dinner. Something devastating is eating at that man, if he has to call her, drop in unexpectedly, then call her again before making up his mind to invite her out. The most hesitant dinner invitation in the history of dating (but maybe it isn't a date).

There are two possibilities, she thinks on her way to the restaurant where they've agreed to meet: He likes Cecilia and maybe doesn't know her as well as it seemed. Or he likes me. Why couldn't he like me?

She'd barely gotten a look at him, still, the nondescript Viberti's physical features are so nondescript as to trigger an inordinate acceleration of the natural oblivion with which the physical features of strangers usually meet in her mind. She's not sure she's interested—when she saw him the other day at the café she wasn't attracted to him, though maybe not repelled either. Since in her current condition of general lethargy almost no man attracts her instantly anymore, she wants to give him a second chance. There's an eighty percent certainty that the nondescript internist is interested in Cecilia, but she has to know if he interests her and how much, just in case it's the other twenty percent.

As soon as she sees him again, she decides no, he doesn't interest her much at all. In particular, the tennis outfit remains a mystery. It reminds her of the game she had as a child in which you constructed figures by combining the heads, torsos, legs, and feet of different people; you could create a bearded man with buxom breasts, the legs of a soccer player, and a ballet dancer's feet.

She tries to steer the conversation toward Cecilia, to see if she's the crucial reason the internist has come this far after all. But nothing doing, she can't get blood out of a stone, where blood is a revelation or a secret and the stone is Viberti, a rock that remains hard and impenetrable throughout dinner. This man eats sushi with pathetic suspicion, chewing each bite two hundred times. She'd like to take his hand and reassure him: "It won't hurt you, go on, eat, don't worry." To pass the time, she begins telling him the Japanese version of Enrico Fermi's life, and maybe Viberti believes it.

She's asked herself many times what it is that compels her to fictionalize her relationship with Enrico Fermi that way. It's a story in which there are no mother-of-all scenes, and even though she has problems with the concept of maternity, she likes climactic showdowns. The story with Enrico Fermi, at least in its latest versions, seems to be composed of nothing. When she thinks back, when she thinks about the time she spent with him, the first thing that comes to mind is the question: "What were we doing all that time?" What they did resurfaces in bits and pieces, darting, fish-like memories, intact and glistening, too wily to swallow the bait, only dynamite can catch them and in catching disintegrates them. The dynamite is the thought of having thrown away the best years of her life.

More than anything else, the nondescript Viberti appears to be very tired. Doctors are often very tired. On top of it, they tire easily of people. And at a certain point, while talking about dead fathers, Viberti seems to shut down completely. So she says they'd better go, she doesn't want to stay up late. She gets up, goes to the ladies' room: let him take care of paying.

Leaving the restaurant, she finds him giggling alone out on the sidewalk and the evening takes an unexpected turn. Maybe it's the hot sake, but Viberti has become less nondescript and more simpatico. Maybe even tipsy. His shoelace is untied, and even though he's been on his knees for ten minutes, he says, he can't manage to retie the knot. Shoelaces, he says, have it in for him. So

Silvia kneels down and quickly ties it for him. But the end of the lace is much longer than the one on the other shoe. "Your knot," Viberti says, "looks like an overcooked Japanese noodle."

"Don't you dare talk about my knots that way," she says, giggling. What's stopping her from taking him home with her? What's stopping her from introducing him to the tea ceremony?

All the way back they mimic the faces of the people they pass and then burst out laughing. By the time they reach the door to the building, they don't seem anything like the two serious, sedate, rather glum individuals who ate at the counter at the Japanese restaurant.

And as usual, once the tea ceremony starts, it's as if, in her head, Silvia had been aiming for that ending from the beginning of the evening. Even if it's just a fuck, everything is weighted with meaning, afterward. And while that meaning should be examined and revealed, instead it remains inevitably mysterious.

This is the part that for me is really hard to explain: not so much the impact of the change of heart, but its unexpectedness. Until a moment ago Silvia had been fed up, bored, and not at all intrigued by Viberti. Then all she has to do is come out of the restaurant and find him a little tipsy, and she feels a sudden tenderness which is a kind of fraternal kinship, a destiny they have in common the moment the reserved, controlled internist loses his reserve and control and starts acting like an idiot.

All told, they act like idiots together three times.

Ten days later Silvia is having dinner at Carla's house, Stefania is there, too. Carla has an eleven-month-old son, the *spitting image* of her. Now, certainly children may resemble their parents, but they shouldn't be perfect miniatures. Clone wars? No. At the same time, looking at these two human beings who are like two peas in a pod, seeing how happy they are, you wonder if that's the secret: replicate yourself instead of trying to be pointlessly original. Silvia wonders about it, though obviously being identical to her mother would be impossible, because her mother is one of a kind.

The nondescript Viberti sent her a text message a few days ago, making up an unmistakable excuse not to see her anymore, and she felt an unmistakable relief. Her disappointment over this heralded ending is a relative disappointment—an annoyance more than anything else; she'd like to have the guts to see the men who show up in her life only once. Instead, she seems to have to verify two, three, or even four times what she already knew the first time, namely, that they don't interest her. It must be a form of premature senility, a kind of deafness toward feelings or dementia of attraction that makes her keep asking life, "What? What? Can you repeat that?" even though she's heard the answer clearly. In particular, there's the exasperation that all this is becoming a habit, virtually the rule; men she couldn't care less about approach her, she doesn't discourage them because she doesn't want to be alone, she goes to bed with them because she sees no immediate reason not to, and she watches them disappear over the horizon with no regrets.

Carla's baby loves to eat. When mealtime comes, he begins moving his hands frantically, as if he were turning two faucets, opening the flow of dinner. His eyes are wide, shining. He quivers with joy. Carla plays a game with him: she brings the spoon to his lips, pretends she's about to put it in his mouth, and abruptly takes it away. It seems sadistic, but the baby laughs like crazy. Then he gets a mouthful as a reward. And again Carla pretends to take the food out of his mouth. The baby's father says: "Can you believe it? At eleven months he knows what irony is." The three women send him off to set the table.

An hour later, sprawled on the couch, Stefania starts telling a story: an elderly aunt of hers died and her cousin, an only child, had to empty his mother's house; he took whatever furniture was worth taking and tried to sell the rest—nobody wanted it; he tried to give it away—nobody wanted it; he called a junk hauling service—they said they'd do it but that they didn't pick up items larger than three by three feet; the cousin went and bought a saw—he spent two weekends sawing his mother's furniture up into pieces.

At this point Carla pretends to shoot herself in the mouth.

Stefania is offended.

Silvia laughs, then she doesn't feel like laughing anymore. She feels a tug at her heart. An image of the nondescript Viberti, at her door the first night, comes to mind. She'd asked him if he wanted to come up and he nodded with a kind of resignation, though he immediately started giggling again.

When it's time to leave, Carla squeezes her arm and whispers: "Was there something you wanted to tell us tonight?"

"No, why?"

"Your mind was elsewhere. Are you still worried about Michela?"

Silvia shakes her head. "You have a beautiful baby."

Carla smiles.

On Monday, Cecilia calls to tell her that Mattia fainted at school and was admitted to the hospital. He's all right but they're keeping him overnight for observation, could she stop by their house and pick up some pajamas and bring them to her? So she finds herself alone in her sister's deserted house, and after getting the boy's pajamas from a drawer, invents excuses to linger a little longer, even she doesn't know why. Or maybe she does know: she hasn't seen Cecilia since before the tea ceremony and she'll have to pretend nothing's wrong, she'll be ill at ease and will have to hide it. Not that her sister will necessarily be angry; if she knew about her and Viberti she'd probably start laughing, because that's Silvia's fate, she's destined to make a fool of herself in front of the tragic, severe paragon Cecilia represents.

She checks to see if there's laundry to be hung or if the dishwasher needs emptying or if the beds have to be made. She paces the corridor with slow steps. She sits on the couch in the living room. She's never envied Cecilia's big house, the nicer neighborhood. Now maybe she does. She doesn't feel like living alone anymore. How nice to have a house like that, how nice to see that disorder, so different from her disorder as a woman alone. Could she ask Cecilia to go and live with them? No. There's no room, in every sense of the word: physically, mentally. She could suggest they get a bigger house, all together. Women used to do that. Old spinster aunts who kept each other company. In fact, she and Stefania have jokingly read that fate in their future more than once, as if by saying the possibility aloud they might exorcise it.

Without realizing it, as she sits there daydreaming with a blank stare, she's been twisting Mattia's pajamas in her hands, getting them all crumpled. She puts them in her backpack and hurries to the hospital.

When her father died, Silvia shut herself up in the house, lying on the couch for hours looking at the same patch of blank ceiling, listening to the same song over and over ("Risingson" by Massive Attack). She could no longer eat, each mouthful was always too big and too bitter, she had to have lukewarm or cold liquids that would easily slide down her esophagus. Cecilia came to her rescue, cooking broths and thin soups, providing her with yogurt, and occasionally buying raw fish at a nearby Japanese restaurant—an extravagance, but it was the only solid food that Silvia claimed she was able to swallow.

She spent her days spinning elaborate fantasies. Before dying, her father calls for her and asks her to deliver an envelope to someone. An envelope, a package, a small red velvet pouch. It contains a letter, a book, or Nonna Re's engagement ring. The person is unknown, the address unfamiliar. A woman opens the door, the same age as her father, though she looks at least ten years younger. Behind her, a room full of books. Silvia doesn't have to introduce herself, the woman was expecting her. They smile. She'd recognize that woman's eyes anywhere. Because they recognize her, thanks to her father's stories.

"I was sure you existed."

"May I call you Silvia?"

Cecilia urged Silvia to look ahead. It was practically the same advice she'd given their father after the first operation, and considering how it had all ended up, it wasn't a piece of advice that Silvia took well. Look ahead? Where? At what? But Cecilia was the last person she could afford to be angry with, since without her she would die of starvation.

Then her appetite returned, moderately, though little by little the shopping money petered out and there were no freelance assignments in sight; she had also run out of excuses for missed deadlines. Between February and March she reached a record low in productivity: she couldn't manage to edit more than one sentence a day. She ate at Cecilia's one evening a week, occasionally she skipped dinner, and in general she scrimped to the bone, the last of the money her father had secretly given her was almost all used up. She was so used to turning to him in her times of need, she was so sure she wasn't in any danger, that she never checked to see what she had in the bank. They called her at home to tell her she was overdrawn. She couldn't give up the rent, the heat, and her ADSL, she couldn't give up the occasional night out with her girlfriends. She tried to reduce the rest to a minimum. The day came when she boiled a quarter pound of pasta one night and ate it without sauce, without even a drop of olive oil, and thought the simple flavor of the plain spaghetti was the tastiest in the world.

One sunny, windy spring afternoon she stationed herself behind the trunk of a chestnut tree in front of the building she'd lived in for twenty-two years, her parents' house, the house where her mother now lived alone. She had to wait until her mother left to go and pick the children up at school; it was a day when Cecilia had the afternoon shift, and it was the only one of her mother's errands whose duration she could calculate exactly. She watched her walk away, waited another five minutes, and then headed briskly toward the imposing cherrywood door whose reddish grain formed two large wide-open eyes.

She opened it with her old set of keys. The last few times she'd come to see her parents she hadn't used them, buzzing the intercom to emphasize her position as an outsider. She took the elevator up to the fifth floor and didn't run into anyone, but even if a neighbor had suddenly appeared in the dim vestibule, in the uncertain light of the landing, what would he have suspected? Her mother didn't associate with anyone in the building, no one could report having seen her younger daughter enter the house (specifically, the one she argued with all the time, you could hear them on the ground floor).

The apartment hadn't changed over the years. With two exceptions: when the first daughter had married, her old room was used by her mother on nights when their father would not stop his unbearable snoring (therefore every night; only by snoring could he express his rebellion); when the second daughter left home, her room had been set up for the grandchildren to nap and play in. But since these changes were confined to two inner rooms that were basically hidden, the rest of the house seemed even more changeless and eternal.

No sign of the husband and father's death. It had been two months. Her father had been a drifter in a foreign land where he was barely tolerated, a migrant. With his illness he'd become a minority in a ghetto: assigned to his own cramped space. Her mother had no intention of repossessing the master bedroom where her husband had slept alone until the last night before the final trip to the hospital. The marriage was dead, the husband was dead, the room was dead. The door was closed, the room condemned, and Silvia had no desire to open it, enter it. She roamed around the rest of the deserted house without turning on the lights, without touching anything, careful not to leave any trace. Like a thief, she thought, but that wasn't quite right, because she actually *was* a thief; she roamed through the house like a stranger, a person to whom those rooms meant nothing.

She'd brought plastic bags from home, to put the food in. From the fridge and pantry she took meat, vegetables, packets of pasta, biscuits, bread. Her mother would notice the theft, of course. She would immediately think of her and wouldn't accuse anyone else. Maybe she would talk to Cecilia about it, and she and her older daughter would exchange a meaningful look, just a quick glance, and wouldn't comment any further because it would be too ridiculous and painful. Or maybe not, maybe she was overestimating them. They would talk about it at length and her mother would make Cecilia look into it. Cecilia would look into it and she would confess immediately. Cecilia would say, Don't be silly; she'd give her some money. And she would live on her sister's charity until her next assignment. And she'd start working full-time again, and would at least have enough money to get by.

After filling the two plastic bags and setting them near the door, she lingered in the house. She tried to feel some emotion. She tried to cry, but it was no use. Maybe she thought the house itself would move her, that it wasn't necessary to enter her father's room. But she realized for the millionth time that her father had lived in that house as a guest. This was confirmation of it: she hadn't been looking for it, but she'd found it.

She left the building with her shopping bags, without encountering a soul. She walked unhurriedly to the corner, turned it, and found a deserted street in front of her, the promise of a clean getaway, a successful venture, and thought maybe she wouldn't do it again. It had been a childish thing to do.

Instead she continued doing it. She went shopping at her mother's house at least once a week for several months, till autumn. If her mother noticed it (how could she not notice?), she hadn't told anyone. She hadn't told Cecilia, or if she had told her, Cecilia had suggested that she act as if nothing had happened (Cecilia often suggested acting as if nothing had happened, besides, it was better that Silvia steal from her mother than from a supermarket).

The horror and fascination of being late; she can't remember the first time she felt that shiver, but she knows it's by far the strongest emotion she can afford to feel these days. Motionless on the couch for weeks, after the death of her father, she went through a period of indulgence. On the phone with editors at the publishing houses, she engaged in orgies of excuses, hopelessly entangling herself in a web of lies. At that point being late had become a way like any other to get by, to let the world know she was still alive. As Cecilia fed her sashimi and yogurt and cooked broths and baby pastina and semolina soups for her, she went on accruing missed deadlines. She came up with the most improbable excuses to put off for hours or days the consignment of work that she wouldn't be able to complete even in weeks or months. It's taken her years of diligently meeting deadlines to make up for that month of madness and win back the publishers' trust. When she misses a day of work and the specter of being late rises up in front of her, waving its white shroud and rattling its chains, she feels a stab of fear in the pit of her stomach. And she starts counting the number of pages again, updating the daily quota that will allow her to finish on schedule.

It's been twenty days since her fling with the nondescript Viberti and she still feels like she's fallen behind, even though the fling itself didn't consume any of her working hours, since it took place entirely in the evening. Chalk it up, perhaps, to the usual tangle of meaningless thoughts, as well as to that damned tome on Hindu mythology, that meteorite she allowed to hit her, which she has to finish polishing up by mid-July. If she's behind schedule, those three harmless nights aren't responsible. She has thirty days of work left, she could add a weekend to make sure she finished on time.

She's therefore planning to work on a certain Saturday afternoon when she suddenly falls into a deep, dreamless sleep on the couch, and sleeps like a log for three straight hours. As far as she knows, only children nap like that. A phone call from Cecilia wakes her at six. She's confused, dazed, but pretends to be wide awake, as if she were afraid of being yelled at, by her sister moreover, for having wasted the afternoon. Cecilia doesn't notice anything, she's excited about her own news, she wants to tell her that she took the boy to summer camp, even though he'd been in the hospital twelve days earlier.

"Good for you, Ceci, he won't have any problems, you'll see."

"He's been playing soccer every afternoon."

"Really."

"Going to camp meant so much to him. But, you know, the minute I leave him I get anxious."

"You're an hour's drive away. But there won't be any problem . . . And Michela?"

She manages to get Cecilia's mind off Mattia by having her tell her about Michela's study holiday and then finally gets rid of her.

She takes a shower. Her breasts are swollen; she must be getting her period. She gets dressed, she goes out with her girlfriends and some other people, they go to eat and then to see *The Day After Tomorrow*. She'd been the one to insist on it, she chose the film and persuaded everyone that it wasn't the usual apocalyptic trash. After ten minutes, however, she slumps down in the seat.

Stefania wakes her when a new ice age has descended over the world and the actors are moving around in the blizzard, muffled up in bulky yellow snowsuits.

"What's the matter with you?"

"I'm working too hard."

She works all day Sunday without ever going near the couch or the bed for fear of falling into a stupor again. Ever since morning, she's known exactly what she's going to start thinking once she calls it quits. As if an unwelcome letter had been delivered and she hasn't wanted to open it all day.

At seven she saves and closes the file she's been working on, makes some tea, and picks up her datebook. The nondescript Viberti had been careful. She'd told him to be careful. She saw him. She saw him the second night. She saw him the third night. Traces of that precaution were left on her sheets. The first night, they'd made love on the floor, in front of the couch. Right afterward he'd gone to the bathroom, presumably to wash up.

She's never kept track of the date of her last period, ever, in her whole life. Cecilia, of course, is the one who marks a little cross on the calendar. Though Stefania, unpredictably, does, too. Carla is so regular she doesn't need to.

The hell with it, it'll come. Still, just to pass the time while the tea steeps, what day was it? A Monday morning, toward the middle of May: she'd awakened at six with stomach cramps and stained pajamas. She'd gotten out of bed, trying not to fully wake up, toddled into the bathroom, rinsed off, got a tampon and clean panties. She'd been about to go back to bed, sleep until eight. But something drew her to the living room window. At night she keeps the shutters lowered only in the bedroom, she likes the light coming from the other room in the morning. Outside it was daylight, and there was a gray cloud in the pale sky above the rooftops that was constantly changing shape: a flock of birds that swelled and contracted rhythmically in the morning air.

So, it was five weeks, almost. So she is late. She's been eight or nine days late before. She could be late even longer. She could be late by a month and still not be pregnant. She suspects it's just a way to neglect her work, to create excuses for herself, to sabotage the mammoth book of Hindu mythology, substituting one delay for another. She'll wait a week and then think about it. But since Thursday is a holiday and she might decide to go to the beach with Stefania (if she's caught up with her work), since it could ruin a couple of days in a bathing suit, she'll get it on Wednesday night, it's bound to happen.

The next day she tries not to think about it, she's able to work well but her breasts are still swollen and she's tremendously sleepy; she's worried. She sleeps wearing panties and a tampon. Nothing happens.

Tuesday morning at eight she shuts off the alarm clock without thinking and goes on sleeping. She sleeps until ten, gets up with anxiety buzzing in her head like a persistent fly. At ten twenty she goes to the pharmacy and buys a pregnancy test; it's the first time, it's not the pharmacy she usually uses. They ask her if she wants two, she doesn't get it, she says no. Afterward she realizes it was a trap (to see if she was *worried* about being pregnant or *trying* to get pregnant).

She returns home. She opens the box: the object looks like a marking pen, the morning seems like a normal workday, but instead of editing proofs with a highlighter, like you used to do—coloring the uppercase letters that should be lowercase and vice versa pink or blue—she's about to take a pregnancy test. She's thirty-two years old and it's never happened to her before. She hasn't considered herself particularly fortunate because of it, but maybe she has been?

She removes the cap, holds the tip under the stream of urine for five seconds as instructed, leaves the bathroom, and waits. The tip turns pink, the first control line in the display window turns blue. The second one turns blue as well. Surely it's wrong. She has to do it again. The reason she's never gone to that pharmacy is because they're unreliable, they have old merchandise, expired stuff.

She goes out again, she feels a little dizzy, she stops for coffee and a croissant, she can't manage to drink the coffee, the aroma alone makes her feel like throwing up. She orders a cup of tea, sits down, tells herself: Calm down now, okay? Calm down. Stern, angry. Eyes fixed on the marble tabletop. She drinks the tea, eats a bit of the croissant.

She goes to her own pharmacy. She asks for the test kit, mortified. The pharmacist smiles, asks if she wants two. "Of course," she says. She also buys a toothbrush.

At home she repeats the test. It's a different brand, but that one also looks like a highlighter. It turns pink and then blue. Then blue again. Why always those colors? Who decided? It's not possible, she can't be pregnant.

She's shaking. It's eleven fifteen and she hasn't started working yet, the Hindu mythology book stares at her from the desk. Never mind looking inward, thousands of Bodhisattvas are pointing their finger at her.

She thinks about doing the third test right away, but instead she calls Stefania at her office, asks to have lunch with her. The moment she says the word "lunch" she feels nauseous. Stefania can't meet her, she asks if something happened, if something's wrong.

"No, everything's okay, talk to you later."

She hangs up and the next instant she panics. She calls Stefania back, tells her she's afraid she's pregnant, she had a fling with someone she'll never see again, she's a moron, she screwed up, can't she see her right away?

Stefania asks how it could have happened, doesn't wait for an answer, tells her to take a pill, half a pill, she'll be there as soon as possible. If she really is pregnant, maybe taking a Xanax isn't the best idea.

She does a search on the Internet, ends up on a site where she reads testimonials written by pregnant women subject to panic attacks: some say you can take Xanax, others say you can't. She jumps up from her chair, paces the length of the room breathing heavily.

Stefania calls her back, tells her not to take Xanax, that maybe you're not supposed to.

She lies down on the couch, gets up again. She slips a Japanese cartoon that the children gave her into the DVD player. It's called *My Neighbor Totoro*, and it's so slow that it's relaxing. One deep inhalation; one deep exhalation. She tells an imaginary companion the story of *Totoro*. Once upon a time there were two sisters and a daddy; their mommy was sick.

She gets up, turns off the TV. She walks around the room, recites out loud the story about Xanax that Cecilia is always repeating: the woman who arrived in the ER claiming she'd taken "the axe."

After half an hour Stefania arrives, but she's more frightened than Silvia is. She grabs the pill that Silvia left on the table, breaks it in two, and swallows half of it with a glass of water. She has her tell her everything; then she starts to cry.

"Stefi, you can't cry, I called you because I needed someone to talk to, you can't start crying, too."

"You have to talk to your sister about it, you have to call her right now. You have to let her help you." Because keeping it, of course, would be crazy, but Stefania doesn't have the courage to say so, and wants Silvia to be the one to say it first.

"I can't," Silvia says, shaking her head.

"I'm sure she'll know what to do in a case like this."

"What are you saying?"

"She's a doctor! She *knows*!"

Then Silvia begins to cry.

"I can't talk to her about it, I can't. She has plenty to worry about, believe me. I just can't."

They sit on the couch, holding hands. "This is the first time something this big has happened to us, right?" Stefania says.

Silvia nods. "The first time."

"Will you tell me what happened? Tell me who he is?"

At Michela's First Communion, Luca had asked to speak to her, and the following day he'd come to her house and started telling her everything. But not right away, not all at once. It took four visits. The first time, he'd sprawled on the couch, drained, enervated, and at the end of an hour of stammering in a faint voice, he hadn't said a thing. He wasn't wearing his usual gray suit and tie, but all clothes looked good on him, even that blue sport jacket, even those beige chinos. He no longer seemed like a distant hologram but more fraternal; there was no longer any trace of frenzy and panic in him. Nor had he reverted to being the person he always was: present, solid, yet remote. He was a new and different Luca, one who collapsed on the couch and sprawled. He said he was sorry he'd gotten her involved, that Cecilia would never forgive him, that he didn't want to put her in a tight spot and trouble her with their problems. Silvia looked at him in silence and thought back longingly to the frightened man she'd glimpsed the day before.

"I'll make you some tea," she said. He explained that he didn't drink tea, it bothered his stomach, he'd never liked it. A pointless explanation, because Silvia started boiling water, poured two teaspoonfuls of Darjeeling into the infuser, set the cups on a tray. With her back to him, leaning against the kitchenette counter, she murmured that she could keep a secret, she wouldn't say anything to anyone. She added that if he no longer felt like confiding in her, however, it was fine, too. If he'd changed his mind, if the prospect of talking made him uneasy and he no longer felt like unburdening himself, best to just drop it.

It was a trick she knew well, she'd used it dozens of times with her girlfriends, her girlfriends had used it dozens of times with her. Many years later she would use it on her son, so it wasn't necessarily a malicious trick to extort confessions. When used with good intentions, it helped someone who wanted to talk, but who had lost his courage.

Luca shook his head, he was sure that talking would do him good, though until then he hadn't felt like it, and he wondered why he'd felt the urge to tell her everything the day before, at Michela's party. And his answer was that maybe he really wanted her to *not* keep the secret, maybe he wanted her to tell someone.

Silvia laughed. "Some trust you have."

"You're not understanding me." He reddened. "I can't explain it." He slumped down a little more, hanging his head between his shoulders. He looked at his hands in silence. After an hour he left.

He came back the next day. And again Silvia offered him a cup of tea and again he said no thanks. Silvia smiled, began boiling water, poured it into the teapot, shut the lid. She crossed the room, turned on the stereo, turned the volume down low. She really couldn't imagine what Luca wanted to tell her, she'd come up with any number of hypotheses, but the most credible still seemed to be trouble in the marriage. She couldn't guess which of the two was the cause; it seemed so unlikely that either of them would have a lover, people as sensible and levelheaded as they were. Just the idea of it made her laugh, the way two people kissing make children laugh. Seeing Luca among the objects of her daily life reassured her. Nothing serious or irreparable could have happened.

"Yesterday, when I said . . . I meant to say . . ." He stopped, rubbed his forehead with one hand. "I was sure that what I wanted to say would have upset you and that you would tell the people you're closest to. It's normal, it's natural, everyone does it, to try to understand. I can't do it right now, I just can't."

Silvia poured the tea into the cups, set the tray on the table in front of the couch, picked up her cup; the other cup stayed where it was, steaming, gradually cooling, no longer steaming. "Okay," Silvia said, sitting down. "Who was I supposed to tell whatever it is you want to tell me?"

"I don't know. Your mother?"

"My mother?" Her eyes widened. "I barely talk to my mother. How could you think I'd go and tell her anything about you? And why?"

"I wanted someone to know who would tell Cecilia that she was wrong, that she'd done a terrible thing."

"You wanted our mother to tell her?"

"You, your mother, I don't know. I'm just trying to understand why I thought I should tell you. I feel so ashamed. I don't want to tell anyone. I don't want anyone to know about it. I wish it had never happened."

"I'm not following you, I'm sorry."

Luca pulled his phone out of his jacket pocket. He seemed to be searching for a number or a message; he sighed, put it back in his pocket. He shook his head a little, muttered something.

What if after having been the most normal guy in the world, he, too, had become one of those oddballs, what if he had become one of those people who sit on park benches, talking to themselves?

"Maybe you should tell me what it is Cecilia did, otherwise I don't get it."

"It's not easy. I've never felt the way I've felt the last couple of months, this has never happened to me. This person isn't me, this anger isn't me. I think about it all day, I think about it all night, I never would have imagined having certain thoughts. Do you understand?"

"Not really."

"I wanted someone to tell her that she shouldn't have done what she did, I wanted a parent to yell at her. I wanted to share the anger with someone."

"Well, I, in any case, can't go and say anything to anyone, and

I can't reprimand Cecilia for what she did if I do understand, I think, what she did. So, if sharing it with me isn't enough, better not to tell me anything."

This time it wasn't the old trick to affectionately extort confessions. It was a new trick, in which you said exactly what you thought. In part because by this time it was clear that Cecilia had been the one to betray him, and Silvia wasn't sure she wanted to know the details of the story.

"You don't understand, you can't," said Luca.

He got up. He stood there a moment. He said goodbye, and then he was gone.

Cecilia had fallen in love with another man while her father was dying. Silvia placed her empty cup on the tray, beside the one that was still full.

Luca came back after a few days, very upset. "I would have been better off if I'd never met her, hadn't married her, hadn't had the two children we have. Can you imagine? Me thinking such a thing? The best moments of the past ten years, the most precious things I have, destroyed forever. Michela's first day of school, remember how big she was already? We were more nervous than she was as she was getting ready the night before, and that morning I took her picture before we left the house; she was proud, excited. Every so often I look at the photo again and I laugh to myself, happy, you know? And the evening, at dinner, when Mattia began speaking, his first complex sentences with all the words in the right place, and Ceci and I looked at each other and almost started crying: he hadn't gotten a single word wrong. He chatted about cars, he already knew all the models of all the manufacturers, and we pretended not to notice, not to interrupt him, to prolong the moment, but Michela couldn't help herself, she shouted: 'Mattia, you're talking perfectly!' We all burst out laughing. And once at the beach when he defended his sister from two older kids who threw sand at her, and Michela was beaming, and he wanted to continue fighting, furious at us for dragging him away. And that time, in the mountains, when some young people passed us, we were on the shore of a pond, and Michela, behind us, followed them all the way to the other side, she was three or four years old, and when I went to bring her back they were laughing like crazy, saying what a cute little girl she was, she wanted to know which ones were boyfriend and girlfriend, she'd only known them five minutes, and she was saying, 'Don't you like her? Why don't you kiss each other?' in that tiny voice of hers, remember?"

"Oh, I remember, I remember." Silvia nodded. She nodded. And nodded. What else could she do? She could only nod. Until Luca went away, forgetting even to say goodbye this time.

The man she'd glimpsed a few days ago wanted to talk, he needed help, he was seeking advice. This one didn't need someone to talk *with*, he needed an audience, he just had to recite his monologue, he already knew all the answers. Besides, wasn't this whole scene a little too much, if it was just an affair?

Then finally, on his fourth visit, Luca blurted out what he wanted to say, with no second thoughts.

He showed up carrying an umbrella, even though it wasn't raining and wasn't threatening to rain. He sank onto the couch. He sat up straight. His voice went up two octaves, took on a ragged, high-pitched timbre, and ended in a sob through clenched teeth: "We were expecting a baby, Cecilia aborted it, she said she couldn't keep it."

Silvia held up her hands to stop him. "Wait, I don't understand! She was expecting a baby? She lost it?"

"She went and had an abortion, she went alone, without telling me."

"She had a miscarriage . . ."

"NO! NO!" he shouted. "WILL YOU LISTEN TO ME? SHE HAD AN ABORTION! SHE DIDN'T WANT IT!"

"She said she couldn't keep it . . ."

"She meant she didn't want it."

"She told you: I can't keep it. That's all she said."

"She told me she didn't want another child, that Mattia was still having problems, that she didn't have the strength to start all over again. That's what she said. I wanted us to talk about it, I asked her to wait. No use. Ten days later, she'd done it."

"I don't believe it."

The disclosure was so unexpected, the shock so great. Silvia shook her head. When had it happened? A day when they'd seen each other? A day before, a day after? Without telling anyone. She'd made an appointment. By phone? At the hospital? She'd gone by herself. When? What was the weather like? Was it sunny or raining? What had she been doing at that moment? Where were the children? In the morning she'd taken them to school. In the afternoon she'd gone to pick them up. She was calm; she was frightened. Did her mother know? She didn't know. But how could she not have noticed anything? How could her sister have been able to hide it all so well?

She didn't want to hurt Luca, but she wasn't sure she wanted to console him. She had a knot in the pit of her stomach, her old friendly knot, and at the same time she felt lighter, relieved, maybe only of uncertainty. Above all, she was sure she didn't share Luca's anger. She would have been willing to share his grief or pain or sorrow, but anger? Actually, it seemed unthinkable to her that in the face of such an act he would feel only anger, or mainly anger, that he didn't have anything to say about Cecilia.

"Is Cecilia all right?"

"Cecilia is just fine, she doesn't realize what she's done; you'd think she'd gone to the dentist."

"Are you *sure?*"

He nodded.

Silvia started stammering. "It doesn't seem possible that she . . . if she made that decision . . . I'm not against it . . . I'm not opposed in general, but . . . it's a big decision, the way you tell it, it seems like she made a snap decision, just like that . . . without giving it any thought . . . it's not like her, I can't believe it . . . I don't like you saying that . . . that thing about the dentist . . . I don't like it, I don't like it *one bit!*"

She was a little short of breath. But she knew why she felt relieved. Cecilia was no longer the perfect woman, she was no longer infallible, and it was only right that her mother know it. In the end, she did share a little of Luca's anger, though for different reasons: Cecilia never told her anything, she didn't expose herself, she didn't reveal her weaknesses, she wasn't a true friend, and that's why she had no girlfriends—girlfriends bare all to one another. To go and do a thing like that alone. She felt relieved, but it was a fragile relief; her anxiety was stronger. She put a hand to her throat to gauge her heart rate, she tried to think rationally.

"Maybe none of us realized how much Cecilia suffered over the death of our father, for not having been able to save him. I, too, sometimes felt angry with her, because she always seemed so cold when she spoke about Papa's condition, about his prospects— when she told me and Mama what could still be done, as if she were talking about a to-do list, without ever saying there was nothing more that could be done. But those are defense mechanisms, you know? If she did—if she felt the need to do that thing, she must have had her reasons, she certainly has reasons that you have to find out. I understand you're upset, but angry, no, you can't give in to it, you have to be there for her. And don't ever say that thing about the dentist again."

"It's definitely not the worst thing I said." He told her that for a month they'd gone to the park to fight, so the children wouldn't hear them. In a clearing among the trees he told Cecilia she was an animal, a murderer, that she made him want to puke, she was a monster, a hideous thing. He told her she didn't deserve to be the mother of his children. He told her he would have rather she died giving birth.

He relayed all this as if it had nothing to do with him, the dry umbrella still beside him. It was pointless for her to say anything. And in any case, she couldn't take any more, she was too upset. She bent forward and rested her forehead on her knees, her arms limp at her sides. Her heart was pounding in her ears. And to think she'd actually planned to ask him for money. Her heart slowed, swelled with each beat, filled her entire rib cage, became tough and fibrous. Again Silvia imagined her sister, alone—before, during, and after—alone from now on, alone with herself, as she'd never wanted, or been able, to be.

She thought of confessing to Cecilia that she knew everything. In her head she tried out several things she might say to approach her. She never got beyond the introductory phase, in which she struggled at length to justify Luca's choice, as if her brother-in-law's decision to tell her everything incriminated her as well, as if she, with her weakness and frailties, had forced him to break the vow of silence.

But each time she found herself in Cecilia's presence, even before she started to speak, she was certain that she would not raise the subject that day. There were more urgent things, things that were more interesting, less difficult. She had to wait for the right occasion. And not cause additional, unnecessary friction between Luca and Cecilia. She kept telling herself that if she didn't talk to her about it, it was out of a sense of responsibility, not because she didn't have the courage.

Still, she felt a little less like a black sheep; her sister had become more human and fallible in her eyes—a tragic figure, a Medea. And she realized that she loved her dearly, she realized that she cared about her and the children the way you care about a real family. Except superstitiously, to ward off the possibility, she never gave serious thought to the idea that Cecilia and Luca might break up; they were fated to be together.

The day Silvia discovers she's pregnant, Stefania stays over at her house. They talk for an hour in front of the muted TV set. Every now and then they get up to look for information on the Internet. They search for whatever essential facts they need concerning the timing and methods for terminating a pregnancy. They open and close pro-life and pro-choice sites after just a few seconds. They go to bed early; both of them sleep very badly.

The next day is much better. Stefania goes to the office. Silvia phones the editor for whom she's revising the book on Hindu mythology. The editor lets her persuade him to give her two more weeks with surprisingly little argument. Most likely he'd lied to her about the schedule. No matter, the news fills her with joy and gives her an unjustified confidence in the future. Everything will work out.

So the following night, the feast day of the city's patron saint, she goes out with Carla to watch the fireworks. In the middle of the bridge across the river she confesses the truth. Carla wants to know all the details. She wants to know who he is. She wants to know if it's out of the question for them to continue seeing each other. Then she tells her she has to talk to Cecilia about it. In any case. Whatever she decides.

"Have you decided?"

She shakes her head: "I can't think straight."

"Do you want to keep it?" It doesn't even seem like a question; Carla manages to say it in a perfectly neutral tone so that the words don't express opinions, judgments, prejudices, or fears.

"I can't think right now. But I don't think I have any choice given my situation."

"Talk to your sister. Promise me?"

"Why do you all want me to talk to my sister?"

"Because she can help you, she can make it less painful."

She looks at Carla, not comprehending.

"You know in whose hands you could end up? You hear stories about women treated like criminals."

"But I haven't decided anything yet . . ."

"Of course. But, in any case, you should decide."

Talking to Cecilia becomes a way to buy time and reach the inevitable decision. As though Cecilia, as a doctor, possesses enough natural cynicism to state flatly that there is no other choice.

"I'll wait another two or three days. I want to be able to think about it."

On Friday morning she does the third test, just to use it, since she bought it. It turns pink, then blue, then blue.

She decides to go to the shore with Stefania. Staying in the city, she'd spend two days at home going around and around the same subject. At the shore she spends two days at the beach going around and around the same subject. Stefania again urges her to talk to Cecilia. No matter what she decides. "All right, I'll go see her on Tuesday," she says, to stall for one more day.

She works very efficiently all day Monday. In the evening she imagines possible ways to broach the subject with Cecilia, possible ways the conversation might develop. She talks about it at length on the phone with Francesca, who not being face-to-face with her is perhaps more sincere. She tells her that raising a child alone seems like madness, "even though you're not alone, we're here, you know," but she's referring to the other two, since she isn't actually there.

The next day she gets to the ER, goes inside. But when she sees Cecilia at the end of the hall she turns on her heels and flees. Outside it's a normal late-June morning in the city. It's already hot, the sky is overcast, there's not a breath of air. A short walk restores her courage and enables her to return to the ER. But the more she thinks about it, the more difficult talking to Cecilia about an unwanted pregnancy seems. If Cecilia hides her feelings, she won't be able to bear seeing her impassive face. If she crumbles, she won't be able to bear seeing her emotional face. And she isn't even sure she wants advice from her.

She walks for ten minutes, headed back home. She's no longer upset, she no longer feels pregnant. She feels drained, as if it were already over. She's tired, so she gets on a bus, lets her thoughts drift, lets her gaze wander over the city. Despite the grimy, rattling window, the world has never seemed so vivid, its contours so clear and sharp.

If she stayed on that seat for a whole week maybe the jiggling would make her lose the baby. Maybe she'll lose it anyway. She skips her stop, she doesn't feel like getting off, going home, to do what? She continues riding to the last stop, then retraces her route.

She passes the pedestrian zone where Rumi's club is. Rumi has red hair like Enrico Fermi, but unfortunately he's not Enrico Fermi. Enrico Fermi introduced her to so much music! If she were to go to him now, if she confessed everything, maybe he'd take her back. He'd put on "Sweet Song" by Blur and they'd dance in each other's arms in his studio apartment. But the truth is she doesn't want to get off that bus.

The year her father died, following Luca's confession, she'd continued her raids even after her mother left for the shore with the grandchildren and the house wasn't being restocked with fresh food. One day, pacing back and forth in the dark corridor, she began smiling and talking—acting as if she were welcoming a guest to the house and inviting him to sit in the living room, and she pictured herself as the mistress of that house, a person with a real job and a real love life, and in any case something to talk about. The game didn't last long, but she liked it so much that she went back the following day. She imagined discussing with an architect how she wanted to renovate the apartment, she imagined the architect falling in love with the house and with her.

(Many years later, she would want her son to become an architect, and her son would disappoint her, would end up reconstructing different architectures.)

She didn't have the courage to enter her father's room. She stayed in the kitchen and recalled epic fights with her mother. There was a crack in the wood table where her gaze had retreated during those battles. She stood up and went to sit in her father's place, trying to remember how she looked at sixteen, the clothes she wore. Her father would stand on his head to side with her without irritating her mother. She remembered when she'd invited Enrico Fermi to the house on a Saturday afternoon, thinking her parents wouldn't be back before Sunday night; he showed up with a tray of pastries, some they ate, some they threw out the window at passing cars, and some they eventually used in a food fight waged throughout the entire house. Until her mother, whom they hadn't heard come in, appeared in the doorway. The moment their eyes met, Silvia read not anger and disapproval in her mother's stare, but only shock, and realized that if she had caught her fucking on the kitchen table it wouldn't have been more consequential.

She did well in school, so in the end her father forgave her everything. Because he was proud of her, he was very proud of her. And it was in that kitchen that Silvia had found the whole family gathered when she came home from her thesis defense (she hadn't wanted them to go, maybe her father had been offended): Cecilia with her big belly, pregnant with Mattia; Luca; little Michela running around the room; her father and mother. She couldn't remember hugging her mother after that day, not even a few months ago, when her father died. She hugged the air four times, repeating the gesture she'd made. Everyone congratulated her; she'd received honors and her thesis had been recommended for publication.

Then she resumed her pacing around the house, passing the closed door of the master bedroom, each time putting off the act of placing her hand on the handle and turning it. Among the tacky objects her mother adored were two sconces that had cast a dull light in the entry hall from time immemorial: two arms of gilded, worm-eaten wood, the arms of an angel or an infant, which looked like hunting trophies and held the base of a flame bulb in their closed fists. So sweet and disturbing, they might have been cut off some naughty child. Or the child may have been walled up, except for the arms, to keep her still, so she wouldn't leave the house anymore to go who knows where or with whom. Impossible to know what her father thought of that eyesore. She should have asked him and she hadn't. Not that he would have said a word.

She walked resolutely toward the closed door, opened it with an angry gesture, and went inside. Overwhelmed by her father's smell, which rose above the mustiness and the odor of illness, she raised the shutters and opened the window before her strength failed her. She lay down on the bed covered with a white sheet, rested her head on the pillow without a pillowcase, and closed her eyes. She wished she never had to get up again.

Her father's worldly possessions weren't many. The clothes in the closet. A boxful of his works in the attic. A library of science fiction volumes. A rolltop desk with three drawers full of odds and ends. On the bedside table, half buried by packages of medications, Isaac Asimov's *Foundation* trilogy. Her father had told her the story many times, from when she was little: the Galactic Empire is in decline, a dark age lasting millennia is in store for humanity, or at least that's what Hari Seldon thinks, a mathematician who has developed a surefire system of equations to predict the future. Seldon establishes a colony on a distant planet, as far away as possible from the center of the galaxy (where the capital of the empire is located) and names it the Foundation. The Foundation must safeguard human knowledge through the dark age to come, and attempt to shorten its duration. Things go according to Seldon's plan for several centuries, until the appearance of the Mule, a mutant endowed with higher psychic powers. The Mule is the unexpected, that which no future science will ever be able to anticipate. The Mule defeats the Foundation in battle and conquers what remains of the empire. The only hope for free men lies in an ancient prophecy: for centuries it had been rumored that Hari Seldon founded not one but *two* colonies, and that the Second Foundation, hidden away *at the other end of the galaxy*, would save the first one.

When she was a little girl she barely understood it and at the end she would regularly ask if the Mule was good or bad, and if he was bad, why? It wasn't clear to her even now. But her father never answered. The Second Foundation was the high point of the story, for him. The important thing was that she understand clearly *where* the Second Foundation was. Why? That, too, continued to remain obscure. Her father would join the tips of his index fingers together and say: "If the galaxy is made like this," and he twirled his fingers in the air in opposite directions, moving them apart as if following the thread of a large screw, "like a spiral staircase, see? And the First Foundation is here," he had no fingers left to point with so he touched his left hand with his nose, "where will the Second be?" After a while, she'd learned to answer: "In the center." That is, not on the other side, on the right hand. The opposite extreme was the center, the space between his hands (and yet in the galaxy that was where the old capital of the empire was). This story was very important, for some mysterious reason. Listening to her father always generated two conflicting sensations: a feeling of being unique, because he was telling her something he considered important and had chosen to tell it to her; and a feeling of embarrassment, because she was almost certain (not quite) that it was a bunch of crap. And so her anxiety grew, the pins and needles in her fingertips, the shortness of breath.

The same pins and needles, the same shortness of breath that she now felt lying on her father's side of the bed, as the summer evening's air mingled with the air in the room and caressed her bare legs. How many hours had her father stared at the same patch of blank ceiling? In that bed, too, like in the galaxy's spiral, the location of only one of the Foundations was known. The Second was silent, its position was unknown, nobody knew if it really existed, or if it was just a legend.

In August, when her food ran out, she stole a ceramic centerpiece and six saucers decorated with a leaf-and-pomegranate motif from the attic; she also stole a fruit stand from the same set with a pomegranate split in two. They were pieces from her paternal grandmother's lovely dinner service; she thought she'd sell them in the fall. It was unlikely that her mother would notice they were missing, she'd banished her mother-in-law's legacy. Boxes and boxes of items that were nearly new or never unwrapped: a pair of women's brown gloves in butter-soft leather, for example, or a full, sealed bottle of Ferro-China Bisleri liqueur.

In the attic she also found her father's datebooks. Thirty years of appointments, business meetings, deadlines, never a personal note. How could he have resisted the temptation to jot down a thought, a hope, or a regret, or even just a comment on the weather, or the summary of a book. Every so often, an "x" or an asterisk. But there was no mystery: her father was only noting the recurrence of his headaches and when he took his painkillers. She spent hours shut up in the attic, in the acrid dusty heat, in the dim light, sweating profusely. It seemed to her that what was missing from the datebooks was everything that made a life worth living.

She found the *Urania* volume that her father had sent her to look for the year before. It was called *The Resurrection of Warped Dismay*, named after the protagonist, a cartoon producer who died in December 1966, like Walt Disney. She recalled that, according to urban legend, Disney had had himself frozen. And so in the novel, seven hundred years later, in 2666, technology enables the doctors to revive the body of the cryogenically preserved Warped Dismay and cure the cancer in his left lung. In the meantime, however, his cartoons have become the sacred texts of a blood-thirsty fundamentalist sect that has conquered the entire world, and Dismay, appalled and horrified by the cult of *Dumbo, Cinderella,* and *Peter Pan,* becomes a kind of Antichrist.

She remembered afternoons when her father watched tapes of the cartoons with Mattia and Michela, how spontaneous and genuine his enjoyment was. "Come on, Papa, don't laugh like that," Cecilia used to tell him. Cecilia had always treated him like a senile old man, which is why as he got older he always felt more comfortable with her.

Then September came, her mother returned from the shore, the refrigerator and pantry were restocked, Silvia started stealing again. One day she was going down in the elevator after making her usual raid, two full shopping bags at her feet. The elevator stopped on the ground floor, the doors opened, Silvia went out into the lobby.

In front of the mailbox stood a woman with her back turned. She hoped it wasn't her, but it was: her mother. She'd taken out the mail and was looking closely at an envelope. She turned her head, saw her. She turned her head again, went back to studying the envelope. Before she saw her—if she'd seen her—she was in the same position. But now, reading without her glasses, holding the envelope up to her face, almost hiding behind the white rectangle, there was an intention that hadn't been there before. Silvia stood still in front of the elevator door, the plastic bags in her hand. Her mother didn't turn around again, didn't move. Both women stood motionless for a very long time. Then Silvia walked through the lobby behind her mother's back and out onto the drive; she opened the front gate and stepped out into the street.

She made her way painstakingly along the sidewalk, her legs rigid, her joints stiff. The afternoon sun was casting its shadow on the wall and she felt flat and squashed, like that shadow. She crept through the heavy air. She managed to get to the street corner.

There were garbage bins there, she stopped in front of them, set the bags on the ground. She couldn't imagine making it home in that condition. She threw it all away.

Gradually the muscles of her legs relaxed. She remembered afternoons during her childhood when her mother would have a couple of girlfriends over for tea. They seemed so elegant to her, beautiful in a way that was unattainable. High-heeled shoes, of course, but especially the dark pantyhose, the slim ankles and the curve of their calves. How could they have such gorgeous ankles? She and Cecilia didn't have them, no use fooling herself.

She arrived home an hour later. Meanwhile, she'd decided that her mother hadn't seen her. For four and a half hours she watched old episodes of *Friends* she'd borrowed from Carla. She went to bed at two. She couldn't sleep even though she was no longer agitated. Details about her mother's clothing kept popping into her head. Certain bras with rigid cups. Black slips edged with lace. Very dark stockings. Pastel green twinsets. Later on, during the night, she decided that her mother had seen her. How could she ever live down the shame?

The following morning Cecilia buzzed the intercom, an unexpected visit, but its purpose was predictable. Silvia waited for her sitting on the couch, eyes lowered, ready to be humiliated. Cecilia walked into the house and didn't notice her sister's haggard, guilty face; she was focused on the short speech she was about to make: she and Luca were splitting up.

"That can't be!" Silvia said. "You can't."

"Now you have to be the one to help me."

"You two are made for each other," Silvia said. "You can't break up."

"Did you hear what I said? You have to help me now, I'm counting on you."

"You've always gotten along, what's wrong?"

Cecilia's eyes suddenly filled with tears. "Are you listening to me?" She took her hands. "It's over. We can't live together any-more."

They hugged.

Cecilia told her about the last few months: Luca's coolness, his inability to accept that she had a professional life of her own, and that she couldn't give all of her time to the family. She didn't say anything that came close to or even remotely hinted at the abortion. Silvia listened, thinking that sooner or later, through some sudden twist in the story, that chapter would emerge. She listened and waited, as if she were standing at a window. She saw everything go by, but not that. She thought there were plenty of other reasons, and that maybe Luca had made it up. Then she thought, no, he hadn't made it up. Cecilia didn't talk about it, but that was easier for her, she was used to not talking about things. For Silvia, on the other hand, talking came naturally. She could have said: I know everything, Luca told me. What difference did it make now? Cecilia's animosity toward him couldn't possibly get any greater. She could have spoken, but she didn't. So, in the end, the abortion didn't silence her sister. It silenced her. It had to happen sooner or later, that something would silence her. She didn't talk about it that day; she would never talk about it.

Before Cecilia left, however, Silvia confessed that she was broke. She was stealing food from their mother's house. Cecilia laughed: "Good thing you're here to cheer me up."

"You don't believe me? Ask Mama. She saw me."

"No, I believe you. I'll hire you as a babysitter, meals included. I'll need one, these next few months. Sound good?"

And with this conversation, more or less, that terrible year was over and the years of dormancy or cryopreservation began.

She gets back home after riding around the city for three hours, lies down on the couch, turns on the TV, starts the DVD of *Totoro*.

She falls asleep in front of the cat bus with twelve paws. The insistent ringing of the cell phone buried in her handbag wakes her. It's Stefania; she asks how it went with Cecilia, what she told her.

"Sorry, I fell asleep," she says. "Hold on."

She goes to the bathroom, rinses her face, looks in the mirror. She peers at her eyes and doesn't find them as sad and dark-shadowed as she thought.

She picks up the phone again: "Everything's okay. She told me not to worry. To take my time and think it over, I have to be the one to decide. She'll help me, whatever I decide." She wouldn't have the strength to confess the truth right now, she'll tell her later. Anyway it's unlikely, if not impossible, that Stefi would call Cecilia. Her friends are afraid of Cecilia.

She cooks a two-portion package of tortellini, seasons it with butter, and adds a few sage leaves. She's not upset, she's not worried, she's relaxed and very hungry. When she finishes eating, it occurs to her what to do.

She'll go and find the nondescript Viberti. He, too, is a doctor, he's a decent person, he'd even called her to tell her it was best they not see each other anymore. Truthfully, she doesn't necessarily need to know a doctor to get rid of the problem, she knows very well what to do and where to do it. But it's only fair that he be informed. Suppose he sounds frightened, suppose he tells her: "You don't want to keep it, do you?" Well, his reaction would be enough to persuade her.

She takes a day off, she admits to her girlfriends that she hasn't spoken to Cecilia, her sister has enough on her plate. Maybe she'll speak to her erstwhile lover, he's a doctor (a coincidence, nothing to do with her sister), he can help her. Make the procedure less painful for her, as Carla said. Her friends are worried about her, maybe it's *not* a good idea, he's too involved, he might upset her, no matter what his reaction is (it's not clear to her if they're afraid he'll convince her to have an abortion or if they're afraid he'll try to stop her). And they want to know if she's told them the whole truth, if she really hardly knew him, if the affair really only lasted three nights, whether they might not get back together.

But only Carla has the guts to ask her if the guilty party was Enrico Fermi, only Carla has the nerve to say, "Swear to me, please, that you haven't started seeing him again." It's Carla's voice, strained with emotion, and her face—she looks like she's about to cry—that stop Silvia from telling her to go to hell. Or maybe not. She's been so relaxed the last couple of days, so peaceful, that she has no desire to be mean to anyone. She swears to Carla that she hasn't seen Enrico Fermi for a year and that this doctor is someone else, with a different name and a different face, and that it really was an unpremeditated slipup, terribly irresponsible.

Still, she remembers her friends' hostility toward Enrico Fermi, especially toward versions five and six. She thinks it's partly their fault that she's in this mess. Carla in particular never missed a chance to belittle him. Okay, so he wasn't a genius. But maybe she would rather have had a child with him than with an unknown internist. At least the kid would have had red hair.

She tries calling Viberti that same night and the next day, but the cell phone just keeps ringing with no answer. She hangs up before leaving any messages. She thinks of writing him an e-mail, doesn't get beyond "I need to talk to you," and deletes it without sending it. She phones Internal Medicine, they tell her that Dr. Viberti is with patients. Then it occurs to her that rather than talk about it over the phone, it would be better to see him. She decides to look him up at home, and incredibly his address is in the white pages; there's only one Dr. Claudio Viberti in the entire city. Nevertheless, she wouldn't want to go too far, she wouldn't want to seem intrusive. At the hospital she's likely to run into Cecilia, but she knows the place well enough to be able to avoid crossing her sister's path.

So she shows up at the department's check-in desk in the late afternoon, hot and tired, and discovers that the doctor has just left. Rather than go back home, she wanders through the corridors, getting lost, asks the way to the ER to make sure she doesn't end up there, comes out in a parking area strewn with sickly trees, finds herself back outside the main entrance.

And she spots him. Viberti is walking toward her. Then he's running away.

She watches him move away swiftly, his green Lacoste polo untucked. She's left standing there with an idiotic smile on her face, not understanding.

She doesn't understand what's happened. She doesn't know if there was eye contact, if Viberti started running when he saw her. It doesn't seem possible. Why should he run away like that? He can't know anything. Unless he knows something.

There's a row of taxis standing under the trees on the avenue. The drivers are all out of their cars, sitting on the benches, water bottles and makeshift fans in hand.

She gets into the first one on line. Inside it's suffocating, even though the car has been standing in the shade. She'll lose the baby in that cab, or maybe she'll fall asleep.

No, she'll make her way to the nondescript Viberti's house, she'll wait for him at the front door, she'll talk to him. If he wasn't going home, she'll wait for him. She'll find a café with air-conditioning.

She arrives at the address, pays, and gets out. She looks closely at the name plaques on the entry panel. There are a C. VIBERTI and an M. VIBERTI.

She turns. A blue car comes down the street, and it's him, Viberti, at the wheel, driving with a crazed look; he looks at her, sees her, and keeps on going. In fact he speeds up and has to jam on the brakes at the intersection. Then he turns right.

Yes, this time she saw him. She saw that he saw her. He's running away.

The first night: maybe he knows he wasn't careful enough the first night. Maybe he knew it all along and hoped to get away with it.

She feels like giving in to despair, she'd like to think: It's hot, it's the first of July, the heat is staggering, suffocating. It's six o'clock, time to go home. This bastard won't help me. But she's not so tired after all and she no longer feels like she's going to faint. She wants to know why the nondescript Viberti is trying to flee.

She thinks calmly about what just happened. As calm and composed as she's never been in her life. What's going on with her? It must be hormonal. Pregnancy has turned off the little panic dynamo that has been droning in her head since the beginning of time.

It makes no sense to buzz Viberti's intercom, because Viberti is on the run.

She pulls a piece of paper out of her handbag, and leaning against the wall writes:

Dear Claudio, I wanted to talk to you about something important, can you call me? Thank you. Silvia Re (Cecilia's sister). P.S. It's really important.

She buzzes the intercom of M. VIBERTI.
"Yes?"
"I have to leave a message for Dr. Viberti, can you open for me?"
She hears conferring in the background. They won't open.
They open.
On the mailboxes in the building's vestibule, the name plates say: MARTA VIBERTI, II FLOOR—DR. CLAUDIO VIBERTI, V FLOOR. She hears voices in the stairwell. Instead of slipping her note into the mailbox, she takes the elevator and presses the button for the second floor.
On the landing is an elderly lady wearing a pinafore with tiny

blue flowers, and a younger woman who is trying to persuade her to go back into the apartment.

"I was right, you see?" the older woman says triumphantly. "She didn't believe me, but I knew you'd come up."

Silvia apologizes with a smile, she didn't mean to disturb her, she has an urgent message for Claudio, can she tell him to call her?

The lady steps forward, away from the protection and support of the woman behind her; she clings to Silvia, takes her hands, squeezes them. "Of course, I'll tell him."

"Thank you, signora, you're very kind. Tell him Silvia Re was looking for him."

"I recognized you!" the elderly lady exclaims.

"Let's go inside now, Mrs. Marta," the woman looking after her says.

Signora Marta has no intention of releasing her prey. She looks at Silvia, smiling, her blue eyes boring into hers: "How are you?"

"I'm well, signora, I'm very well. And you?" She smiles at the caregiver, to reassure her. "I didn't think you'd recognize me."

"I don't forget people who are . . ." Marta says, lowering her eyes impatiently, searching for the right word as if it had fallen on the floor, ". . . people who are *nice*."

Silvia squeezes her hands, murmurs a thank-you. "I didn't forget you, either." She doesn't know how to extricate herself, she doesn't know if she wants to break away from those eyes. "I'm fine, I've been working hard and I'm a little tired. I'm working for three different publishing houses. Right now I'm doing a book on Hindu mythology. It's kind of boring."

Marta smiles. "We have to do boring things as well," she says. "If you only knew how bored I was with my husband!"

They laugh, clasping each other's hands, laughing with relief, together and for their own reasons. The caregiver smiles, too.

"I'll leave you now, I have to go. But I was very glad to see you again."

"Me, too, very much so," the signora says, "come back and see me." She doesn't let go.

The caregiver has stepped back, waiting, but as soon as she notices Silvia's embarrassment she comes forward again and manages to draw them apart. Silvia admires the delicacy with which she guides the elderly woman, barely touching her.

They go into the house without looking back. Marta is saying: ". . . a friend of Claudio, I recognized her." The door closes by itself, as if there were someone else hidden behind it. Not the nondescript Viberti, unless he came in through the window.

It's comfortable in the lobby, very cool. She can't wait for him there, however, she doesn't feel like having to put on another act. She goes out the door.

She doesn't feel like going straight home either. And there are no cafés nearby with air-conditioning and a view of the building's door.

She sits on a step across the street. She thinks she's passed the point of no return, the point at which you no longer have enough oxygen to return to Earth and so you let the spaceship drift lazily into a black hole toward Alpha Centauri, light-years away, hoping to find breathable air there.

Every now and then she gets up and goes to buzz the intercom, in case Viberti has come in through some other entrance. She can't believe he doesn't want to see her.

She waits in front of the door for an hour and a half. She exchanges a few text messages with her girlfriends, pretending to be at home watching *Totoro*.

The whole story seems so unlikely, she tries imagining that she's seen it all wrong. She thought the man in the green Lacoste polo outside the hospital was him, she thought the man in the blue car was him, but she can't be one hundred percent certain. It's happened to her before—convinced that a stranger was someone she knew, she's had to apologize for making a fool of herself. And if he's not answering the phone, there must be a reason.

But no, she saw him, it was him, and he saw her. He must be frightened, who wouldn't be.

She returns home because a storm is brewing. She'll try again tomorrow.

As soon as she gets home she drinks three glasses of water, she pats the book of Hindu mythology, she feels as if she hasn't opened it in months. Then she lies down on the couch and begins thinking about Signora Viberti. She wonders if she'll ever be like her. Maybe not, in the future there won't be elderly people as lovely as that any longer. She can't seem to express the thought more clearly; she falls asleep.

As if she were on vacation, Friday morning she stays in bed until ten.

Looking in the mirror, trying to make herself presentable, she remembers all the times she's asked herself whether men are scared off by her hair; that's why she wears the black headband, to keep it under control—and that scares men even more. With that wide black headband she seems to be saying: *You're under my control now. You'll end up as my prisoner.* That's what men seem to read in her, and they run away.

Still, it seems only right that Viberti find the courage to speak to her and share in the decision. She tries to reach him all day Friday, sends him an e-mail, leaves messages on the answering machine.

On Saturday she tries again, to no avail. She calls the hospital; the doctor isn't in. She calls his cell phone and his home phone, alternating every five minutes, just so it's clear she won't stop. No answer. So she calls Cecilia, who is on her way to pick up Mattia. Cecilia is more evasive than usual; it's obvious the question makes her uncomfortable. She says she thinks Viberti is actually out of town; he was supposed to take his elderly mother to the country, to get her out of the city's heat. She adds that she's sure to find him on Monday.

The moment her sister says the word "country," Silvia sees before her the name of the place where Viberti went to hide out: San Colombano. The first night, over dinner at the Sino-Japanese restaurant, they'd talked about vacations, and Viberti told her he had a dreary house in a dismal place, a real morgue, which as a boy he used to call San Columbarium when his mother forced him to go there.

To get there, she soon discovers, she'd have to take a local train and then a bus: a half-day's trip; by car it takes only two hours. She doesn't own a car, but Stefania's father does. She calls her.

Stefania resists a bit, then gives in. Half an hour later she comes to pick her up. The car is a metallic gold Lancia Delta that is nearly eleven years old. Her father takes it out of the garage only on Sundays. Stefania can barely reach the pedals, she has to drive right on top of the steering wheel and lean sideways when turning. To be even with her and keep her from craning her neck too much as she talks, Silvia slides her seat forward too. They look like two elderly spinsters on an excursion.

The day is hot, sunny. "San Colombano is just beyond the foothills, the 'mid-elevation' mountains," Stefania says. They discuss this outmoded geographical designation, the *mezza montagna*, telling stories and constructing historical-sociological theories. The mid-mountain is a reassuring place, it doesn't offer the extreme challenges of the mountain, but it's at a higher altitude, more beneficial than the countryside. They're capable of rambling on about any subject for hours on end. They're used to buoying themselves up by talking. And so they arrive in San Colombano without having once mentioned Viberti or discussed what Silvia wants to tell him, or planned how they will find him once they reach the town.

Here it really is cooler than in the city. The town isn't dismal at all. There's a piazza, there's an old café-restaurant. Silvia gets out of the car, enters the café. She asks the barista if he knows the Viberti family, if he knows where they live. The barista gives her directions. She gets back in the car. She says: "Just outside of town, a white house on the left, after the bend in the road."

"How did you know they would know?"

"I didn't know. I didn't even know if this was the right place."

"You mean we came all this way and you weren't sure it was the right place?"

Silvia doesn't answer. Stefania starts the engine again. In the car, silence falls. When they come to the specified spot, Stefania stops. She turns to her friend and asks: "Are you scared? What are you going to do? Do you want me to come with you?"

Silvia shakes her head slightly. No, she's not scared. "I'll get out, I'll tell him, and I'll come back. Wait for me here?"

They hug.

There's a gray fence, a partly open wooden gate, a gravel drive-way that crosses the front lawn. The house is two-storied and the upper story, with a mansard roof, has pale wood paneling. It's a *mezza montagna* house that would be presentable in the mountains.

Viberti's Passat is parked under a shed. There are no doorbells, chimes, knockers. She's about to tap on the door, but she hears voices coming from around back.

She circles the house, passing under the shade of some pine trees, and comes out in the sun, to a more spacious lawn overlooking the valley. There's a lovely view. The nondescript Viberti is sitting at a stone table with his mother. On the table are earthen pots of various sizes, some empty, others filled with soil and dry seedlings.

Viberti sees her, he gets up. Has he turned pale or is that just her impression? Is it the effect of the light that bleaches things for her, coming from the shade, or the contrast with the dark shirt he's wearing? What's certain is that Viberti is speechless.

Silvia apologizes for the intrusion, she apologizes for harassing him. She doesn't mean to hound him. She asks if she could have just a few words with him, no more.

She isn't wearing the black headband this morning, she tied her hair at the back of her neck like Cecilia does, in a stunted ponytail. Viberti still seems very frightened, though. He has no idea what to do.

His mother, however, seeing Silvia, makes a sudden decision. She gets up and without taking off her gardening gloves goes back into the house. The son follows her with his eyes, then he says to Silvia, "Of course, come," and he walks with her to the outer edge of the lawn, where long spikes of blue flowers stick up amid the damp grass.

As I was writing this story I kept thinking about all the things I could have asked my three parents had they still been alive. But that, almost always, is the disadvantage of writing—you write in the future, and you end up being unjust, or maybe just imprecise. You use the few surviving traces, you stitch together remnants of conversations, all the rest is fabricated; and when you fabricate, perfectly plausible, or even probable, variants are discarded for narrative expediency, to avoid causing too much pain, to conceal inopportune details and reveal harmless ones. On the other hand, if I'd questioned my three elderly parents ten or twenty years ago, wouldn't they have treated their memories the same way?

I really don't know what Silvia and Viberti may have said to each other that day at the edge of the lawn and I have no desire to imagine it; or maybe I know all too well what they said and that's the reason I don't feel like recounting it. No, that's not it: I tried and I'm unable to. Besides, what could they have said? They were two predictable people: Silvia, smiling faintly, tells him she's pregnant, but she hasn't come to cause him any trouble; Viberti, dead serious, tells her it's her decision and that he will do his part in any case.

Then he asks her to please sit down at the stone table and wait for him, just five minutes. He needs to be alone a moment, he has something to tell her. Something important. And he remains at the edge of the lawn, looking out over the valley, gathering his thoughts.

Silvia has sat down on the wrought-iron chair, without shifting it, her back to the view. Marta has come out of the house, followed by Angélica with the coffee tray. Silvia thanks her, she explains that she doesn't drink coffee, but she'll gladly take a glass of water, thank you. And Marta sends Angélica back inside.

Marta doesn't seem to notice her son's absence. She's staring at Silvia with a joyful light in her eyes. Who does she think she is? Really one of Viberti's classmates? Or maybe she's mistaken her for someone else. Her son had been married. Has she mistaken her for his first wife?

Silvia compliments her on the house. Such a beautiful location, such a view, such a charming little town. Meanwhile, she feels a chill. Even in the sun it's too cool, maybe she's reverted to the anxious, fearful person she'd always been.

"It was my husband's grandfather who bought it," Marta says. "My husband was one of the most boring people in the world. Not a bad man. I remember him fondly. Oh dear, 'remember' is a loaded word, I don't know if I told you that I have problems remembering lately."

Silvia smiles. She takes a sip of water. She smiles at Angélica, who smiles back to let her know she recognizes her. She feels accepted, like an old family friend. She thinks this woman, Viberti's mother, is the loveliest person she's ever seen. And she wonders why she has that effect on her. Because you could tell she must have been beautiful when she was young? Because she's still beautiful, even though she's more than eighty years old? Because she resembles Viberti? Because her son or daughter might resemble her?

"It's a small town, quiet," Marta says. "It's not fashionable. But you know, at my age, change is impossible. And I don't travel anymore. I'm too old. Besides, I never traveled. My husband traveled alone, on business. But I never went with him. When we came here he would sit there at the edge of the lawn, and read. Then he'd come back and say he hadn't read a word, because the view distracted him."

They laugh. Silvia turns around, following Marta's direction, and sees my father with his back still turned, his gaze perhaps lost in space or maybe with his eyes closed. She thinks of Stefania waiting for her in the car. She takes her cell phone and tries to write her a text message, but her hands are shaking too much. If it's a girl she'll call her Marta, if it's a boy she'll name him after her father.

"My father was a bit like that, too," she says. "He was always reading. We never knew why. We never knew what he was thinking, what thoughts he had, what desires. He was a little boring, too."

Marta shakes her head and Silvia has the feeling she doesn't understand, that she's no longer able to hear, even though she continues speaking.

"It was my husband's grandfather who bought the house. I never met him, he was already dead. My husband barely remembered him. He must have been a boring man. The men in that family were all boring. I knew my husband's father. He was completely senile, but it was obvious that as a young man he'd been *extremely* boring!"

They laugh again. Silvia realizes that she has her right hand on her belly. She realizes that her hand is caressing her belly with a circular motion, and wonders if this is the first time she's doing that. Maybe she's just trying to warm up, maybe it isn't yet a maternal gesture.

Marta notices it, too. She looks at her and asks her with a smile: "Have you already told me what month you're in?"

Then Silvia stands up abruptly, trembling, and says it's really chilly, in that mid-mountain town. "I'll just run and get a sweater from the car, I'll be right back." But she doesn't move.

Marta keeps looking at her.

"I'm at the beginning," Silvia said. "I've only just begun."